"Protection is my job, and I know I blew it before, but I'm not going to make that mistake again."

Her lashes fluttered against her smooth cheeks. "I wasn't in any danger when you left me to do another tour."

"You were in danger of erecting your hard shell again. I'd broken through. I'd made you feel safe and loved, and then I snatched all that away." He skimmed the pad of his thumb along her jaw. "And I never even said I was sorry."

"You did what you had to do." She shrugged, and he put his hands on her raised shoulders.

"Don't. Don't pretend it didn't hurt. Don't pretend I didn't betray your trust, your. . .love."

Her chest rose and fell as she twisted her fingers in her lap. "Liam, I. . ."

He held his breath, waiting for the words he'd needed to hear from her two years ago.

Instead an explosion rocked the car and lit up the night sky.

NAVY SEAL SPY

BY
CAROL ERICSON

Published in Great Britain 2015
by Mills & Boon, an imprint of Harlequin (UK) Limited,
Eton House, 18-24 Paradise Road, Richmond, Surrey, TW9 1SR

© 2015 Carol Ericson

ISBN: 978-0-263-25320-7

46-1015

Harlequin (UK) Limited's policy is to use papers that are natural, renewable and recyclable products and made from wood grown in sustainable forests. The logging and manufacturing processes conform to the legal environmental regulations of the country of origin.

Printed and bound in Spain
by CPI, Barcelona

Carol Ericson lives with her husband and two sons in Southern California, home of state-of-the-art cosmetic surgery, wild freeway chases and a million amazing stories. These stories, along with hordes of virile men and feisty women, clamor for release from Carol's head. It makes for some interesting headaches until she sets them free to fulfill their destinies and her readers' fantasies. To learn more about Carol, please visit her website, www.carolericson.com, "Where romance flirts with danger."

For LRF, my future Navy SEAL

Chapter One

A soft footfall outside the door raised the hair on the back of Katie's neck. With her gaze riveted to the dull silver handle of the door, she watched it go down slowly and then click against the lock.

She spun around on the toes of her low-heeled shoes and launched toward the closet. Good thing she'd mapped out an escape route days ago after studying the layout of the offices. Of course, the closet would be more like a trap than an escape if someone decided to investigate.

Holding her breath, she slipped into the claustrophobic space and crouched behind some boxes. She had a sliced-up view of the office through the slats on the closet door.

The door to the office swung open, and the figure of a man filled the frame. "I didn't expect to see you here this late."

Her heart slammed against her chest, and she rocked back on her heels with her rehearsed excuse running through her head.

A woman answered from the hallway. "I forgot some papers in my office and wanted to do some work at home. What's your excuse?"

The blood rushed to Katie's head, and she planted her hand against a box to steady herself. She pressed her other hand against her mouth to stifle her panting breath. Of course, nobody could see her through the slats and behind the boxes—yet.

The man, Garrett Patterson, responded. "I thought I'd left my office door unlocked and came back to check it out. I had no intention of doing any more work, unlike some people. You work too hard, Ginger. Do you ever turn off that brain of yours?"

Ginger Spann's tinkling laugh sounded close. She must've entered the room behind Garrett.

"Just like a man to think a woman has to turn off her brain to relax or…enjoy herself."

The door to the office clicked shut, and the soft sounds of rustling material floated across the room.

Katie swallowed, poked her head out from behind a box and squinted through the slats on the closet door. She couldn't see heads, only bodies, and those bodies were doing some naughty things to each other.

If she wasn't in hiding, she could record this encounter and turn it over to Human Resources—if they had an HR department and if she was a snitch. Neither was the case.

As Garrett pushed Ginger against the desk, she groaned, and Katie almost groaned along with her. How long would she be trapped here while these two went at it?

Garrett murmured. "I never thought you were interested before, even though I tried my damnedest to entice you. I've been waiting a long time for this, Ginger."

"Mmm, so have I, Garrett. So have I."

Someone gasped. Garrett? Who knew cold, uptight Ginger Spann had the moves to bring a man like Garrett to his knees?

Garrett slumped across the desk, and Katie drew back from her peephole as his face appeared in her line of sight. His mouth gaped open, and his eyes bugged out of their sockets.

What was Ginger doing to him, and could she give lessons?

Then Ginger shifted from beneath Garrett's body and pushed him to the floor, where he fell in a heap, his pale face still turned in Katie's direction.

Katie drove her fist against her mouth. Garrett looked... dead.

Ginger straightened her pencil skirt and smoothed her hands over the fabric. She crouched next to Garrett's body, but Katie couldn't see her face.

Ginger must be in shock. Her movements, slow and deliberate, didn't look like those of someone who'd just had a guy drop dead on top of her.

Katie watched, her mouth dry, as Ginger felt for his pulse. Then Ginger's hand plunged into his pocket.

Katie froze, afraid to move one muscle, as Ginger searched Garrett's body. What the hell was she doing? Why wasn't she calling 911?

When Ginger rose to her feet, Katie gave a silent sigh of relief. Maybe Ginger was just trying to cover her backside—literally. As far as Katie knew, Garrett was a married man. She knew nothing about Ginger's marital status, although rumors had been circulating about her and the big boss. The woman was as cold as an icicle.

Katie heard the tones of cell phone buttons, and her stomach dropped. Once the EMTs swarmed this place, what chance would she have of escaping? It could be hours. She could be discovered.

"We've got a problem." Ginger's sharp tone was a one-eighty from her breathy pillow talk with Garrett. "I got here all right, but Garrett Patterson was here before me."

Ginger paused and then lashed back. "How the hell am I supposed to know? I couldn't risk it. He's dead."

Katie swallowed.

"This is your problem. You're the one who lost your

badge in his office. Send one of your minions over here to help me out. Now."

She must've ended the call because she'd stopped talking. Ginger moved toward the door and out of Katie's sight, but Garrett's dead eyes still stared at her in her hiding place.

Both she and Garrett had stumbled on more than they'd bargained for. Garrett had forgotten to lock his office door when he'd left for the day, and Katie had been careening down the hallway looking for an unlocked door.

Garrett's action had gotten him killed, and hers had gotten her trapped—but had also confirmed her suspicions about her place of work. Now, if she could only get out of this situation alive.

A soft tap on the door had Katie's heart hammering again.

The door opened and Ginger whispered. "Did anyone see you?"

"No. Besides, I have an excuse for wandering the halls at this hour."

"You're an idiot. How did you manage to lose your badge?"

A pair of legs encased in gray pants with a black stripe up the side came into Katie's line of vision. Security.

"My plastic badge holder cracked on one side. It must've fallen out, but at least I figured out where."

"Yeah, you're a real genius. Get a new badge holder. Patterson was already suspicious. Finding your badge in his office would've amped up his suspicions even more."

The security guy whistled and crouched beside Garrett's lifeless body. A hand with a bird tattooed on the back reached for Garrett's throat. "How'd you do him?"

"As far as you're concerned, he had a heart attack."

"With his fly down?" The security guard chuckled.

"That's why you're here. Set it up."

"Fingerprints?"

"Don't worry about fingerprints. I have every right to be in Garrett's office, and nobody's going to be doing a criminal investigation here if you stage it correctly."

The guard hoisted Garrett's body up and dragged him out of Katie's view. Unfortunately, the two conspirators exchanged very few words as they positioned Garrett at his desk and straightened up the office.

Katie hadn't noticed a security guard's badge when she'd first entered Garrett's office, which seemed like hours ago now, but she hadn't known what to look for. It was the first time in two weeks of searching that she'd discovered an unlocked office, and she'd meant to take advantage of it.

If she'd found that badge first, there's no telling what she could've discovered about her employer, Tempest… and Sebastian's suicide.

"That should do it." The security guard cleared his throat. "Should I close his eyes?"

"Why? People die with their eyes open all the time."

"I don't know. He looks kinda…surprised."

"He was."

Katie shivered. Why kill Garrett unless she suspected him of returning to his office to get the security guard's badge? Why would he do that? Was it because he had his own doubts about Tempest?

The security guy's shoes squeaked as he crossed the floor. "Should I discover him tonight?"

"Let someone else discover him tomorrow morning. Keep a low profile."

"He's a married guy. His wife might come looking for him or start calling around."

"Garrett's wife is out of town." Ginger made a clicking noise. "He must've told me that ten times this week."

"Then he's someone else's problem."

Ginger brushed past the closet door, and Katie's heart stuttered as she caught a whiff of Ginger's light, citrus perfume.

"I'm leaving first. Wait at least a minute and then get lost."

"Should I leave the door locked or unlocked?"

"Leave it unlocked—the easier for someone to find him tomorrow morning."

"I hope this works."

"Of course it'll work. I didn't slit his throat. The drug I gave him mimics a heart attack, and that's all you need to know."

The door clicked open and shut, and Katie eased out a short breath. Ginger terrified her—even more now.

The security guard hummed a tuneless song as Katie closed her eyes and counted the seconds until his departure. Her muscles ached with tension.

Just when she thought she'd be holed up in the closet all night, she heard the door open and close and blessed silence descended on the office. Leaning her forehead against the nearest box, she released a noisy sigh.

She shifted her stiff body and pressed her eye against the slat in the door. As far as she could see, the room looked empty, not that she expected Ginger or the security guard to pop out from behind the desk—but she wouldn't put it past them.

Unlike Ginger, she had no reason to be in Garrett Patterson's office, so she shrugged out of her sweater and wiped down the boxes and the inside of the closet door. Still using the sweater, she pushed against the door to open it and crawled out.

She straightened up and then immediately swayed to the side when she caught sight of Garrett slumped in his chair, his eyes still open. She crept toward the desk and reached across the body to shuffle through the contents on top of his blotter. The security guard must've found his badge.

Like most employees at Tempest, Garrett worked on a laptop that he must've already taken home for the evening.

Her fingers tripped across the edge of a notebook shoved beneath the blotter. She pulled it free and thumbed through the pages of what looked like an appointment book.

As she wiped the desk clean with the sweater, it caught on the arm of Garrett's chair and she yanked it free. She didn't want to get any closer to him than she had to.

She shoved her arms into the sleeves and tucked Garrett's spiral notebook into the pocket. Grasping the door handle with the sleeve of the sweater pulled over her hand, she took one last glance at the room. If she'd had her cell phone with her, she could've caught the whole scene on video. Of course, if she'd had her phone with her and it'd buzzed, she could be dead right now.

She pushed down on the handle and inched open the door. The hallway stretched to her right toward the stairwell, and she slipped from the office and tiptoed down the hallway. She'd already checked these other doors earlier— all locked.

When she reached the metal door to the stairwell, she pulled the sleeve of the sweater over her hand again. She didn't think the authorities would be checking for fingerprints out here, but she didn't want to be connected to this floor in any way. She'd already tampered with the security camera, and she'd fix its footage later.

Anxious to put as much distance between herself and Garrett Patterson, she charged through the door. She took the stairs two at a time on her way down and then stumbled to a screeching halt as a man materialized in front of her.

A scream roared from her lungs and then ended in a squeak on her lips as she looked up into the bluest eyes she'd ever seen—or at least the bluest eyes she'd ever seen since the last time she'd locked lips with the man who broke her heart.

Chapter Two

Adrenaline pumped through Liam's body as he reached out to grab the woman barreling into him. She tipped back her head, her perfect lips forming a perfect O, and his adrenaline kicked up another notch.

He whispered the name of the woman who'd been haunting his dreams for two years. "Katie-O."

"You!" Her dark eyebrows collided over her nose. "What the hell are you doing here?"

"Me?" He didn't know whether to give her a shake or a kiss, so he settled for smoothing the pads of his thumbs along her collarbone as he still held her by the shoulders. "What are *you* doing here?"

"Always answering a question with a question." She shrugged him off. "I work here."

His eyes narrowed, and his senses kicked into high alert. "You work for Tempest?"

"Shh. Don't tell anyone. It's top secret." She held her finger to her lips, and her eyes sparkled in the dimness of the stairwell.

He'd never known when to take Katie seriously—that had been one of their many problems during their brief acquaintance. Her dramatic words and gestures were over the top, but they held an ultimate truth. If she did, indeed, work for Tempest, then her work was top secret.

"In what capacity, the recreation adviser?" Last he'd heard, Katie was designing video games.

She removed her finger from her lips and shook it under his nose. "Not so fast. I asked you what you were doing here first."

He studied her face in the low light. She was angry with him about the way they'd ended things. He couldn't trust her. Hell, he couldn't trust anyone.

He lowered his voice and put his lips close to her ear. "What do you think I'm doing here?"

She twitched back from him. "The last time I saw you in San Diego, you had one more tour of duty as a navy SEAL. So, you're either here as a consultant or you're training to be an...agent."

"Brilliant deduction."

"Which is it?" She wedged her hands on her hips, as feisty as ever.

"It's top secret." He winked at her.

The door above them scraped open, and Liam pulled Katie into his arms, lunging for the recessed area between the two sets of stairs. A shaft of light from the hallway crept across the landing above them as the door widened.

A footstep landed on the cement floor, and heavy breathing echoed through the stairwell.

Liam held Katie tighter.

The silky strands of her black hair got caught on the scruff of his beard as he held her head against his chest with one hand. If she wondered why someone's presence in the stairwell had sent him scrambling for cover, her curiosity didn't lead her to break away from him or call out to the stranger.

The intruder shuffled onto the landing as if he was peering down the stairs. Then he backtracked and let the fire door slam shut.

Liam remained still for several more seconds, holding Katie, inhaling the sweet fragrance emanating from her skin.

Still in his arms, she tilted her head back, and he could see the pulse in her throat beating wildly. Had his actions frightened her? Aroused her?

Her voice was a low whisper. "Wh-why did you do that?"

"I'm not sure I'm allowed in this building, and I'm bucking for a perfect training score."

"If you're not supposed to be here, what are you doing in this stairwell?"

"Are you allowed in this building?"

"I work on the first floor."

"What are you doing on the fourth floor?"

She pushed away from him and crossed her arms. "Uh, ladies' room—they're on the even-numbered floors only, and the one on the second floor is out of order."

His gaze dropped to her arms crossed over her chest, her fingers biting into her upper arms. She was lying.

"Then maybe we didn't have to hide. I could've said I was visiting you."

"No!"

The word was out of her mouth before he finished his sentence.

He could almost feel the waves of heat coming from her cheeks as she twirled a lock of hair around her finger. "I—I just think it's better if Tempest doesn't know that we were...acquaintances. Don't you?"

The minute Katie-O had plowed into him, he'd had no intention of revealing his relationship with her to Tempest, and he never would've allowed her to do it, either. The fact that she'd come up with the deception first made his life a lot easier...and made him a lot more suspicious.

He raised his eyes to the ceiling and tapped his chin. "I suppose that's probably for the best. Tempest is a covert agency that forbids you to tell anyone where you work. Is it that way for you, too?"

"Absolutely." She puffed out a breath. "I had to sign all sorts of forms and agreements to keep my employment here under wraps—even from my closest family members."

"Even from Sebastian? He's like a brother to you. I can't imagine you'd keep anything from him."

Her pale skin blanched even more and her huge, dark eyes sparkled with tears. "Sebastian's dead."

Without thinking of anything but taking her hurt away, he gathered her in his arms again. "I'm so sorry, Katie. I hadn't heard."

He hadn't heard much of anything in the past two years since he'd seen her. He'd been deployed for another year in Afghanistan and then immediately plucked from the navy for…another assignment.

She sniffled against his chest but didn't offer up any details. If she didn't want to talk about Sebastian, he didn't want to ask her to elaborate on the death of the man who'd been the only person she'd called family.

"Is that why you took a job with Tempest in the middle of Idaho, to get away from everything?"

Stepping back, she grabbed both of his hands, her nails digging into his flesh. "Don't tell anyone here that you know me."

He'd be more than happy to keep her secret, since that meant she'd be keeping his. "You have my word, Katie."

"And don't—" she flung his hands away from her "—call me Katie."

He opened his mouth to find out what she wanted him to call her, but she spun around and disappeared down the stairwell.

KATIE RAN HER tongue along the inside of her dry mouth as the announcement from the Giant Voice system blared from the speaker in the corner of the office where she shared cubicle space with other employees from various departments.

"All-hands meeting in the building S cafeteria. Report immediately to the building S cafeteria."

Katie removed her access card from her computer and grabbed her purse from the desk drawer. Hooking it over her shoulder, she joined her coworker Samantha in the line of people heading for the office door.

Samantha cupped her hand over her mouth and dipped her head toward Katie. "What do you think this is all about?"

"I have no idea." Katie's gaze ping-ponged among the faces of her other coworkers filing out of the office into the hallway. Their expressions registered everything from boredom to curiosity to fear. The fearful ones, she'd come to realize, were either total newbies like her or long-termers, but she hadn't yet figured out what they had to fear.

"Hey." Samantha tugged on Katie's purse strap. "Do you think all hands include all the hot guys who are over at the gym training every day?"

"I thought we weren't allowed over at the gym."

"Don't be such a Goody Two-shoes, KC. I told you I'd heard there was hot man meat over there, and I was going to check it out." Samantha smacked her lips. "And I'm here to tell you the reports didn't lie."

"You're going to get yourself fired, Samantha." If spying on the agents got Samantha fired, then she couldn't even imagine her punishment for spying on a murder.

Samantha shrugged. "Whatever. This job sucks, anyway. Too many rules, regulations and restrictions, and not a damned thing to do out here in the middle of nowhere."

"The pay's good."

"That's about the only perk." She dropped her voice and moved close to Katie again. "And you can't tell me you think Mr. Romo is anyone who remotely resembles a normal boss."

"Quiet." Katie glanced around at the other Tempest employees streaming into the cafeteria. Maybe Samantha didn't want to keep this job, but Katie had to keep it—even now that Liam had turned up. Maybe even more so.

How had Liam gotten involved with Tempest? She bit her lip and blinked the tears from her eyes. Probably the same way Sebastian had gotten involved, but she hadn't come here to save Liam McCabe.

She came to get justice for Sebastian, and she wouldn't allow anyone to stand in her way—not even Liam.

As she shuffled into the cafeteria, Katie noticed the security guards at each door. She studied their faces, impassive beneath their caps, and wondered which one had helped Ginger last night. If she could get a look at the backs of their hands, she'd know for sure.

"I feel like I should be mooing." Samantha tossed her hair back and then nudged Katie's shoulder. "The man parade is here. This must be important."

Katie jerked her head to the left and watched a line of impressive men, with one woman in their midst, snake through the side door and line up against the wall. Facially, they weren't all handsome, at least not like Liam, who possessed the classic good looks of a California surfer, but all of them had incredible builds with muscles that went on forever and an air of quiet competence. And these were just the new recruits.

Man meat, indeed.

Had Liam picked her out of the crowd as easily as she had him? As she studied his face across the room, he looked up and met her eyes as if he knew exactly where she'd been standing all along.

Closing her eyes, she allowed herself one delicious shiver as she relived their meeting in the stairwell last night and once again felt Liam's arms around her. He'd smelled precisely as she remembered—fresh like an ocean breeze, manly and strong.

Her eyelids flew open. And now he was part of Tempest— the enemy.

Pradeep Singh tapped the microphone at the front of the room, and the other managers lined up behind him. Their boss, Mr. Romo, was absent as usual. Ginger took a position to Pradeep's right, folding her hands loosely in front of her, the business suit, glasses and chignon sending a demure, professional vibe.

But Katie knew better.

"Hello, everyone." Pradeep waved his hands. "There are some seats up front, but we won't keep you too long."

Not many in the crowd took him up on his offer, so he continued.

"I know some of you have been hearing rumors this morning, and some of you early risers heard sirens and may have even seen the ambulance."

Katie swallowed and hung on to her purse strap. *Here it comes.*

Pradeep cleared his throat. "I'm sorry to report that one of our own, Garrett Patterson, died at the compound last night."

A few gasps and oohs and aahs rippled through the room, and Ginger leaned toward Pradeep, covering the mic with her hand as she whispered something in his ear.

Pradeep nodded once. "Garrett had a heart attack in his office last night—in this very building on the fourth floor."

A wave of sympathetic murmurs swirled through the cafeteria, but Katie felt the air brimming with tension. Was it just the fact that a coworker had died in the building, or did the Tempest employees sense something more? She glanced around the room at the concerned and sad faces— emotions totally in keeping with the announcement.

She continued to scan the crowd and like a magnet, her eyes locked on to Liam's. Even from this distance she could feel the intensity of his gaze. He'd probably taken note that Garrett had keeled over on the fourth floor—the floor she'd been exiting when she bumped into him on the stairwell. Liam didn't miss much—except when it came to emotion.

Ginger stepped up to the mic next. "We'll be taking up a collection for flowers for Garrett's wife. The memorial service will be back East, so please pay your respects with a little donation."

Katie clenched her jaw at Ginger's phony, saccharine tone. Pradeep droned on for a bit more, but she'd tuned out. They'd put the heart attack story out there, and apparently had no trouble selling it to the EMTs who'd responded this morning.

Would that be the end of it? Could she phone in an anonymous tip to the police to check for some sort of heart attack-inducing drug?

"Earth to KC." Samantha snapped her fingers in front of Katie's face.

Pradeep had stopped speaking, and the crowd had begun shuffling back to their work areas, talking in low voices.

"Psst." Samantha pinched her arm. "Let's exit the same way the agents are exiting."

"A coworker just died and that's all you can think about?"

"Between you and me—" Samantha looked both ways "—Garrett had a roving eye. The few times I talked to him, he couldn't seem to keep his gaze at eye level, if you know what I mean."

"So he deserves to drop dead at his desk for being a perv?"

"Was he at his desk?" Samantha cocked her head. "I didn't hear them say where he was."

Katie shrugged. "Pradeep said he was found in his office, so I just assumed he was at his desk."

Samantha herded her across the room to the farthest exit door where Liam and the other agents were headed. Would Liam think she was trying to get close to him?

She and Samantha jostled for position, and someone bumped her purse from behind. Gripping the strap, she glanced over her shoulder.

"Sorry." Liam dropped his eyes to her purse and then stared straight ahead as if she was just another Tempest office worker—not someone who'd shared his bed for eight delicious months two years ago.

As the workers fanned out into the hallway, Samantha poked her in the back. "You see? It worked. One of them actually said something to you."

"Yeah, he said sorry for bumping into my purse after you pushed me in front of him."

"Well, that's a start."

"Start of some trouble. We're not supposed to be fraternizing with those guys." Katie flashed her badge at the reader by the office door, and the red light turned to green.

"I'd like to fraternize one or two of them." Samantha winked and then ducked into her cubicle.

Katie dropped into her chair and hunched forward to open her bottom desk drawer to put her purse away. As she wedged it into the drawer, she noticed the corner of a white card sticking out of the side pocket.

Pinching it between two fingers, she pulled it free. The words jumped out at her.

Behind the bleachers at noon.

She recognized the writing as Liam's, and her heart skipped a beat. Should she risk it? She might be able to wheedle some information out of him. She had special ways of handling Liam McCabe—or at least she used to.

She had to find out what he knew. The notebook she'd

snatched from Patterson's office last night had been a bust—just a bunch of abbreviations, a series of numbers and meeting notes.

The rest of the morning crawled by. Samantha popped in to let her know she had to bail on lunch for a meeting with her boss in accounting, which saved Katie from bailing herself.

When the clock on her computer read ten minutes to twelve, Katie grabbed her purse and ducked into the lunchroom to get her sandwich from the fridge. She'd better have some cover for being out at the track on her lunch hour.

Glancing at the gray skies, she turned up the collar of her jacket and crossed the quad. If it started raining, she'd have to abandon the meeting with Liam, and he'd have to reschedule it—or not. What did he want with her, anyway?

She slipped behind the building on the north side of the quad, put her head down and marched toward the gym that had a track behind it. Tempest had taken over an old high school for its compound and had remodeled most of the buildings on campus, even adding dorm-type living quarters for the recruits, but the track and the indoor pool had been maintained.

Employees were allowed to use the gym, but only before and after regular work hours. Tempest wanted to keep the agent recruits and the rest of the employees apart, unless the job directly involved the agents—hers didn't, not yet, anyway.

A few people were jogging around the track, and she realized one of them was Liam. She settled on the second to last row of the bleachers and pulled out her lunch and a book. Ignoring the runners, she ate her sandwich with her book propped open on her knees.

Liam broke away from the track and started jogging up and down the bleachers. On one of his trips down, his pace slowed as he passed her. He panted. "Underneath the bleachers."

She wadded up her brown paper bag and stepped down from the second row. She wandered to the trash can at the back of the bleachers, tossed away her trash and then ducked beneath the bleachers, stepping over the bars criss-crossing the open space. She could still hear Liam's feet as they rang against the metal steps above her.

Less than five minutes later, Liam joined her beneath the bleachers, steam rising from his flesh, damp with sweat. His musky scent pulsed off him in waves, drawing her in, making him seem closer than he was.

His blond hair, away from the sun and surf, had darkened to a burnt gold, but his blue eyes still sparkled like the ocean on a clear day. She curled her hands into fists to squelch the urge to run her fingers through his hair.

"What do you want?" Angry with herself for responding to him in the old familiar ways, her tone came out as harsh as the raw, cold day.

"That guy, Patterson, died in his office on the fourth floor."

She brushed a speck of dirt from the sleeve of her jacket. "Yeah, I know. I was at the same meeting as you."

"You—" he leveled a finger at her "—were on the fourth floor of building S last night, flying down the staircase like you'd seen a ghost."

"Well, I didn't see Garrett Patterson, if that's what you're implying, and if I had, I would've reported his... death instead of chatting about old times with you in the stairwell." She widened her stance and dug her heels into the rubber track beneath her feet.

"Old times? I don't remember any walk down memory lane. You were too busy telling me to keep my mouth shut about knowing you...KC Locke."

"Have you been checking me out?"

His eyes flickered. "If we're going to pull off this pretense, I figured it was best if I knew what you were calling yourself."

"KC Locke." She stuck out her hand. "Nice to meet you."

He took her hand and circled the inside of her wrist with his thumb. "KC, Kathryn Claire Locke—that's the name you used when you were in the foster care system. How does Tempest not know that you started calling yourself Katie and changed your last name to your mother's maiden name, O'Keefe, when you left the system?"

"Shh. I have friends in low places."

"Yeah, more like you used your mad skills with a computer." He tightened his grip on her wrist. "Are you going to tell me what you're doing here under an assumed name?"

She leaned in close just to catch another whiff of him. "I'm going to tell you that Garrett Patterson had a heart attack, and I wasn't there when it happened."

Dropping her hand, he lifted one shoulder. "Don't play with fire, Katie."

"You should've warned me about that two years ago in San Diego." She hunched into her jacket and stepped out from beneath the bleachers.

With her hands stuffed in her pockets and her head down to ward off the chilly wind, she strode toward the track to cross it. Would he come after her? He couldn't. They couldn't be seen together out in the open.

She wandered across the track, sniffing back the tingles in her nose. Then a sharp voice interrupted her daydreams.

"Stop right where you are, or I'll drop you where you stand."

Chapter Three

All of Liam's senses ramped up to high alert but instead of charging from beneath the bleachers to defend Katie like he wanted to, he flattened his body against the metal bars that crisscrossed his hiding place. He wouldn't be doing either one of them any favors by rushing out to protect her. Besides, a Tempest security guard wouldn't shoot an employee in cold blood...would he?

He peered through the bars, his heart hammering against his chest at the sight of Katie with her arms in the air, a weapon pointed at her back.

A woman's voice cut through the air. "Meyers, put down that gun."

The security guard lowered his weapon as he stammered. "I—I—I'm sorry, Ms. Spann, but civilian employees aren't supposed to be out here on the track."

Ginger Spann waved her long fingers in the air. "The infraction of that rule is certainly not punishable by death. Turn around, dear."

Katie turned to face the duo, and Liam had to give her credit. She didn't shift her gaze once in his direction, although she had to know he was still ensconced beneath the bleachers.

He couldn't see her expression since the security guard

was now blocking her face, but he could feel ice coming off her in waves, making the chilly air even crisper.

"What is going on? I come outside to eat my lunch in the fresh air and I'm held at gunpoint?" She shook her empty sandwich bag, which she'd pulled from her pocket, in the security guard's face.

"I agree, KC." Ginger tilted her head to one side. "It is KC, isn't it? Down in programming?"

Katie worked in programming? That made total sense… and could be useful.

"That's right, and you're Ginger Spann. I just saw you at the all-hands meeting."

"So sad about Garrett Patterson. Maybe that's why we're all on edge." She turned to the security guard. "Meyers, apologize to Ms. Locke."

Meyers shifted from one foot to the other. "I'm sorry, ma'am. It's just that we have strict orders about this area of the—"

"That's enough, Meyers. You can return to whatever it was you were doing before you scared the wits out of Ms. Locke."

"Yes, ma'am." Meyers spun around, and Liam caught a glimpse of the man's tight mouth as he walked toward the gym.

Seems he didn't care much for Ginger's tone, but then, who did?

His departure gave Liam a clear view of Katie's face.

Her wind-tossed, dark hair blew across her face, and she scooped it into a ponytail, holding it over one shoulder. "I'm really sorry about venturing this far. After the news about Garrett, I just wanted to get out of the building for lunch and get some fresh air. I wasn't paying any attention to where I was going, and when I looked up I realized I was way out here, so I just sat on the bleachers to eat my sandwich."

Ginger raised her suit-clad shoulders. "No harm, no foul. It's just that we have training going on out here for potential agents. You knew that, right? Everyone knows that, I suppose."

"That's the buzz, anyway."

The wind gusted, and Ginger tugged at the lapels of her suit jacket.

She wasn't dressed for a turn around the track in this weather. Had the security guard spotted Katie first before calling Ginger? If so, had he seen her emerge from beneath the bleachers?

"It's chilly out here. Let's walk back together."

Liam twisted his lips. That was a less-than-subtle way to get Katie out of this area.

As the two women turned and took the path back to the office buildings, Liam let out a long breath.

What was Katie doing working for Tempest in what amounted to an undercover situation? That was *his* job.

If she was here in a legitimate position as a programmer, why would she come on under an assumed name? She'd called herself KC when she was a teenager in foster care, had switched to the more formal Kathryn when she became an adult and started working and then settled on Katie, which suited her a lot better than Kathryn or KC.

Now she was KC again.

KC was the wild child, the rebel, the illegal hacker, even though she dressed like an office drone. Did calling herself KC have some significance here?

He narrowed his eyes and peered between the bleachers at the empty track. He'd skipped lunch to run a few miles, so he'd better work up a sweat to bolster his story.

He slipped between the slats and hoisted himself on top of the bleachers. Lifting his knees almost to his chest, he began running the stairs. A few trips up and back and sweat dampened his gray T-shirt and beaded his brow.

As he slung his towel around his neck, he peered at the office buildings in the distance. What kind of game was Katie playing with Tempest?

She had to know that if she lost even one round of that game, it could mean her life.

KATIE TOOK A deep breath and hunched over the sink in the bathroom. For a minute she thought Ginger was going to follow her in here. The woman gave her the creeps, and that had been before she'd watched her kill a man in cold blood in midcoitus.

Ginger had shown a lot of interest in Katie's work. Had asked her several questions about programming and what programming languages she knew.

Katie splashed some cold water on her face even though her cheeks still stung from the crisp air outside.

She blotted her face with a paper towel and then crumpled it in her fist. Ginger had no reason to suspect her. Neither she nor the security guard had seen Liam crouching beneath the bleachers.

Meyers—had he been the same guy who'd assisted Ginger last night? He'd been wearing black gloves so if he did have the bird tattoo, she couldn't see it. The voice sounded similar and besides, how many guards did Ginger have that would willingly be an accomplice to murder?

She tossed the paper towel in the trash and straightened her shoulders. Ginger didn't scare her. She still planned to gather more evidence against Tempest and then report the agency to…someone. She hadn't gotten that far in her plan yet.

Her head swiveled back toward the mirror, and she ran her hands through her wind-tossed hair. She'd thought Liam McCabe was the kind of man to turn to in dire straits, but not if he was working with the enemy.

Or was he?

Sebastian certainly hadn't known what he was getting himself into.

She pushed out of the ladies' room and turned the corner to catch the elevator down to her floor. The phone rang just as she stepped into her cubicle, and she spent fifteen minutes dealing with a software issue.

"Where did you disappear to for lunch?" Samantha hung on the corner of her cube.

"I wandered around outside for a bit. How was your meeting?"

Samantha rolled her eyes. "A huge waste of time, and Larry didn't even buy me lunch, the cheap bastard."

"That's just wrong."

"Cute jacket." Samantha tilted her head. "Do you have the sweater you borrowed from me yesterday?"

"Oh, yeah. It's hanging in the closet." Katie jerked her thumb at the metal black cabinet behind her that had a bar and a couple of hangers.

Samantha reached past her and opened the door. She shook out the cream-colored sweater she usually kept on the back of her chair for the days when the office got too chilly—like today.

"I hope you sew."

"What?" Katie clicked on an email reminding her about database maintenance tomorrow night and then deleted it.

"There's a button missing, and I swear it wasn't missing when I gave the sweater to you yesterday."

Katie spun around in her chair. "Really?"

Samantha thrust the sweater at her and a few scraggly threads marked the spot where a square button had been.

"I'm so sorry. Do you have a replacement for it? I can sew it back on."

Samantha laughed. "I'm just kidding. I might have an extra button for this old thing at home. I'll sew it back on when I find it."

"I'll check my car. I didn't bring it in to my place last night. I wore it to my car and tossed it in the backseat so I wouldn't forget it today."

"Don't knock yourself out." She draped the sweater over her shoulders. "It's just my office sweater. I wouldn't actually go out in public wearing this thing."

"The buttons are kind of cute."

"These?" She plucked at one of the shiny squares. "They're hideous."

Samantha retreated to her own cubicle, and Katie dug into her work. She hadn't figured out a way around the Tempest firewalls yet, but she would. She'd been something of a hacker before she went legitimate, and while changing a few grades didn't compare to the type of security Tempest had in place, she had confidence in her skills. She'd already figured out how to mess with the security cameras and the access cards.

She stretched and wandered to the window, folding her arms as she rested her forehead against the glass. She couldn't quite see the track from here, but she could see the edge of the gym, and the movement over there meant the agents were training again.

She knew they slept here. They had living quarters behind the compound out there. Some of them wouldn't make the cut, and they'd be sent home after signing some nondisclosure agreement. They agreed not to talk about their training, and they walked away with a nice severance bonus—at least that's what she'd heard.

She had no doubt Liam would pass every physical test they threw at him. When she'd met him in San Diego, he'd been a SEAL—conditioned, primed and at his peak.

From the looks of him today in his T-shirt and running shorts, he was still at his peak. She chewed on her bottom lip. Maybe she should warn him. But warn him about what? She had no idea really what Tempest was up to. She just knew it was no good, and maybe Liam knew that, too.

She couldn't believe he'd turn on her, but then she wouldn't have believed he'd leave her stranded, high and dry in San Diego, while he returned to the Middle East for another tour. He'd promised her he was done.

She snorted and squiggled her finger through the mist her breath had left on the window. Men like Liam were never done. Men like Sebastian.

She needed another break. She dipped back into her cubicle and dragged her car keys from her purse. Tapping on the side of Samantha's cubicle, she said, "I'm going out to my car in case anyone's looking for me. I'm going to look for that button."

"I don't care about the stupid button, KC."

"I know, but it's bugging me now, and I need a break, anyway."

"If you remember, get me a diet cola from the vending machine downstairs. I'm gonna need some caffeine if I'm gonna get through this boring stuff before I leave tonight."

Katie patted the pocket of her jacket where she had a few dollar bills. "No problem."

She made her way to the parking structure, where cars still took up the majority of the spaces. Most of the employees took off around five o'clock, except for the diehards, people like Ginger and Garrett and Mr. Romo. Nobody ever saw much of Mr. Romo, and nobody ever called him anything but Mr. Romo, but he presided over Tempest from the top floor of the building like some omniscient being. She'd caught sight of him a few times, and he always seemed to be staring at her, but that was probably because he had the oddest, light-colored eyes.

Katie had her doubts he ever left the compound.

She clicked her remote, and her horn beeped once. She went straight for the backseat, running her palms along the leather. Then she lay on her stomach and scanned the floor for the shiny button. She even slipped her hands between the seat cushions.

Her fingertips skimmed the edge of a long-lost nickel. She pulled it free and tucked it into the pocket of her slacks.

Blowing a wisp of hair from her face, she shimmied out of the backseat and slid behind the wheel of the car. She scooped a fistful of quarters from the cup holder to make sure she had enough money for Samantha's soda and one for herself.

Then she tilted her head back against the headrest. When had she lost that button? She hadn't been too many places after borrowing the sweater from Sam at the end of the workday.

She'd worked late in her cubicle after everyone had left to give herself time to do her weekly roaming of the hallways. She'd finally lucked out when she discovered Garrett Patterson's door unlocked—at least she'd considered herself lucky until Ginger had murdered Garrett.

Could she have lost the button hiding in that closet?

Or was it worse than that? She pressed her fingertips to her lips as she recalled the sweater getting caught on Garrett's chair as she wiped her prints from his desk.

No point in returning to his office even if she could get in. If she'd lost the button there, it was either hidden or someone had found it and disposed of it. A button was a button, and it could've come from anywhere.

She scooted from the car and deposited the rest of the change into her pocket. She slammed the car door and leaned forward to peer at her reflection. This dry weather wasn't doing her hair any favors—not that she had cared about her appearance here at Tempest one iota until Liam had shown up on the scene. The man still caused her blood to simmer despite her resolve not to let him affect her. She couldn't afford the distraction.

A movement reflected in the glass caught her eye, and she spun around. The blank headlights on the rows of cars parked in their orderly places stared back at her.

She cocked her head, listening for the beep of a remote or the slamming of a car door. Her own heavy breathing answered her.

Maybe someone had just come back to his car to get something or take a break. Nobody at Tempest had any reason to suspect her of snooping. Sure, Ginger and Meyers had caught her near the track, but she wouldn't be the first female employee at Tempest to try to get a better look at the buff recruits as they went through their paces.

Wiping her palms on her slacks, she strode toward the parking structure's elevator and jabbed the button. When the doors closed, she released a sigh and sagged against the wall of the elevator.

It had been a long time since she'd practiced this cloak-and-dagger stuff. She'd stopped hacking shortly after turning eighteen. Sergeant Liz Humphries, the cop who'd taken an interest in Katie while she'd still been in the foster care system, had undertaken the chore of teaching her right from wrong and more important at the time, the difference between a juvenile record and an adult record.

The same woman had encouraged a rebellious Sebastian to enlist in the Marine Corps. Liz had been a surrogate mother to both of them, creating an unbreakable bond between them at the same time—unbreakable until Sebastian's death.

She blinked back tears as she crossed the courtyard between the parking garage and the office building. As soon as she had proof that Tempest was responsible for Sebastian's death, she'd blow this organization sky-high. And if Liam was still with Tempest, she'd blow him sky high with it.

She swung by the lunchroom and fed her dollar bills

and coins into the soda machine. With a can in each hand, she returned to her office on the first floor. She swiped her card and sailed through the free-standing desks at the front of the office toward the cubicles in the back of the room.

She leaned into Samantha's empty cubicle and placed the can on the edge of her desk in the only spot not covered with papers.

Something gleamed under the lamp on Samantha's desk blotter, and Katie reached out and smoothed her fingers along the edges of the square button.

She blew out a breath. Samantha must've found it in the office. Maybe it had fallen off the sweater in her cube before Katie had even borrowed it.

She returned to her own cubicle and popped the tab on her soda. She had one bug fix to take care of, and then she planned to do a little digging into Liam's file if she could get in there. She'd hacked into other recruits' files but had never found Sebastian's. Of course, Sebastian had been a full-fledged Tempest agent and not just a recruit. She hadn't discovered that database yet.

She laced her fingers and cracked her knuckles over her keyboard. "Just give me time."

A gust of Samantha's flowery perfume announced her presence. "Thanks for the soda."

"You're welcome. I see you have the button. If you want, I'll sew it on for you."

Samantha held up her hands, wiggling her fingers, topped with long, blue fingernails. "Despite these nails, I'm rather handy with a needle. Don't worry about it."

"Where'd you find it? I bet it was in your cube all along. It had probably come off even before you loaned the sweater to me."

"No, it didn't." Samantha put her lips to the can and took a sip. "Someone found it and returned it to me."

"Really?" Katie's hands hovered over her keyboard. "Someone actually found a button and knew it was yours?"

"Said he'd noticed the sweater on me before because his sister had one like it." She shrugged. "Maybe he'd been checking me out."

"He?" Katie dropped her hands to her lap, threading her fingers together so tightly the knuckles turned white.

"One of the security guards."

A muscle ticked in Katie's jaw. "Which one?"

"The big guy with the tattoo of a bird on his hand—Meyers."

Chapter Four

Katie took a quick swig of her soda, and the carbonation fizzed against the back of her throat, making her eyes water. "Where'd he find it?"

"Outside the ladies' room."

"That's just weird that he knew it belonged to you."

"I don't know. The buttons are kind of distinctive—ugly but distinctive. Like I said, he said his sister had one like it. Whatever, I got the button back and you're off the hook." She raised her can and disappeared into her own work area.

Katie closed her eyes and wrapped her hands around the sweating can. Meyers had a tattoo of a bird. He'd been the one helping Ginger in Patterson's office and the one who had held her at gunpoint on the track. Now he'd found Samantha's button.

Was he pulling for employee of the month?

Pressing her damp fingers against her cheeks, she let out a long breath. So, Meyers found the button outside the ladies' room, recognized it as Samantha's and returned it to her. Nothing odd about that. He'd notice an attractive blonde like Sam, had probably been checking her out and maybe thought this was his chance to talk to her.

If he had found the button in Garrett's office, would he really run around the company trying to find its owner? Would they be that obvious?

Her computer blipped and an instant message popped up in the lower right-hand corner of her screen.

What r u really doing at Tempest?

A trickle of fear crept down her spine. The usual name that accompanied an instant message read *user*. This could be anyone testing her. Someone had seen her with Liam at the track.

She typed where the blinking cursor invited.

Who is this?

You have a tattoo of a mermaid just above your right pelvic bone.

Even sitting at her desk, she squirmed at Liam's reference to her tattoo. The man had gotten to know her body very well during their time together in San Diego.

She typed her response.

R u going to rat me out?

Same stairwell at 8 tonight.

What choice did she have? If she refused to meet him, he just might let her real name drop, and then Tempest would make the connection between her and Sebastian. KC Locke had no history with Sebastian Cole, but Katie O'Keefe did. She'd worked too hard to scrub her background and identity. She didn't need Liam McCabe to come along and blow it all up.

Not that she really believed Liam would expose her. Even if Liam knew her true purpose here, he'd never do anything to harm her. Although he'd bruised her heart, he'd move heaven and earth to protect her, and she'd do the same by telling him to run as far away from Tempest as he could.

The rest of the afternoon flew by with her joint efforts at doing her real job and continuing her assault on the firewalls Tempest had set up. Whoever had put them in place was damned good.

She jerked her head up and blinked her eyes when Samantha banged on the side of her cubicle. "Whoa, take it easy."

"I've been saying your name and tapping on the edge of your cube for the past minute. It's quittin' time, girl. A few of us are going to the Deluxe Bar for a couple of cocktails. Do you want to join us?"

"I'll pass. I have a problem to work through, so I'm going to stick around until I figure it out."

Samantha saluted. "Now that's what I call dedication. If you figure it out quickly, join us. We'll be there for a few hours."

"Will do. Have fun."

When Samantha left at five-twenty, Katie got a bag of chips from the vending machine and returned to her desk, slumping in her chair as she ripped open the bag.

"Are you working late?"

She glanced up, and her heart skipped a beat as Meyers's form filled the opening to her cubicle, his two hands wedged on either side of the edges as if blocking her exit.

She swallowed her chip and wiped her greasy fingers on a tissue. "I can get more work done when it's quiet."

"I just wanted to apologize for this afternoon. Management keeps us on our toes about protecting that area where the recruits are housed."

"I understand."

"We're kind of damned if we do, damned if we don't.

We're supposed to keep a close eye on it, but then we get in trouble for overreacting."

"Didn't mean to get you in trouble. I'll be more careful where I wander around next time."

"Yeah, just, sorry."

"Me, too."

He scratched the heavy stubble on his chin, causing the bird on his hand to move its wings. "Samantha leave for the day?"

"Uh-huh." She stuffed another chip in her mouth to end the conversation.

"Does she have a boyfriend?" He stared at his thumb while picking at his cuticle.

Her tense shoulders dropped. So, he had a thing for Samantha and probably *did* know the button he'd found belonged to her and used it as an excuse to talk to her.

"Nope." Not that she wanted to give Meyers false hope, but he wasn't Sam's type, anyway, and after his complicity in Patterson's death last night, she sure as hell wouldn't let Samantha date him.

"She likes those recruits, huh?"

Her spine stiffened again. He sure was keeping tabs on Samantha. "Oh, I wouldn't say that, no more than any other woman around here."

"I'll let you get back to work. Just wanted to apologize for drawing my gun on you this afternoon."

"Thanks." She swiveled her chair in front of her keyboard and popped another chip into her mouth, listening for the office door to close behind Meyers.

She worked for a few more hours, glancing at the time on her computer every ten minutes, not able to concentrate on anything. She'd never get through Tempest's firewalls with her mind on Liam.

At ten minutes to eight, she scrubbed the history on her computer, including her instant messages. Then she logged off and snatched her access card from the card reader on her computer. She had a date in a stairwell.

She headed for the elevator like she did every night, but when she got off·at the second floor, she entered the stairwell instead of heading to the exit for the parking garage. She jogged up two flights of stairs and ducked beneath the staircase.

A door above her scraped open, and she held her breath until Liam came into view.

He joined her, huddling so close she could smell the fresh scent of his soap and the mint of his toothpaste. He placed his lips close to her ear. "Did you get rid of those instant messages we traded?"

"Of course. I should be asking you that."

"I had a good teacher show me how to cover my tracks on a computer." He touched his finger to her nose.

She jerked her head and he dropped his hand. "Would you really blow my cover?"

"To keep you safe and get you away from Tempest? Maybe."

She caught her breath. Did he realize the danger at Tempest, or was this some kind of trick?

"What are you talking about? We both work for Tempest."

"Under somewhat assumed identities."

"Are you telling me they don't know you're Liam McCabe, former navy SEAL and all-around badass?" She narrowed her eyes.

"I like that description. Maybe I'll put it on my next business card."

She punched his arm, her fist meeting rock-solid muscle. "Be serious."

"They know I'm Liam McCabe, former navy SEAL, and they know about my badassery." He raised an eyebrow. "But that's where my identity ends as far as Tempest is concerned."

"What does that mean? What else is there?"

"What happened last night in Patterson's office? Why were you up here?"

She sighed. Maybe if she started answering some of his questions, he'd start answering some of hers.

"I've been searching Tempest at night, trying to find unlocked offices, looking for evidence. Patterson had left his office unlocked last night, and I slipped inside."

Liam pressed the heel of his hand against his forehead. "And you found him dead?"

"Worse than that. He came into the office while I was there, and I had to hide in the closet. Ginger Spann followed him, and...and she murdered him."

His body stiffened. "Are you sure? How?"

"She injected him with something that mimicked a heart attack. I heard the whole thing, Liam. Then she got some security guard in there to help her—the same security guard who pulled a gun on me at the track."

"They didn't see you?"

"No."

He took her by the shoulders and squeezed. "Why are you doing this, Katie? What's Tempest to you? And I want the truth. Tempest isn't some high school or hapless government agency that you can hack into for fun and games."

Staring into Liam's blue eyes, she felt safe for the first time since arriving at Tempest. He didn't seem that surprised about the murder, and he was obviously hiding something from Tempest. She could trust him. She could always trust Liam, except when it came to staying by her side.

She closed her eyes and let out a shuddering breath. "It's Sebastian."

"Sebastian? You told me he was dead."

"He is—and Tempest killed him."

"What? How? You have proof of this?"

"One question at a time." She placed her hands against his chest, and his heart thundered beneath her palm.

"He killed himself, Liam." Her nose stung, and she sniffled back the tears.

Liam's touch on her shoulders turned into a caress, and he pulled her snug against his body. "I'm so sorry, Katie. Was it the drugs again?"

She wrenched away from him. "Absolutely not. He'd been clean and sober for years. It was Tempest."

"You keep saying that, but how was Tempest responsible for his suicide?"

"They recruited him to be an agent—just like you— and after he'd made the grade and had worked for them for just over a year, he killed himself."

Her words slammed against his brain, and he blinked to clear the fog. Sebastian Cole was the Tempest agent who'd killed himself? He'd known about the agent but didn't know his name…until now. He didn't want to color Katie's perceptions or lead her on, so he kept his tone as neutral as he could.

"Why are you laying his suicide at Tempest's gates?"

She threw up her hands and took a half turn in the small space. "Because I saw him before and after. He was in a good place. He was thrilled Tempest wanted him. While he was in the marines, he'd heard rumors about the covert agencies and how much good they accomplished under the radar."

Liam pressed his lips into a thin line. As a SEAL he'd heard the rumors, too, but it was Prospero, not Tempest, who ruled the shadow operations. Tempest had always been second best, and then the agency had turned to the dark side, but no one knew to what extent.

"Then what? He came here?"

She nodded. "Yes, he came here as a recruit. I saw him once after he completed the training and already there was something off about him, but he seemed happy so I was happy."

A pulse danced in his jaw and he rubbed it into submission. Did Tempest start in with the recruits while they were still in training? "What was off about him?"

"He seemed a little detached, distant. I chalked it up to the covert nature of his training and work." She fluttered her lashes. "R-reminded me of you when you first got back from a mission."

Great. If she'd thought him detached and distant when he'd been a SEAL, what would she think of him as a covert ops agent?

"You saw him again?"

"It was worse the next time, the last time I saw him." Her bottom lip trembled, and he wanted to kiss away her pain. "He was angry, cold, closed up. He pushed me away."

God, just like he'd done when he'd decided to do another tour of duty while she'd been busy planning a life with him. Katie-O deserved so much more. This fearless woman at least deserved the truth.

He looked her straight in the eyes. "And then he shot himself in France while he was on an assignment."

Her mouth dropped open, and she took a step back. "How do you know that?"

"That's what I'm doing here, Katie."

"You're here because of Sebastian's death?"

"Partly."

Crossing her arms across her chest, she tilted her head to one side. "You're not a navy SEAL anymore, are you?"

"I'm working for another covert agency."

She snorted before he could finish. "That's swell. So you're over here, what? Stealing their secrets to success?"

"Katie." He grabbed her fidgeting hands. "Tempest is

bad news. It's not just Sebastian's suicide we're investigating, and no, I didn't realize the dead agent was Sebastian Cole. Another Tempest agent went on a rampage and had to be stopped. Another agent is on the run."

"What is Tempest doing to them? What's going on?"

"Drugs, brainwashing, mind control."

"I suspected as much." She sagged against him. "Why? What's their goal?"

"Their overall goal? We're not sure yet, but their goal for the agents is just that—mind control."

"To turn them into robots that'll do whatever they're told, no matter how unscrupulous." Her dark eyes widened. "That's what Sebastian was, some kind of robot."

Tears streamed silently down her cheeks, and she did nothing to stop them or wipe them away.

He cupped her face with his hands and smoothed his thumbs across the wet trails on her flushed skin. "I'm sorry, Katie. I know how much Sebastian meant to you."

Her body jerked, and she grabbed two handfuls of his jacket. "And what are you? Some kind of canary in the coal mine? If your…agency already knows what Tempest is doing to its agents, why do you need to be here to experience it firsthand?"

"We know what Tempest is doing, but we don't exactly know how, and we don't know when it all starts. It was important for someone to infiltrate the compound."

"Why does it have to be you?" Her voice rose, almost on a wail. "Why does it always have to be you?"

He put two fingers to her soft lips. "Shh. It's going to be okay. What's not okay is your presence here. You need to quit and leave as soon as possible."

"You need me." She wiped her sleeve across her nose. "I'm getting close to hacking through Tempest's firewalls. When I do, I can bring them down financially. I can hit them where it hurts. I'll make them pay for what they did to Sebastian."

The fire in Katie's eyes practically lit up the dim stairwell, and a thrill zapped his body. This was exactly why he'd fallen in love with this woman, exactly why she terrified him.

He pressed his lips to her hot forehead. "The computer stuff would be great but not necessary right now, not worth your safety."

"I am safe. I went through a lot of trouble to get this gig, and I'm not giving it up —for anyone. Did you give up your job for me?"

A flash of heat claimed his chest and crawled up his neck. He hadn't. He'd done what he believed was his last mission for his SEAL team, was ready to settle down with Katie when he got the call. They'd needed him, needed him more than Katie with her prickly, standoffish attitude.

"No, I didn't."

"Exactly." She pushed the hair from her face, pushing his hands away at the same time. "I have a job to do here. I have to avenge Sebastian's death, and I'm gonna do it with or without you."

How the hell could anyone resist a woman like Katie?

"Then we work together. You keep me posted and I'll keep—"

Katie grabbed his wrist and dug her fingernails into his flesh, while pointing at the ceiling.

Then he heard it—someone jiggling the handle on the metal door on the floor above. Good thing he'd rigged it.

Katie dragged at his arm and whispered. "We need to get out of here."

"He won't be able to get in for several minutes because I jammed the door. Let's go downstairs."

Placing his hand on the small of Katie's back, he propelled her down the stairs ahead of him. They passed the third floor and headed to the second, which was on the same level as the bridge to the parking garage.

He jerked his thumb at the door.

She shook her head and pointed down. Then she leaned in close, her hair tickling his chin, and whispered, "I have to do some cleanup on the security camera footage and my access badge."

Katie had a brain that wouldn't quit and a body to match.

"What time are you leaving? It's probably not safe in that parking structure after hours."

"Are you kidding? Nobody can get on and off this compound with the tight security Tempest has. Only employees are allowed in the parking structure."

"That's what worries me."

They jogged down one more flight. Placing his hands against the metal door, he cocked his head and listened. He inched the door open and peered through the resulting crack. All clear.

He grabbed Katie around the waist and turned her toward him. "Be careful. This ain't no video game, Katie. This is life and death."

"I know that." She touched his face with her fingertips. "Don't let them do anything to you, Liam. Don't let them change you."

"Don't worry." And then he did something he'd been dreaming about for the past two years. He kissed Katie O'Keefe, intrepid sleuth, hacker extraordinaire, woman of his dreams, on the mouth.

Chapter Five

Katie slipped back up to her cubicle and dropped to her chair, her fingers pressed to her buzzing lips. Even a quick, hard kiss in a cold stairwell from Liam McCabe beat any other lip-lock she'd experienced in the past few years.

She squared her shoulders and stuck her card into the card reader on her computer. The kiss didn't mean anything—just his way of sealing the deal that they'd work together on this thing. She didn't want to jump back into a relationship with Liam, anyway. She had life-and-death matters to take care of now.

She logged on to her computer, and her fingers flew across the keyboard. She'd broken into the security cameras weeks ago, which allowed her to freeze the cameras and erase certain inconvenient images. That capability allowed her to wander around the facility at night, as long as she stayed a few steps ahead of security.

Would security make anything of the jammed door? Given the high level of paranoia around here, most likely. She and Liam would probably have to find another secure meeting place. She'd check out the online map of the buildings and the surrounding area to look for something.

Once she adjusted the footage from the security cameras, she got into the access badge area, located her badge code and erased the recorded swipes of her leaving and entering her office area. If the rigged stairwell door sent someone on a quest to identify late workers and trace their movements, she'd be safe. According to the computer codes, she'd never left her office.

Liam didn't seem to have an access badge, so how he managed to wander around the compound at night, she didn't have a clue. But Liam could do just about anything he put his mind to, and the thought of working with him excited her.

She wrapped up her work and headed to the parking garage. As she strode across the quad to the structure, her nose twitched at the smell of a cigarette. Her steps slowed as she picked out two figures lurking near the entrance to the garage and a pinpoint of light glowing in the dark.

Tensing her muscles, she drew closer, and one of the men turned his head in profile. She instantly recognized Liam. He'd been worried about her leaving late, but who was smoking the cigarette next to him?

She cleared her throat and clutched her purse under her arm.

The cigarette smoker spoke first. "It's okay, ma'am. It's just us recruits from across campus."

"Oh, I was wondering who was out here so late." She pointed at the cigarette, ignoring Liam. "I don't think smoking is allowed on the facility grounds."

The man threw back his head and laughed. "If it's not even allowed on the facility grounds, can you imagine the consequences if the powers-that-be found out a recruit was smoking?"

"Is that what you two are doing over here? Sneaking smokes?"

He crushed the cigarette against the side of the parking structure. "Kinda like middle school, huh? That's what I'm doing out here, anyway. I'm Dustin, by the way, and this is Liam, and I don't know what the hell he was doing here."

"I'm KC, and I really don't think we're supposed to be fraternizing."

Dustin snorted. "You mean like the school dance in the gym? The employees stand on one side and the recruits stand on the other like a bunch of wallflowers? Just like middle school."

He held up the butt of his extinguished cigarette. "You won't tell the principal, will you? Principal Romo, or worse yet, Vice Principal Spann?"

She shrugged her shoulders, made stiff by Dustin and his irreverent comments. Was he trying to trap her? Trap Liam?

Liam had obviously been lurking around the parking garage to keep an eye on her as she left the property, and Dustin had discovered him. Or had he followed him?

"Whatever you do is your business."

He held out the butt. "You wanna take this with you? Destroy the evidence? Help a brother out?"

She folded her arms, tucking her hands beneath her armpits. "I—I…"

"Let's go, man." Liam took the cigarette from Dustin's fingers and plowed his toe into the loose rocks on the ground. He dropped the butt onto the rocks and with his boot, covered it with more rocks. "We have a long day ahead of us tomorrow, and you still need to rinse that tobacco smell out of your mouth."

"Okay, okay." Dustin held up his hands in surrender. "I'm just messin' with you, KC. If you don't rat me out, I won't rat you out."

She forced a laugh and regretted the fake tone. "I won't rat you out, but all I'm doing is leaving work after a long day."

"If you say so." Dustin's eyes shifted from her to Liam.

Liam nudged Dustin's arm. "Let's get back before lights out."

As she passed them, Liam said, "Have a nice evening, ma'am."

She put her head down and scurried to her car, looking neither right nor left. She didn't want to run into anyone else.

Liam had taken a big risk hanging around to see her off. Was Dustin even a smoker or was it all a ploy to get them in his confidence? She had no intention of playing that game.

She trusted no one here—no one except Liam.

As soon as she dropped onto the seat of her car and closed the door, she sank against the backrest and relaxed her muscles. She had to pick up the pace on her efforts to hack through Tempest's computer system. She couldn't take much more of this stress. She'd much rather be in San Diego with her chocolate lab, Mario, working on the newest video game.

Of course, Liam's appearance on the scene and knowing they were on the same team had just brightened the situation considerably.

She'd have to show him some pictures of Mario. They'd been looking for a dog together before he'd up and decided to abandon her. And then in the dark days after Liam had left, Mario had found her. They'd found each other. Figured one lost soul would seek out another.

God, she missed that little guy.

She sighed and cranked on the engine. Her tires squealed on the cement as she wound her way down the parking structure. She followed the long road out toward the guard shack and waved to the attendant on duty as he raised the parking arm for her.

Tempest's facility was located about five miles from a small town on one of the many lakes up here. The residential area, where most of the Tempest employees lived, fanned out from the town with the more expensive homes farther afield and situated at the lake's edge. Tempest employees, retirees and ski resort workers populated the town and environs since the logging company had closed down several years ago.

As she sped down the highway, she glanced at the illuminated numbers on her dashboard clock. It had been over three hours since Samantha had left the office. She and the others had probably deserted the Deluxe by now. Thankfully, she still had a half a bottle of wine in her fridge. After the day she had, she could use a glass or two. She needed two just to turn off her brain.

She took the turnoff for the town, anyway, and rolled through the quiet streets. A couple of cars were parked in front of the bar—not enough to make it worth her while.

She swung out of town and hit the highway again. She lived in an apartment complex peopled with a few Tempest employees and a gaggle of retirees from California—more functional than fancy, but private.

A set of taillights up ahead had her tapping her brakes. Traffic often clogged this road, the only one into and out of town, but not usually at this time of night. As she crested the hill behind two other cars, a flood of lights illuminated the night sky.

Red-and-orange emergency lights revolved, looking almost festive. The cars ahead of her blocked her view of the accident, and she slowed to a crawl as the cops directed single-file traffic to the left.

She drew abreast of the scene and rubber-necked just like everyone else. A single car sat smashed and battered at the side of the road. Looked like a tow truck had dragged it up from the ravine.

As she inched past, she shivered at the back window with cracks running from one side to the other. Then her heart stopped and she slammed on her brakes. The car behind her honked, but she barely noticed.

A large, yellow O on the back of the windshield had caught her attention. Samantha had gone to the University of Oregon and had proudly displayed her alma mater's sticker on the back of her blue sedan. Was that car blue? She couldn't tell in the lights.

She swerved to the right, just ahead of the accident scene and threw her car into Park. She scrambled from the car, flinging out her arms to catch her balance. Her heels crunched against the gravel as she made her way toward the crumpled car.

A police officer stopped her progress. "Hold on, miss. You need to stay back."

"I think I know that car. Is it a woman? Is she okay?"

"It was a woman, but I can't tell you any more, miss. You'll have to get back in your car and move along."

Standing on her tiptoes, she peered over his shoulder, her heart pounding a mile a minute. "Is it a blue sedan? Was a blonde driving the car? Is she okay?"

"Miss—" he spread his arms out "—you're going to have to move along now."

"Okay, okay." She plowed a hand through her hair, her gaze shifting across the street. If she dashed across the highway, she could sneak around the perimeter the back way.

She spun around and walked back to her car. When the cop's attention had returned to directing traffic, she scurried across the road, dodging between the creeping cars all slowing down to get a better look.

She stumbled back down the highway on the other side of the street. Once clear of the accident scene, she ran back across the road.

She slipped past a tow truck driver and zeroed in on the crippled car. Her knees weakened as she recognized Samantha's blue sedan. Her gaze tracked to the stretcher beside the ambulance. An EMT was securing a strap around a form tucked beneath a white sheet.

In a daze she walked toward the stretcher, shaking off someone's grasp. When she reached the side of the stretcher, she saw silky locks of blond hair, streaked with blood, hanging over the side.

She gulped for a breath but it wasn't enough. The night grew darker around her, and she sank to her knees.

Chapter Six

Liam held his plate of egg whites in one hand as he scanned the cafeteria. Dustin was right. This was all reminiscent of middle school, and he'd better go sit with the popular kids so he wouldn't be an outcast. He didn't want to appear different, and he didn't want Dustin to think he was avoiding him because he'd discovered him hanging around the employee parking structure last night.

He pulled out a chair, and his plate clattered as he set it on the table. He nodded to the other men and stabbed a clump of scrambled egg with his fork.

Dustin eyed him over the rim of his coffee cup. "Did you hear the news?"

Swallowing, he shook his head. "Did they up the number of pull-ups on us?"

Charlie, sitting next to Dustin, flexed his biceps. "Let 'em try. I'm ready."

Dustin rolled his eyes. "Another Tempest employee bit the dust."

Liam almost choked on the orange juice going down his throat and managed to turn it into a cough. "Really? Another heart attack? Maybe the stress of working here is getting to the civilians."

"It was an accident out on highway 26—a woman."

Liam wanted to jump up and throttle Dustin to get him

to talk faster, but he felt the other man's dark eyes on him, studying him. "That's too bad. Single car or were there more people involved?"

"Single car. She plunged into the ravine off the highway, no seat belt."

Charlie waved his fork in the air. "I heard she'd been drinking at the Deluxe."

Pain throbbed against Liam's temple, and the eggs tasted like chalk in his mouth. He couldn't ask the name of the employee because he really wasn't supposed to know any names, and he couldn't tip his hand in front of Dustin by asking if it was KC.

"That sucks." He shrugged. "I just hope they don't pull us into another all-hands meeting for some announcement."

He wolfed down the rest of his breakfast and traded war stories with Charlie on their way to the classroom. They had geo-political studies this morning—nothing he hadn't already covered as a Prospero agent and with a lot more content thrown in, including the US perspective, which seemed to be missing from Tempest's lessons.

Max Duvall, the agent who'd broken free of Tempest, had told them the agency used foreign operatives as well as Americans. This coursework must've been designed for an international student body.

He took his seat in the classroom and logged on to the computer. Then, using tricks he'd learned from Katie, he switched to an anonymous identity and instant messaged her.

Katie-O, you okay?

The cursor blinked at him, mimicking the pulse ticking in his throat.

No answer. She could be away from her desk. He checked the time. Maybe she started late.

He gave her a few more minutes and had to switch to his own identity for the lessons, but he couldn't concentrate on a damned thing.

Maybe someone had seen them at the track. Maybe she hadn't been able to fix the security cameras. Maybe Dustin had reported them. Any number of things could've gone wrong, and they all marched through his brain, pounding against his skull.

He wished Tempest would have another of those gatherings to let them know what was going on, but this case was different from Garrett Patterson. This so-called accident happened away from the facility.

He tapped a key on his keyboard and nothing happened. The groans around the room told him others were having the same problem with their computers.

Mills, the instructor, rapped on the lectern. "It seems we're having some difficulties with the computers in here. I'm going to make a call to IT. You can take a break until then."

Liam stretched and glanced around the room. He needed more info about that accident last night, but didn't want to show undue interest and didn't want Dustin to overhear him.

He wandered out of the room, following a group of guys on their way to the vending machines. The agents in training could get their sugar fixes there, since the recruit diet banned sugars, fats and high-sodium foods.

He braced his hands against the snack machine, studying the candy bars, his ears attuned to the idle chatter. But they had bigger concerns than an accident involving a civilian.

"I've heard the psych test can get you discharged immediately."

"I'm going in showing my aggressive side. I've heard that's what Tempest wants."

"What about you, McCabe? You worried?"

He cranked his head to the side. "About the psych evaluation this afternoon?"

"As a former SEAL, you've probably already been deconstructed and put back together again, anyway."

"I'm not too worried. Let's face it. If you don't have the psych makeup for this job, then you probably don't want the job."

They grumbled amongst themselves but didn't offer him any opportunity to bring up the accident.

Mills poked his head into the room. "We have someone from IT. Those of you having problems, we need you to log back in to your computers."

Liam punched a button for a chocolate bar and strode out of the lunchroom. He hoped this geek couldn't tell if he'd been accessing the computer as an anonymous user.

When he returned to the room and saw the geek, he tripped to a stop. The relief that surged through his body almost had him dropping to his knees.

Katie, dressed in a pair of navy blue slacks and a white blouse was sitting at a computer in the corner, tapping away at the keyboard. Even though he missed her tight jeans, wild hair and black nail polish that she'd sported when they were together in San Diego, he'd never been so happy to see anyone in his life. She didn't look up when he walked into the room.

Mills said, "Here's another one. His computer's in the last row."

Katie leaned back in the chair, stretching her legs in front of her. "You guys need to restart these computers every day. We do automatic downloads, and if your computers are off, they're not going to get the downloads. Some of the stuff you're running in here is out of date."

Mills shoved his glasses to the top of his head. "Our class time is almost over, and the recruits have physical training next, so we'll just call it a morning."

She pushed back from the chair, her gaze flicking in his direction. "That's probably a good idea, but I need each of the guys who were having problems to stay and log in for me so I can run the updates."

"Yeah, they can be late to PT." Mills counted the computers with the blue screens. "Just three more. Jensen, Chang and McCabe stay behind. The rest of you get ready for PT."

Liam had a feeling Katie would get to his computer last. He could wait for her all day, but he might not like what she had to say. If she'd taken the risk to disrupt the computers in this room for a chance to talk to him, it couldn't be good.

She finished fiddling with Jensen's computer. Mills left as Katie sat down with Kenneth Chang, a man of few words and fewer social graces. He grunted in response to Katie's questions and practically charged out of the room when she finished repairing his computer. A guy like that would pass Tempest's psych exam with flying colors.

"Now, let's have a look at yours." She slid into his seat, brought up a document and typed the word *bugged*?

He drew up a chair next to hers. "No. I've been worried sick about you. I heard about the accident, but I couldn't get any more information out of anyone without looking suspicious. Thank God you're okay."

Her fingers trembled as they hovered over the keyboard. "I'm not okay. My friend Samantha Van Alstyn was killed in that crash."

"I'm sorry. I heard there was drinking involved."

She gripped his wrist in a vise. "They killed her because of me."

His heart slammed against his rib cage. "What does that mean?"

"I borrowed Samantha's sweater the day before yesterday. I was wearing it in Patterson's office a-and I think I lost a button by his desk. Meyers, our favorite security guard, returned the button to Samantha."

"So they think Samantha was in that room? Why would they assume she witnessed the murder? She could've lost it there another time."

"Samantha was in accounting. She had no reason to be in Patterson's office."

"If he was putting the moves on Ginger, how do they know he hadn't brought other women to his office?"

"I don't know. You're making these suggestions as if these people are rational beings. They thought there was a chance she was in that office, and they took care of the problem."

He dug his fingers into his left temple. "God, it could've been you."

"How could I be so stupid to leave behind evidence like that button?"

The pain in his head sharpened. "Do they know you and Samantha were friendly? Are they going to think she told you something about Patterson's death?"

"If she told me something about the murder, wouldn't they expect me to hightail it out of here?"

"Maybe, but she didn't leave Tempest and they took care of her, anyway."

"They could've just figured Samantha was seeing Patterson but hadn't been in his office during the murder. They got rid of her as a safety measure."

Liam tapped his chin. "Tempest doesn't like loose ends."

The handle of the classroom door turned, and Liam jumped back from Katie and crossed his arms as her eyes widened. "Yeah, it was running a little slow right before the crash."

"You're missing three updates, so I'm going to run those for you right now."

The door eased open, and Dustin poked his head into the room. "Hey, look who's here."

"Yeah, my computer died along with a couple of others." Liam lifted his shoulders.

Putting his finger to his lips, Dustin glanced over his shoulder. "Don't worry. My lips are sealed or I'd have some explaining to do of my own about my nicotine habit."

Liam clenched his jaw. He'd had enough of this guy's veiled threats and innuendos. "Look, man, if you want to tell someone I was walking about the facility last night and got as far as the employee parking garage, knock yourself out."

"Same goes for me. You're the one who started the conversation last night." Katie punched a few more keys.

"I'm just messin' with you." Dustin turned his fingers into a gun and pointed it their way. "Hey, Hamilton sent me to find you, so you can get in a workout before the psychologist starts shrinking our heads."

"Be right out." Liam nodded at his computer. "You need me for anything else?"

"Nope. Just restart your computer, don't forget your access card and have a nice life." Katie gathered her notebook and papers and stuck her pen in the spiral binding of the notebook.

Dustin stepped aside to let her pass, rolling his eyes at Liam.

Liam logged off the computer and snatched his card out of the reader. "Okay, I'm ready to work up a sweat."

After two hours of running, doing sit-ups, push-ups, pull-ups and weight training, Liam returned to his room to shower and get ready for his appointment with one of the docs. Usually a psych eval involved word association, the Rorschach and various situational questions—nothing Prospero hadn't trained him to handle.

Tempest had already run the recruits through this ringer before, thinning their ranks in the process. He didn't know what to expect this time, but Prospero had prepared him for anything.

Since Tempest didn't want the recruits comparing notes, head psychiatrist, Dr. Nealy, herded them into a waiting area with snacks, reading material, DVDs and video games, where they spent the time until their own appointments. Dr. Nealy had a staff of several psychologists to perform multiple evaluations at the same time—a regular assembly line of head-shrinking.

As he entered the holding pen, he nodded to Dustin and Charlie, grabbed an apple and plopped down in one of the beanbag chairs in front of a gaming system. Maybe Katie-O had worked on this game.

The sweater incident and Samantha's death had him rethinking Katie's role in this investigation. Tempest must be all kinds of paranoid if finding a woman's button in Patterson's office had driven them to murder.

Of course, maybe he and Katie were all kinds of paranoid. Samantha could've drunk too much, gotten into her car and driven off the road all by herself.

The door to the waiting area swung open, and Nealy's assistant called out four names. She hesitated at the door as the recruits filed out of the room. "Remember, gentlemen... and lady, no discussing the evaluations before or after."

Nah, if he had to bet on the paranoia winner, it'd be Tempest.

By the time he'd finished his apple, played a few levels of the video game and leafed through a sports magazine, the assistant was back with another four names—his among them.

He and the other three men followed her into the hallway, where she deposited each of them in an office. At the last door, she turned to him.

"At the end of the session, Dr. Harris will escort you out of her office, and you'll return to your room."

"Why would I do that? Don't we have range this afternoon?"

Her lips formed a tight smile. "I'm sure I don't know, McCabe. Those are the instructions I have."

His pulse jumped. Why would the recruits be going back to their rooms? How long were they expected to be quiet about the evaluations and why?

She opened the door for him, without looking in the room, and he stepped into the dim office. He blinked, taking in the couch against one wall, the chair beside it and the person behind the desk.

She didn't stand as he took another step into the room. Instead, she studied him over the rim of her glasses, like a specimen under a microscope.

This was gonna be fun.

He raised his hand. "I'm Liam McCabe."

"I know who you are. I'm Dr. Harris."

"Where do you want me to sit, Dr. Harris?"

"The couch, please. I'll take the chair."

"Do I have to lie down?" He snorted, but she didn't crack a smile at his attempt to make a joke.

"You can do whatever you like, Liam. You like being in control, don't you?"

She'd jumped right in on the analysis.

He sank into the soft cushion of the couch and crossed an ankle over his knee. "Who doesn't?"

She finally rose from behind her desk, a tall woman whose thin frame made her appear even taller. She pulled the chair closer to the couch and sat, her knees almost touching his.

"But you have to give up some control when you're in the US Military, correct?"

"Sure, yeah, of course, for the greater good of the unit and all that."

She slipped a pencil between two tapered fingers and tapped it on her knee. "You did exhibit a few issues with... excessive violence, didn't you?"

Prospero had planted that little nugget in his file. Tempest seemed to like its agents a little on the outlaw side.

He pinned her with a hard gaze. "It's war. It's violent."

"I get that, Liam. Nobody's judging you here, but I do want to hear more about the incident."

He started reciting the story that Prospero had fed to him. This was his third account of the story, and he stuck to the script. Embellishing could only lead to trouble.

Dr. Harris held up her hand, cutting him off. "That's your conscious remembrance of the event."

"Yeah?" He drew his brows over his nose. What did she have up her sleeve?

She held up her pencil and twirled it slowly between her fingers. "I want to get to the subconscious truth of the incident. I'm going to hypnotize you."

Chapter Seven

Samantha's boss, Larry Turner, hovered at the entrance to Katie's cubicle, his hands shoved into the pockets of his khakis. "I just can't believe it. Sam wasn't even a heavy drinker."

"And if she was so drunk, why'd her so-called friends let her get in the car?"

Larry hunched his shoulders. "I think she left later than they did. One of the guys said she'd been flirting with a stranger."

Katie's stomach dropped, and she folded her arms across her midsection. Had this stranger slipped her something? "D-did the police talk to him?"

"I'm not sure. All I'm hearing is rumor right now." He kicked the empty box at his feet. "I had to talk to her mother today, father's dead. I asked her if she wanted me to pack up Samantha's personal effects and send them to her."

She'd come to realize that Tempest employees shared similar backgrounds—orphans, loners—just like her and Sebastian. "That's not a very pleasant task. Do you want me to help?"

"Funny thing is her mother didn't want Sam's stuff. Said she'd come out later to pack up her apartment but told me I could trash the stuff in her office. Did they have a strained relationship, or what?"

"I have no idea. Samantha never talked about her mother."

"Well, she sounds like a real piece of work to me." Larry nudged the box toward Samantha's cubicle with his foot and ducked inside.

Less than a minute later, he emerged, dangling Samantha's sweater from his fingertips. "Do you want this? You seemed to wear it more than she did."

Katie swallowed. Had other people noticed that, too? She never wanted to see that sweater again as long as she lived.

"No, thanks. I don't think I could wear anything of Samantha's after what happened. In fact, I'm feeling pretty sick to my stomach right now."

"If you worked for me, I'd send you home. You should take off."

"I think I will." She would've gone home if she hadn't been desperate to talk to Liam and tell him about the missing button. It hadn't taken much to incapacitate those computers and to figure out which one belonged to Liam. It had been risky and Dustin had caught them again, but the look on Liam's face when he'd seen her in the classroom had been worth it. Even if he no longer loved her, that look confirmed that he at least cared about her deeply. Or maybe it just meant he didn't want to see her dead.

Okay, that was a start.

"Are you sure you don't need help with Samantha's cubicle?"

"She didn't have much stuff in here. You go home."

She called her boss and logged off. As she walked across the quad to the parking structure, she shaded her eyes and gazed in the direction of the recruits' compound.

At this time of day, you could usually hear the shots from the range. The buildings were soundproof so you had to be outside to hear the gunfire, but she heard nothing from that direction. The recruits had an indoor area for shooting, as well. She should know because she'd worked on some of the computerized scenarios, but usually they split the recruits into outdoor range and indoor training. Not today.

A little flutter of fear winged its way across her chest. The psych exams. Dustin had mentioned something about the psychological testing. Was it starting already? Was Liam safe?

If she lost Liam to these people, too, she'd shut this place down single-handedly if she had to.

She hesitated before punching the button to call the elevator car. Shut the place down? She could do that. She'd incapacitated her entire high school at the end of her junior year just because—computer systems, lights, bell schedule, the works. It had gotten her suspended, but the challenge had given her a thrill. Imagine the thrill of shutting down Tempest?

She stepped into the elevator and as the doors began to close, a large hand slapped the edge. The doors jerked back open, and Meyers stepped into the car.

She clutched her purse and gave him a weak smile.

"Sorry about that. I have to check on that car alarm on the top floor."

"That's okay. Sorry I didn't see you coming."

"Pretty distracted, huh?"

Had he been privy to her daydreams about bringing Tempest operations to a crashing halt? Maybe Tempest read minds, too.

"Umm, yeah."

"I mean about Samantha—terrible accident."

"It was. I just couldn't concentrate, and my boss told me to go home."

"Yeah, I think all the people drinking with her last night stayed home today, too."

"Do you know anything more about what happened than we're hearing from the rumor mill?"

"Probably not. She went out with some coworkers, got behind the wheel when she probably shouldn't have and went into the ravine."

The elevator jostled to a stop at her parking level, and she straddled the door. "Did you hear anything about a guy she met at the Deluxe?"

He raised his eyes to the ceiling. "Didn't hear that but it wouldn't surprise me. Samantha was a pretty girl."

"She was." The doors closed, and she stood staring at the elevator. Car alarm? She didn't hear any car alarm.

Twenty minutes later, she coasted to a stop across the street from the Deluxe Bar. She hadn't planned on coming here, but when she'd passed the off-ramp for the town, she couldn't resist.

The cops who'd investigated the accident scene may have talked to the employees at the Deluxe, but the cops didn't know what she knew about Samantha's employer.

Stepping out of the car, she buttoned her coat. The bar stayed open all day. Just after three o'clock, she had a jump on the happy hour crowd.

She pushed through the front door, and a few heads turned before their owners got back to the serious business of pickling their livers. With the stools on either ends of the bar occupied, she hopped up on one in the middle, hooking her heels on the footrest.

The bartender braced his hands against the bar, hunching his shoulders. "What can I get you, sweetheart?"

"I'll take a club soda with some lime." She had no intention of sharing Samantha's fate.

His brows shot up. "If you're thirsty, why don't you go to the quick mart on the next block? You can get a sixty-four-ounce drink for a buck."

"Are you in business to sell drinks, or what?" She slapped a five-dollar bill on the bar.

He shrugged and filled a glass with club soda. He jabbed a slice of lime with a cocktail toothpick, dropped it into the clear, fizzing liquid and added a straw. "That's two-fifty."

She slid her money toward him and sipped her drink.

When he wandered past her again, she said, "Were you working when that woman was in here yesterday? The woman who died in the accident?"

He crossed his arms and leaned against the register behind him. "You a cop?"

Before coming to work for Tempest, that question would've been ludicrous since she favored heavy black eyeliner, black nail polish, tight jeans and boots most of the time. Her slacks, sensible heels and demure makeup made it a reasonable query.

"I'm not a cop. The woman was my friend." She dabbed her eyes with a cocktail napkin and didn't even have to fake it.

"Sorry." He stroked his beard. "The cops were around this morning trying to put blame on my bar for serving her excessive drinks. I told them and I'm telling you, she had two drinks in here last night and a whole lotta food. I had her credit card receipt to show them."

"I didn't think that sounded like her. Could someone else have been buying her drinks, maybe promising her a ride home that didn't pan out?"

"I have no clue. Her group sort of drifted away one-by-one, and she and another guy stayed later."

"Was he a regular here?"

"Not here. I figured he was part of the work group." He tapped her glass. "Can you handle another club soda or did you just come around for some answers?"

"I guess I just wanted to find out for myself what happened." She jabbed her straw into the ice at the bottom of the glass. "Did she leave with that guy?"

"I didn't notice, and my waitresses couldn't tell the cops, either. Just sad all the way around."

She slid from the stool and pocketed a buck-fifty, leaving a dollar bill on the bar. "Thanks."

"Hey."

She turned at the door.

"Drive carefully. I don't want this place getting a bad reputation."

"Thanks for your concern." She stepped into the cold air and shivered. If Samantha had two drinks only, her autopsy would show that level of alcohol in her system. Had the stranger slipped her something?

She refused to believe the coincidence of Samantha getting into a car accident on the very day Meyers returned that button to her. Tempest had long tentacles, and she could feel them tightening.

It was still early, and the happy hour crowd hadn't descended on the bar yet. The Tempest employees probably wouldn't be up for cocktails after Samantha's accident. Management hadn't called another all-hands meeting to announce Samantha's death, but the news had spread like wildfire, anyway. Tempest probably wanted to distance itself from the accident and not remind people that two employees had died in a matter of days.

She pulled away from the curb, checking her rearview mirror. A small car appeared from around the corner a block behind her. She couldn't lose the car even if she wanted to, since her place was a straight shot down the highway. Unless she wanted to veer off toward the lake, it looked as if she'd have company on the way home.

Her clammy hands gripped the steering wheel as she accelerated. She sped past the turnoff to the lake, and her heart jumped when the car that she thought had been following her took the off-ramp.

She blew out a breath and turned up the radio. Who was the paranoid one now?

With absolutely nobody following her, she pulled into the parking lot of her apartment complex.

A text message came through her cell and she pounced on it. After reading an alert from her bank, she tossed her phone into her purse.

Liam did say he'd try to text her, although she had no idea how he planned to accomplish that. Maybe he'd fail the psych test—for not being psycho enough—and Tempest would kick him out. What kind of outfit did he work for that would send him into the lion's den? These people could do anything to him, and then who'd save him?

She grabbed her purse and pushed the car door open with her foot. If it came to it, she'd do her damnedest to save Liam herself.

She collected a few bills and a slick circular from her mailbox and then jogged upstairs to her place. She shoved the key in the dead bolt and froze. She always locked the dead bolt.

She tried the door handle, which was locked. Would the police come out if she told them she'd locked her dead bolt and it was now unlocked?

She pulled the key free from the dead bolt and stuck it in the door handle, turning it slowly.

The door creaked as she eased it open, pushing it wider. She hung on to the doorknob and poked her head into the living room. Holding her breath, her gaze tracked around the room. Nothing looked out of place, but that didn't mean anything.

She left the door open and stepped into the room, clutching her keys between her knuckles like a weapon.

She'd taught Liam a few computer tricks, and he'd taught her a few tricks of self-defense.

She crept into the room, thankful for the first time she'd chosen a one-bedroom place. She toed off her shoes in case she had to make a mad dash for the exit, and then tiptoed toward the hallway. She peered into the empty bathroom first and then scooped in a breath and braved the bedroom, even checking the closet and under the bed.

She rushed back to her front door, slammed and locked it. She stood with her back against the door, breathing heavily, surveying her living room. Nothing was out of place, and yet…something didn't feel right.

The blood rushed to her head, and she launched off the door, making a beeline for a small area rug on the floor in front of the gas fireplace. She dropped to her knees and swept the rug aside. Using her fingernails, she worked her fingers into a crack between two loose floorboards. She pulled one up and reached into the floor, heaving a sigh as her fingers brushed the edges of Patterson's notebook. She gripped the cover and pulled it free, shaking the dirt from the pages.

She had to show this to Liam. Maybe he could make some sense of Patterson's notations. Hugging the book to her chest, she rose to her feet.

She tossed the notebook onto her kitchen counter and grabbed a plastic container of leftover pasta from the fridge. She popped the lid and shoved it into the microwave.

She didn't know how much more of this cloak-and-dagger stuff she could take. Couldn't Liam's agency order an autopsy for Patterson? With her as an eyewitness, that could be enough to shut down Tempest.

Chewing her lip, she watched the bowl of pasta spin around in the microwave. She knew Liam had loftier goals than just closing down operations for Tempest. He wanted to dig at the truth. He wanted to know Tempest's purpose and design for its agents.

When the pasta was done, she dumped it on a plate, poured herself a glass of red wine to make up for the tee-totaling at the bar and sat down with Patterson's notebook open on the table.

Why had he gone back to his office, and why had Ginger been so afraid he'd get his hands on Meyers's badge? She must've had some reason to suspect Patterson's loyalty to Tempest.

Patterson had been a big deal, had been one of the people directly reporting to Mr. Romo, a geo-political strategy guy who pinpointed the trouble spots for Tempest. If he hadn't been on board with Tempest's plans, he could've just resigned. It had to be more than that. Or maybe once you worked for Tempest, the only way to quit was in a coffin.

Patterson's chicken scratch blurred on the page, and it had nothing to do with the wine. She needed a new set of eyes reading this thing. She needed Liam.

She stowed the notebook back in its hiding place and washed the dishes. Then she put a small load of laundry into the washing machine and sat down at her laptop.

Before taking the gig at Tempest, she'd contracted to design a video game for her friend's company. Over the next few hours as she coded explosive traps and hidden viruses, she wished she could do the same to the Tempest facility.

Yawning, she put away her work and checked her phone once more for a message from Liam. If he didn't think he could get through to her, he shouldn't have even raised her hopes. Now that sick feeling in the pit of her stomach wouldn't go away. What had happened at the psych eval?

She put her wineglass in the sink and gathered her clothes from the dryer, folding them into her laundry basket. She hoisted the basket, balanced it on one hip and shuffled to her bedroom, where she dropped the basket on the floor near her dresser.

She collected four pair of underwear in one hand and pulled open the top drawer of her dresser. She caught her breath, and the underwear fell to the floor.

She was no neat freak, but she always shoved her panties to the right side of the underwear drawer and her bras to the left. Now they intermingled in a silky, frothy, rainbow kaleidoscope. A rash of goose bumps danced up her arms. It wasn't the fact that someone had run his hands through her underwear that creeped her out, or even the fact that someone had been in her apartment—it was what it meant.

Tempest was on to her.

Chapter Eight

Liam crouched at the side of the track and raked through the dirt with his fingers until they met the smooth edges of the phone he'd buried there earlier.

Prospero and his boss, Jack Coburn, weren't expecting any calls from him while he was undercover at Tempest. In fact, he'd get yanked off this assignment in a matter of seconds if Coburn discovered his risky behavior. Right now he didn't care.

He turned his back to the housing unit and cupped his hand around the phone as he dialed Katie's number. Nobody expected the recruits to be out and about after the psych sessions, after the hypnosis and their first dosing with the T-101. They'd called it a vitamin, but he knew better.

Prospero had given him an antidote to the T-101, and he'd undergone intense training in resisting hypnosis. He'd been fully conscious through the entire ordeal, including the injection of the T-101.

This was going down, and it was going down hard.

After five rings, Katie picked up the phone, her "hello" breathless and tentative.

"It's Liam. Are you okay?"

"I'm not okay. Someone was here."

He gripped the phone. "Don't say another word. Walk outside or go sit in your car. I'll wait."

She sucked in a breath, and then he heard movement and rustling over the phone.

"I'm back."

"Are you sitting in your car?"

"I'm out by the pool."

"Is it safe?"

"There's a group of people out here. Why am I outside? Do you think the person who broke into my place bugged it?"

"Could be."

She swore under her breath. "That's all I need."

He wiped a hand across his brow. "You know for sure someone broke into your place? Why would they want to tip you off?"

"They probably don't want to tip me off. Whoever broke in was careful. I had my suspicions when I discovered the dead bolt wasn't locked, so I checked out everything, and nothing was out of place."

"Are you just going off the dead bolt, then?"

"You didn't let me finish. I didn't notice anything out of place until I went to put my laundry away. Then I saw that someone had messed up my lingerie drawer."

"Your lingerie drawer?"

She sighed. "You know, underwear, bras."

"Since when did you start folding underwear in your drawer or folding anything anywhere?"

She clicked her tongue. "I have a system in that drawer, and it was messed up."

"Who knew?"

"Are you taking this seriously, Liam?"

"Deadly. That's why you're outside crashing someone's pool party." He saw a light from the recruit housing and sidled up next to the fencing. "Maybe they suspect you because you and Samantha hung out."

"Maybe Dustin ratted us out, and Ginger put two and

two together—she intercepted me at the track and Dustin discovered you hanging around the parking garage just when I was leaving. She also asked me a bunch of questions about programming in general and my work in particular on the way back to the offices."

"It could be anything or nothing. She could be taking precautions, and now you need to do the same. You have to quit, Katie."

"I'm not quitting. I'm too close to breaching their firewalls. Do you know the damage I can do to that facility once I have their computer systems at my fingertips?"

"You're not going to do any damage if you're dead." His harsh tone grated against his own ears, and the silence on the other end of the line engulfed him in guilt. "I'm sorry, Katie-O. I'm just telling it like it is."

"I know the risks, just like you." She cleared her throat. "What happened today in the psych evaluation? Why'd it take you so long to call me?"

"This is my job. I'm on assignment."

"Answer the question, McCabe. What happened out there today?"

"Dr. Harris tried to hypnotize me."

She gasped. "Tried? You obviously didn't succumb or *you'd* be dead."

"I can resist hypnosis. I told her the same story about how I got into trouble with my SEAL team that I'd told before. I even embellished the violence a little to make her salivate and to make it appear that I'd been holding back before."

"She didn't suspect anything?"

"If she had, she wouldn't have had the nurse or whoever that was inject me with their secret formula."

"Liam!" She choked. "They injected you with something? What did it do to you? Are you okay?"

"It did nothing. I have the antidote running through my system already. The T-101 won't have any effect on me."

"T-101?"

"That's what Tempest calls this serum."

"And th-that's what made Sebastian crazy?"

"He's not the first agent to kill himself, Katie. Another agent, Adam Belchick, was the first, and another agent probably would've taken himself out if he hadn't been killed first."

"We have to save the rest of them, Liam. We can't allow Tempest to ruin their lives."

"I'm working on it, Katie-O, but it's hard when I'm worrying about you at the same time."

"Where are you? How'd you sneak out?"

"I'm at the track. Everyone's conked out, but I gotta go. Are you going to quit your job?"

"No. When is your assignment over? What's your goal?"

"Find out how Tempest plans to use these juiced-up agents and destroy its capacity to do so."

"That's my goal, too, and I'm aiming for the head honcho."

"Mr. Romo?"

"Yep."

"Have you ever seen him?"

"A few times. Have you?"

"He's off-limits to us."

"He's off-limits to us, too. Maybe he doesn't exist."

"Oh, he exists. Do you think you saw an imposter? Someone's calling the shots, and it's not Ginger Spann." He kicked at the root of a bush growing beside the fence. "Have you noticed that helipad on top of building S?"

"No."

"I think that's the way Romo gets on and off the facility."

"We need to stop this, Liam."

He heard someone shout in the background, and his heart flip-flopped. "What's that?"

"The party's getting rowdy out here. Anything else?"

"Just be careful."

"You, too."

He ended the call and dropped to his knees. As he kicked dirt over the hole where he'd placed the phone, he swore to himself.

Why'd he ever let that woman go? If she gave him another chance, he'd keep her close forever...if they both came out of this alive.

KATIE WALKED INTO the office, her gaze focused straight in front of her, looking neither right nor left. She didn't want to catch anyone's eye and have to wonder if he'd been running his hands through her underwear the day before.

Had someone seen her go into the Deluxe? What had they hoped to find at her place? Did Ginger realize that Patterson's notebook was missing? Did she even know he had a notebook? She had to get that thing to Liam. He'd know how to decipher it.

She'd taken on this assignment by herself with the expectation that she'd find out why Sebastian killed himself and then exact revenge for it. How quickly she'd come to rely on Liam as soon as she'd discovered his presence here.

But Liam was that kind of guy. She'd always been strong and independent, so it took a real alpha male to get her to give up control and rely on someone else. She'd met her match in Liam, and then he went away.

She should've been strong enough to adjust to that, too, but his abandonment had opened up all those old wounds of a mother who'd left her on the steps of St. Anthony's Catholic Church in Imperial Beach at three days old.

She scooted her chair closer to her desk and logged in to her computer. She had some bug fixes to attend to, but she planned to devote a big chunk of her day to breaking through Tempest's firewall.

She got so deeply into her work, the telephone ringing on her desk startled her, jangling her nerves.

"KC Locke, program development."

"KC, this is Ginger Spann, and I have a proposition for you."

Katie swallowed and peeled her tongue from the roof of her mouth. "Oh?"

"I've been hearing good things about your work and figured you were an excellent fit for this particular project."

"What project?" She pressed a palm to her chest to steady her fluttering heart. Was this some kind of trick?

"I'll let Mr. Romo explain it to you."

Katie closed her eyes. "Mr. Romo? It must be important."

"It's very important, and I believe you're the person to take it on."

"What about Frank?" Someone had to bring her boss's name into this discussion.

Ginger's laugh tinkled over the line. "Frank is a capable manager, but he's not at your level of programming knowledge, is he?"

Katie swallowed. What did Ginger know about her level? Had she been looking into her background? The background she'd carefully cleansed?

"I...well, all my work comes through Frank."

"You surprise me, KC. I thought you'd jump at the chance to do more than the bug fixes Frank hands off to you."

She would jump at this opportunity if she hadn't just witnessed Ginger murdering a coworker.

"Of course I'm interested, but I want to keep my job. I don't want Frank thinking I'm going over his head."

"I'll worry about Frank. Meet me in front of the executive elevator in fifteen minutes."

Ginger ended the call, not waiting for a response.

Katie slumped in her chair, biting her bottom lip. What did this all mean? It could be the perfect opportunity to get close to Mr. Romo and get the keys to the castle. Or it could end in disaster.

She sat up in her chair and exited a few programs. When had she ever been one to steer clear of disaster if it held out the tiniest bit of hope that she'd get what she wanted in the end?

Ten minutes later she was standing in front of the executive elevator, clasping a notepad to her chest. This elevator stopped at the floor that housed the executives' offices and above, including the top floor occupied by Mr. Romo. You needed a special access card to operate the elevator, which Ginger most certainly must have.

A sharp click of heels against the tile floor announced the woman's arrival, right on time.

"I hope you haven't been waiting long, but your early arrival shows your eagerness. I had expected a little more enthusiasm from you on the phone."

Katie lifted her shoulders to her ears, still gripping the notebook. "I'm new here. I don't want to get on the wrong side of Frank."

"Frank doesn't have a wrong side." Ginger flashed her card at the card reader and stabbed the call button. "He's reliable but a bit of a slug."

Katie had no intention of throwing her boss under the bus. This could all be some kind of test of her loyalty. "He's a good manager."

"Ah, KC." The elevator doors opened and Ginger gestured her through with a flourish of her arm. "Playing it safe."

With her coworkers dropping around her, what choice did she have?

When the doors closed, Katie turned to Ginger. "This is a programming project, I assume?"

"Yes, a very exciting one I think you'll enjoy."

"Why me?"

Ginger clicked her tongue. "We do a very thorough background check here at Tempest."

If Katie expected more of an explanation, the thin line of Ginger's lips put that to rest.

The elevator skimmed past the executive floor and came to rest on the top level. The helicopter pad Liam had mentioned must be right above this level on the roof.

The doors whisked open and Ginger pressed the button to keep them ajar. "After you."

Katie stepped into the hallway, her heels sinking into the plush carpet.

Ginger breezed past her, one finger in the air. "This way."

Katie followed her to the end of the hallway, past several closed doors. The hushed atmosphere had her whispering. "Does anyone else have an office up here?"

"Mr. Romo occupies all the offices on this floor." Ginger winked. "He likes to spread out when he works."

They had reached the end of the hallway, and Ginger tapped on a thick wooden door. The handle clicked, and KC glanced up and spotted the camera. Mr. Romo had seen their approach. He wouldn't take any chances.

Ginger ushered her into the office first, where the thick carpet continued to silence their footsteps.

Katie took two hesitant steps into the room while a man rose from a sofa on the side of the room, lifting his computer from his lap and holding it with both hands. "Come in, come in."

Katie didn't necessarily expect Mr. Romo to be seven

feet tall with steam coming out of his ears, but the middle-aged compact man with the friendly smile and neat beard took her by surprise. He'd looked bigger from afar. Only his eyes, a light blue, marked his appearance as anything but ordinary.

Ginger closed the door with a click. "Mr. Romo, this is KC Locke. KC, Mr. Romo."

Mr. Romo placed the laptop on a sofa cushion next to him and dusted his hands together. "A pleasure to meet you, KC. Please, take a seat."

Since he didn't offer to shake hands, Katie took a chair across from the sofa, and Ginger sat in a chair next to hers.

Her gaze darted around the comfortably appointed room, more a lounge than an office, and then settled again on Mr. Romo, who'd resumed his seat.

"Water, coffee?"

"No, thank you."

He clasped his hands around one knee. "You're probably wondering what this is all about. We tend to be rather secretive here at Tempest."

"Ms. Spann mentioned something about a programming project, but I'm not sure why you tapped me for it."

"Really?" Mr. Romo tilted his head, looking somewhat like a bird with his close-cropped black hair resembling downy feathers. "Come, come, KC, let's be blunt. You're a hacker, aren't you?"

Katie widened her eyes to feign surprise. She hadn't scrubbed that part of her background at all. She'd figured an organization like Tempest would be attracted to rather than repelled by any hint of criminal activity in someone's past.

Her instincts had paid off.

"I-is that a problem?" She waved her hand. "All that's in my past. I can assure you all my programming is on the level today."

Except for when I'm trying to breach your firewalls.

Mr. Romo and Ginger exchanged a glance, heavy with a meaning that eluded her. Then he sat forward, resting his elbows on his knees. "That's not a problem at all, KC. In fact, we're hoping you can use some of those…skills to help us out."

She drummed a pen against her notepad. "I'm not sure I understand."

Ginger reached across and patted her shoulder. "Don't look so nervous. We're not going to ask you to hack into a bank."

Mr. Romo's unnervingly light eyes actually twinkled when he laughed along with Ginger, as if he hadn't ordered the murder of two of his employees in the space of one week.

"Nothing like that at all. It is a little—" he steepled his fingers "—unorthodox, but then you know Tempest is an unorthodox organization."

Licking her lips, Katie pinned her hands between her bouncing knees. "What's the project?"

"It involves spying on our employees." Mr. Romo delivered the line with a smile still hovering about his mouth, as if this were a big joke among the three of them.

She could play that game to get on the inside. If Romo offered her unfettered access to the computer system, she could wreak a severe amount of havoc in no time. Then she and Liam could get the hell out of here.

"Is that legal?"

Ginger snorted. "You can drop the act, KC. We've looked at your file, and you didn't seem all that concerned about the legality of your actions before. Why worry about it now? You have Mr. Romo's approval. That's all you need."

"Then count me in." Katie leaned back in her chair and

spread her arms out to her sides. "And if this is some kind of trap, you got me."

"No trap, young lady, but I appreciate your caution." Mr. Romo pulled the computer back into his lap and started tapping on the keyboard.

"This does come with some hazard pay, right?" KC jumped from her chair and paced to the window overlooking the facility. She could just make out the recruits in training. "I'm taking a risk if an employee finds out and brings some government agency down on our heads. I'll be taking the fall, not you."

Without looking up from the laptop, Mr. Romo snapped his fingers in Ginger's direction. "Ms. Spann will see to that."

Katie glanced at Ginger, who stretched her lips into a smile. "Of course, KC. You'll be compensated for your efforts, but we expect to see results."

"Oh, I'll get you results. When do we start?"

"Right now." Mr. Romo tapped his laptop screen. "I want you to start with these two."

Katie sauntered across the room to the couch and leaned over Mr. Romo's shoulder.

The blood roared in her ears, and she stifled a gasp as she stared into the clear blue eyes of Liam McCabe.

Chapter Nine

Mr. Romo cranked his head around, his dark brows colliding over his nose. "What's wrong?"

Katie could feel Ginger practically breathing down her neck. She cleared her throat. "I've seen those two before."

"Where? They're recruits." Mr. Romo's pale gaze skewered her.

Ginger sat on the arm of the couch. "Did you see them at the all-hands meeting?"

"No." Liam wouldn't mind if she squealed on him to gain some street cred with these two. She took a deep breath. "I saw them out by the employee parking garage when I left the other night."

"What were they doing?" Mr. Romo's quiet tone sent a chill down her spine.

"They were just standing there talking. The one guy, the black guy, was smoking a cigarette." She jabbed her finger at Dustin's picture on the screen.

Had Liam misjudged Dustin? The recruit couldn't be spying for Romo if Romo wanted her to spy on Dustin. Or maybe she'd walked into one big trap.

"Did they say anything to you?" Ginger moved to her side and placed a hand on Katie's arm.

"We exchanged a few words. I guess the guy with the cigarette didn't want anyone to see him smoking."

"And the other one? The blond?" Mr. Romo flicked his manicured fingers at Liam's picture. "What excuse did he give?"

"I don't know. He didn't say much. Did they do something wrong? Why do you want me to spy on them?"

"You don't need to worry about that part, KC. We'll give the directions, and you'll follow. Do you think you can do that?" Ginger's fingers curled into her arm, her nails poking at the flesh beneath the material of her blouse.

Katie nodded. "Of course. How do you want me to monitor them?"

"Through their computer log-ins at first. Each recruit has a laptop and an access card. We want you to track what they're doing on their laptops—the obvious things like emails and websites visited and then anything else you can dig up, anything they might be trying to conceal."

"I can do that."

Ginger loosened her grip, and her touch turned into a caress. "We knew you could, KC, and we figured with your criminal background you wouldn't blink an eye at the request…if we held out a little monetary incentive."

Standing up, she broke away from Ginger. "Criminal background?"

"Well, you did lie to us about your past activities, about your juvenile crimes, didn't you?" Ginger shook her finger in her face. "That in itself is a crime—fraud."

"Are you threatening me?" Katie widened her stance and crossed her arms across her chest and wildly beating heart. Ginger played hardball.

Mr. Romo stood up between them, hands out. "Let's dispense with the ugliness and be frank. If you don't tell on us, we won't tell on you. That gives us all a little skin in this game, but a whole lot to gain."

He cupped his hands and gestured to them to move in closer. Ginger took a step toward him, and he curled his arm around her waist and pulled her next to him. "Your turn, KC."

Katie suppressed a shiver and shuffled toward him. Putting his arm around her waist, he dragged her into the circle. Ginger sidled up next to her and wrapped her arm around Katie's waist, as well.

As much as she wanted to, Katie couldn't stand there with her arms hanging at her sides so she put one around Mr. Romo, holding on to his suit jacket with two fingers and placing the other lightly around Ginger's back.

Mr. Romo tightened the circle by pulling them so close, Katie could make out white flecks in the irises of his blue eyes. Was that what made them so light?

"Ginger and I are in this together to do what needs to be done to protect Tempest, and as a result make this world a better place, and we're happy to have you along for the ride, KC." His hand slipped from her waist to her hip, his fingers resting on the curve of her backside.

Her stomach roiled, and she had a sudden urge to puke in the middle of the circle of trust. And she would have except for the stronger urge to warn Liam that Mr. Romo had him in his crosshairs.

LIAM SAT IN the back of the classroom and logged in to his laptop. Physical training this morning had been exhausting. He'd had to keep up with all the recruits who'd had their first dose of T-101 the day before.

He'd have to wrap up his work here soon or it would become apparent that the T-101 was not having its desired effect on him.

As soon as his computer powered up, he launched the instant messenger. He didn't expect to see any messages from Katie. She'd warned him that her messages might pop up automatically when he logged in and he might not be alone when they did.

He looked around the room at the other recruits logging in to complete assignments left over from yesterday because of their extralong psych evaluations. As far as he knew from questioning the other recruits, he'd been the only one subjected to hypnosis. The psychologists might be using different methods for different recruits, or he'd been singled out.

He typed a message to Katie.

You there?

Apparently, she'd been singled out, too, if they'd searched her apartment. As he stared at the blinking cursor, he wondered what her place looked like.

Back in San Diego, she'd had a mishmash of stuff in her apartment. She'd called her tastes eclectic, but he'd come to the conclusion she had no specific taste at all. She just loved stuffing her apartment with all the odds and ends she'd collected on her travels—items to remind her of the places she'd been.

She'd make a boatload of money as an independent contractor hiring out her programming skills, and then take off for a month or two—until she'd met him. Then she'd been ready to settle down and like an idiot, he'd taken off. Sure, his team had needed him, but it never occurred to him that Katie-O had needed him more.

She'd been the epitome of the cool chick—casual, rootless, free-spirited. She'd sported a stud on the side of her nose then, a pierced belly button and that mermaid tattoo. How the hell was he supposed to know that he'd break her heart by leaving?

But he did know, deep down. Katie put on that tough-girl act because that's what she'd needed to do in the past to get by. She'd let her guard down enough with him so that he could see the soft squishy insides beneath the hard shell.

And he'd let her down. He'd be damned if he'd do it again.

The screen flickered and a message popped up.

They're on to you.

He jerked his head up and scanned the room. He asked her how she knew that, and his heart pounded while he waited for her response.

Five minutes later she replied.

We need to meet tonight.

Stairwell?

Parking structure at 9.

The rest of the afternoon and early evening passed in a blur of assignments, tests and nutritional guidance, which was a joke. Who needed good nutrition when you were being jacked up with some chemical formula that altered the composition of your brain and body?

During their downtime after dinner, most of the guys watched TV or played video games—probably a few of Katie's designs. The pool and Jacuzzi stayed open all night, and some of the guys wandered around the facility for a change of scenery. He'd be wandering around the facility, too, the parking structure to be exact.

At ten minutes to nine, he slipped out of the recruits' compound and hugged the edges of the buildings on his way to the employee parking structure. He'd better not see Dustin Gantt out for a smoke again.

He headed for the same spot where he'd seen Katie yesterday and ducked into the shadows.

A few minutes later she appeared at the edge of the

quad and strode toward the parking structure. When she got within a few feet of him, he whispered her name.

She didn't even break her stride. "Follow me upstairs to my car."

"Cameras?"

"Not a problem."

They didn't say another word as they marched up the stairs to the second level of the structure. A lone car huddled in a space in the middle of the lot, and as Katie aimed her remote at it, the lights blinked once in welcome.

He climbed into the passenger seat of the small car and shoved the seat back as far as it would go, and he still had to bend his knees. "Could you find a smaller car?"

"I paid cash for it and never registered it—just another way to cover my tracks."

"You'd make a better Tempest agent than half those recruits." He jerked his thumb over his shoulder.

"Not once they get all juiced up." She grabbed his arm. "I have all kinds of news for you."

"I figured you did. How do you know they're on to me?"

"I'm working with them."

His eyebrows shot up. "What does that mean?"

"I met Mr. Romo, Liam. I'm in. He and Ginger want me to join the dark side and start spying on Tempest employees. I'm thinking that's why they broke into my apartment and maybe even bugged it, but it looks like I passed with flying colors."

"I don't know, Katie-O. That doesn't sound safe. They could be playing you."

Her nails dug deeper into his flesh. "You're the one who's not safe, Liam. They want me to spy on you."

His eyelid twitched. He'd failed. His first assignment for Prospero and he'd failed. "Why? Did they indicate what had made them suspicious?"

She flicked the keys in the ignition. "They're not going

to let me in on those details. I did tell them I'd seen you and Dustin by the parking structure the other night."

"Great. Thanks."

"I wanted to ingratiate myself with them, let them know they hadn't made a mistake by approaching me. They already suspected you, anyway."

"And Dustin."

"Yeah, looks like you were wrong about him."

"Maybe, maybe not." He covered her hand resting on the steering wheel with his. "Like I said, maybe they're playing you. Maybe they're playing both of us, and Dustin is in on the gig."

"I don't think so, Liam. They're giving me the keys to the castle."

"Computer access?" He squeezed her hand.

"They want me to start with you and Dustin. It's perfect."

"If it's not a setup." He traced the ridges of her knuckles. "What's he like, Romo?"

"Ordinary except for his eyes. They're such a light blue, especially for his coloring. He has black hair and an olive skin tone."

"Maybe they're contacts just to freak people out."

"I don't think he needs the eyes for that." She huffed out a breath. "I'm going to use my newfound freedom to poke at their firewalls. I'm going to find out their master plan."

"Did they wonder why you jumped in with both feet and no questions asked?"

"I made it about money and they made it about blackmail."

"Blackmail?"

"I lied about my background on my application and during the interview. Ginger implied they could file charges or something."

"I don't think so."

"I pretended to believe her, anyway. They couldn't exactly threaten my life if I didn't play along, although you and I both know that's the takeaway."

Knots tightened in his belly. "You're in over your head, Katie-O. Just leave. Now."

Her jaw dropped. "No way. I have them right where I want them."

"You know what these people are capable of. They can make you believe whatever they want you to believe."

Turning toward him, she placed her hands on his thigh. "This gives me a chance to protect you, too. If they suspect you, I can throw them off your scent."

"You don't need to protect me, Katie." He threaded his fingers through hers. "Protection is my job, and I know I blew it before, but I'm not going to make that mistake again."

Her lashes fluttered against her smooth cheeks. "I wasn't in any danger when you left me to do another tour."

"You were in danger of erecting your hard shell again. I'd broken through. I'd made you feel safe and loved, and then I snatched all that away." He skimmed the pad of his thumb along her jaw. "And I never even said I was sorry."

"You did what you had to do." She shrugged, and he put his hands on her raised shoulders.

"Don't. Don't pretend it didn't hurt. Don't pretend I didn't betray your trust, your...love."

Her chest rose and fell as she twisted her fingers in her lap. "Liam, I..."

He held his breath, waiting for the words he'd needed to hear from her two years ago.

Instead, an explosion rocked the car and lit up the night sky.

Chapter Ten

The blast slammed Katie's head against the seat and seemed to lift the car.

"Liam!"

His arms came around her. "My God. Are you okay?"

"What was that? What happened?"

"It was some kind of explosion, and it was close." He pointed to the gaps between the parking structure levels. "I can see the smoke."

She covered her ears, which were pounding. "We have to get out of here. We can't be seen together."

He pulled her into his arms and kissed her hard on the mouth. "Be careful. I'm not losing you again."

Then he slipped out of the car and disappeared.

She sat, gripping the steering wheel for a few minutes, frozen. She couldn't just drive out of the structure as if nothing had happened. She had every right to be here, since she'd worked late.

She got out of the car on shaky legs, and the acrid smell of smoke engulfed her. She choked and headed for the stairwell.

Sirens wailed in the distance. Someone had already called the fire department.

She headed toward the side of the parking structure and peeked through the gaps. Gasping, she jumped back.

Flames engulfed one side of the small building across the way, and chunks of cement and twisted metal littered the quad.

It had to have been a bomb. Had Tempest figured out a new way to get rid of more pesky employees?

The blare of the sirens drew closer, and Katie hit the stairwell and jogged down the steps. At least Liam had been with her at the time of the explosion, so she didn't have to worry about him.

His words had turned her insides to jelly and made her breathless until the blast had ruined the moment. It had brought them both back to reality. They needed each other right now—not as lovers but as colleagues.

When she reached the bottom of the structure, she pressed her palms against the metal door. When she'd peered from above, she hadn't noticed the fire threatening the parking garage, and the door still felt cool to the touch.

She cracked it open. The debris and smoke in the air made her eyes water, and she squinted at the mayhem the blast had caused. The fire trucks had reached the scene, and knots of people clustered on the outskirts of the quad.

Covering her mouth and nose with one hand, she pushed through the door and picked her way across smoldering chunks of the building and shards of glass.

"Ma'am! Ma'am! Are you all right?"

One of the firemen had spotted her and rushed to her side. "You need to keep your distance."

"I'm fine. I was in the parking structure, in my car." She stumbled, and the fireman caught her arm.

"KC? Oh, my God, are you okay?" Ginger flew toward her, grabbing her hand. "Is there anyone else in the garage?"

Apparently, she'd become Ginger's new best friend once she'd decided to spy for her and Mr. Romo, and her new bestie seemed genuinely shocked by the scene around them. If the Tempest cabal hadn't engineered this little bonfire, who had?

Liam's agency wouldn't be this in-your-face. He'd already explained that they were forming a trap around Tempest and would wait it out for the proof.

"KC?" Ginger squeezed her hand. "Anyone else?"

Katie shook some soot and white powder from her hair. "N-no. I didn't see any other people or cars in the parking structure. I was already in my car, but I had to see what was going on. Does anyone know what happened?"

"One of the firemen mentioned something about a gas line here. I hope nobody else was burning the midnight oil, like you."

"I didn't see anyone. What blew up?" She eyed the main office building, which had a few broken windows but no other damage.

"It was the small utility building next to the parking structure."

"Were all these people in the main building?" She nodded toward the clutches of people, murmuring together and staring at the scene with shocked faces.

"A few of them. Everyone got out safely, as far as we know. No injuries, nobody in the utility building. The guys over there are the recruits. I think they felt the explosion all the way across the facility. They certainly heard it."

Katie scanned the crowd of men near the fire engines and let out a breath when she saw Liam's face among them. Of course, he'd be here just like all the rest of them.

She touched Ginger's arm. "Mr. Romo? Is he okay?"

"He's fine. The building rocked a bit but he's high enough that the explosion didn't affect him or any of the windows in his office. He got out quickly, though. We both did." Ginger covered her hand with her long, tapered fingers. "He made quite an impression on you, didn't he?"

Katie tipped her chin to her chest. "He's the type of man who commands a room."

"He certainly does. Women want him and men want to be him, as the saying goes." She stroked Katie's fingers and held her gaze, her glossed lips parted.

Katie looked away as heat surged up her chest and burned her cheeks. Was Ginger coming on to her or suggesting that *she* wanted Mr. Romo? She hadn't known what to make of that weird group hug in Mr. Romo's office, but his wandering hands had grossed her out.

Ginger gave a low chuckle and pinched Katie's chin. "Don't worry about it, KC. Mr. Romo has that effect on all women. But rest assured, he's safe and secure right now and will be happy to hear you're the same."

Katie swallowed. "I'm sure he'll be relieved that *all* of his employees got out safely."

"Of course, but especially you, KC." Ginger had turned to watch the firemen douse the flames with their hoses, her sharp profile in relief against the orange glow of the fire. "You're one of us, now."

Ginger strode toward the other employees, waving her arms and barking orders. Katie slumped. What the hell had she gotten herself into?

LIAM RETURNED TO his housing unit along with the other recruits still yammering about the explosion. If they all really believed some faulty gas line caused that blast, they didn't deserve to be covert ops agents. Given the current climate here, if Tempest hadn't set off that explosion, one of its enemies did.

He'd meant what he said to Katie, that she'd make a better agent than half these guys. It didn't surprise him that Ginger Spann had recognized how valuable Katie's skills could be to an organization like Tempest. It didn't surprise him, but it did worry the hell out of him. She'd officially entered the lion's den, and he'd do everything within his power to make sure she came out of it without a bite.

"Hey, man, you up for some Worldwide War?" Charlie jerked his thumb at the video game room.

"I'm dead tired but knock yourself out." He slipped into his room and flicked on the light. His gaze swept across the four corners of the ceiling. Katie had assured him that she could take care of any cameras or bugs, especially now that she'd been invited into the inner circle.

He still planned to watch his back. Ginger Spann and Mr. Romo had obviously made him, or at least they had their suspicions. What had tipped them off?

Dr. Harris—it must've had something to do with his session with her yesterday. Maybe he'd gone overboard in proclaiming his love of violence and rebellion.

He stripped down to his boxers, tossing the notebook Katie had pressed into his hands while they were in her car onto the bed, and ducked into the bathroom to brush his teeth and splash some water on his face. He could use a shower to get rid of the acrid stench of the fire that lingered in his skin and hair, but beneath that smell lurked another scent—wildflowers and warm California sunshine.

Katie-O's lips had felt soft and juicy beneath his. The kiss had been natural and right—and he planned to repeat it.

He shut off the lights overhead and clicked on the lamp clipped to the headboard of his bed. He crawled between the sheets, his head sinking against the pillow. He closed his eyes for a few seconds and then dragged Garrett Patterson's notebook into his lap.

Katie had confessed she couldn't make heads or tails out of Patterson's notes, but Patterson must've wanted to protect the information or he wouldn't have hidden it beneath his desk blotter.

Ginger and Romo probably didn't have a clue that this notebook even existed. Patterson must've been hiding it from his bosses.

He flipped open the cover. For all he knew it could be a detailed accounting of all the women Patterson had sexually harassed at Tempest.

His gaze ran down the first page—numbers and more numbers. Prospero had required training in code-breaking...and he'd been at the top of the class. Katie should excel at this sort of thing, but she'd always maintained she didn't have the patience to review or fix anyone else's software codes. Her mind always leaped ahead to how she'd create it from scratch.

He trailed his index finger along the columns of numbers in decimals. Another column next to that one contained sets of four numbers.

He rubbed his eyes and brought the notebook closer to his face. Snorting, he smacked the paper. He wouldn't even call this set of numbers a code. The four numbers clearly represented dates—months and days, no years. Katie must be slipping.

He studied the dates, which meant nothing to him—no holidays, nothing of significance. He'd have to run them on his laptop, which Katie had also promised to protect.

He stared at the other numbers through half-closed eyelids and then gave up. His brain was as blurry as his eyesight at this point.

He dragged himself out of bed and slid a dime from his nightstand. He climbed on top of the bed, reaching for the vent in the ceiling. Using the dime, he unscrewed the plate over the vent and then shoved the notebook in the open space. He replaced the vent and dropped back onto the bed.

He'd have to get Prospero something they could use and

quick. He couldn't fake one more dose of T-101. Tempest would either expel him for not being susceptible to the formula…or they'd kill him.

THE FOLLOWING MORNING his alarm startled him awake. He rolled onto his back and eyed the vent—GPS coordinates. The first set of numbers indicated locations and the second set, dates. Why would Patterson be hiding that information from Mr. Romo?

He rolled out of bed, took a quick shower and dressed in gym clothes. They had a five-mile run this morning before breakfast. After that it was anyone's guess what they'd do. If Tempest had planned and executed that little fireworks display last night, there would be some fallout from it—maybe another conveniently dead body.

At least it wouldn't be Katie's.

He joined a couple of the other recruits in the hallway and they headed out to the track together.

Liam started stretching and warming up in the chilly morning air. Hamilton liked them all to start together, so the guys scattered on the grass waited for the slow starters to show up.

Liam rose from his stretch and sprinted up the bleachers. At the top he peered across the facility to the damaged building. Would the employees be going to work in their building with the broken windows today? The fire department probably gave them the all-clear already. The windows were boarded and the debris shoved off to the side.

He glanced at the field where Mills and Hamilton had their heads together, and a ripple of excitement ran through the recruits.

Now what?

He jogged down the bleachers and approached Charlie talking with two other guys.

"What's going on? How come we haven't started the run yet?"

Charlie raised an eyebrow. "Dustin Gantt is missing, dude, and they think he blew up the building last night to escape."

Chapter Eleven

"So you were right about him. I'm only sorry you didn't approach me sooner. Maybe I could've prevented this." Katie sat in a chair across the room from Mr. Romo and Ginger, with her knees together, hands folded in her lap.

Ginger paced the room, sparks of rage shooting from her green eyes. "You saw him in that area the other night, didn't you, him and McCabe? They must've been setting it all up then."

"McCabe?" Katie drew her brows over her nose. "Is he missing, too?"

"Exactly, Ginger." Mr. Romo clicked his tongue. "If the two of them were involved in this together, McCabe would've escaped with Gantt."

"I don't like it. I don't like him." She wedged her hand on one slim hip. "We thought he'd be a perfect specimen. He far outpaced the other recruits in every physical pursuit. So why didn't the T-101 have the desired effect?"

Katie blinked. She wasn't supposed to know what T-101 was. "T-101?"

Mr. Romo shot Ginger a look that could freeze her on the spot if she weren't already as cold as ice. "A highly concentrated vitamin supplement we administer to the recruits to improve their physical prowess."

"Oh." Katie spread her hands. "Maybe it didn't do anything for him because he's already at the top of his game."

"Are you an expert on health and nutrition now, KC?" Ginger strolled toward Mr. Romo and dropped a hand on his shoulder in a proprietary way.

Did Ginger think she had designs on the irresistible Mr. Romo? She seemed to encourage it on the one hand, and now she'd gone all territorial on her...and him.

Katie was still trying to process Dustin's betrayal of Tempest. What did it mean? Maybe Liam's agency wasn't the only one trying to infiltrate Tempest. But if Dustin was working for someone else, what good did that blast do other than afford him a distraction to escape?

Dustin must've figured out enough about Tempest to realize that a recruit couldn't just up and quit at this point in the training.

Ginger snapped her fingers. "Are you listening?"

"Sorry, I was thinking about the best way to track Gantt's computer use."

Mr. Romo almost beamed at her. "You see, Ginger, our girl is on it."

Katie flashed him a broad smile, but her stomach did a flip. "I do have a question, if you don't mind. Why didn't Dustin Gantt just quit? Why go through all that trouble to leave Tempest?"

Mr. Romo shifted his light gaze toward Ginger. "It's in their contract. Once they reach a certain point in their training, they lose a large portion of their signing bonus."

She shrugged. "Just seems kind of extreme to me."

Mr. Romo tapped his head. "Dustin Gantt had issues, obviously."

"Do you even know for sure he's the one who did it? Maybe it's just a coincidence—the explosion and his departure."

"KC, we're not paying you to theorize. We're paying

you to spy." She clapped her hands twice. "Now, go find out what Gantt was up to before he made his spectacular exit. We expect a report back at the end of the day."

"I'm on it." Damn, she'd appeared too eager, but any normal person would have questions.

Mr. Romo beckoned her with a cupped hand. "Come here, KC."

Katie forced her legs to move, although they felt like lead. She approached Mr. Romo's realm, just close enough to encounter a wave of his spicy cologne. Then she planted her feet in the dense carpet.

His lip twitched but his blue eyes looked like chips of ice. Then he rose slowly from the couch and gathered her in his arms, again resting one hand against the curve of her hip.

Every muscle in Katie's body tensed as her arms hung at her sides.

Mr. Romo gave her a squeeze and then released her. She stumbled back.

"I'm a hugger." He lifted one powerful shoulder. "Isn't that right, Ginger?"

Ginger laughed. "I think you're a little overwhelming for *our girl*, Mr. Romo."

Katie gritted her teeth. In normal circumstances, she'd haul off and smack Mr. Romo in the face. But these weren't normal circumstances, and these weren't normal people. Did Ginger call him Mr. Romo while she was straddling him in bed, too?

"I—I'm just not used to hugging in a work environment."

Ginger took two long steps toward her and cupped her face with one hand. "You're not used to much hugging or personal contact at all, are you? You poor, lost lamb. We know all about your background in the foster care system, shunted from one uncaring home to another. We're going to make that all go away for you, KC. You have a place with us."

As long as you do what we tell you to do.

The unspoken thought hung in the air between them, but Katie heard it as clearly as if Ginger had shouted it in her ear.

"I appreciate that, Ginger."

Ginger's touch on her cheek turned into a caress. "We'll take care of you, KC. Now get to work, dear."

Katie backed out of Mr. Romo's office and then sped down the hallway to the executive elevator. Ginger had paused it, so all Katie had to do was punch the button for her floor.

When the doors closed, she slumped against the wall of the elevator car, a bead of sweat trickling down the back of her neck.

What kind of game were these two playing?

She had no doubt Ginger and Mr. Romo had a thing going on, but what role did they expect her to play in their relationship?

Ginger alternately acted jealous and seductive.

When the elevator landed on her floor, she squared her shoulders and strode to her cubicle. As if she didn't have enough incentives to wrap up this job, the prospect of working with Romo and Ginger on a daily basis just amped up her motivation tenfold.

Liam must know about Dustin, but what did he think about his defection? The man had been playing a part when she'd run into him and Liam near the parking structure. He must've been worried that she and Liam would report him. Was that why he acted when he did? He'd destroyed the maintenance building but hadn't done much more damage than that. Had he been planning an attack on a larger scale but abandoned it because Liam had discovered him?

She'd do her research on Dustin, all right, but she had

no intention of turning any findings over to Mr. Romo. If Dustin Gantt had any info about Tempest's nefarious plans, Liam would want to know about it.

She pulled her chair up to her computer and glanced at the time in the lower right-hand corner of her screen. The recruits should be in the classroom about now, but she never texted Liam first in case someone was hovering over his laptop.

He'd wasted no time, though. When she launched her instant messenger, a note was waiting from Liam. One word:

Dustin?

She explained to him that the official word was that he was off the rails and caused a disruption to escape the facility and break his contract.

He responded:

Same here. Need to see you.

She assured him that she could arrange that. After all, wasn't she part of the inner circle now?

A few hours later, after clearance from Ginger, Katie made her way to the training facility. She had some work to do on the recruits' laptops.

Ginger had already called ahead for her, so when she entered the classroom, Mills didn't blink an eye. He glanced up from his desk once and said, "Do what you have to do. Gantt's computer is the one in the third row."

She retrieved the laptop. "I'm going to take this into the empty classroom next door, and I'm going to have to get a couple of these guys to leave class and join me with their laptops."

"No problem. They're doing independent study right now. Just call 'em out as you need 'em."

"Thanks." She tucked Dustin's laptop under her arm and left the classroom without stealing one look at Liam.

After giving Gantt's laptop the once-over, she'd call another recruit in here first to keep suspicion away from Liam.

She checked the obvious on Dustin's computer—browsing history, cookies, files. The guy was no idiot, but everyone left a trail on their computers whether they knew it or not, and not every hacker knew how to reveal that hidden history—but she did.

She'd have to do the heavy work back at her office. She powered off his laptop and snapped the lid shut.

Then she checked her list and decided to call in Charlie Beck for the hell of it. She poked her head into the classroom where the recruits were clicking away on their keyboards. "Charlie Beck?"

A young guy looked up from his work, eyes wide, cheeks flushed.

Wow, did she strike the same fear into the hearts of Tempest employees as Ginger Spann did? She'd truly reached inner-circle status. Mr. Romo would be so proud, he'd likely give her another hug. So she'd better keep this to herself.

"Sh-should I bring my laptop?" Charlie stood, halfway crouched over his desk.

"That's the point, cowboy."

Charlie's blush deepened at the scattered guffaws from his fellow recruits.

He followed her into the other classroom, carrying his laptop awkwardly in front of him.

She patted the desk next to hers. "Just put it here."

"Are we all under some kind of investigation because of Dustin Gantt?"

"Not really, nothing to worry about, but honestly, if you

think you might want to break your contract it's best just to talk it out instead of blowing things up and running away."

"Oh, yeah, hell, I'd never do that."

She pointed to his laptop. "Could you please log in to your computer?"

"Uh, I didn't log out. I just closed it."

She suppressed a sigh and smiled. She didn't want to be another Ginger. "That's perfect. Just wake it up and we'll get to work."

Charlie had been working on a paper about political unrest in several West African countries.

She waved her hand at the document. "You can close out of this and open your browser."

He saved the file and launched a browser. "Do you need me to do anything else?"

"Just switch places with me."

"Sure." He clambered out of the chair that was too small for his long, lanky frame and held out the chair for her.

"Thanks." She settled herself in front of Charlie's laptop and opened his browsing history just to look busy. A number of porn sites cropped up in the list.

He coughed. "You know, some of the other guys were messing around with my laptop. I didn't visit those websites."

"I don't care." She flicked her fingers at the screen. "That's not what I'm here for, anyway. I'm just making sure you don't have a particular virus on your computer, but those are just the types of websites that harbor bugs and viruses."

"I didn't know that. I'll make sure those guys don't get to my computer again."

"Also, you can never really delete your browsing history, so you'd better be careful." She cleared her throat. "I mean, those other guys need to be careful."

"Yeah, yeah. I'll put out the word."

She could've eased Charlie's fears since she didn't think Mr. Romo would care if the recruits were visiting porn sites, just as long as they all took their vitamins and turned into good little robots.

She checked out a few more areas of Charlie's computer, actually found some malware, probably from those porn sites, and ran a fix.

"I think that'll do it." She restarted his computer. "So, what's everyone saying about Dustin Gantt?"

"We can't believe it. I can't believe it. He seemed like a cool guy, really gung-ho. He was the only one who came close to McCabe in the physical fitness department, until that last day."

"His last day of PT?" She unplugged Charlie's laptop and snapped the lid closed for him.

"Yeah, he really lagged behind. McCabe, too. They both seemed slower that day. Hell, even I did more pull-ups than McCabe. That was a first for me."

"Maybe Gantt just lost interest and decided to split and make a splash while he did so."

Maybe the T-101 didn't have an effect on Dustin, but he must've been planning his escape before the injection of the drug.

"I don't know. Crazy way to go out." He scooped his laptop from the desk. "You finished?"

"You're good to go. Can you please send Liam McCabe in here with his laptop?"

"Sure." He turned at the door. "Ms. Locke? You're not going to mention those websites, are you?"

She ran her fingertip across the seam of her lips. "My lips are sealed."

"Thanks, ma'am."

She paced the room for the next several minutes until Liam came through the door. It took an iron will not to rush across the room and throw herself at him. He looked so damned good and safe and normal. She needed a huge dose of normal right now after slinking out of Mr. Romo's lair.

Liam snapped the door closed behind him. "How'd you manage this visit?"

"In addition to collecting Dustin's laptop, I told them I could put some tracking software on yours."

He walked to the desk where she had her purse and set his computer on top of it. "My stomach's been in knots thinking about you with those two. I just can't get past the idea that they're on to you and setting you up for something."

"I really don't think so, Liam." She had no intention of telling him about the creepy sexual vibe she'd been getting from both Ginger and Mr. Romo. He didn't need anything else to worry about.

He pointed to his laptop. "Shouldn't we at least pretend to be working on the computer in case someone comes in here?"

"Yeah, although I requested privacy." She took a seat at the desk, and he pulled up a chair next to hers.

She turned the laptop toward him. "Go ahead and log in."

He reached past her, and she watched his strong fingers move across the keyboard while she inhaled his fresh scent. He didn't need any heavy cologne to increase his allure.

He glanced her way. "Anything else?"

She blinked and focused on the screen. "Nope." She accessed his browsing history, hoping not to find any porn sites there. "You were wrong about Dustin. What do you think about him now?"

"I'm not sure. Maybe something happened here that spooked him. The T-101 injection could've been the last straw, and maybe he's not susceptible to hypnosis so he was able to put two and two together."

"The T-101 didn't have any effect on his system."

"How do you know that? I didn't notice."

"Charlie told me. You were probably too concerned about your own behavior to notice Dustin's." She skimmed the websites he'd visited. "No porn."

"Excuse me?" His brows shot up, disappearing beneath the lock of sandy-blond hair that fell over his forehead.

"That idiot Charlie had been visiting porn sites on his company laptop. Who does that?"

"An idiot." He ran a hand through his hair. "So, Dustin got freaked out by a few things, figured Tempest wouldn't let him out of his contract and caused a distraction to escape. I plan to look him up when we get out of here, but I have something else to tell you."

She jerked her head to the side. "What?"

"I figured out the code in Patterson's notebook, which really wasn't much of a code."

"You did?" Leaning over, she took his face in her hands. "I knew I could count on you. I looked at it for two minutes and got dizzy."

He turned his head, placing his lips against her palm. "Patience is not your strong suit, Katie-O."

"Ain't that the truth? What did all those numbers mean?" The kiss had scorched her flesh, and she dropped her hands into her lap, curling that hand into a fist as if to capture the kiss for later inspection.

"They're GPS coordinates and dates—months and days."

She slumped in her chair. "I missed that? Seems kind of obvious now. Where are the locations, and what's the significance of the dates?"

"That's—" he reached over to the keyboard and launched a search engine "—what I'm hoping we can discover right now. Anything we put in here, you can get rid of, right? Nobody will know I've been looking up those coordinates on my computer?"

"Just call me the cleaner." She huffed on her fingernails and polished them on the front of her blouse.

"You know what I'm going to miss most about being here at Tempest with you?" He flicked her collar. "These blouses and slacks."

She smacked his hand away. "This is proper office attire."

He grinned the grin that had reeled her in from the moment she'd met him at Sebastian's party over three years ago.

"You ready for those coordinates now?"

"Do you have the notebook?"

He tapped his head. "It's all in here. Ready?"

"Show-off." She positioned her fingers on the keyboard. "Shoot."

He reeled off the first set, and she entered the coordinates into the website she'd accessed.

Hunching forward, Liam peered at the monitor. "Djibouti, the capital city of the Republic. Follow up on that address."

She entered the address for the African city and read aloud. "That's the address of the Parliament Building there."

He poked at the screen. "Get another tab going and input this date."

She clicked open a new browser page and typed in the date that Liam recited from the recesses of his photographic memory. She scanned the bits and pieces on the screen. "Nothing."

"Okay, enter that date along with the Parliament Building in Djibouti."

This time the search engine returned several news stories about two African leaders who'd been killed when their cars had exploded as they were leaving a meeting at the Parliament Building in Djibouti.

She covered her mouth and turned to Liam. "Do you think Tempest was responsible for that?"

"Let's do the next one."

He gave her a location, and this time it came back to Montevideo in Uruguay. When they matched the location, a street in a gated community, to the date, they got no hits.

Liam wouldn't give up. He continued to rattle off different search combinations until a news story about the death of a prominent Uruguayan judge popped up.

She let out a breath. "Tempest's handiwork again. What are they trying to accomplish with these assassinations besides the obvious?"

"I don't know, but the two dates we entered occurred in the past. Patterson's dates included month and day only, no year, so I just assumed the dates took place this year. There are dates on those notebook pages still in the future."

She clasped the back of her neck and squeezed the hard muscles on either side. This project had turned into so much more than getting revenge for Sebastian's suicide, and she was in way over her head.

Liam rubbed her back. "Are you okay, Katie-O? This is some pretty heavy stuff."

"I'll do what I can, Liam."

"You know why Sebastian died now. You know my agency is going to do everything in its power to put a stop to Tempest's activities." He stroked her hair. "You've done enough. We never would've had this intel if you hadn't been snooping around Garrett Patterson's office, putting yourself in danger. You can go home now, Katie."

She tilted her head. "Do you really think Mr. Romo and his sidekick are going to allow me to leave now? I'm part of their inner circle. They own me."

The corner of his mouth twitched. "They don't own Katie O'Keefe *or* KC Locke. Nobody owns either of those women."

"I'm not leaving here without you. So whenever you're done, I reckon that's when I'll wrap up."

He tugged on a lock of her hair. "Stubborn girl."

"You'd better get back. You can finish up when you return to the classroom, as long as nobody can see what you're doing. I can erase every trace of every keystroke."

"I think I can manage, but let's look up one more date here—one in the future."

The first location they searched for brought up another street, this time in Berlin. She jotted it down. "I'll search for any notable people at this address when I get home."

"There are only three more, all in the future. Do the last one on Patterson's list, and we'll call it a day." He closed his eyes and retrieved the coordinates.

She entered the numbers, and the location flashed onto the screen. She didn't need to look up this address or the occupants or the date.

It was the White House.

Chapter Twelve

The tap on the door made him jump from his chair, his adrenaline still coursing through his system after their discovery. He righted the chair as Katie called out, "Yes?"

Mills poked his head into the room. "Are you done in here yet, Ms. Locke? The recruits have lunch and psych."

Liam's stomach dropped. This new psych session had been slipped in at the last minute, thanks to Dustin. He had a feeling they were in for some heavy-duty hypnosis and probably another shot of T-101. Their loyalty had to be secured.

"I'm not quite done, but I can finish up what I'm doing without Mr. McCabe's help."

Mills worked his jaw back and forth before the words spilled from his mouth. "The recruits aren't supposed to allow their laptops out of their sight when they're not locked up in the classrooms."

Katie stopped tapping away on the keyboard and let her gaze travel up and down Mills's body. "I'm here on business for Mr. Romo. If you care to call him and verify, I'll be happy to wait."

Mills flushed up to the roots of his buzz cut. "I don't want to bother Mr. Romo. When you're finished, please return Mr. McCabe's laptop to the classroom. I'll be waiting for you so I can lock up."

"Will do." She flicked a glance at Liam. "Thank you for your cooperation, Mr. McCabe."

"You're welcome. Thanks for making my laptop faster."

"We'll see about that. I'll check in on your progress in a day or two."

"Got it." He gave her a mock salute and followed Mills out of the room and back into the classroom to retrieve his backpack and assignments.

Mills dropped into his chair and blotted his forehead with a tissue. "Between me and you, McCabe, that Ms. Locke is another Ginger Spann."

"You think? She seemed nice enough."

"Cold, bossy, just like Spann. She's definitely Romo's type, if you know what I mean—physically and every other way. He likes the tall, slender women, brainy types."

Liam almost tripped to a stop at the door. Gripping the doorknob, he twisted his head over his shoulder. "I don't know what you mean."

"You didn't hear it from me, but Romo and Spann are an item to put it politely, and I wouldn't be surprised if he had Ms. Locke lined up as a younger, newer model."

Liam lifted his stiff shoulders. "As long as it doesn't affect me."

"Yeah, not you guys." Mills's features had twisted into a sneer. "But when Romo sets up one of his lady friends, he gives her carte blanche over the rest of us. It's highly illegal on all levels—bed the boss and get all kinds of perks."

Liam's blood simmered, but he pasted on a smile. "Not my business."

Mills shook his head and blinked as if coming out of a rage-induced trance. "Of course not. Not mine, either. Just blowing off a little steam—just between us, eh, McCabe?"

Everyone around here walked on eggshells, afraid of retribution from Romo. Mills had let his anger loosen his tongue.

"Sure, Mills. Like I said, it's not my concern."

He walked back to his room, his mind racing. Had Katie not noticed Romo's attention, or had she just neglected to tell him about it? Maybe Mills just didn't like female authority. Katie had nettled him, and nobody liked Ginger Spann, so Mills was attributing their power to sleeping with the boss.

He had to put his concern for Katie on the back burner for now. She could handle Romo's advances. He had to get to his phone and deliver this new info to Prospero, whether or not he got reamed by his Prospero bosses for sneaking a phone onto the facility. This information couldn't wait. If Prospero could tie Tempest's agents to these other assassinations, they'd have a good case to make with the CIA for shutting down Tempest completely and revoking its funding.

He hung his backpack on the chair and washed his hands. Maybe he'd have some time after lunch and before the psych session to dig up his phone.

Lunchtime was buzzing with more talk of Dustin. To prove their superior insight, most of the recruits were now insisting they suspected something fishy about the guy. Liam kept his mouth shut.

Dustin had been using the cigarettes as an excuse for being in locations where he had no business being. How soon had he caught on to Tempest's true intentions? It had to have been before the T-101 injection, but that was probably the icing on the cake.

Would they be subjected to another dose this afternoon? A light sweat broke out on his skin. The docs at Prospero had no idea how long the T-101 antidote would work. Would there come a time when the formula would find an accepting host in his body? Then what? Would that be enough to compel a decent man to launch an attack against his own country?

"That leaves the field free and clear for McCabe."

"Huh?" Liam looked up from his turkey sandwich into the eager eyes of Charlie Beck.

"Gantt was the only one who could challenge you during PT. You're going to be the top dog now, free and clear, no challengers."

Not once they all got pumped up with T-101.

"I guess Gantt's body was a lot more fit than his mind."

"Yeah, yeah. He must've been nuts, right? Why else would he go out that way?" Charlie's voice carried an edge of hysteria that he probably didn't even notice.

Was he having his own doubts? Liam's gaze darted among the faces at his lunch table, and the smiles seemed tight and strained, the jaws tense. Were they all getting it now?

It would make his job a whole lot easier when it came time to roll.

He picked up his plate. "I'm going to try to squeeze in some fresh air before the psych sessions start, clear my mind."

Tammy, the lone female recruit, nodded toward the cafeteria door where one of the Tempest security guards stood with his arms crossed. "I think you're going to have a problem with that."

A few of the recruits at the table murmured. "Are they locking us in now? Damn Gantt."

Liam stacked his plate on a tray by the door and approached the security guard. "I'm done. Can you step aside?"

"Mr. Moffitt wants to make sure all recruits are in the waiting room by one o'clock."

Moffitt was the assistant to Hamilton, the physical trainer. Liam tapped his watch. "It's twelve-forty. I'm just going to get some fresh air."

The security guard's eyes slid from Liam's face to

the table of restless recruits behind him. "Yeah, sure, of course."

He stepped aside, and as Liam strode away from the cafeteria, he heard the guy get on his cell.

Liam made it to the track without seeing another soul, and then suddenly two figures emerged from the buildings on the other side of the facility. As they drew closer, Liam could make out their security guard uniforms and their equipment belts. Tempest believed in arming its security guards with more than pepper spray and a pair of zip-tie handcuffs.

So he was allowed to get his fresh air, but not without an escort. He could forget about calling Prospero on the phone, buried in the dirt on the other side of the track.

For show, he walked around the track, anyway, while the security guards stationed themselves on either end of it. Did they expect him to jump the fence and make a run for it toward the kiosk at the entrance to the facility? Gantt must've slipped through the gates when the fire trucks were on their way in to respond to the blast.

He and Katie would have to manage their own way out. He wouldn't be leaving her behind—not this time.

After making a point of walking around the track a few times and staring at the sky, Liam returned to the recruit facility and the claustrophobic waiting room, where even Charlie wasn't playing video games.

The mood had changed for the recruits. Gantt's escape had planted ideas in their heads, ideas that they'd dismissed before as preposterous.

Did they finally understand that they couldn't leave at this point of their own free will? Couldn't break their contracts? They'd owe Tempest money back from their signing bonuses, but Gantt must've realized that wouldn't be the only consequence of his defection.

Mr. Romo had to be aware of the rumblings, and he'd

take action. It would push up the schedule for indoctrination. Once Tempest had thoroughly drugged and brainwashed the recruits, they wouldn't want to leave. They'd be tied to Tempest for life. The only way out—suicide, like Sebastian and Adam, total, crazed rebellion like a previous agent, Simon Skinner, or escape like Max Duvall from whom Prospero had gotten the bulk of their intel.

He nodded at a couple of the other guys and grabbed a sports magazine, burying his nose in the pages. He didn't want to talk to anyone. At this point he wouldn't put it past Tempest to monitor the recruits' every move. If they didn't trust him enough to get a breath of fresh air on his own, they must be in extreme paranoid lockdown mode.

Time to make a move, take what they had and get the hell outta Dodge.

The monitor opened the door and called in the first four recruits for their sessions. He'd just been bumped up the list, along with Charlie and Tammy. Again he was the last drop-off along the hallway and again Dr. Harris awaited him.

"Hello, Liam. Take a seat." She gestured toward the couch. The chair he'd occupied last time had been removed.

He sank on the end cushion of the couch, across from her chair. "You must want me to lie down this time since the chair is gone."

"You're very observant." She tapped the end of her pencil on her knee.

He spread his hands. "That's why I'm here. Spies are supposed to be observant, right?"

"You seem…hostile today."

"I suppose I don't like being tailed by a couple of security guards when I'm out for a walk."

"You understand what's going on."

"Dustin Gantt."

"That's right. He put lives in danger. We can't allow that to happen again."

"Understood." He snapped his fingers. "He wasn't your patient, was he? Mr. Romo's gonna wonder why one of his shrinks screwed up and didn't see the signs in Gantt."

One corner of her mouth lifted. "Don't worry about me. How'd the vitamin shot make you feel last time?"

"Good." He raised his eyes to the ceiling. "Strong. Sharp. Tempest should put that stuff out to the general market. They'd make a mint."

"It's reserved for our agents. Are you ready to go under again?"

"Sure, as long as you don't make me dance like a chicken."

"I did that last time."

He smacked his knee and rocked back on the couch in an enthusiastic show for the first glimmer of humor he'd seen from any of the Tempest drones.

Her lip turned up again in that half smile. "Let's get to work."

She tried the same trick on him with the eraser end of her pencil tick-tocking in front of his face. He imagined weights pulling at his lids and allowed them to droop over his eyes, all the while keeping his mind clear. Prospero had trained him well, not that he'd ever been susceptible to hypnosis.

When she believed he'd gone under, her questions and suggestions dealt with the recent past this time. She encouraged him to talk about Dustin Gantt, asking him his true feelings about Gantt and his escape. Did they really expect to get at any truths this way? Romo seemed to have an inordinate amount of faith in hypnosis.

He made sure to let his disgust of Gantt's actions seep into his narrative. He also revealed his encounter with Gantt near the parking structure just so he didn't come across as too perfect since he'd never reported that encounter.

Dr. Harris finished up her questions and brought him out of what she thought was his hypnotic state.

"How do you feel, Liam?"

"Good. Relaxed."

"Great. Are you ready to feel even better?"

"Another vitamin shot?"

"That's right." She twisted around and picked up her cell phone. "He's ready."

Liam's muscles tensed up. He hated this part—too many uncontrolled variables. Did that antidote have a long shelf life or did it wear off? The Prospero doctors hadn't had enough time to figure out much before he had to join the next Tempest recruitment.

A nurse walked through the door, pushing a cart in front of her. "Are you ready, Mr. McCabe?"

"As ready as I ever am for a needle poking me in the arm." He rolled up his sleeve.

The nurse shot a quick glance at Dr. Harris. "This time the injection is going into your buttocks. Sorry, but can you please stand, turn around and pull down your jeans and underwear?"

The pulse in his jaw ticked. "Ah, sure."

He pushed off the couch and turned to face the wall. *Why the change?*

He unbuttoned his fly, hooked his thumbs in the elastic band of his briefs and yanked down his pants and underwear.

She swabbed a spot on his right buttock. "This will sting a little."

He gritted his teeth as the syringe went into his flesh. He expected to feel no reaction, just like last time. What he got was a surge of adrenaline and darkness crowding his peripheral vision.

"Whoa." He swayed toward the couch and flung out his hand, which hit a picture on the wall.

The nurse grabbed his arm and eased him onto the couch, his pants and briefs still twisted around his thighs. "Just relax, Mr. McCabe."

"Is he going to be okay?" Dr. Harris hunched forward in her chair as he fought to focus on her face swimming before him.

From somewhere far away, he heard the nurse's voice. "I administered a double dose, just like you requested."

Chapter Thirteen

Katie took a deep breath and hugged her file folder to her chest as she waited next to the executive elevator. She'd been dreading this appointment all day, but she'd come prepared.

She'd had no contact with Liam since he'd left for lunch and another appointment with the psychiatrist. After Dustin Gantt's escape, Mr. Romo would be coming down hard on the recruits, but Liam had a plan in place. He'd told her nothing the psychiatrist did, including shooting him up with T-101, would have any effect on him.

The clip of Ginger's heels echoed down the corridor as she approached the elevator. She pushed her glasses on top of her head as she drew next to Katie and flashed her badge to call the elevator car. Lifting one sculpted, carefully groomed eyebrow, she glanced at the file folder. "Fruitful afternoon?"

"Absolutely." Katie raised her hand at a passing co-worker from programming, but the person looked away and scurried past the elevator.

Word had gotten out. She'd been lumped in with Ginger Spann. Mr. Romo had plucked her from the obscurity of the worker bees and had elevated her to the secret society of executive elevators and private afternoon meetings. It's what she'd hoped for, what she'd planned for once she figured out the lay of the land at Tempest, but it made her feel…unclean.

The doors whispered open, and Ginger gestured with her hand. "After you."

Katie retreated to a corner of the elevator, still gripping her folder and staring at the lighted numbers even though they would make only one stop.

"You're discreet, KC. I like that." Ginger touched a finger to her lips and stretched them into one of her stingy smiles.

"I have to be discreet. If it gets around that I'm digging into employees' computers, this operation would be a total failure."

"You enjoy it, don't you? You like the thrill of the forbidden." Ginger crossed her arms and wedged a shoulder against the mirrored wall.

"I admit it." Katie blew a lock of hair, which had escaped from her chignon, from her face. "I like solving other people's puzzles. That's what hacking is—solving a puzzle someone else put into place."

"But those computer programs are supposed to be impenetrable for a reason. Face it. You love breaking the rules." She shook a finger at her as the car landed on Mr. Romo's private floor. "You naughty girl."

"Rules are meant to be broken." Katie tossed her head, and her loose bun came undone in a shower of bobby pins.

"Exactly." Ginger's eyes lit up and Katie relaxed her shoulders, knowing she'd given the appropriate response— one that Ginger had been waiting for from her, one that had solidified her membership in the covert triumvirate.

As Katie ducked to retrieve the pins on the floor of the elevator, Ginger placed the toe of her shoe over one of them. "Leave them. Mr. Romo will like your hair like that."

Katie raised a flushed face to Ginger. "I—I don't, I'm not…"

Ginger patted her hot cheek. "Oh, I know you're not trying to seduce Mr. Romo, KC. Don't worry. That's not what he thinks, either."

Katie was about to blurt out that Mr. Romo was the creepy, sexual harasser in this triangle, but she pressed her lips into a thin line. If she wanted to keep this position and help Liam, she'd have to suck it up and make nice with Romo.

But she'd have to draw the line somewhere—wouldn't she? How far did spies go to secure their mole status? Did they ever sleep with the enemy?

There's only one man she wanted to sleep with right now, and he was somewhere on the other side of this facility getting his head shrunk.

Ginger rapped her knuckles on Mr. Romo's open door. "We're here for the three o'clock meeting."

"Wonderful." Mr. Romo rubbed his hands together, and even this seemingly innocent gesture had knots forming in Katie's gut.

He stood up and gestured to the chair across from his regular spot on the couch.

Without waiting for an invitation, Ginger sat on the other end of the couch, crossing one long leg over the other.

Katie perched on the edge of the chair, resting the manila folder on her knees, her muscles coiled. She didn't want either one of them taking her by surprise.

Mr. Romo picked a piece of lint from the lapel of his dark jacket. "What did you find out about Dustin Gantt, KC?"

Katie flipped open the folder and positioned her index finger on the first bogus bullet point she'd created for Gantt.

"Well, if you had any lingering doubt that Gantt was responsible for the explosion, his browsing history should dispel it." She tapped the page. "He'd done a little research on gas lines. He'd also found a map of the facility."

Mr. Romo leaned back, lacing his hands behind his neck. "Good, good. Did he have any contacts on the outside?"

"No. I found one email account belonging to him with one of the free providers, but he'd followed instructions before arriving here and had deleted the account. There was no suspicious activity on that account before he reported to training."

"What about instant messaging with anyone within the company?" Ginger hunched forward. "Was he communicating with anyone? Samantha Van Alstyn?"

"Samantha?" Katie jerked her head up. "Why would Dustin Gantt be communicating with Samantha?"

Ginger's eye twitched. "She seemed overly interested in the recruits. You knew her. Didn't you notice that?"

"I think Samantha was overly interested in the recruits' hot bods, nothing more." She allowed her folder to slide off her knees as her mouth dropped open. "Oh, my God. You don't think Gantt had anything to do with Samantha's accident, do you?"

"How could he?" Mr. Romo had reached over, placing a hand on Ginger's thigh.

Was that a love tap or a warning to keep her mouth shut about Samantha?

Ginger cleared her throat. "Of course not. Gantt was still here when Samantha had her unfortunate accident, but perhaps Samantha was distraught over something Gantt mentioned to her."

"You're grasping at straws, Ginger. Samantha didn't know Dustin Gantt, and there's a way to trace deleted instant messages." The lie rolled off Katie's tongue. "Gantt had no instant messages other than to Mr. Mills regarding some classroom assignments, messages he never bothered to delete."

"Ahh." Mr. Romo tilted his head back and raised a fist in the air. "Isn't she magnificent, Ginger?"

"She is, indeed." Ginger dropped her hand to Mr. Romo's knee to mark her territory again. "What did you do about McCabe?"

"Do about him?"

Ginger tsked. "Don't let us down now, magnificent KC. Did you check out his computer?"

"Of course. I planted some tracking programs on his laptop so that I can monitor his keystrokes while he's in the classroom. You might be barking up the wrong tree there. I didn't note any unusual activity on his computer."

"Keep looking." Mr. Romo smoothed his thumb across the back of Ginger's hand. "Anything more to report on Gantt?"

"I'm still looking at him, too. In fact, I was going to ask you if it was okay if I took his laptop home with me tonight to do some work over the weekend."

Mr. Romo tilted his head at Ginger. "Does he have anything confidential on it?"

Ginger shook her head. "Frank, KC's boss, cleaned everything off just like he does for every employee who leaves."

"I can verify that." Katie held up her finger. "There's nothing on Gantt's computer except for his assignments."

With his unusual eyes crinkling at the corners, Mr. Romo said, "You are adorable, KC. No plans but work this weekend? A pretty girl like you?"

Nobody had ever called her adorable before. When she'd recovered from the shock, she peeled her folder from the floor. "Not a lot of socializing to be had in this town. I figured that's why Tempest chose this location—the dearth of distractions."

"We create our own social life." He winked at Ginger, who smiled like a sleek cat who'd just lapped up the last of the cream.

Katie held her breath, waiting for him to invite her into their social whirl. She didn't have to wait long.

"Any time you feel like joining us, just let Ginger know." He stood up and stretched his powerful frame. "No pressure. I know you're a little shy. Maybe you're more comfortable with computers than people."

She stood up and met his gaze at eye level. "Mr. Romo, I'm here to do a job, and I'm more than happy to help you in any way I can. I'm not really looking for…anything else."

Her muscles tensed, bracing for his anger. She shouldn't have challenged him, but wasn't that what a normal employee, under normal circumstances, would do when her boss started making inappropriate suggestions?

His lips twisted into a smile. "I appreciate your dedication to the job, KC. Come, let's have our group hug to reinforce our commitment to each other and to Tempest."

That wasn't too bad. Katie let out a measured breath and stepped in for the embrace. She could put up with this nonsense as long as Romo understood she wanted nothing more from him…or Ginger.

Ginger curled her arm around Katie's waist and drew her into the circle.

Mr. Romo placed his arm lower than Ginger's and tucked Katie against his side. His hand dropped to her backside, and he dug his fingers into her flesh beneath the gabardine of her slacks.

As she gasped, he pressed his forehead against the side of her head and growled. "You'll do whatever I want whenever I want it."

Then he stuffed his tongue in her ear.

KATIE CLUNG TO the toilet seat and retched for the third time. She staggered to her feet and hunched toward the mirror, staring into her red-rimmed eyes. "Sissy!"

She splashed cold water on her face and brushed her teeth. Then she flipped down the toilet seat and sat, digging her elbows into her knees.

A little tongue action from Romo and she'd collapsed like a tent in a windstorm. Of course, she'd waited until she got home for the complete breakdown.

In his office she'd blushed and stammered and pretended it's what she'd wanted from him all along, but claimed she didn't understand the situation since he seemed so close with Ginger.

They'd both gotten a big kick out of her naïveté, and Ginger assured her she wanted nothing more than for the three of them to form an intimate relationship. Katie pretended shock and insisted she needed time, and blah, blah, blah.

She didn't have to go far to convince either one of them since Romo seemed to think he was God's gift to womankind, and Ginger shared his assessment of himself.

She had discovered one thing—there's no way she could submit to Romo even for God and country. She'd have to get out of there before that eventuality took place.

And she had a plan, if only Liam would contact her. She figured he couldn't get to his phone. Post-Dustin, Tempest had the recruits under a microscope.

In the meantime, she had Dustin's laptop, and she intended to conduct a real investigation and find out where he went. Liam and his agency could use whatever info Dustin had dug up while a recruit.

She crept out of the bathroom and poured herself a glass of water. She still didn't even know if Tempest had her place bugged. It would give her some small satisfaction for

Mr. Romo to see the effect his attentions had on her, but she also knew it could be dangerous. *He* was dangerous.

He didn't just want people to work for him and do his bidding, he wanted his chosen employees completely under his control, sexually and every other way.

A tremble rolled through her body, and she shook it off. She sat cross-legged on her couch and pulled Dustin's computer into her lap and got to work.

She hadn't found any of that stuff on his computer that she'd reported to Mr. Romo and Ginger. She hadn't even checked his private email, but all recruits had been given explicit instructions to disable their accounts and not send or receive email while in training.

After a little investigating, it appeared that Dustin had followed orders—at least until he blew up the maintenance building. What had driven him to the conclusion that he'd have to escape or die at this point in his training? Had he recognized a kindred spirit in Liam and had tried to reach out to him? She'd probably ruined that moment between them at the parking structure.

She uncurled her legs and stretched them in front of her. A car alarm whined from somewhere outside, and she stopped short on her way to the kitchen. That car alarm belonged to her.

Stuffing her feet into a pair of clogs, she grabbed a jacket from the hook by the front door and swept her keys from the coffee table. She locked her door behind her and jogged downstairs to the parking garage beneath the building. The lights on her compact flashed as her alarm whooped it up.

She unlocked the car with her remote to stop the alarm and crept along the side of it, inspecting the windows. Had someone tried to break in to the vehicle? Her heart began to hammer almost as loudly as the alarm, and she glanced over her shoulder.

Her gaze darted to the dark corners of the garage where the overhead lights had burned out. She'd never noticed those missing lights before.

She locked her car and as she turned, an arm grabbed her around the waist, and a hand clamped over her mouth.

She bucked and raised her leg to stomp on her attacker's foot, just like Liam had taught her, but he blocked the move with his knee.

The man whispered in her ear. "Shh, shh. I'm not going to hurt you."

Relief flooded her body, and she slumped against Liam's chest. "Oh, my God. You scared the hell out of me. What are you doing out? Did you escape? Did something happen during the psych evaluation?"

Liam loosened his hold and turned her to face him with rough hands. He studied her through narrowed slits, his face a cold mask.

"Who the hell are you?"

Chapter Fourteen

The beginnings of Katie's smile froze on her lips. Her laugh gurgled to a stop in her throat.

Liam hadn't moved one taut muscle. His blue eyes glittered at her with a dangerous light.

"Stop messing around, Liam. I don't appreciate these kinds of jokes, especially after the day I had." She tried to jerk away from him but he held fast, his face, lined with confusion, inches from her own.

"Liam McCabe. I'm Liam McCabe."

Fear punched the words out of her. "Stop it. Just stop."

He tilted his head to the side as if deciphering a puzzle. "I know you. I had your address stamped in my memory. I had the make and model of your car stamped in my memory."

Full-blown panic coursed through her body. "What's wrong with you? It's me, Katie-O. God, don't play games with me, not now."

"I'm not playing games. Are you going to turn me in? Are you going to call someone to send me back to that place? I'm telling you straight up. I'm not going back."

"Liam, Liam." She pressed her palm against his unshaven cheek. "What happened? Don't you know me? I'm Katie O'Keefe. We're working together. We're…together."

Still holding her close with one arm, he dug his fingers into his left temple. "If you're lying to me, I'll..."

His eyelids flew open and he skewered her with his blue eyes, darker but eerily similar to Mr. Romo's—like there was nobody home.

She sobbed. "Please, Liam. I'm not lying to you. How did you escape from the facility? Why? Are they after you?"

His gaze tracked past her face, peering into the dark recesses of the garage. "Would they look for me here? It's the only address I knew, except for one in San Diego, and we're obviously not in San Diego."

She sniffed. "That's your home, *our* home. They're not going to look for you here, but they will look for you. How did you get out? Do they know you're missing?"

"I took out a security guard." He stepped back, and for the first time she saw his uniform. "He won't be discovered for a while."

"Good. Then you have time. What do you remember? You were fine this morning. We met. I talked to you."

"I need answers. I'm suffering from some kind of memory loss or amnesia. We can't stand in this garage all night. Is your place here or are you living with someone?"

"I live alone here, but we can't go up to my place. It might be bugged. You told me that, Liam."

"I need food or...something. I feel sick, agitated."

"It must've been the T-101. It got to you this time."

"T-101?"

She bunched the front of his shirt in her fists. "I know where we can go. There's a group of cabins not too far from here, close to the ski resort in Sun Valley. We'll rent one of those."

"Why can't we just drive, leave?" He'd clamped one hand on her shoulder.

He still didn't trust her.

"We can't. You'll understand why when I explain everything to you."

"If you try to take me back there…"

"You'll kill me." She put her fingers to his lips. "I don't plan on taking you back to Tempest."

"Tempest?"

Tears stung her nose and gathered at the back of her throat. She couldn't do this without Liam. Maybe he was right. Maybe they should just run. But the real Liam would never forgive her if she turned tail and took off when their work wasn't finished. He still had all those successful older brothers of his to live up to.

She squared her shoulders. "I'll explain everything." She unlocked the car. "Get in the backseat, on the floor. I'm going back up to my place to get my purse and throw a few things in a bag. It's Friday, and I'm going on a weekend getaway."

He finally released her and stepped back into the shadows. "I'll wait for you somewhere else."

She spun around and raced back to her apartment. She threw a few things into a suitcase and packed Dustin's laptop, along with her own. She dragged a blanket from her bed and then removed the floorboard in front of the fake fireplace and withdrew a bundle of cash, wrapping it in the blanket.

She'd learned a lot from Liam, and now it was her turn to teach him a thing or two.

FIFTEEN MINUTES LATER the woman—Katie—returned with a suitcase and her purse. Could he trust her? Every fiber of his being told him he could, but then he'd lost his memory so who could say he hadn't lost his gut instincts, too? But what choice did he have right now?

He had the security guard's gun, a little cash from the guy's wallet and numbers—addresses and telephone numbers and license plate numbers—dancing across his brain but not much else. As soon as Katie had said his name, he'd retrieved it. As soon as he'd seen her face, he'd recognized it.

All was not lost.

She whispered into the darkness. "Liam?"

He stepped forward from across the garage. "I'm here."

"Thank God. I thought you might've taken off."

"You're my lifeline, Katie, the only hope I have."

"Then get on the floor of the backseat. I have no idea if anyone's following me or watching me."

She'd popped the trunk of her car, and he lifted the lid for her and hoisted her suitcase in the back. Then he climbed into the backseat, and she threw a blanket in after him.

As she started the car, he folded his frame onto the floor. "You couldn't have found a bigger car?"

"Funny, you already asked me that once before."

She reached into the backseat and pulled the blanket over him. "That should help."

"How far away are these cabins?"

"An hour or so, not much more than that. Are you still hungry?"

His stomach growled. "Starving."

"I'll swing through a fast food drive-through once we get closer to the resort town. I don't want anyone asking questions about what I ordered and how much."

"Are you a spy, too?" He tucked the blanket around his frame, inhaling the scent of wildflowers that brought a rush of memories tumbling across his mind—kisses, soft skin, bodies melded together. Her body. No wonder he couldn't forget her.

She snorted. "I wasn't until fairly recently, but now I'm in a tangled web, and your memory loss has just tightened the noose."

"I'm not a complete blank slate. I do remember certain things—I know I'm a covert ops agent for Prospero."

"Propsero?"

His pulse quickened. "You don't recognize the name?"

"You never mentioned the name of your agency to me. I've never heard of it, but then I'd never heard of Tempest, either."

"Tempest—that's the place I escaped from."

"It's also a government agency. You were working undercover there for Prospero. Tempest is drugging its agents. You had an antidote, but something must've gone wrong this time."

His head pounded with the assault of information. "Okay, stop. Let me process this. You just drive."

She turned on the radio and tuned in to a country station. "This is for you. I prefer alternative rock and old punk."

He closed his eyes against the soft blanket and listened to the music as the car rocked back and forth. It was probably the first time he'd unclenched his jaw since the moment he'd woken up in that bed with no memory of who he was—just adrenaline coursing through his body and a sharp sense of danger.

He'd taken care of those two security guards as if they'd been ninety-eight-pound weaklings instead of two roided-out meatheads armed to the teeth. When he'd hopped the fence, he'd been able to clear it completely, avoiding the electrical field. With the address in town imprinted on his brain, he'd run the five miles to Katie's apartment building in record-setting time.

What the hell had happened to him?

After a while the car veered to the right, and Katie reduced her speed.

"Fast food ahead. It's a burger place. What do you want?"

"Everything."

The car bumped over the curb into a parking lot and slowed to an idle.

Katie buzzed down the window. "Three deluxe cheeseburgers with everything, two large fries, onion rings, chicken strips, two apple pies and a large vanilla shake, please. Oh, and a sugar-free lemonade."

The speaker gurgled something back, and she rolled forward.

He tucked the blanket around his shoulder in case the cashier decided to peek into the backseat of her car. "I hope you plan to share some of that with me."

"It's all for you. I'm a vegetarian."

"Of course you are."

She paid for the food at the next window. The rustle of paper bags and the smell of deep-fried everything made his stomach growl again.

The car lurched forward, took a few turns and accelerated uphill.

"We're almost there. Stay out of sight while I book the cabin. They're scattered along a hillside on the edge of a forest, so nobody will see us going inside. They're designed for privacy."

She parked, left the car and returned a short time later. "All set."

"Did you use a credit card?"

"I paid cash."

"Damn, you're good."

The tires crunched over gravel as Katie wheeled the car toward the cabin. "This is a nice spot. I saw these weeks ago when I was driving around one weekend."

The car stopped, and she opened the door. "I think we're good. Nobody's renting the next cabin over. I stressed that I wanted peace and quiet."

"That's exactly what I need right now." He threw off the blanket and rose stiffly from his cramped position half on the floor, half on the backseat. He staggered out of the car where Katie was already pulling her suitcase from the trunk, holding bags of food in the other hand.

"Let me get that." He took the suitcase from her and set it on the ground, looking at his surroundings. He took a deep breath of pine-scented air, crisp and cold. If anything could set him straight, this natural environment could do the trick.

Ducking back into the front seat, Katie grabbed the drinks from the cup holders. She hunched into her jacket and stomped toward the front door of the cabin. "It has a kitchen, too, so we don't have to go out for food, just groceries."

She pushed open the door and turned on a lamp, which bathed the room in a soft, yellow glow. "Rustic."

"Looks a lot better than the room I woke up in tonight."

Wedging her hands on her hips, she said, "I still don't understand how you got out of there."

He parked her suitcase in the corner of the room, next to the stone fireplace, and shrugged. "Super-human strength."

In the dim light of the cabin, Katie's face drained of all color.

"What's wrong?"

"It's the T-101. It got to you somehow."

"You mentioned that before. T-101 is some kind of formula Tempest is using? Why wouldn't it get to me?" He took the bags of food from her limp hand and placed them on the counter that separated the kitchen from the living room.

"You told me your agency—Prospero—had given you an antidote."

"I guess it didn't work." He ripped open the bag with

the cheeseburgers and sat on a stool at the counter. "Sit down and have a piece of lettuce."

"I see you're getting your bad sense of humor back. That has to be a good sign." She hopped onto the stool next to his and stuck her straw in the lemonade. "The thing is, the antidote *did* work, Liam. Today is not the first time Tempest administered it to the recruits."

"That's what we are, recruits? What are you doing there? Are you a recruit, too?"

"One question at a time. You eat and I'll explain." She puckered her lips around the straw and sucked up a sip.

He repositioned himself on the stool, damned glad that he and Katie were *together*, as she'd put it. He just didn't have the willpower to resist her charms, or was that the T-101 talking?

As he stuffed his face, she did a thorough job of explaining how they both ended up at Tempest, he working undercover for Prospero and she working under an assumed identity to investigate her friend's suicide.

If she glossed over answers to his questions about how they didn't realize each other would be at Tempest and how he didn't realize the Tempest agent who had killed himself was a mutual friend of theirs, he couldn't complain. He'd get the details later, or maybe his sieve of a mind would be able to fill them in. Things were shaping up more and more in his brain.

When she got to the part about Tempest's past and future assassinations, he tapped his head. "I still have those numbers right here. It may take me some time to make sense of them, but they're in my data bank."

"That's because you—" she dabbed something from his chin with the corner of a napkin "—are a freak of nature with a photographic memory."

Wrapping his finger around a strand of her wavy hair,

he pulled her face close to his. "It saved my life. It brought me to you."

Her dark lashes fluttered, and her plump lips curved into a smile.

He kissed that smile, slanting his mouth over hers. He slipped his hand behind her head, tangling his fingers in her thick hair and deepening the kiss. His erection throbbed and ached.

He could take her right now on top of this counter, on top of the remnants of his dinner. He drew her bottom lip into his mouth, between his teeth. She squeaked as he lifted her from her stool, pulling her between his legs, crushing her body against his.

Through the fog of his lust, he felt Katie's body, rigid and tense, not soft and compliant. He became aware of his hand yanking her hair and his thighs pinning her legs together.

He jerked back, blinking. "I'm sorry."

"I-it's okay." She put a shaky hand against his chest and then swept her tongue across a spot of blood on her bottom lip.

"My God, I hurt you." He jumped from the stool and grabbed a napkin from the counter. He soaked it with water and then leaned over the counter to dab her lip. "I don't always make love like a caveman, do I?"

A pink tide flooded her cheeks. "Sometimes, but you usually have a little more finesse than that."

"I know this is going to sound like some kind of lame excuse, but the T-101 made me do it."

"I believe you." She covered his hand with hers. "My lip's fine. Are you finished eating?"

"Yeah, and beginning to feel human again."

HE REALLY DIDN'T remember they'd called it quits. Was it so wrong to play house with him a little longer and reap the benefits? Although his advances had been a little rough, she had tingles in all the right places—and a few wrong places.

He started gathering the wrappers of his food and then twirled an onion ring around his finger. "Are you sure you don't want something? The rest of these onion rings? Some fries?"

She wrinkled her nose. "Most likely cooked in animal fat."

He chomped on the onion ring and raised his eyes to the ceiling. "Definitely animal fat."

"I had dinner before you set off my car alarm, anyway. I'm good." She rewrapped one of the burgers and put it in the fridge. Running her hands under the water, she asked, "So, you see why it's important that we stick around and finish the job."

"We need to try to destroy the facility and warn the other recruits, but I don't understand why you need to be involved anymore."

"Are you kidding me?" She grabbed a paper towel and dried her hands, turning to the side to watch him. "I guess you forgot that you'd started to put your faith in me that I could handle this job."

He closed his eyes and dug his fingers into his shoulder.

"Are you all right?" She stepped forward in case he toppled over, not that she could catch him but she could at least break his fall.

"Feels like I'm coming down from some incredible high." He pointed to the sink. "Can you get me a glass of water? Maybe I can flush this stuff out of my system."

"Is your memory returning?" She ran the water until it turned cold and filled a glass.

"Bits and pieces. I remember some of the recruits. I still don't remember the session that brought me here."

She handed him the glass, and their fingers brushed for

an electric instant. Their eyes clashed. Would he throw her on the counter like he'd obviously wanted to do ten minutes ago?

He took the glass and gulped down half of the water.

"I don't understand why the T-101 had that effect on you. It must be the antidote in your system. The other recruits got injected and it didn't affect them like you."

"Not that we know of." He downed the rest of the water, and she filled the glass again and handed it to him. "For all we know, the recruits are running amok."

"I wonder when they're going to find out you made your escape."

This time he sipped from the glass, watching her over the rim. "What's that going to mean for you if you return?"

"If?" She brushed stray strands of hair back from her face. "You mean *when*. I have to go back there, Liam. They have nothing to connect me with you other than the fact that they'd instructed me to spy on you. If I disappear now, my life will be in as great a danger as yours."

"And you don't think your life is in danger by returning to that hellhole?"

"I'm one of the chosen ones, the teacher's pet."

His jaw hardened. "What exactly does that mean? This Romo character sounds like a psycho. If he's not the brains behind Tempest, he's following orders like a good little psycho soldier."

"I can handle him." Her stomach twisted into knots as she mouthed the lie. She could no more handle Mr. Romo and his kinky desires than she could tell Liam the truth—that they were no longer a couple.

"Come here." He opened his arms and she went willingly, resting her cheek against his erratically pounding heart. "We have the weekend to think this through, right? By the end of that time, I will probably have regained most of my fleeting thoughts and shifting truths and can make some sense out of the whole mess."

She wrapped her arms around his waist and hugged him with all her strength. One weekend to pretend Liam McCabe was all hers again.

He kissed the top of her head. "Did the hotel clerk at the front desk say the fireplace was operational?"

"Not only operational, but there should be a cord of wood on the back porch and some kindling."

Tilting her head back with a finger beneath her chin, he brushed his lips across her mouth. "What are we waiting for?"

He released her and strode toward the back door off the kitchen.

She tossed the rest of the trash and wheeled her bag into the bigger of the two bedrooms. She'd snagged the smallest cabin—a two bedroom, one bath—but she had no intention of sending Liam to the other bed.

He called from the other room. "I got the wood. You okay?"

"I'm changing. I'll be right in."

"Wish I could change. Bring a couple of blankets with you."

She kicked off her clogs and peeled her jeans from her body. She pulled on a pair of black flannel pajama bottoms with pink lips on them and shimmied into a black camisole. Then she yanked a blanket off the queen-size bed and walked into the living room, dragging it behind her. She tripped over it when she saw Liam crouched in front of the fireplace, stoking the flames in nothing but his white briefs.

He cranked his head around. "I think this is going to work. Hurry up with that blanket. I had to get out of that polyester uniform, and now I'm cold."

"That's because you're half-naked." She draped the

blanket around her shoulders to cover her peaked nipples beneath her camisole—and her response had nothing to do with being cold. In fact, it had gotten extremely warm in here.

He stood up, the fire crackling behind him, his blond hair resembling a halo, and spread out his arms. "Nothing you haven't seen before, Katie-O."

"Do you remember calling me Katie-O, or is it just because I mentioned that nickname to you before?"

"Oh, I remember. I remember a lot of things." His slow smile ignited a flame in her belly. "Like that mermaid tattoo right above the sweetest spot in the world."

The flame licked at her insides, and the blanket dropped from her shoulders.

"Hey, we need that. I'm half-naked, remember?"

She swallowed. "How could I possibly forget?" Dipping down, she plucked up the blanket and walked as if in a trance toward Liam in his underwear.

He curled an arm around her and pulled her flush against his body, warmed by the fire. His erection bulged against his briefs, and she didn't know if it was the effects of the T-101 or her hand skimming between his powerful thighs.

He cupped her face with one hand and swiped his thumb across her throbbing lips, following up with a kiss. Then he stepped back and tugged on the blanket. "Is there another one of these in the bedroom?"

She swallowed as the cold air rushed between their bodies, raising goose bumps across her skin. Had he backed off because he was afraid the T-101 would turn him into an animal? Or had he just remembered that they hadn't been a couple at all because he'd left her?

"Yes. I'll get it."

"You stay here and warm up." He rubbed the gooseflesh on her arms. "I'll get it."

He brushed past her on his way to the bedroom, and she turned to admire the view of his broad shoulders tapering to a narrow waist and the thin cotton of his briefs clinging to his muscled buttocks. She just got warmed up.

She called after him. "What happened to your butt?"

He emerged from the bedroom with another blanket thrown over his shoulder. "What do you mean?"

"I saw the edge of a Band-Aid poking from the waistband of your underwear." She crouched down and spread out the first blanket on the floor over the throw rug.

"I have no idea." As he approached the fireplace, he dropped the other blanket and reached around to press his fingers against his backside. "Something happened because it's sore back there."

On her knees in front of the fireplace she patted the bed she'd made with the blanket. "Come on down here, and I'll have a look—if you insist."

The grin spread across his face as he joined her on the floor, stretching out and rolling onto his stomach, his tanned flesh at her fingertips. "I do insist."

She trailed her hand down the smooth skin of his back, her fingers making a detour around the scar on his side, courtesy of the Taliban. Hooking her fingers around the elastic of his briefs, she pulled them down, exposing the sculpted contours of his buttocks with one small plastic strip stuck to the top of the curve.

"What is it?"

"Hmm? What?"

He twisted his head around, his blue eyes smoldering beneath half-closed lids. "The Band-Aid. You're supposed to be looking at whatever's beneath it."

"Oh, I am." Her fingers played along the hard muscles of his backside, and she had the pleasure of watching him squirm. Then she picked at the edge of the plastic strip with her fingernail and peeled it back.

She sucked in a breath. "It's the site of an injection. It must be where they shot you up with T-101."

"Really?" He shifted to his side, propping his head up with one hand and stretching out his other arm. "Because last time, they shot me up in my shoulder. I still have that mark."

She rubbed the spot on his arm with two fingers. "Why would they change the injection site...unless the nurse just wanted you to drop trou?"

"Yeah, I have that effect on women."

"Watch yourself." She pinched his solid biceps and then sat up straight. "I got it—bigger muscle."

"Bigger injection."

"They'd decided to give you a higher dosage because the previous one didn't have the desired effect."

"This one didn't have the desired effect, either. Unless I ran around the track at the speed of light or lifted the corner of a small building before I collapsed on my bed, that extra dose was pretty much a waste of good T-101— until I took out their security guards and leaped over a tall, electrified fence."

"If you don't remember what happened, do you think they were able to question you?"

"I doubt it. I think the shot made me black out. If it didn't kill me, I don't think they expected me to wake up and escape."

She massaged his shoulder. "Thank God it didn't kill you."

"Thank God I didn't kill you."

"Since you had my address and license plate number emblazoned on your brain, it made sense that I was friend, not foe."

"I knew the second I wrapped my arm around you that you were friend." He turned his head and kissed the fingers that were prodding his shoulder. "In fact, I knew you were a lot more than friend. I could feel it in my...soul."

"You could tell that by cinching an arm around my waist and clapping your hand over my mouth?" She raised an eyebrow, but a thrill danced across her skin. They'd always had an electric current running between them, and she'd felt it again from the moment she bumped into him in the stairwell—two years apart vanished in a second.

"I could tell because my arm around you felt natural and right." He rose to his knees and dragged an ottoman in front of the fire. He leaned against it and tugged on her arm. "Join me, unless you're scared."

"Scared of what?" She crawled to his side, dragging the blanket with her, and settled next to him.

"Afraid of my Hercules-size strength and prowess." He draped an arm around her and tucked her against his body, where her head fell against his chest.

She stretched out her legs until her toes peeked from the bottom of the blanket. She wiggled them, luxuriating in the warmth of the fire and the feel of Liam's bare skin beneath her cheek.

"I told you before. You weren't hurting me and you didn't scare me."

"But this is nicer, huh?" He stroked her hair. "Slow and easy. It's been a while, and now we have all night."

"It hasn't been that long." She carefully threaded her fingers through his, holding her breath.

"Not that I can remember, but I'd have to bet we weren't getting it on in the hallways of Tempest, and from the looks of my room I wasn't a new arrival there."

She released a long breath. "I guess it has been a while."

"Let's not take it too slowly." He nudged her into his lap. "C'mon over here, woman."

She straddled him, placing her hands on his shoulders. "Are you sure you can handle it? I mean, just over two hours ago, you barely knew your own name and were threatening me with death."

"I'm feeling better with each passing minute. All that junk food and the water helped. The adrenaline has stopped pumping, and my head isn't so foggy."

"And the memories?"

"Slowly but surely. I should be fine by the end of the weekend."

"Then, what are we waiting for?" She twined her arms around his neck. If he'd wanted her as much as she'd wanted him, he'd forgive her this deception.

Tipping his head to the side, he kissed her throat. "You smell like wildflowers. You always smell like wildflowers."

"I roll around in them, naked." Her head fell back, and he buried his face in the crook of her neck.

"That I'd like to see, Katie-O." As he traced his tongue around the indentation in her throat, he slipped his fingers beneath the straps of her camisole. "Lift up your arms."

She obeyed, and he pulled the top over her head and tossed it over his shoulder onto the couch behind them. He cupped her breasts, circling her nipples with the pads of his thumbs.

She closed her eyes and parted her lips as she panted out his name. Rocking forward, she pressed her thighs against his erection.

A breath hissed out between his clenched teeth, and he sank his fingers into her hips, positioning her.

She looked into his face, and their eyes locked. Slipping a hand behind her neck, he pulled her close and kissed her—softly at first then with more and more urgency.

He shifted his body so that she slid off him. Then he wrapped his hands around her waist and pulled her down so that her back was flat against the floor.

"How are you still wearing pajama bottoms?"

"Probably for the same reason you're still wearing your underwear."

"On the count of three?"

She nodded, hooking her thumbs in the waistband of her pj bottoms.

"One, two, three."

She yanked off her bottoms and underwear in one flourish while Liam smiled down at her, his briefs still covering his essentials. She hit him over the head with her clothes. "Cheater."

He ran his hands down her body, placing his palms against her inner thighs. "I want this all about you for now."

She melted under his touch, and her legs fell open for him.

He positioned himself between her thighs and stroked her swollen flesh with the tip of his wet finger. His tongue followed, and she plowed her fingers through his hair, urging him on.

Since she'd already been fantasizing about Liam all week, the stroke of his tongue on her heated flesh sent her to dizzying heights within seconds. Her muscles tensed as all feeling centered in her core. One by one her worries melted away—Tempest's plans, Mr. Romo, Liam's memory loss. She let each one of them go.

They were back in San Diego, back when she'd been planning a life with someone for the first time ever, back before Liam had left her for another taste of honor and duty—one more scribble on the McCabe wall of pride.

He slipped his hands beneath her derriere and tipped her pelvis toward his exploring mouth.

The warmth invaded her body, seeping into her taut muscles and turning them to molten lava. Then the pleasure zigzagged through her body and when it tossed her from the precipice, she screamed her release.

As she rode out the remnants of her orgasm, Liam kissed her thighs, her belly, her breasts and took possession of her mouth and kissed her until she'd dissolved into a quivering puddle of goo.

He smiled against her lips. "I do remember that scream."

She sucked in his bottom lip. "You're not exactly quiet yourself."

"I don't remember at all. You're going to have to show me."

"I think I can do that—" she bucked him off her body and tapped her fingers along his rock-hard shaft "—big boy."

She scooted down the length of his body and took him into her mouth. She cupped his backside, skimming her fingernails across his skin.

He moved against her, in and out, his hands fisting in her hair. When she had his head thrashing from side to side, he jerked away from her.

"You're making me crazy. Let's put an end to this slow and easy stuff. I need to be inside you…now."

She kissed the side of his hip. "I was thinking the same thing."

He flipped her onto her back, and she didn't even need the fire anymore to stay warm. She was burning up.

He entered her in one smooth movement, filling her up and claiming her for his own. She hooked her legs around his thighs and he plunged deeper. He wouldn't last long enough to make her come again, and then suddenly he shifted his position until he was rubbing against all the right bits.

Had he known this trick two years ago?

Hot coils tightened in her belly, and her breasts ached as she clenched her jaw, ready for the explosion. It came. She came.

He came.

He growled just like a caveman as he drove into her, lifting her bottom from the blanket they'd spread beneath them.

Throwing back his head, he moaned as he spent himself completely.

"Shh." She smoothed back the hair from his damp forehead. "You're going to wake the bears."

He kissed her nose and her ear and then rolled to his side, yanking the blanket over both of them. "Whatever happens at Tempest, this night was well worth the price... and we're not done yet."

She stretched and yawned like a very satisfied cat. "I'm going to brush my teeth and get some water. You?"

"Same. Let's move this party to the bedroom. I'll see about the fire."

About fifteen minutes later they slipped between the sheets of the bed, and Katie snuggled against Liam's side. Maybe this had all been a huge mistake. How could she ever let this man out of her life again after this night?

Would she have a choice?

He'd left her before to join his navy SEAL team on a mission to free a doctor who'd been imprisoned for helping the US Forces. Now he and his Prospero team had to save the White House. What chance did her love have in the face of that calling? And did she even have the right to expect him to give up the calling?

She sighed and burrowed her head against his shoulder.

His breathing had deepened, and his chest rose and fell with every breath. He murmured something in his sleep.

He'd lied. He'd fallen into an exhausted sleep and not even another shot of T-101 could rouse him. They were finished...for now. And that was okay. She just wanted to drift off in the protection of his arms.

The next morning she awoke with a start. As she rubbed

her eyes, Liam's handsome face came into focus. He'd been watching her sleep.

She brushed her knuckles across the hard plates of his pectoral muscles and the light dusting of hair scattered across them. "It's heaven to see your face first thing in the morning. It's been a while, and I missed it. I missed you."

He quirked one eyebrow and trapped her fingers in his hand.

"Katie O'Keefe, you're a stone-cold liar."

Chapter Fifteen

She woke up fast. Her eyebrows shot up and she tried to snatch her hand away from his, but he had a tight grip.

"What do you mean?"

She managed a convincing tone, but the two red flags on her cheeks gave her away.

In one quick move that would do any juiced-up Tempest agent proud, he'd rolled her onto her back and straddled her hips, pinning her with his thighs. "We were not together before your infiltration of Tempest and hadn't been together for about two years."

She gulped, her Adam's apple bobbing in her delicate throat. "You understand why I had to tell that little lie, right?"

"Enlighten me."

"You had no memory. You'd just escaped from a situation you didn't completely understand, and you knew my address. You didn't know who I was. I could've been the enemy. I diffused the situation the fastest way I knew how."

Cocking his head, he studied her face. "You could've just told me we were friends or even exes—the truth."

"A friend doesn't carry the same emotional weight as a lover, and why would I tell you we were exes? That would give you even more reason to distrust me. Is the interrogation over now?" She bucked her hips to dislodge him and it only made him hard.

He clamped down on his bottom lip but didn't budge. "Kind of sadistic lying to some poor SOB who'd lost his memory, don't you think?"

"I did it for your own good." She gave up the struggle to get him off her, crossing her arms behind her head. "I'm glad your memory returned and that you're feeling better. You can sleep in the other bed tonight."

"Is that what you think I want?" He traced a finger from her pouting lips, down her neck, between her heaving breasts, along her flat belly and then outlined her mermaid tattoo.

She squirmed at his touch. "You called me a liar."

His fingers dabbled back up to her breasts, and he tweaked her nipple. "You are."

She squeaked. "Then if I'm such a big, fat liar, you can sleep in the other bed, away from my big, fat lies."

"Did you hear me complaining about your lies?" He rose to his knees, his erection protruding in front of him. He brushed the tip along her skin, and she closed her eyes and gripped the iron bars of the headboard above her.

"No," she whispered.

"Turns out, I kinda like the lie, and I really like that you used it to get me into bed."

Her lids flew open. "I did not...exactly."

He hovered over her face and nibbled on her earlobe. "Turn over."

Still trapped between his legs, she struggled to roll onto her stomach. He helped her and then brushed the hair away from her cheek so he could see her face, flushed with desire, her eyes half-closed. She curled her fingers around the bars of the headboard again, and he pressed his lips against the corner of her mouth.

Then he laid a trail of kisses from the nape of her neck,

down her back and along one creamy cheek of her luscious derriere. Hooking an arm around her waist, he hoisted her up to her knees and entered her from behind.

Having her wrapped around him felt just like coming home. Her body moved with his, accepting every inch of him. He reached around and stroked the moist folds of her flesh, close to where their bodies were joined together.

She arched her back and then exploded around him. He continued to drive into her as she quaked and trembled on her knees. His release came hard and jagged, ripping a cry from his throat.

He folded on top of her, and she collapsed beneath him. He kept moving against her, the soft flesh of her backside pressing against his thighs, keeping the fire burning in his belly.

He didn't want to go back to his world—didn't give a damn about Tempest, didn't want to return to Prospero, didn't care what his brothers thought of him—just wanted to drown in the pleasures of this woman.

"You're crushing me." She wriggled beneath him, and he hardened once more inside her.

He couldn't blame the T-101 for that. He turned onto his side, taking her with him, still maintaining their connection, spooning against her back. He cupped her breasts and toyed with her nipples.

"Is this my punishment for lying?" She captured his hand and pulled it down between her legs. Using his fingers, she traced along the seam that joined their bodies.

He undulated his hips, growing inside her, and she moaned, soft and low. He could take her again, right now.

The ringing of Katie's cell phone on the nightstand shattered the heavy sensuality that had encompassed the bed... and his brain.

Katie made no move toward her phone, instead taking one of his fingers and using it to pleasure herself again.

But the insistent ringing had brought him back to reality. He pulled away from her, out of her, dousing cold water on their hot emotions. "You need to get that."

By the time she'd come out of her haze and fumbled for the phone, it had stopped ringing.

"Who was it?"

She squinted at the cell, sucked in a breath and then turned the display toward him.

He read the words with dread beating against his temples. "Ginger Spann."

"They know." She dropped the phone as if it were contagious. "They know by now that you escaped and that has to be why she's calling me. She wouldn't call me on a Saturday unless it was urgent."

He picked up the phone with two fingers and swung it in front of her face. "Then you'd better call back."

"Do you think they'll ping my phone to find out where I am?" She dragged the sheet up to her chin and stared at him over the edge with round, bright eyes.

"They might, but they definitely will if you ignore Ginger's call." He tapped the phone against his chin. "You took the weekend to get away from it all. They already think you're some sort of computer geek, right? It shouldn't be a stretch for them to think you took off on your own. Offer to come back in the office if they need you."

"I thought you didn't want me going back there."

"I don't. They're not going to make you come back. Anything you can do at this point you can do remotely, but make the offer, anyway." He squeezed her shoulder. "Are you ready?"

She nodded and tapped Ginger's name before putting the phone on speaker. It rang once before Ginger picked up.

"KC, thanks for calling back so quickly."

"I was in the shower. What do you need, Ginger?"

"Another recruit left the facility—Liam McCabe."

Katie gasped. "You and Mr. Romo were right about both of them—Gantt and McCabe. How did you know? I saw nothing in McCabe's computer usage."

"It was something else, something I can't tell you about, KC."

"I understand completely, Ginger."

Katie's obsequious, butt-kissing tone made him sick to his stomach. Who knew his computer-hacker girl had such amazing acting chops?

"Obviously, you didn't see him wandering around the town or anything, or you would've called us…right?"

"Wandering around the town? Why would a recruit escaping from the facility be wandering around the next town over, waiting to be discovered?"

"We have reason to believe McCabe is not in his right mind."

"How did he escape? I thought we were watching the recruits after Gantt's stunt."

That use of *we* was a nice touch. He smiled at Katie and nodded.

"He… I can't tell you that, either, KC."

"Did he hurt anyone? Is everyone okay? Mr. Romo?"

Liam rolled his eyes.

"He did hurt people. He's a dangerous man, but Mr. Romo is fine."

"Have you called the authorities?"

"Yes, yes, of course we notified the police."

Liam mouthed to Katie, *Liar.* Tempest would never bring the local authorities into its business.

"Do you want me to come in, Ginger? Is there anything I can do to help?"

"No need. I just wanted to warn you, give you a heads-up, and if you're still working with Gantt's computer, dig deeper and see if you can find a connection between him and McCabe."

"I definitely will and if you change your mind—I'm there."

Liam held his breath. She'd almost reached the finish line and Ginger hadn't asked her about her location.

"So sweet of you to offer, KC, especially after the little incident in Mr. Romo's office yesterday."

Liam jerked his head up, drawing his brows over his nose. Katie hadn't mentioned an incident, but then he hadn't given her much time.

She glanced at Liam, her face reddening. "Oh, it was just a misunderstanding."

"Mr. Romo has…particular tastes, and he deserves to be indulged. I do indulge him, KC. He had his eye on you from the moment you arrived at Tempest and had instructed me to find out what you could do to help us. That's the main reason we brought you in—he knew you were special."

A dull pain throbbed at the base of Liam's skull. What the hell kind of particular tastes was Ginger going on about? Katie would not meet his eyes. It had to be bad.

Katie rushed her words. "My talents matched up with what you needed, so it worked out for everyone."

"We're glad to have you in our inner circle. *I'm* glad to have you, so don't ever worry about making me jealous. There is no room for jealousy between me and Mr. Romo. I hope that eases your mind and you're willing to relax and enjoy what Mr. Romo has in store for you."

"I—I'm sure I will, Ginger. It's like I told you…"

"I know. You're shy, you're unsure of yourself. Mr. Romo saw that in you, and he's eager to awaken you. He'll set free your desire to serve. You'll get immense pleasure from catering to Mr. Romo's needs."

Liam curled his hands into fists and punched the pillow on his lap. Through a fog of rage, he only half listened to Katie ending the call through her blushes and stammers.

She paused for a long time and then looked up with a half-smile. "At least she didn't ask where I was."

"How long has that stuff been going on, how far has it gotten and why didn't you tell me about it?"

"It just started, really, and you had enough to worry about."

"Damn it, Katie." He chucked the pillow across the room. "You cannot go back there. You don't know what Romo is capable of. He might even drug you. He probably uses T-101 himself to keep up with his particular tastes, as Ginger politely put it."

"I think I'm safe for now. Mr. Romo has his hands full with Gantt's defection and now yours."

"Yeah, I know what he wants his hands full of, and stop calling him *Mr.* Romo like you have some kind of respect for him."

"I can't think of him any other way. I figured Ginger called him Mr. Romo even when they were between the sheets." She punched him in the arm.

"You're making jokes about those two in bed?"

She tilted her head, gathering her messy hair in one hand. "You act like that's worse than what they've already done and what they have planned for the White House— whatever that is."

"And you're acting like it's nothing at all." He grabbed her hand. "Don't put on the tough act with me, Katie. Romo is a dangerous character."

"I know that, Liam. That's why we need to put him out of business." She squeezed his fingers. "I'm not a recruit. I can come and go as I please."

"For now. Do you really think Ginger Spann has any freedom?"

"She doesn't want freedom from Mr.—from Romo."

"Maybe not now, but we don't know what happened to

make her this way. Who knows? Maybe she was a sweet, shy little geek at one point, too."

"Let's talk about this later. I'm starving." She leaned forward and kissed him full on the mouth. "I'm going to shower first if you don't mind. Then I'm going to run out for groceries. I think it's best if you stay hidden for now, don't you?"

"Probably. Do you think there's a clothing store in town?"

"There are a couple of ski runs here. Even though they're not open yet, I'm sure the town has clothing stores. Write down your sizes for me."

"Get me a baseball cap and some sunglasses, too, something I can use as a disguise."

She stumbled off the bed, dragging the sheet with her. "So, when did you recover your memory and do you have all of it back?"

"I started regaining bits and pieces last night. The food helped, the water helped, the sex helped a lot."

Her hands outlined a circle in the air. "I mean all of it. When did you remember we'd split up?"

"This morning when I woke up." He told her the lie with a straight face. In fact, he'd remembered how stupid he'd been two years ago as soon as he'd taken her into his arms in front of the fire.

And he had no intention of repeating his stupidity. He'd never let this woman go again even if it meant he'd failed in his mission for Prospero. He could handle failure. He couldn't handle losing Katie again.

KATIE FACED THE warm spray, massaging the soapy washcloth over her body, parts of it still sensitive from Liam's touch. He'd reclaimed her with...vigor.

She felt a petty sense of pleasure about his jealousy over Mr. Romo. Sure, the man was lethal, but having some kind of relationship with him was about the least lethal position he could take. In fact, any true spy worth her salt would take Mr. Romo up on the offer and strike when he was at his most vulnerable.

Not that she planned to suggest this to Liam. He'd go ballistic. Her lips curved into a smile as she splashed water on her face.

But she still needed to get back to work. She had a facility to shut down, and Liam needed to warn the other recruits and set them free from their bonds.

He'd infiltrated Tempest for Prospero, not only to get intel, but to hamper their operations and interfere with the flow of agents out of the academy. The agency had already executed several successful hits, and the CIA had never suspected the complicity of Tempest agents in those assassinations.

She and Liam had a chance to seriously damage Tempest's operations. She wanted to do it for Sebastian, for Samantha and for all those other agents.

She ended her shower and pulled on a pair of jeans and a black sweater. She planned to burn all of her slacks, blouses and low heels when she escaped from Tempest.

She picked up a pair of black motorcycle boots and walked to the living room where Liam had built up the fire again.

He turned around and leveled a finger at her. "Now that's the Katie-O I remember—tight jeans, lots of black and boots. All you're missing is the dark purple nail polish and black eyeliner."

"No point in putting on the nail polish only to remove it by Monday." She dropped to the ottoman and pulled on her right boot. "I'll be happy to see you out of that uniform."

He winked. "You already did."

"You have a dirty mind, McCabe."

He chuckled. "I wrote down a list of clothes and sizes, if you can find them."

"I'll do my best. Are you going to call Prospero?"

"To report my failure?"

"I'd hardly call what you achieved a failure. You got on the inside, identified the other recruits and decoded Patterson's notes. We're still going to bring down the facility."

"Not at the expense of your safety."

She put on her other boot and stomped her feet. "You didn't invite me along on this operation. I came on my own. You do what you need to do, and I'll do what I need to do. So, you're not calling Prospero?"

"I don't have a phone, and I'm not using yours to call in."

"I can try to pick up a disposable."

"It's on the list." He crossed the room to the kitchen, grabbed a piece of white paper and waved it at her. "I'm way ahead of you."

"That's why you're the spy and I'm not."

"You could've fooled me. You're doing a helluva job so far."

She snatched the list from his hand and stood on her tiptoes to kiss him. "Can you hold out until I get back?"

He slipped a hand beneath her black sweater and caressed her breast through her bra. "For this?"

"One track mind. You sure that T-101 is out of your system? I meant, can you wait for food?"

"I can always eat the leftover burger in the fridge." He pulled her into his arms. "Be careful out there, Katie-O."

As she drove away, she saw the curtain at the window fall into place. She'd been counting on Liam's help for her plan to shut down Tempest, but he couldn't step foot on the place now. They'd figure out something. She refused to leave this alone and walk away now.

Driving the two miles into town, she kept one eye on

her rearview mirror. Ginger had given no indication that she suspected her of being out of town, but Elk Crossing was too close to the Tempest facility for comfort.

She made her first stop at a clothing store where she managed to find a pair of jeans, some long-sleeved T-shirts and a flannel shirt. She picked out a baseball cap with an elk on it and a black stocking cap that could be pulled down to mask the face.

She ducked into a ski shop for a scarf and a pair of sunglasses, but not even the convenience store had a disposable cell phone. Then she hit the grocery store and bought enough food for a couple of breakfasts, lunches and dinners. They didn't need to go out to any local restaurants. There weren't enough people in town yet to be inconspicuous.

She loaded the grocery bags into the trunk and tucked the clothes in between the bags.

She slid into the front seat and as she reached for the ignition, she heard a different kind of click next to her ear.

"You make one false move and I'll blow your head off."

Chapter Sixteen

Her heart galloped in her chest as she gulped for air, staring straight ahead. She didn't dare look in her rearview mirror in case he offed her for being able to ID him. On the off chance she had a run-of-the-mill criminal in her backseat, she stammered. "T-take my purse. Take my car. I haven't seen you, and I'm not interested in seeing you."

"I don't want either of those things, although the car might come in handy later. And I don't give a damn if you see me or not."

She shifted her gaze to the mirror and her mouth dropped open. "Dustin Gantt."

"The one and only. Now take me back to that little love nest you're sharing with McCabe."

Her nostrils flared. "I don't know what you're talking about."

"Drop it. I tracked your car there. I saw you from the woods."

"How?"

He hunched his shoulders. "I didn't leave Tempest empty-handed."

"What do you want from us? We're on the same side." She felt like banging her head against the steering wheel. She'd been so cocky and sure of herself, and she'd failed Liam.

"Maybe, maybe not. I want answers."

"Then get that gun away from my head, or I'll have to assume you're working for Tempest."

He practically growled. "After what those people did to me? They're lucky I didn't blow up the whole damned place."

"You didn't want to kill anybody. That's why you hit the utility building."

He grunted. "I wouldn't say that. I just didn't want to kill anyone who didn't deserve it—and there are plenty there that do."

He lowered his weapon and she released a long breath. "Thank you. Liam wanted to find you, and now you've found us."

"Why'd he want to find me?"

"He figured you'd discovered something about Tempest, and he wanted to pick your brain. We really are on your side."

"Then take me back to that cabin."

"I need to tell Liam first."

"No!" He waved the gun again and she instinctively ducked. "Why do you think I didn't approach you at the cabin when I had the chance? McCabe is lethal. But now you're my insurance. I don't know what game you two are playing, but I'm not taking any chances until I find out. And if you don't take me with you, I guess I'll make an anonymous call to Tempest, because if McCabe is here with you, chances are Tempest would be very interested in that piece of news."

"Okay. I'll take you to the cabin."

"Don't try anything stupid, Ms. Locke. Just because I'm not pointing my gun at you doesn't mean I can't remedy that situation in about a half a second."

She licked her dry lips. "I believe you."

She maneuvered the car back on the winding road to the cabin. As the manager's cabin came into view, she said,

"Get down in the backseat. For all the manager knows, I arrived here alone, and he doesn't need to know anything else."

Gantt slid down in the seat as she drove the back road to the cabin. Wouldn't Liam be surprised?

She screeched to a stop in a hail of gravel and dust in front of the cabin.

Gantt popped up behind her. "Why'd you come in so hot?"

"I'm nervous, okay? I have a man in my backseat with a gun pointed at me."

"Get out, slow and easy."

She opened the car door and planted one booted foot on the gravel. Gantt was beside her in a second, poking her in the ribs with the gun.

"You don't need that thing." She swiveled toward the trunk.

"Where are you going?"

"I have groceries back there." Her eyes widened as Liam appeared behind Gantt. Gantt's own eyes flicked when he noticed her expression, but already it was too late.

Liam had wrapped one arm around Gantt's neck, knocking his other against Gantt's wrist, dislodging his weapon with a sharp blow.

Katie dropped to the ground and grabbed the gun. She jumped to her feet, clutching the weapon in one trembling hand.

Gantt choked and clawed at Liam's forearm, pinned to his throat. "Let me go. All I want is answers."

"Nobody holds a gun on my woman." He kneed Gantt in the back, bringing him to his knees. "Katie, give me that gun before you shoot the wrong person."

She handed it over, glancing at Gantt doubled over in the dirt. "He didn't hurt me."

"Good, and now maybe I won't hurt him once he tells

me what the hell he's doing here." He waved the gun at Gantt. "Get up and head toward the cabin."

Gantt staggered to his feet, and Katie reached out to help him up.

Liam snapped. "Get away from him. Go ahead of us and unlock the door."

His tone brooked no disagreement. She jogged up the two steps to the cabin and unlocked the door, swinging it wide for Liam and his prisoner.

When they all got inside, Katie held up her finger. "I left the groceries and your clothes in the trunk."

"Leave it for now." He pointed the gun at one of the chairs in front of the fireplace. "Take a seat, Gantt, and start spilling."

Gantt collapsed in the chair, rubbing his throat. "You know all there is to know, McCabe. I busted out of the prison they called a training center."

"I need to know a lot more than that, Gantt, and I'm the one with the gun."

"You should know what happened better than anyone. Some pretty little nurse shot me up with a vitamin. Ha! If that was a vitamin, I'm the grand wizard of the Ku Klux Klan."

"It didn't affect you?"

"Oh, it affected me all right." He turned to Katie. "Ms. Locke, can I get some water?"

"You can call me Katie, and…"

Liam sliced his hand through the air. "He can wait a few minutes for the water."

"Liam…"

He shot her a look that cut to the bone. Maybe she wouldn't make a good spy, after all.

"How did it affect you, Gantt?"

"Knocked me out. Gave me weird dreams. When I came to, it took me a good fifteen minutes to remember who I was and what the hell I was doing in that place. Nobody else seemed bothered by it, and then you saw them at PT the next day—running like Usain Bolt and lifting weights like the Incredible Hulk. I'm no genius but I put two and two together."

Liam nodded. "Yeah, T-101 is no vitamin."

"T-101?"

Liam ignored him. "But it must've been something before that. You didn't plan your escape and that explosion in one day."

"I overheard a conversation between Hamilton and Moffitt. I had left my access card in my computer in the classroom. Mills wasn't there, but the door was ajar. Their voices were hushed, so of course I listened."

Katie held her breath as Liam asked, "What did you hear?"

"Crazy stuff. They were discussing our class of recruits and how they thought they'd respond to training and hold up in the field." He cleared his throat. "Normal stuff until they started mentioning all the Tempest agents who'd gone off the rails. I know all about post-traumatic stress, but the things they were talking about?" He shook his head. "Crazy stuff."

"You started planning your escape then?" Liam had relaxed his grip on the gun, but he still looked ready to pounce.

"I did. The night I ran into you at the parking garage, the plan was in its final stages." He hunched forward, his hands gripping his knees. "I almost confided in you that night. I knew you were different from the others."

"How?" Liam narrowed his eyes.

"First of all, if that fool Hamilton couldn't tell you'd already had some training or experience, he should lose his job."

"I was a SEAL. He probably put it down to that."

"I know, but there was something else about you. And then I could tell the vitamin shot hadn't affected you, either. You could still almost just keep up with the other guys, who were all pumped up on that stuff. T-101. But not quite."

"So, why didn't you? Confide in me?"

Gantt leaned back in the chair and winced. "It was that night at the parking garage when Ms. Locke, Katie, showed up."

Katie folded her arms. She knew it had been her fault. "Why did that stop you?"

He waved his finger between her and Liam. "You two obviously knew each other, and that made me have doubts about McCabe. I'd heard rumors about your...connection with Mr. Romo and that piece of work Ginger Spann. I thought it might be a setup. It might still be a setup."

Liam plucked at the rumpled guard shirt he was still wearing. "Yeah, I'm actually a security guard for Tempest."

"They know you're missing?"

"They do now."

Gantt chuckled. "Serves 'em right."

The tension seeped out of Katie's shoulders. The men seemed to be done circling and sniffing each other. "Can I get Dustin that water now?"

"Sure, if he promises not to toss it in my face."

"Man, I'm going to be too busy drinking it. That choke-hold you executed did a number on my throat."

"Like I said—" Liam winked "—nobody holds a gun to my woman."

Katie filled a glass with water from the tap and handed it to Gantt. "How have you been surviving out here?"

"Easy." He took the glass from her hand and downed half of it. "I'm a survivalist."

"How'd a survivalist end up taking a job with the government?" Liam shoved Gantt's weapon in the back of his waistband.

"Tempest never presented itself like that to me. I mean, I knew it was a government agency, but they emphasized that they flew under the radar. I guess I didn't realize how far under the radar a government agency could fly."

"You'd be surprised."

Gantt swirled the remaining water in his glass. "Are you going to tell me your story, McCabe?"

"Someday."

"That day had better be sooner rather than later if you expect my help taking down that facility."

Liam's expression never changed except for a flicker in his eye. "What makes you think that's our plan?"

"You wouldn't still be here if it wasn't." He jerked his chin toward the window. "You have a car, cash. If I'd had those things I'd be at the Mexican border by now."

"You're good, Gantt. Too good for Tempest."

Katie stuck her hand up in the air and waved. "Can I get those groceries now? I'm starving."

Gantt rose from his chair, but Katie held up her hand, palm forward. "Both of you guys are in hiding. I can handle the groceries."

She made two trips to bring in the groceries and Liam's clothes. She parked the bags on the counter and started pulling out the food. "I have bacon if one of you wants to cook it. I'll whip up some scrambled eggs and someone can oversee the toaster.

Liam raised his hand. "I think I'm qualified to watch the toaster."

"I can do the bacon." Gantt joined her in the kitchen and began banging the cupboard doors, looking for a skillet.

She shoved the toaster toward Liam and dropped a loaf of wheat bread next to it. "See to the toast, toast boy."

Liam untwisted the tie on the package. "Gantt, where were you staying all this time?"

He jerked his thumb at the side door. "In the woods."

While Gantt told Liam what he'd taken from Tempest and how he'd used it, Katie made the scrambled eggs and cooked some potatoes in the microwave. She diced the potatoes and cooked them in the leftover bacon grease.

She piled two plates with eggs, potatoes and bacon. "How's the toast coming along?"

"Four slices done and buttered."

She set the plates on the table for Liam and Dustin and then scooped the rest of the eggs onto a plate for herself.

They all sat down at the kitchen table, and Dustin pointed to her plate. "That's all you're having?"

She opened her mouth and Liam cut in. "She's a vegetarian."

Dustin broke off a piece of bacon and waved it at her. "You'd do okay in the woods. I could show you a lot of edible plants and berries, but you gotta watch some of those berries—poisonous."

"Thanks, I'll keep that in mind the next time I'm stranded in the woods."

"You keep hanging out with this guy—" he pointed his fork at Liam "—and that might be sooner than you think."

"Nope. She's getting out of here."

Katie rolled her eyes. "I'm not leaving, Liam. Now that we have Dustin here, we have a better chance than ever of stopping Tempest in its tracks."

"I'm in." Dustin stabbed a piece of egg, his jaw tight.

She grabbed Liam's wrist. "I haven't even told you my plan yet. I have unlimited access to Tempest's computer system now. Do you know what that means? Do you know how much power that gives me?"

"But Gantt and I can't even be there with you."

"You can be close. There are woods all around that facility." She leveled a finger at Dustin. "Who better to hang with in the woods than Mr. Survivalist himself?"

"Having you back in that nest of vipers with the head snake makes my stomach turn."

Gantt dropped his fork. "Mr. Romo? You got close to Mr. Romo? So the rumors were true?"

"Some of the rumors were true. He and Ginger invited me into their inner circle. They're trusting me with their computer system, but I'm not buddy-buddy with them."

Gantt gulped down some orange juice. "I heard it's not a buddy Mr. Romo wants. Or maybe it is, but it's a particular kind of buddy if you get my drift, and—" he glanced at Liam "—no offense."

"Oh, I can handle that part." She flicked her fingers, wishing Dustin hadn't reminded Liam of Mr. Romo's designs on her body. "That part of the initiation is off in the future. I'll be long gone by then—if Liam allows me to carry out this plan."

"Shoot." Liam pushed his plate away. "Let us in on this big plan."

She took a big breath and gripped the edge of the table. "I'm going to infiltrate the facility's main computer system and shut down everything—electricity, network, phones. You're going to tell all the recruits what's really going on, and once we have everyone out of there, we're going to do what you'd planned to do all along, Liam. We're going to blow the place sky high—literally."

Chapter Seventeen

Liam just about choked on his eggs. "You can do all that from a computer?"

"Pretty much, but I'm going to need your help with the recruits and the…uh…explosives."

Dustin got up from the table and gathered the plates. "I don't get it. If you have to be at Tempest to do all this stuff, where are you going to be? Once those systems start to shut down, aren't Romo and Spann going to figure out it's you?"

"What he said." Liam stretched his legs in front of him. "And how do you blow up several buildings from a computer?"

"Like I said, I figured you two could come up with something for that." She brushed some crumbs from the table into her palm.

"What makes you think I'm hell-bent on destroying the Tempest facility? I'm here to gather intel." He shifted his gaze away from Gantt and his intent stare.

Katie folded her arms on the table and hunched forward. "Don't you think the intel you already gathered is sufficient cause to shut down the compound?"

"I think it's time that I checked in with—" he glanced at Gantt hanging on his every word "—checked in."

"I've been thinking about that, Liam. We're not too far

from Sun Valley. There have to be stores there with throw-away phones. I could head out there this afternoon and be back before dark."

"By yourself?" Every cell in his body protested. All this talk of blowing up Tempest and taking down computer systems gave him a strong desire to tuck Katie back into that bed and pull the covers over her head. Thankfully, she couldn't read his thoughts right now.

"Nobody is going to know me in Sun Valley. I doubt Tempest has spies covering the entire state of Idaho. I'm coming with you. I even have a disguise."

Gantt ducked his head. "I'm going to sit this one out. I need to get back to my camp in the woods. I have a cache of weapons buried out there. I'll work out a way for us to get close to Tempest, and once Katie shuts down the computer system, we can take care of the rest."

Crossing his arms, Liam studied Gantt's face. He had to trust the man at some point. He couldn't haul a captive around with him everywhere.

Katie spread her hands. "We'll meet back here for dinner?"

"This ain't no house party, Katie." Liam pushed back from the table and drained the rest of his orange juice.

"I realize that, and just to bring us all back to reality, who gets the gun?"

Gantt lifted a shoulder. "You can take it... I have others."

"You *are* good, Gantt. Did you take more than guns?"

"How the hell else are we gonna blow that place to smithereens?"

LIAM REFUSED TO stuff his body on the floor of the backseat again, but he slumped down in the passenger seat, pulling the baseball cap over his eyes, until they cleared Elk Crossing.

The temperatures dropped even more, but the snow was a no-show even at the higher elevations.

Katie turned the heat on higher. "We might get lucky and find a phone in a convenience store on the way to Sun Valley and spare ourselves the drive."

"I don't mind the drive, and maybe I'll find some decent jeans over there." He poked himself in the thigh.

"You don't like the ones I picked out for you?"

"Is there such a thing as dad jeans? If so, I think I'm wearing them."

"Please, you look sexy in anything."

"I was thinking the same thing about you in those slacks and blouses buttoned up to your chin. No wonder Romo had singled you out." He reached over and tucked her wild hair behind her ear. "What did you think of Gantt?"

"I believe him. I trust him. Do you?"

"His story rings true, but I'm not sure he'll be at the cabin when we return."

"You're naturally suspicious. He'll be there. He really wants revenge on Tempest, don't you think?"

"Yeah, but he's a survivalist, and survivalists usually work alone. That's what surprises me about his employment with Tempest. His type usually doesn't trust the government."

"Maybe he got sick of living on roots and bark."

Liam drummed his fingers against the console. "Just makes me wonder what line Tempest fed him during the recruitment phase. They could've been more upfront about their objectives with someone like Gantt."

"Do you really think Gantt would go for...whatever it is Tempest is trying to accomplish with these assassinations?"

"I'm not sure, Katie." He skimmed his knuckles along her thigh, the denim of her jeans soft and worn. "Until I get the list of executions to Prospero, we have no idea what connects the victims. Some of these killings have been off the radar, set up as accidents."

"Will your agency be able to figure it all out?"

"We have some amazing analysts on board. I'm sure they'll see a pattern." He punched at the radio buttons. "Alternative rock?"

"Out here?" She snorted. "I doubt it. Go for the country. I can live with it—I did before."

"Before…" He traced the edge of her ear. "I never said I was sorry for leaving."

"Yes, you did. You said it a million times before you left."

"Before…they were just words before I left. Words I said to make you feel better, to make myself feel better." He smoothed his fingertip along the hard line of her jaw. "I never said sorry after, when I really meant it."

Her long lashes swept over her eyes. "You freed that doctor, didn't you? When I heard about it on the news, I knew it was you, your team. That doctor risked his life to help us, and then you risked your life to save him."

He stared past her out the window, recalling the doctor as they'd found him—filthy, gaunt, signs of torture on his body. That doctor had helped them, and they had to rescue him.

"Oh, I realize you can't acknowledge it, but I know it was your team, and for a little while I felt better about your abandonment."

His gaze shifted back to her face. "Only a little while?"

"Only when I wasn't missing you so much it hurt." She sniffed.

"I would've come back to you, Katie."

"I couldn't trust you anymore, Liam. You'd left me just like all the rest, just like all those families who'd promised to be my forever."

"Biggest mistake of my life. I want a do-over."

"I can't get punched in the gut again."

"Is that a no?"

"Our first convenience store." She veered off the highway and wheeled into the parking lot, dodging his question like a pro. "Maybe they sell phones here."

They walked into the store. Liam nodded at the clerk. "Do you sell prepaid, disposable phones?"

"We sure do, but I gotta warn you. The cell reception is bad here. You probably have to head into Sun Valley to get some decent air."

"That's where we were headed, anyway." He strolled to the aisle the clerk indicated while Katie stood before the refrigerators. "Do you want something to drink?"

"Soda." He pulled one of the phones from the rack and read the instructions. He had no idea if Prospero would even pick up from an unknown number, even if he did have all the right codes.

He met Katie at the register, and she pulled out her wad of cash to pay. He owed this woman more than money when all this was over, but she didn't seem to want anything more from him— probably wouldn't even take the money.

She put her drink in the cup holder and started the engine. "Do you want to continue to Sun Valley and have lunch? Pretend we have a normal life for an hour or two?"

"Sure. Gantt's not expecting us until later, anyway—if he shows up at all."

She hit the road and turned down the radio. "How did you end up with Prospero after leaving the navy? Or can't you tell me that?"

"I can tell you anything, Katie-O. You've earned it." He popped the tab on his can of soda and took a fizzy sip. "Prospero recruited me at the end of that last mission. I went through a training academy, similar to Tempest's but worlds apart in goals, objectives and methods."

"You mean they didn't drug you?"

"And no creepy leader. The man who heads up Prospero is admirable, a role model, one of the good guys."

"Your last mission was just two years ago. You haven't been with Prospero long, have you?"

"This is my first mission." He took another swig of soda to wash away the taste of failure in his mouth. "I was chosen because I'm new, young, unknown. Maybe they should've gone with a more experienced agent."

"You haven't failed, Liam, and you're not going to. Even Prospero must've realized there was a chance the T-101 would affect you. They must've warned you that you could become a Tempest agent for real. They knew the risks, and you were willing to take those risks for your agency."

The turn-off for the resort appeared, and Katie maneuvered the car onto the road that led to the main resort area.

Liam pointed to a few of the mountainsides with white dusting. "Looks like they're going the man-made route for some of the runs."

"Good, then we should be able to get lost in the crowd."

They rolled into the town and agreed on a restaurant that served just about everything. Once the hostess seated them in a corner booth, Liam pulled out the phone.

"I'm going to give this a try. I have Prospero's phone number memorized along with the access codes I need to get through."

The waitress hovered at their table and he ordered another soda while Katie requested some hot tea. When the waitress left, he punched in the Prospero number. He listened to a series of beeps and responded with the appropriate code. He went through this process two more times before he reached a ringing phone on the other end of the line.

He released a pent-up breath when he heard the clipped British tones of an analyst he knew. "Agent ID, please?"

Liam cupped his hand around the phone and recited his agent ID.

"This is Analyst Sharpe. How can I help you Agent McCabe?"

"Xander, you can cut the formal stuff. I need help."

"You're supposed to be in the Tempest training camp out in Idaho. What happened?"

"It was the T-101. They gave me a super dose of the stuff and I freaked out—lost my memory, escaped from the facility."

"You obviously recovered your memory. Did you get any intel before you abandoned ship?"

A muscle ticked in Liam's jaw. "I didn't abandon ship. I temporarily lost my mind and yes, I got some names and dates of assassinations, some that were staged as accidents, so maybe those were off our radar."

"Good job, Agent McCabe." Xander paused. "Can you relate that information to me now?"

"I have GPS coordinates and dates. Are you ready?"

"Fire away."

"And Xander?"

"Still here."

"The last set of coordinates is the White House."

"Got it. Ready to receive."

Katie waved the waitress away as Liam closed his eyes and retrieved the numbers from Patterson's notebook.

"That's it." A light sheen of sweat had broken out on his forehead, and he blotted it with a napkin.

"One more thing, Liam. Coburn's going to want to talk to you. Can he call you on the phone you're using?"

"Yes."

"He'll get back to you within the hour. Stay put."

He shoved the phone to the side of the table and gestured to the waitress. "The boss is going to call me back."

"That's good, right?"

He nodded and ordered a bowl of chili and some corn-bread from the waitress. Katie opted for some lentil soup and more hot water for her tea.

When the chili arrived he plunged his spoon into the steaming bowl. "What have you been up to the past few years? I know you're still in San Diego, and I know you're still designing video games. Have you been…dating?"

"Here and there. You?"

He stuffed down the jealousy. "Not much time for that with my schedule."

"I should tell you, though, I'm in love."

Her words slammed against his chest, and his hands curled into fists. Was this some kind of joke? After the way they'd made love last night, she'd made him feel like the only one—just as she was for him.

She smirked and pulled out her phone. "You deserved that, and I can't help myself. I'm a cruel witch."

She held out her phone to him. "I'm in love with this guy."

He'd never been so happy in his life to see a picture of a chocolate lab puppy, grinning from one floppy ear to the next.

"You got a dog."

"His name is Mario. A neighbor found a litter of aban-doned puppies and of course, I had to take one in—one abandoned puppy to another."

He took the phone from her and traced his finger around Mario's head. "He looks like a handful."

"He is."

"Who's taking care of him?"

"The same neighbor who found him and kept his sis-ter for herself. So he's having a holiday with his sister."

"But you miss him." He touched the corner of her turned-down mouth.

"Of course."

The phone on the table buzzed between them, bringing him back to his reality. He answered the phone with a code word, and Jack Coburn responded with the corresponding code word.

"You okay, McCabe? No residual effects from the T-101?"

"No, sir. None that I can detect."

"We'll get you a full medical when you get back. Good work on the coordinates. I think you just prevented an attack on the White House, son."

"I think so, too, sir. I'm sorry that I compromised the rest of the mission."

"How so? You didn't compromise anything."

"I let my feelings of disorientation get the best of me, and I escaped from the facility."

"I don't see that as a problem, McCabe. Where are you now? How are you surviving without money, a car? We don't even have any safe houses out that way."

Liam's gaze tracked to Katie, pouring herself another cup of tea. "I have some help on the outside, sir."

Coburn sucked in a breath. "Can you trust him?"

"With my life." He winked at Katie as she looked up. "Will we try to infiltrate another way?"

"Hell, no. We've still got you."

He glanced at Katie and shrugged. "What do you mean?"

"They double-dosed you with T-101 and you flipped out. In their eyes, the fact that the drug had its desired effect and you were able to escape is all good."

"I'm not sure I follow, sir."

"You're going back in, McCabe."

"Sir?"

"You go back to the Tempest facility with your tail between your legs, apologize for running off half-cocked and now you're more committed than ever to fulfilling your duties as a Tempest agent. They might still suspect you, but the fact that you returned is going to speak volumes to them."

He tried to ignore Katie's wide eyes. She couldn't hear Coburn's words, but his face must be betraying all kinds of emotions.

And the last one she'd see was satisfaction. Coburn was giving him the opportunity to redeem himself and the operation, to snatch victory from the jaws of defeat. And more important, he wouldn't have to send Katie back there on her own.

"Sounds like an excellent plan, sir. I'm on it."

"Now that we have further proof of Tempest's plans, you know the endgame, don't you, McCabe?"

"Alert the recruits and destroy the Tempest facility." Just as Katie had guessed.

Coburn ended the call with his assurances that any effects of the T-101 would be countered once he returned to the fold—if he returned to the fold.

"You look…happy. Is your boss giving you a bonus or something? Since I'm the one who got the notebook at great peril to my health and well-being, are you going to share that bonus?"

"I got a bonus, all right. I get to return to Tempest." He popped the last piece of cornbread into his mouth.

Katie's own mouth dropped open. "What does that mean? How can you possibly return to Tempest?"

"I do it as a contrite recruit who overreacted to the vitamin shot."

"You're willing to go back and poke the bear?"

He grabbed her hand. "I'll feel a lot better about having you go back there if I'm there with you."

"If they let you live." She reached out and twisted the front of his shirt in her fist. "I don't like it. They might continue to dose you with T-101 and then restrain you. What happens then?"

"It's my job, Katie. I'll figure it out."

"I'm scared." She covered her hands with her face. "I can't lose you, Liam, not again."

"Then we'd better make sure our plan works. Now get me and Gantt back to your place, so that he can set up in the woods and I can wander back to the facility on my own on Sunday."

They paid up and got back on the highway to Elk Crossing. When they arrived at the empty cabin, Liam placed the gun and his phone on the kitchen counter next to a piece of paper.

He picked up the paper and turned it toward Katie. "It's a map of the woods. Looks like Gantt's campground."

"And you thought he wouldn't be here."

"He's not here."

"It's not six o'clock yet, and he left us directions to his campsite. Do you think he wants us to go get him?"

"We're not doing that. We're not walking into a possible trap."

"I think the guy is trustworthy."

"We'll see."

They waited for over an hour, during which time Katie cooked some pasta and had him chopping tomato, basil and garlic.

He pulled his phone toward him. "After six, no Gantt."

As she stirred the pasta in the boiling water, Katie bit her bottom lip. "You don't think he's planning to double-cross us, do you?"

"What happened to trusting the guy? He's ten minutes late, and now he's in league with the devil?"

"Well, what do you think?"

"I think he probably thought better of joining a team,

since it worked out so well for him last time. The guy's a loner and he'll stay a loner."

"He still may show up."

The time ticked on and still no Gantt. They ate the pasta and some salad and saved the leftovers for Gantt.

"We're going to have to leave without him tomorrow morning, Katie. I need to get back to Tempest and turn myself in."

Her nose wrinkled as she washed up the last of the dishes. "I just don't get it. He was so gung-ho to take his revenge on Tempest."

"The guy is an enigma. I don't know what happened, but I'm going to keep that gun under my pillow tonight."

He built up the fire again and they sat before it, filling each other in on the details of their lives in the past two years. He didn't know how he was going to convince her to take him back, but he was determined to be a part of her life again.

And he knew one method of persuasion that she couldn't resist. He took her face, warmed by the fire, in his two hands and kissed her mouth thoroughly. "Let's go to bed."

After they'd made love, he tucked her against his side and put the gun within reach on the nightstand. If Gantt or anyone else was lurking outside and decided to break into the cabin in the dead of night, he'd get a nasty surprise.

But the night passed without incident, and Katie cooked up the last of the eggs the next morning.

He hunched over the counter, Gantt's map between his hands. He flicked his finger at an X with a circle around it. "I wonder what this is."

Katie leaned over his shoulder, holding a plate of steaming food. "Looks important."

Liam snapped his fingers. "Gantt said he'd taken several weapons from Tempest and buried his cache. I wonder if they're here. Maybe he left them for us, and they'd definitely come in handy."

"So, we *are* going to his campsite before we go back?"

"I think it's worth the risk."

"Just like you think returning to Tempest is worth the risk. Seems like you think a lot of things are worth risking your life over."

"A lot of things for me, but not you. You're not going to risk your life, so you drive me to the edge of these woods down the road and wait. I'll see if I can find his cache of weapons. If not, I'll be back at the car as soon as I can. If anything else happens, you leave me."

"Yeah, right."

"I mean it, Katie."

"Gotcha."

He tugged on a lock of her hair. Stubborn woman wouldn't do a thing he told her to do.

They cleaned up the cabin and Liam changed back into the security guard uniform. Rolling up the sleeves, he said, "That's one thing I'm looking forward to back at Tempest—my own clothes."

"If they let you live long enough to change into them." Katie dropped her purse at the front door and rushed into his arms. "I don't want you to go back there."

He crushed her to his chest and stroked her wavy hair. "I don't want you to go back there, either."

She murmured into his shoulder. "It's different for me. I didn't escape. I'm not under suspicion."

"You don't know that. Don't get too complacent, Katie. Be careful."

"I will, and I'm not giving them much time to get suspicious. As soon as I'm able and you're ready, we're shutting it down."

They packed up the car, and Katie checked out.

When she got back behind the wheel, Liam asked from

the backseat, "Did the manager mention anything about Dustin?"

"Didn't say a word about him or you. Asked if I'd enjoyed my stay and despite everything, after the two nights we shared, I couldn't wipe the smile off my face when I told him I'd had the best two days of my life."

"He must've figured you'd led a boring life up to this point."

"I wish." She pulled away from the cabins and when she'd made the turn to the main road, he climbed into the front seat and smoothed Gantt's map on his knee. "Just a half a mile to the next turnout on your right."

"Is his campsite far from the road?"

"Maybe a quarter of a mile in. Shouldn't take me more than ten minutes in and ten minutes out, depending on the terrain. Give me another ten minutes to dig where X marks the spot, so I'm talking forty minutes tops. I'm not back here in forty minutes, you take off."

She didn't respond, even after he stared at her profile for several seconds. He heaved out a breath and tucked the map into his pocket. He then checked the chamber of the gun and held it loosely in his lap. He had to prepare for an ambush, but if Gantt had buried a stash of weapons, he wanted to get his hands on them.

Katie pointed ahead. "There's the turnoff."

When she parked, he turned to her and kissed her hard. "I'll be back in forty."

"I'll be here."

He slipped from the car pushing the door closed and then crept into the woods, Gantt's map burned into his brain. They'd done some tracking and survivalist training at the Prospero academy, so he had a handle on this.

He noticed some freshly broken twigs and dirt covering newly fallen leaves, indicating that someone had come this way recently. Gantt had planned to return to his site when he and Katie had left for Sun Valley. Maybe he should've insisted that Gantt come with them just to keep an eye on him.

Several feet from the campsite, Liam circled around from the other side, bordered by a dense thicket of trees. He crept forward, watching the ground to avoid dry leaves and twigs.

As he drew abreast of the campsite, he looked up, searching for a break in the trees and a clear view of the space.

He crouched forward, peering through a gap in the branches.

He'd just found Dustin Gantt—tied to a tree, his throat slit.

Chapter Eighteen

Katie hummed to the country song on the radio and glanced at the clock on the dashboard. Fifteen minutes and counting. As if she'd leave Liam in there after forty minutes or forty hours. She'd never leave him.

The tap at the window sent her straight to the roof of the car. She jerked her head to the side, and the relief coursing through her body almost made her weak. She hadn't realized how tense she'd been since Liam had loped off into the forest.

She unlocked the door and he burst into the car, his breathing heavy, his face flushed.

"What's wrong?"

"Hit it! Hit the gas."

She cranked on the engine and peeled away from the turnout, her back tires fishtailing and spewing gravel and dirt in their wake.

She didn't say another word until they made it to the highway. Gripping the steering wheel, she finally asked, "What happened back there?"

"Someone killed Dustin Gantt."

She gasped and tightened her hold on the steering wheel. "You saw him."

"Someone had slit his throat."

The blood pounded in her temples, and she panted for air.

"I'm sorry," Liam said as he rubbed her thigh.

"Did you see anything else?" Her voice seemed unnaturally high and disembodied to her own ears.

"I didn't stick around to see anything else. Believe me, I wanted to dig up that cache of weapons, but I thought someone might still be watching the area. I couldn't even be sure they didn't have a drone in the area. All I could think of was getting back to you and getting you out of there."

"How did they find him?"

"Not sure. The tracker was tracked."

"Oh, my God." She placed a hand over her thumping heart. "What if they had tracked him when he was at the cabin with us?"

"If they had, they would've stuck around and waited for us."

"Do you think Dustin told them anything about us?"

He didn't answer her, and she slid a glance at his white face and hard jaw.

After several seconds he passed a hand across his face. "Dustin Gantt didn't give them anything—guaranteed."

She was afraid to ask more, so she drove on. "Nothing changes, Katie. Drop me off somewhere before you get to your place, and I'll make my way back to Tempest this afternoon. You go back into work as usual Monday morning. Got it?"

"I do. And don't worry about those weapons." Tears stung her nose. "I'll get you access to whatever you want. Dustin showed us the way, and now they have even more to answer for."

The trip passed too quickly and all too soon, Liam was directing her off the road.

He turned to her and grabbed her by the shoulders. "Whatever happens in the next forty-eight hours, just know that I love you, Katie-O."

He slammed the car door before she could respond, so she whispered it to his back as she watched him through the window. "I love you, too, Liam McCabe."

SHE SMOOTHED HER hand along the front of her pleated, gray slacks and pressed the button of the elevator in the parking garage. Stepping inside, she pushed the button for her level with her knuckle.

She hadn't seen any ambulances, fire trucks or armed guard this morning, so whatever they'd done to Liam, they'd done it privately and under cover of Tempest security.

Her gut knotted as she got off on her floor and forced her feet to move one in front of the other to her office.

Her ears tuned in to the idle chatter from the help desk bullpen and the other cubicles, but the only discussion of murder and mayhem she heard came from people recapping their weekend TV viewing.

She sat in front of her computer and logged in. Two instant messages popped up. One came from Liam:

I'm in.

She closed her eyes and took two deep breaths.
The second one was from Ginger:

Urgent, call when you get in.

The tension seized her muscles once again. Ginger and Mr. Romo must want to discuss these latest developments with her.

Since Liam's message had come in earlier, she didn't dare answer him now. Instead, she responded to Ginger that she was in the office and ready to meet.

She jumped at the alacrity of Ginger's response:

Elevator now.

Her fingers itched at the work to be done on the computer system, but she wanted the details on the return of the Prodigal Son, so she snatched her access card from her computer's card reader and headed out to the executive elevator.

In a first, Ginger beat her to it and greeted her with a grim smile and a bland question. "Did you have a nice weekend?"

"I did, thanks. You?"

"No."

The elevator doors opened, and Ginger ushered her in first. They rode in silence.

As soon as the doors opened on Mr. Romo's floor, Ginger blew out a noisy breath. "McCabe returned."

"What?" Katie tripped to a stop in front of Mr. Romo's office door. "Why did he do that?"

Ginger nudged her into the office with a little push. "Sit."

She greeted Mr. Romo and sat in her customary chair across from him as he balanced his laptop on his knees. What did he do on that thing all day?

Folding her arms across her chest, she asked, "When did McCabe return?"

"Yesterday, late afternoon, disheveled, a little worse for wear, but contrite." Mr. Romo snapped his laptop shut.

"Where had he been?" Katie scooted to the edge of her chair, arms still crossed.

Ginger wedged one slim hip against the arm of the couch, next to Mr. Romo. "Wandering around the woods, apparently, still wearing the guard uniform he'd stolen off Meyers's back."

"Did he tell you why he escaped?"

Mr. Romo stroked his beard with two fingers. "He had a bad reaction to our vitamin formula, went a little crazy."

Katie narrowed her eyes. "Do you believe him?"

"Maybe." Mr. Romo exchanged a look with Ginger that made her believe one of them wasn't buying it.

"Do you think the same thing could've happened to Dustin Gantt? The vitamin hit him the wrong way and he lost it?"

Ginger's eyes flickered at Gantt's name. "But you told us there were indications in his browsing history that he'd been planning some kind of escape."

"That's true." She'd really just wanted to mention Gantt's name in their presence to gauge their reactions, and Ginger hadn't disappointed.

"And you said McCabe had no such indications." Mr. Romo drummed his fingers on top of his laptop. "That's still the case, isn't it, Katie? You didn't discover anything more about McCabe over the weekend, did you? No connection to Gantt?"

She'd discovered all kinds of delicious things about Liam over the weekend, but she'd be damned if she'd share any of it with them. "Nothing and no association with Gantt, but I did discover additional info about Gantt. He'd been doing some research on survivalist websites. What do you think that means?"

Mr. Romo flicked his fingers in the air. "We don't care about Gantt. What's done is done. If he attempts to reveal any top secret information he learned here, we'll go through the appropriate authorities."

They obviously hadn't gone through any appropriate authorities to murder him, which was why Gantt's disappearance was suddenly off the table, a nonissue.

"What's going to happen to McCabe? A-are you going to fire him or whatever you call it?"

Mr. Romo spoke up, a little too loudly. "He's too valuable to discharge—a prime specimen, former navy SEAL, and now apparently loyal as hell."

"We don't know if that's the real reason he returned." Ginger rested a hand on Mr. Romo's shoulder. "It could be some sort of ploy."

Mr. Romo's cold eyes grew icier as he rolled his shoulder, shrugging off Ginger's hand.

Ginger snorted in a quick breath, her nostrils flaring. *Someone would pay for her dissension in front of the new girl.*

"How can I help?" Katie folded her hands in her lap, all eager schoolgirl. "What do you want me to do?"

"Watch him through his computer activity as you'd planned to do. He rested last night and is ready to resume his regular schedule today, including classroom instruction." Mr. Romo smiled, and the ice in his eyes cracked just a little. "Report anything suspicious back to us, of course."

"Of course." She twisted her fingers into knots. "Are you going to try a different vitamin formula on him?"

"Perhaps."

Ginger rose from the couch and stepped between her and Mr. Romo. "That's not your concern, KC."

Mr. Romo hunched forward and nudged Ginger's hip to get her to move to the side. "She's just trying to be helpful, Ginger."

Ginger's eyes blazed for a moment before she eked out a tight smile. "Of course she is."

Ginger Spann was a liar. She'd claimed to harbor no jealousy over Mr. Romo's interest in her, but there it was—in her eyes. And it could mean trouble.

Hopefully, Katie would be long gone before Ginger could unleash the green-eyed monster.

Katie hopped up from the chair. "I'll get right to work tracking McCabe and anyone else you need to look at."

"You're a good little soldier, KC." Ginger took her arm

and began maneuvering her out of the office. If this was to avoid Mr. Romo's creepy group grope-hug, she was all for it.

"KC," Mr. Romo called from his position on the couch, and Ginger had to stop hustling her out of the room, even though her fingers still dug into Katie's arm.

"Yes?" *No hug, no hug, no hug.*

"We'll find a place for you in our new situation."

"New situation?" She shook off Ginger's hold.

"Because of all the problems we're having with the recruits here, we're speeding up their training. They'll be ready to roll in their new positions within the week."

"I hope you do—have a place for me. I feel like I've come home."

Ginger was back, placing her hand on Katie's back this time. "That's wonderful, now, first things first."

Ginger practically shoved her into the elevator, and then held the door open with one hand. "Tell me, KC. Did you ever run into someone named Sebastian Cole when you were being shunted from foster family to foster family in San Diego?"

Katie's heart slammed against her rib cage and she could barely breathe, but she furrowed her brow and tilted her head. "Sebastian Cole? No, I don't think so, but it's possible. Is he someone you know?"

"Yes, someone I knew."

"If you have a picture of him I might recognize him, but it's been almost ten years since I left the system."

"I don't have a picture, just wondering." She let her hand slide from the door, and the elevator closed with Ginger still staring at her.

She slumped against the side of the car. What was that all about? Had Ginger been doing more investigating? Katie hadn't wiped out her time in the foster care system in San Diego, but she'd cleansed any connection she and

Sebastian had in that system. There was no way Ginger could tie them together, but she had to watch her back. Ginger was on the warpath.

She dropped into the chair at her desk and logged in to her computer. With the recruits shipping out soon and Ginger giving her the once-over, she and Liam didn't have any time to lose. It was obvious that Mr. Romo accepted Liam's story, and Ginger had her doubts. As long as Katie could keep shoring up Liam's credentials, she could keep Ginger and Mr. Romo at bay.

Maybe she could shut down the facility as early as tonight. Would Liam be ready?

She couldn't wait to see him again. She'd have to devise some plan to go out to the recruit barracks.

A couple of keystrokes later and she'd brought down a few more of the recruits' laptops. She shot off a quick email to Ginger that she needed to investigate something on McCabe's laptop, and Ginger's okay came through in a flash—maybe too fast.

Katie gathered her notebook just to look official and made her way across the facility to the recruits' area.

She hovered at the doorway of the main classroom just as Mr. Mills was taking a seat behind his desk.

She tapped on the door and he looked up, unable to mask the scowl that had twisted his features. "You again?"

"Sorry. I was monitoring the laptops and noticed some irregularities. Somehow there are viruses that are sneaking through, and they're disrupting the automatic backups."

"Maybe Romo should worry less about computer viruses and more about the mental health of the recruits around here."

A chink in the armor? Katie wedged her shoulder on the doorjamb. "Are you talking about Dustin Gantt? I'd heard he hadn't been too stable when he walked through these doors to begin with."

"Is that what Mr. Romo tells you behind closed doors?" This time he didn't even attempt to keep the sneer out of his tone.

She shoved off the door and strolled into the classroom, and Mills's eyes popped at her approach, already regretting his words.

"I—I mean if Mr. Romo believes Gantt was on the edge, it must be true."

"If that's how you feel about Mr. Romo—" she sat on the edge of a desk "—why don't you leave Tempest?"

"I'm perfectly content here."

She shrugged and flipped her ponytail over her shoulder. "Doesn't sound like it. Is there someone other than Gantt having…difficulties?"

"Not that I know of."

"McCabe…"

Mills jumped from behind his desk. "I didn't say anything about McCabe."

Katie widened her eyes. "No, I did. His is one of the wonky laptops. Will he be coming to class soon?"

"They'll all be showing up in about ten minutes. Do you want to set up in the other classroom again?"

"That'll work. Can you send McCabe over first?"

"Why him?" Mills was gripping the edge of his desk.

She and Liam just might have an ally in Mr. Mills. He was looking out for Liam. He was worried about him, afraid she had some kind of torture in store for him for escaping.

"No reason. I need to see him and Kenneth Chang."

"I'll send McCabe over first with his laptop and Chang next."

"I appreciate that, Mr. Mills." She hopped off the desk and tucked the notebook under her arm. Turning when she reached the door, she said, "You really should think about leaving Tempest."

She went into the other classroom and paced the floor until Liam showed up. She almost ran across the room and jumped into his arms.

"Have a seat and log in to your computer, Mr. McCabe."

He let the door slam behind him. "Have I been a bad boy again, Ms. Locke?"

"The worst."

He sauntered toward her, placed the laptop on a desk between them and leaned forward. In a husky voice, he said, "I think I prefer you wearing decidedly fewer items of clothing."

Her gaze darted over his shoulder at the door. "Quiet."

"I thought that was quiet."

"Sit down, log in and tell me what happened."

He complied and started talking. "I staggered back through the gates yesterday afternoon. The guard at the gate freaked out, pulled a gun on me. I babbled on about losing my memory, losing my mind, and he called good old Dr. Nealy."

"Nealy? He's the head psychiatrist?"

"Yeah, a real mad-scientist type. I have no doubt in my mind he knows all about the effects of T-101. I'm not sure about the others."

"What did Nealy do?"

"Talked to me, deemed me sane enough to return to my room and then called Romo."

"Did you see Romo?"

"Apparently, he reserves that favor for you and Ginger."

She pinched his forearm. "Shut up."

"Did they tell you about me?"

"Yes. In a twist, I got the impression that Romo believed you, and Ginger did not."

"That's because she's tougher than he is. He hides away while she does all the dirty work."

"You might be right." She held her bottom lip between her teeth while she tapped some keys on his keyboard.

"What's wrong?" He scooted his chair closer.

"I think…" She twisted her ponytail around her hand.

"You think what?" He toyed with her fingers as they rested on the keyboard. "We're in this together, Katie-O. You can't keep things from me, not anymore."

"Like how I feel about you?"

He squeezed her fingers. "Like that."

"Is that why you left? Because I never told you I loved you?"

"I left because I was an immature idiot. I knew how you felt about me. Your actions couldn't have been clearer. That's all I should've needed. I still had to go on that last mission, but I should've insisted that you wait for me."

"And I should've told you I loved you, because I did and still do—with all my heart, and now we have to get out of here, Liam. The plan is to speed up your training and ship you out of here before any more of you go off the rails."

"I figured that. Is that what was worrying you before?"

She had to be able to trust him, to confide everything to him with no fear. "I think Ginger has it in for me now because she's jealous of Mr. Romo's…admiration for me."

"Admiration?" He raised his brows until they disappeared beneath the golden lock of hair curling over his forehead. "Is that what they're calling wanting to get in someone's pants these days?"

"That's what I'm calling it. She'd claimed she wasn't the jealous type, but she lied. She asked me about Sebastian today."

"How the hell did she put that together?"

"She hasn't put anything together—yet. I never scratched my background in the San Diego foster care system, and Sebastian shared that same background. Let's face it, that background is something that's very attractive to Tempest, isn't it?"

"That's for sure. She's just grasping at straws, but we don't want to waste any more time."

"Prospero isn't like that, is it? I mean, look at your family—the four of you boys, rambunctious, competitive, close, parents still married after thirty years, can't get more all-American than that."

Her tone must've sounded as wistful as she felt because Liam brushed a knuckle across her cheek. "And I took that family away from you when I left."

She shook her head. "They never belonged to me in the first place."

"Sure, they did." He grinned. "You should've heard the scolding I got from my mom for letting you go. She said even with the nose ring, you were the best thing that ever happened to me. And I didn't even tell her about the tattoo."

She sniffed and then Liam snatched his hand back when the door to the classroom opened. Chang looked inside. "Mills told me you need my laptop."

"I'll be calling you in about five minutes, okay?"

"Whatever."

She wrinkled her nose. "Full of charm, that guy, but you know what?"

"What?" He logged off his computer.

"I think we can use Mills."

"Mills can't stand you."

"Because he can't stand Mr. Romo and Ginger. He thinks I'm part of their axis of evil." She crossed one leg over the other and tucked her hands between her thighs so she wouldn't start pawing Liam. "He actually criticized Mr. Romo to me. Backtracked like hell after, but he'd already put it out there. He might be helpful when it comes time to get the rest of the recruits out of here."

"Tomorrow. Can we start tomorrow? With the information Gantt gave me and your magic tricks on the computer, I think we can shut this place down tomorrow night."

"I think so, too. I'm ready."

He chucked her beneath the chin. "Then why the sad face?"

"What happens to us after Tempest?"

"I have a brilliant idea, but I'll save it for later. Don't worry, Katie-O. I'm not leaving you again."

Chapter Nineteen

The following day Katie did bug fixes for Frank in between checking the computers for the major systems on the facility—electric, networks, telephones, security. She could shut them all down with a few clicks on her keyboard.

Liam planned to approach Mr. Mills today, perhaps even show him Garrett Patterson's notebook and the significance of his notations. Mills and Patterson had shared several interests and had lunched together on occasion. Maybe Patterson had even relayed some of his fears to Mills about the direction Tempest was taking.

And when it was all over? She couldn't wait to hear Liam's brilliant idea.

She'd reported to Mr. Romo that since tracking Liam's keystrokes, nothing had jumped out at her as being unusual. She'd protect that man with her last breath if that's what it took.

The hours dragged by, and a heavy air hung over the office. Clouds had been gathering all day, ominous dark clouds threatening the first snow of the season. But the atmosphere inside carried the same sense of breathless anticipation—or she was just projecting.

If any of the civilians had heard about another recruit's escape from the compound and subsequent return, they weren't talking about it. They weren't talking about much of anything. Could just be the midweek doldrums settling in.

She'd received two instant messages from Liam, one indicating that Mills was in and one giving her the green light for tonight.

The electricity would go first. In case facilities put some type of generator into play, she'd take down the network next—no computer access. She'd already been playing with jamming the cell tower and virtually putting a halt to all cell phone calls into and out of the facility. The security systems had been a piece of cake—all cameras would be disabled, all security doors deactivated.

She had plans to meet Liam outside the facility once she'd shut it down, and he'd have free rein to set up the explosive devices. She'd leave her car here, if necessary. Otherwise, she'd blow past the parking kiosk at the main gate, which would also be disabled.

She plucked her cell phone from her purse and brought up her photos. She tapped one of Sebastian, enlarging it, and traced over his face, his big smile. She whispered. "This is for you, brother."

The five o'clock hour crept up, and Frank stopped by her cubicle. "Are you working late again, KC?"

Stretching her arms over her head, she nodded. "Do you have anything else for me?"

"Nah, I got the word." He winked. "You're Mr. Romo's and Ginger's now."

She gulped, her hands dropping to her lap. "What does that mean? I still work for you, Frank."

"I know you're taking orders from them now, and that's okay. No worries. Hey, we all gotta climb that ladder somehow."

A flash of heat claimed her chest. "I'm not trying to

climb any ladder. I'm working on a special project for them."

He held up his hands. "Hey, whatever. No worries. I'm heading out of here. See you tomorrow?"

"I'll be here, same time, same place."

"Have a good one." He saluted.

Ugh, did everyone in the entire company think she was in some weird relationship with Ginger and Mr. Romo? Why hadn't Romo ever bothered to conceal his proclivities? And Ginger seemed proud of their affair. What self-respecting working woman would get confirmation out of sleeping her way to the top?

The sounds of the office packing up and leaving for the evening had her blood percolating. They planned to give everyone a chance to clear out, even Mr. Romo and Ginger.

Once the Prospero analysts put together those puzzle pieces from Garrett Patterson's notebook, and the CIA got some of the other Tempest employees to spill their guts, the gloves were off. The CIA would come down hard on Tempest and the likes of Mr. Romo and Ginger and all the doctors working on the T-101 formula.

There would be a formal investigation into Patterson's death and Samantha's and Dustin Gantt's, if they ever recovered his body.

All that had to happen and would happen, but Prospero couldn't wait for the formal investigation. Outside of anything sanctioned by the CIA or anything legal, for that matter, Tempest had to be stopped now—and Liam was the man to do it.

Katie had all the processes set up and ready to go. She'd kept the security cameras running so she could monitor everyone's departure.

How had Dustin put it? They didn't want to hurt anyone who didn't deserve it. For most of the people working at Tempest, it was just a high-paying government job that required secret and top secret clearance. They hadn't signed on for assassination and murder—Samantha hadn't.

She finished up the bug fixes Frank had given her just to occupy her time and her mind—the software programs they managed would never benefit from these fixes.

The sun had set, still obscured by the clouds, and the night got darker, the clouds more threatening.

She watched the last of the Tempest employees leave the building. She tracked the final cars on their passage from the parking structure.

Then she took a deep breath and put the first aspect of the plan into motion. She shut down the security cameras for everyone but her. Then she got to work on the access card system, virtually unlocking every door at the facility, making even high-security areas accessible to anyone. She'd already played with this system earlier in the day to give Liam access to the materials he needed.

She put the electrical system in jeopardy next, timing the shut-down of different areas, so security wouldn't be thrown into a panic.

Her fingers hovered over her keyboard. Next...

"Working late again?"

A chill dripped down Katie's spine as she looked up into the cool, green eyes of Ginger Spann.

"I usually do." She tapped the last key on her keyboard to complete the electrical shutdown, and still holding Ginger's gaze, she double-clicked on the program that would bring down the network.

"Stop clicking away on that keyboard, KC, and come with me."

"Come with you?" Luckily, Ginger was not computer savvy and wouldn't have the slightest clue what Katie had up on her screen, even if it wasn't turned away from Ginger's prying eyes. "I was just wrapping up, getting ready to leave for the night."

Ginger's eyes glittered with a strange light. "Oh, but tonight is the night."

Was she drugged up? Katie's heart did a double-time beat in her chest. *She knew.*

"The night for what? It's a Tuesday, no maintenance scheduled, no backups to monitor."

Ginger reached forward and stroked Katie's hair. "Get your mind off computers for a few minutes. Tonight's the night you're going to join Mr. Romo."

Dread thumped against the base of Katie's skull, but she still had work to do. She entered the shut-down code for the network and put it on a timer. Nothing was going into or out of this facility.

She finally logged off her computer and swiveled her chair around to face Ginger. "I don't understand. I thought I could go at my own pace with all that."

"Your pace is too slow. Mr. Romo has a comfortable area off his office. He and I spend a lot of time there, and now we want to share that time with you."

Could she pretend to go with her and then make a run for it at the elevator? She couldn't escape from her cubicle without doing physical harm to Ginger—not that the idea didn't appeal to her, but she didn't even have any weapons except for the scissors in her desk drawer.

"I don't know, Ginger. I'm not ready." She plucked at her dark slacks and prim blouse. "I'm not dressed for it."

Ginger chuckled. "Don't worry about that. You won't be dressed for long."

Why tonight of all nights? It couldn't be a coincidence. Katie tucked her access card into her badge holder, left it on her desk and retrieved her purse from her desk drawer for the last time.

"I—I'm afraid I'm going to be such a disappointment to Mr. Romo. I'm not what he thinks I am."

"Maybe not. We'll see."

Hooking her purse over her shoulder, Katie pushed back from her chair. She followed Ginger, with her perfect posture, down the passageway between two rows of cubicles into the help desk bay.

Katie snapped her fingers. "Oh, wait. I left my access badge on my desk."

"Won't do you much good tonight."

"Oh?"

"For some reason, the door to this office didn't respond to my access badge. I walked right in."

"That's not right. Do you want me to look into that?" She'd taken several steps away from Ginger back to her cubicle. If she could stash those scissors in her purse, she might have a fighting chance.

Ginger placed a fingertip on her chin. "Can you really do something about the access badges, KC? I thought you were a computer programmer."

Katie's heart skipped a beat. She'd fallen into a trap. "Well, a lot of security systems are computerized, so it's the same thing."

"Imagine that."

Katie slipped around the corner into her cubicle, eased open her desk drawer, lifted the scissors and dropped them into her purse. She grabbed her badge holder and clutched it in her hand as she returned to Ginger, patiently waiting by the office door.

"You wouldn't want to forget your badge. How would you log in tomorrow morning and be able to do all of those amazing computer acrobatics that Mr. Romo loves so much?"

Katie managed a weak smile but her stomach churned with fear. Ginger had the look of a predator toying with her prey.

She lagged behind Ginger as they approached the executive elevator. Ginger stabbed at the button, but it remained dark, and the elevator didn't shift into action.

"Well, look at that. The access badges and now the elevator. What next?"

"This probably isn't a good night to get together. Facilities will be working all over the building if there are problems." She started backing away from Ginger. If she turned and ran now, Ginger might just think she was afraid of having sex with Mr. Romo. If she went along with Ginger, how would she get out of that office? Liam expected her to be off the grounds by now.

"Nonsense. Whatever facilities is up to, they know better than to disturb Mr. Romo. We'll take the stairs."

She took Katie's arm, but Katie spun away from her, clutching her purse to her chest, reaching inside for the scissors.

"You can't run from us, KC."

Katie heard the distinctive click of a gun safety, the same noise she'd heard from Dustin Gantt's gun as he hid in the backseat of her car a hundred years ago.

Katie turned slowly, brandishing the scissors in front of her. She stared down the barrel of the gun Ginger had pointed at her.

"Wh-what's going on?"

Ginger's jaw hardened. "Go ahead of me in the stairwell and keep your mouth shut."

Katie glanced outside before tugging open the door of the stairwell.

Where was Liam and what was he doing? If all went as planned, he'd be blowing up this building in less than twenty minutes—and now she was trapped inside.

Chapter Twenty

All of the lights went dead in the recruits' training area, but nobody cared. Half of the recruits were ready to bolt, half had jobs to do and the remaining staff had been restrained or were oblivious to the mutiny around them.

Gantt's escape and Liam's breakdown had already planted seeds of mistrust in most of the recruits' minds. Mills had been an easy convert, just as Katie had predicted. He'd been friends with Garrett Patterson, and Patterson had been hinting at Tempest's dark deeds.

The recruits trusted Mills, trusted what he had to say. Mills was ready to lead the majority of them out of here as soon as the fireworks started to distract security and the parking attendant at the kiosk. Liam warned the recruits that the CIA would most likely be conducting interviews with them once they were out of here and since they'd done nothing wrong, it was in their best interests to come clean about all their suspicions regarding the activities at Tempest.

Now Liam and a few diehards—Charlie, Tammy and surprisingly, Chung—were ready to set the explosions that would allow the rest to go free.

He eyed the helicopter on the top of Katie's building. Romo and Ginger would most likely escape unless he could get a jump on them, but he was willing to let them go and catch up with them later to get all the recruits out of here safely.

He even had a speech prepared over the loudspeaker to warn them of the coming disaster. Not that Romo and Ginger didn't deserve to die for what they'd done to so many people, but he was no judge, jury and executioner. He'd let the CIA handle those two, unless by some miracle he could capture them first.

"Are we ready?" Charlie's shaved head gleamed in the darkness.

Tammy responded. "When the explosions go off here and the remaining psychologists stagger outside, we round them up, right?"

"Right. I'll count down from ten and then it's go time."

Their breaths huffed out in the night air as Liam barked out the countdown. "Three, two, one, go!"

They each ran off to their positions, and a series of explosions rocked the ground. Smoke, shouts, screams and confusion swirled around him—chaos, just what they needed.

Before he reached the office building he glanced behind him in time to see the gates go down and the parking kiosk go sky-high.

He crept around the perimeter of the building and planted the explosive devices in the spots designed to do the most structural damage to the building. Maybe he could force Romo and Ginger out of the building before they had time to prepare the helicopter.

Katie was supposed to be monitoring the parking garage to make sure all the cars got out, but he decided to do a quick reconnaissance of the structure. His gaze swept the empty bottom level, and then he jogged up to the second level. His heart stopped before his feet did.

Katie's little car still huddled in its familiar spot. Had she left it here? Gone out on foot?

When would she have had time to do that? She couldn't still be here. She'd shut down all the systems, just as she'd promised.

Uneasiness caused a cold sheen of sweat to break out over his body, and he pulled the weapon from his waistband, the gun made possible by Katie's manipulation of the security access system. The woman was a genius.

He was going up to get Romo and Ginger. If they wouldn't come out, he had the exploding building as a backup. If they made their escape in the helicopter, the CIA could take care of them later.

He crept past the executive elevator and entered the stairwell. He took the first flight of stairs two at a time and then almost tripped over a shoe on the next landing.

He crouched down and swept it up in one hand. Black, round toe, sensible heel—exactly the type of shoe Katie O'Keefe would laugh at, but exactly the type KC Locke had been wearing in her undercover role as computer geek.

KATIE COVERED HER ears at the next explosion. Everything was going as planned—except this. She glanced at Romo and Ginger in the corner, heads together, whispering.

"The explosions are getting closer, you know, headed this way."

Mr. Romo clicked his tongue. "KC, KC. McCabe isn't going to blow up this building with you in it, is he?"

"I guess the laugh's on you because I'm not supposed to be here. He doesn't know I'm in here."

"It's too bad, you know. We really did trust you. We wanted you to be one of us—until one of our loyal employees spotted you in Elk Crossing."

"The same employee that killed Dustin Gantt?"

"No, actually, a different one—your hapless boss, Frank Norton. He tattled on you, imagine that. Not right away or we would've shut you down as soon as you returned from your weekend getaway. You must've done something to annoy poor Frank."

Ginger tugged on the lapels of her jacket, sniffing. "Of course, as soon as he told us he saw you in Elk Crossing, the same location as Dustin Gantt, we knew something was wrong. The same weekend Liam McCabe mysteriously disappeared, and you never mentioned once to us that you'd been out of town. Maybe if you had, we wouldn't have suspected anything amiss, even after Frank told us where he saw you."

"Really? You wouldn't think anything was amiss that I was in the same place where you murdered Dustin? And how did you kill Samantha?"

"That was you, wasn't it?" Ginger clasped her hands in front of her. "You were wearing that poor girl's sweater the night Garrett died."

"The night you killed him." She jerked her thumb at Mr. Romo. "Does he know you and Garrett were making out on his desk at the moment you killed him?"

Ginger laughed and exchanged a glance with Mr. Romo. "Who do you think gave me the instructions? And as for Samantha, she was a slut who was ready to go home with the first guy she met at the Deluxe. Too bad he happened to work for us."

Mr. Romo stroked his beard. "What organization does Liam McCabe represent? He's too well equipped, too well trained to be on his own. Do you two work for the same agency? Is it the Company?"

"I told you, sweetums. She's here for Sebastian Cole, aren't you? Maybe McCabe is, too. You listen to your brother too much, my love. He's obsessed with Prospero."

Katie pressed her lips into a thin line. "You'd better start thinking of making your way out of here. Can't you hear the explosions? They're coming closer."

"While it would serve you right for betraying our trust

to leave you here in this building while McCabe blows you up, you're more valuable to us alive."

Katie licked her lips. "What do you mean?"

"You do have the kind of skills we need, and after the disaster of this night, we'll need good people to rebuild." Mr. Romo had opened a closet door and dragged out a jacket and a bag.

"What are you talking about? I'm not going to work for you." Her laugh reached an almost hysterical level.

"You will and you'll enjoy it, and you'll enjoy me." He ran a tongue around his full lips. "I haven't forgotten about that aspect of our relationship, either. You'll do what I tell you to do at the computer during the day, and you'll do what I tell you to do in my bed at night."

"You're crazy. That'll never happen. I'd rather see us all blow up first."

Ginger crossed the room and swung open a door next to the windows. A cold gust of wind whooshed into the room.

"What is that? Where does that lead?"

Ginger waved the gun. "To the helipad. We're all taking off and there's not going to be any explosion, at least not for us. Maybe McCabe will just *think* he blew you up. That's good enough for me."

Katie dug her feet into the carpet. She'd ditched her shoes in the stairwell in the hopes that Liam might find them, like Gretel leaving crumbs. "I'm not going anywhere with you."

Ginger strode toward her, smacked her face with the back of her hand and jabbed her in the small of her back with the gun. "Get moving."

Maybe she could jump out of the helicopter, overpower them.

She shuffled toward the door with Ginger prodding her in the back. "I-is there a pilot?"

"Mr. Romo handles the chopper himself."

Romo was slipping into a bomber jacket and slung the bag over his shoulder.

Ginger urged her up the stairs, and when Katie reached the roof, the wind whipped her ponytail across her face.

Mr. Romo joined them as another explosion lit up the night sky. "You keep her here while I start the bird and for God's sake, stay clear of the blades."

He put one foot on the runner and ducked into the chopper. One second later, his body flew backward, knocking into them.

Katie fell to her knees and looked up to see Liam looming in the doorway of the chopper. "Grab the gun, Katie."

Ginger had dropped her weapon, and both women lunged for it at the same time. Ginger's long fingers curled around the handle first, but Katie grabbed the back of Ginger's hair, pulled her head back and then smashed her face against the cement. Ginger's grip slipped off the gun, and it fell over the edge of the roof.

The next explosion rocked the building and threw Katie onto her side.

"Hurry, Katie! Get up. Jump into the chopper. I'm not leaving you."

Ginger was pulling up to her knees, moaning, her face bloody.

Katie hopped to her feet and stepped over her, skirting Mr. Romo's unconscious form.

Liam reached out of the chopper and pulled her inside, flipping switches on the control panel of the bird. As she fell into the seat, she saw Mr. Romo reach for a holster on his calf.

She screamed. "Liam!"

The blades whirred above them and as Mr. Romo staggered to his feet, one of the blades thwacked his back. The next one that hit him knocked him from the roof.

Ginger's keening wail merged with the whine of the chopper as it lifted off.

KATIE'S FINGERS TANGLED with Liam's across the space between their chairs. She didn't exactly know what she was doing here in Florida, but Liam had asked her to come with him, and she'd follow him anywhere.

The door to the office opened behind them, and a tall, angular man strode through it, his energy filling the room, creating tension, excitement.

Liam jumped to his feet. "Sir, this is Katie O'Keefe, the woman I told you about. Katie, this is Jack Coburn, the head of Prospero."

Coburn nodded and slipped into the chair behind his desk, a lock of almost black hair falling over one eye. He pushed it away impatiently. "That was some amazing work you did for us, Katie. Liam's right. He told me all about you."

"Liam's the one who saved the day, or I'd be working for Mr. Romo about now."

"Romo's dead."

She dipped her chin to her chest. "And Ginger Spann?"

"She'll be headed to federal prison once the CIA is finished questioning her." He steepled his fingers and watched them over the top. "Do you know who Mr. Romo was?"

Liam shrugged. "I'd never laid eyes on him the entire time I was there until I kicked him out of his own helicopter."

"You know who Caliban is, right?"

"Was Romo Caliban?" Liam glanced at her. "Caliban is the mysterious head of Tempest. Was that him, sir?"

"We have reason to believe Romo was Caliban's brother."

"Wait." Katie plowed her fingers through her loose hair. "Why is his name Caliban?"

"It's just a codename, a cover, just like Romo." Coburn tipped his chair back and wedged one foot on his desk. "Caliban oversees the entire Tempest organization. We don't know who he is, but Romo came out of nowhere to head up operations of their training facility in Idaho, so we suspect Caliban is a highly placed government official."

"That's what nepotism will get you. Romo didn't do a very good job." Her lips twisted when she recalled the fate he had in store for her.

"A buffoon, more interested in…other things, but he did have an eye for a good programmer, and Liam has been singing your praises ever since we released him from the hospital."

"Where everything was fine, all T-101 out of his system, right?" She took his hand and didn't care if Coburn saw it or not.

"That's right." He squeezed her fingers. "But listen to Jack. He has an offer for you."

"For me?"

"We could use someone with your skills at Prospero, Katie. Would you like to work with us or at least think about it, so this guy—" he jabbed a finger at Liam "—will stop bugging me?"

"I'd love to work for Prospero."

"Thank God. I'm sure you're good, Katie, but mainly we have to make this guy happy. He did a helluva job for us, and we want to keep him around."

"So do I." She grinned like an idiot.

Coburn pushed back from his desk. "This is my office, but it's also my home, and my wife would curse me out in Spanish if I let you go without inviting you to lunch first. So, you two talk it over and join us when you're ready."

As soon as Coburn snapped the door closed behind him, Katie launched out of her chair and landed in Liam's lap. "You did that? You suggested he offer me a position with Prospero?"

"I had to think of some way to keep you close." He wrapped his arms around her waist and kissed her throat.

"Have I ever told you I love you?" She tilted her head, and her wild hair, free from the loathsome ponytails, cascaded over her shoulder.

"You know, I think you let that slip out once by mistake, but just in case it never came out of your mouth again, I committed it to memory."

"You don't have to commit it to your amazing memory, Liam McCabe, because I plan to tell you daily."

He nuzzled her neck. "Mmm, that's okay but I like it better when you show me, but whether you tell me or show me, it doesn't matter because I'm not going anywhere, Katie-O."

She snuggled farther into his lap, showering his face with kisses. She didn't require his assurances anymore, and maybe he didn't require hers, but she never wanted to hold back from this man again. They had each other's backs—and that was coming home.

* * * * *

"Damn, you're gorgeous," he said.

"Thank you. But, so help me, David, if you come inside, I won't get any work done."

At that, he laughed. He leaned over, brushed his fingers down the side of her face, slowly moving over the curve of her cheek, along her jaw to her mouth, where he ran the pad of his thumb over her lips. "If that's meant to scare me off, it's not working."

She dipped her head, rubbed her cheek along his fingertips. "It is your condo. I have no right to tell you when you can be here."

"I'm not staying," he said. She pushed the door open but didn't move.

A gust of wind blew her hair into her face and she shoved it back. "Okay."

"Unless you want me to."

THE REBEL

BY
ADRIENNE GIORDANO

Published in Great Britain 2015
by Mills & Boon, an imprint of Harlequin (UK) Limited,
Eton House, 18-24 Paradise Road, Richmond, Surrey, TW9 1SR

© 2015 Adrienne Giordano

ISBN: 978-0-263-25320-7

46-1015

Printed and bound in Spain
by CPI, Barcelona

Adrienne Giordano, a *USA TODAY* bestselling author, writes romantic suspense and mystery. She is a Jersey girl at heart, but now lives in the Midwest with her workaholic husband, sports obsessed son and Buddy the wheaten terrorist (terrier). For more information on Adrienne's books, please visit www.adriennegiordano.com or download the Adrienne Giordano app. For information on Adrienne's street team, go to facebook.com/groups/dangerousdarlings.

Chapter One

"Come on, boy. Another quarter mile and we're done."

Larry McCall whistled for Henry, his black Lab, who needed exercise more than Larry, to move along. Sunrise illuminated the sky, streaking it in shades of purple and orange that made even a grisly homicide detective marvel at the beauty of nature on an early fall morning.

With Henry busy sniffing a patch of dirt, Larry paused a moment, tilted his head back and inhaled the dewy air. Another two weeks, all these trees would be barren and the city would come in and scoop up the leaves. At which point, his body would make excuses to stay in bed rather than hoof it through ten acres of fenced-in fields on Chicago's southwest side.

Half expecting Henry to trot by him, Larry opened his eyes and glanced to his left, where the dog always walked. No Henry. Since when had he gotten subversive? Larry angled back and found Henry still at the spot he'd been sniffing a minute ago. Only now he was digging. Hard. Terrific. Not only would he have dirt all over him, but he'd also probably snatch a dead animal out of the ground and drop it at Larry's feet. *Here ya go, Dad.*

Not happening. He whistled again. "Leave it," he said in his best alpha-dog voice.

His bum luck was that Henry had alpha tendencies,

too, and kept digging. He'd have to leash him and pull him away before a dead squirrel wound up in his jaws.

Years earlier the city had torn down three low-income apartment buildings—the projects—because of the increased drug and criminal activity surrounding the place. All that was left was the fenced-in acreage that made for great walking. Problem was, there could be anything—rodents, needles, crack baggies, foil scraps—buried. *Needles. Dammit.* Larry hustled back to the dog before he got stuck. Or stoned.

"Whatever you found, Henry, we don't want any part of. Leave it."

He snapped the leash on, gently eased Henry back and was met with ferocious barking. What the hell? His happy dog had gone schizo.

"What is it, boy?"

Holding the dog off the hole he'd started, Larry bent at the waist to focus on something white—dull white—peeking through the dirt.

Henry barked and tugged at the leash.

"Okay, boy. Relax. Let me look at it."

He led a still-barking Henry to a tree, secured the leash around it to keep him at bay and walked back to the spot. Using the handkerchief he always carried—yes, he was that old-school, so what?—to protect his hands, he cleared more of the loose, moist dirt from the top, and more white appeared. He tapped the surface. Solid. Rock solid. And Larry's stomach twisted in a way it only did on the job.

Stop. Twenty years of working homicide told him he should. Right now. *Don't go any further; call it in.*

Birds chirped overhead, the sound so crisp and incessant it sliced right into his ears. Henry apparently had riled 'em good. Still squatting, Larry scanned the desolate area. Beyond the fence at the end of the last quarter mile, the early-morning rush began to swell on Cicero.

Henry barked again. Normally calm as a turtle, he wanted to dig.

Larry cocked his head to study whatever peeked through the dirt, and once again his stomach seized. After all these years, only one thing futzed with his stomach.

Crime scene.

But, truth be told, he had a tendency to overthink things. Something else years on the job had done to him. Hell, he could be staring at an old ceramic bowl. And how humiliating would it be to call this in and have it wind up being someone's china?

Just hell.

Henry barked again, urging him on, and Larry gave in to his curiosity and pushed more loose dirt around. At least until he hit a depression and his finger, handkerchief and all, slid right into it. Gently, he moved his finger around, hitting the outer edges of the depression, and a weird tingling shot up his neck. His breathing kicked up.

What'd this dog find?

He cleared more dirt, his fingers moving gently, revealing more and more of the surface of whatever was buried here. Once again, his fingers slipped into the depressed area and he knew. Dammit.

He'd just stuck his finger into an eye socket.

Chapter Two

Five Years Later

Surrounded by four hundred guests, seven of them sitting at her table in the ballroom of Chicago's legendary Drake Hotel, Amanda studied a giant photo of a fallen firefighter that had flashed on the screen behind the podium. Without a doubt, she'd botched his nose.

Ugh. How embarrassing. Any novice artist, particularly a sculptor, would see the slight flare of the man's nostrils. She slid her gaze to the sculpture, her sculpture, a gift to the widow of Lieutenant Ben Broward, who'd died three months ago after running into a crumbling building to save a child.

The child had survived.

Ben had not.

And Amanda's gift to his widow and their children was now worthless. At least in Amanda's mind. Had the flaring nostrils been that obvious on the photos she'd been given? Later, when she arrived home, she'd swing into her studio and check. Just to satisfy herself.

Darn it.

Sitting back in her chair, she eased out a breath and made eye contact with Lexi, her interior designer friend who'd originally suggested she attend this fund-raiser and meet Pamela Hennings and Irene Dyce, both politically connected—and extremely wealthy—women. Amanda's idea to donate the sculpture had come after seeing an interview with Lieutenant Broward's wife and children. She couldn't give them the man back, but maybe the sculpture would bring some sort of peace. Not exactly closure because Amanda didn't buy in to that whole closure thing. What did that even mean? Tragedy was tragedy and she doubted Ben's family would ever fully recover.

Mrs. Hennings leaned closer to speak over the chatter and the sound of clanging silverware filling the room. "Amazing likeness, dear."

"Yes," Mrs. Dyce said from the other side of Mrs. Hennings. "Beautiful work, Amanda."

"Thank you."

Not that she believed it after spotting her mistake, but coming from Mrs. Hennings, the wife of Chicago's most brilliant defense attorney, a woman notorious for her good taste, Amanda, as she always did, graciously accepted the compliment, allowing it to momentarily smother her doubt.

At least until she looked at that nose again. Would the widow notice? Would she see the blunder every time she chose to look at the piece? Would it drive her insane? Gah.

The woman couldn't spend years looking at a nose butchered by the artist. Amanda couldn't allow it. She'd redo the piece. That was all. She'd make time to fix her mistake.

Done.

Over.

Move on.

A waiter slid a slice of cherry cheesecake in front of her. Any other day, she'd happily indulge, which of

course wouldn't help her lose that extra ten pounds, but
a girl had a right to sugar. Simple fact. But after the beating she'd just given herself, she wasn't sure her stomach
could handle a rich dessert. Gently, she nudged the plate
away, opting instead for a sip of water.

"Evening, Miss LeBlanc."

She glanced up to where a large, barrel-chested man,
late fifties perhaps, stood behind her. "Hello."

"I'm Detective Larry McCall. Chicago PD. Homicide."
He gestured to the vacant chair next to her. "Mind if I
sit?"

Oh, boy. What was this?

Whatever it was, she was thankful he wasn't the man
who'd been sitting beside her all evening. *That* man, a
financial planner from one of the city's big banks, had
disappeared more than thirty minutes ago after she flatly
told him, no, she was not interested in doing "hot" things
in his bed. What an idiot. With any luck, he'd found a
woman willing to take him up on his offer.

She held her hand out. "Of course. Someone was sitting there, but he's been gone awhile."

Hopefully, for good.

The detective glanced across the table to where Lexi
sat with her boyfriend, Brodey, another Chicago homicide detective and also the brother of one of the Hennings & Solomon investigators. Seemed to Amanda that
the Hennings clan had a connection to just about everyone in this city.

"Junior," Detective McCall said, nodding a greeting.

"Lawrence," Brodey drawled.

And how amusing was this? Clearly these two were in
some kind of twisted male peeing match, and Amanda
did everything in her power not to roll her eyes.

Detective McCall dropped his bulky frame into the chair beside her. "I'll move if he comes back. Sorry if I'm interrupting."

"Not at all. What can I do for you, Detective?"

"I checked out your bust."

Amanda bit her lip, stifling a smile as the detective replayed in his mind the last seconds—wait for it. *There.*

He smacked himself on the head, then did it again, but he laughed at himself all the same. Instantly she liked him, liked his ability to find humor in embarrassing situations, liked his acceptance of his blunder without making a fuss.

"I apologize," he said. "This is what happens when you put a guy like me in a place like this. I insult nice women."

And he had the rough-around-the-edges grit of one of those throwback detectives she liked to watch on reruns of *NYPD Blue*.

"Well," she said, "lucky for you I'm not easily offended. And what's worse is that I figured out immediately you meant the sculpture and not my—" she looked down, circled her hand in front of her chest "—you know."

"The sculpture. Yeah. It's really good."

Aside from the botched nose.

"Thank you."

"No. I mean it's *really* good. I knew Ben. Good guy. Great guy, actually. His wife is the daughter of…" He shook his head, waved it off. "Never mind. Doesn't matter. The sculpture is…accurate. Scary accurate."

Hmm… Having been approached by detectives before, Amanda felt the puzzle pieces beginning to come together and she readied herself to ruin Detective McCall's evening. "I had a few photos from different angles to work from."

"Yeah, I guess that helps. Listen, do you ever do forensic work?"

And there it was.

As suspected, the detective wanted her help on a case. Probably doing an age progression on a missing child or working with a witness to identify an attacker. Because of budgeting woes and a lack of funds for full-time forensic artists, police departments sometimes hired outside the department.

None of it mattered. She'd have to turn him down. "I'm sorry, Detective. I do have an interest and have taken some classes, but it's not work I feel comfortable with yet."

McCall, apparently ignoring her refusal, leaned in. "I've got this case…"

He has a case. On countless occasions throughout her childhood she'd heard those very words from her mother, a part-time forensic artist. Amanda held her hand up. "I'd like to help, but I have little experience in forensic work. I'd do more harm than good."

"No, you wouldn't. Trust me. It's a cold case. Five years now. No leads. All we have is a skull and some hairs found where it was dug up. That's all that's left of her."

"Her?"

"The medical examiner thinks it's a female. Maybe late teens or early twenties."

"I see."

"I actually found her."

Amanda gawked. Couldn't help it. "You found the skull?"

The detective shook his head as he let out a huff. "Craziest damned thing. I was out walking my dog in that vacant spot near Midway, and Henry started digging. I'll never forget it. Whoever this girl is, she and I are a team. I made sure I kept her case. It's mine."

"That's admirable, Detective. Really."

He shrugged. "We have a sketch done by one of the department artists, but I don't know. Maybe she got it wrong because no one is coming forward to claim this girl and we didn't get any hits from DNA. I'm a father. It makes me sick." He ran his hand over his thinning, gray hair as he scanned the ballroom and the people moving toward the exit. "I saw what you did with the sculpture of Ben and thought maybe you could help us out."

Amanda glanced across at Lexi, hoping to grab her attention with the *save me* stare. No luck there because her friend was busy whispering in Brodey's ear. By the look on his face, he liked what he was hearing. A flash of something whipped inside Amanda. At odd times, she missed the comfort, the familiarity, the *knowing* of an exclusive relationship. Casual dating didn't provide any of that.

But a pity party wouldn't get her assistance from Lexi or Brodey. To her right, Mrs. Hennings and Mrs. Dyce were in deep conversation about scheduling a lunch, so there'd be no help there, either. For this one, she'd fly solo. Try once again to nicely let the detective know she couldn't help him. As much as she felt for him, she wouldn't—couldn't—risk involvement. She faced him again, meeting his gaze straight on. "Detective, I'm sorry. It's just not what I do. I've never done a reconstruction before. I could ask around, though, and see if any of my colleagues might be interested."

McCall hesitated and studied her eyes for a few seconds, apparently measuring her resolve. He must have received her message because he nodded, his jowly cheeks shaking with the effort. "I'd appreciate that. Thank you. I want to give this girl her name back."

And, oh, that made Amanda's stomach burn. Ten years ago, her mother would have loved this project.

A lot had changed in ten years.

Movement from Amanda's right drew her attention to Mrs. Hennings placing her napkin on the table. "I'm sorry to say, it's past my bedtime." Mrs. Hennings touched Mrs. Dyce's shoulder. "I'll call you in the morning and we'll figure out a day for lunch."

"I'll be at the youth center. Call me there."

"Will do." Mrs. Hennings nodded at Lexi. "And I'll have David call *you* about his new home. He needs help. Just don't tell him I said that."

Lexi laughed. "Your secret is safe with me. And thank you. I'm excited to work with him."

Then Mrs. Hennings turned her crystal-blue gaze on Amanda. "My son has just moved back from Boston. Lexi will be helping him on the redesign of his condominium. I'd love to have him look at your artwork. He's starting from scratch." Her lips lifted into a calculating smile only mothers pulled off. "Whether he likes it or not, he's starting from scratch."

And from what Amanda had heard from Lexi, when Mrs. Hennings made a request, you should not be fool enough to deny her. When it came to Chicago's upper crust, Mrs. Hennings might be their president.

"Of course," Amanda said. "I'd love to. Lexi and I have worked together several times. Your son can come by my studio and look at some of my paintings. Or we could do a sculpture. Whatever he likes."

The older woman reached to shake Amanda's hand. "Wonderful. I'll have him call you."

"OH, COME ON, David," Mom said. "I know you can be charming."

David Hennings sat in the kitchen of his parents' home, his hand wrapped around a steaming mug of coffee, and faced down his mother, a woman so formidable and connected the mayor of Chicago kept in constant communication with her. She might be able to sway masses, but she was still his mother and, at times, needed to be told no.

Otherwise, she'd control him.

And that wasn't going to happen.

"Mom, thank you for your never-ending encouragement."

She scoffed at his sarcasm. "You know what I mean."

Yes, he did. As much as he liked the usual banter between them, he didn't want to hear about whatever scheme she had going. Not on a Monday morning when he had a to-do list a mile long, including meeting with the contractor renovating his new condo. Yep, after two weeks of living under his parents' roof, because even he couldn't be rebellious enough to break his mother's heart by staying in a hotel, he needed to get that condo in shape so he could move in.

As usual, Mom kept her piercing eyes on him and with each second she slowly, methodically chipped away at him. This look was famous in the Hennings household. *This* look could possibly bring down an entire nation. He blew air through his lips, part of his willpower going with it. "Have you talked to Dad about this?"

"Of course."

Lying. He eyed her.

"Well, I mentioned it. In passing."

David snorted. "I thought so."

After attending a fund-raiser for a fireman's fund the night before, his mother had gotten it into her head that Hennings & Solomon, the law firm his father had founded, should have their investigators look into a cold case. An apparent homicide. All in all, David didn't get what she wanted from him. All she knew about the case was what she'd overheard at the dinner table. One, some detective had a skull he couldn't identify. Two, the detective wanted a sculptor to do a reconstruction.

That was it.

A reconstruction alone would be no easy task if an artist didn't have training in forensics. And who knew what kind of credentials this particular artist had?

David might not have been a criminal lawyer like his father and siblings, but he knew that much about forensics.

Mom folded her arms and leaned one hip against the counter. "We can help. I know we can."

For years now, the two of them had been allies. Unlike his siblings, when David needed shelter, he went to his mother. He adored her, had mad respect for her. No matter what. Through that hellish few months when he'd destroyed his father's dream of his oldest son joining the firm because David had decided civil law—horrors!—might be the way to go, his mother had pled David's case, tirelessly arguing that he needed to be his own man and make his own decisions.

And Dad had given in.

It might have been butt-ugly, but the man had let David go.

That was the power of Pamela Hennings.

David slugged the last of his coffee because, well, at this point, the extra caffeine couldn't hurt.

"Okay," he said. "You do realize I'm not a criminal

attorney, right? And, considering I don't even work at Hennings & Solomon, I'm guessing I'm not the guy for this assignment."

"Your father said Jenna and the other investigator, Mike what's-his-name, are too busy. And *you* said you were bored. Since your new office won't be ready for a couple of weeks, you can do this. *We* can do this."

Cornered. Should have known she had a counterattack prepped. So like his mother to use his own words against him after he'd complained the night before that the contractor doing the renovation on his new office was running behind. Had he known that, he'd have stayed in Boston another two weeks before packing up and moving home to open his own firm.

"But I'm meeting with my contractor this morning."

"By the way, as soon as you're done with him, you need to call Lexi."

"The decorator? Why?"

Mom huffed and gave him the dramatic eye roll that had won lesser actresses an Academy Award. "Interior designer, dear. And what do you mean, why? I told you I arranged for her to work with you. Because, so help me, David, you will not be living the way you did in Boston with all that oddball furniture and no drapes. You, my love, are a grown man living like a teenager. Besides, Lexi's significant other knows the detective from last night. When you talk to Lexi, get the detective's name. He'll help you. We'll get Irene Dyce in on this, as well." Mom waggled her hand. "She was at the fund-raiser last night and overheard the conversation. I'm about to call her to set up lunch and you can bet I'll mention it. Between her and her husband, they know half this city. It's doable, David."

He sat forward and pinched the bridge of his nose. By now he should be used to this. The bobbing and weaving his mother did to confuse people and get them to relent. "What is it exactly you want me to do?"

She slapped a business card in front of him. "Talk to the artist. I got her card last night. I told her you were about to move into a new home and might need artwork."

"Seriously? You're tricking her? And how much is *that* going to cost me?"

"David Jeremy Hennings, just shush. I needed a reason to contact her again. And it's not a trick if you hire her. Just have her do a painting or something. That's only fair."

If he wound up buying something, his mother was paying for it. That was all he knew. Sighing, he picked up the card. Amanda LeBlanc. Nice name. Good, solid name. "Why do I need to talk to her?"

"She told the detective she couldn't do the sculpture. I think she's intrigued, though. She might just need a push. And you, my darling, excel at the art of the push."

He held up both hands. "Mom, please don't strain yourself with all these compliments. First I'm charming, and now it's persuasive. This might all go to my head."

"You need to zip it with the sass. For God's sake, you're the intellectual around here. You love research and history and combing through information to reach a conclusion. This case would be perfect for you."

"I'm no investigator."

"But you don't have to be. All you need to do is get the ball rolling. Think of the people we have at our disposal. Russ is an FBI agent. I'm sure he'd help."

Now she wanted to drag his sister's boyfriend into this. Great. Given David's strained—as in they drove each other nuts—relationship with Penny, he and Russ hadn't gotten off to the greatest of starts.

Inspired, Mom boosted herself away from the counter and sat in the chair beside his. *It's over now.* When she got charged up like this, there'd be no denying her.

"David, I want you to think about this. You moved back to Chicago to be part of this family again."

"Mom—"

"Shush. I love you, but you've always had an issue with feeling like the odd man out."

Damn, she's good.

"If you'd really like to be included in all those nasty dinner conversations about criminal cases, this is the way to start. So far, the firm's quasi cold-case squad has solved two murders. Two, David. Do you know how many nights I've had to listen to your father, Zac and Penny re-hash those cases?" She held up her hand. "A lot. This is your chance to finally be part of the conversation. And, frankly, I want this. For the first time, I get to be part of the conversation, too, and I like it. I'm not your father's socialite wife anymore. I'm more than an *appendage*."

Academy Award winner Pamela Hennings. "Cut that out. You've never been an appendage. He's terrified of you. Everyone knows that."

"Everyone knows I'm his wife and that, yes, we have a strong relationship, but I've never had a job, David. All the charity work and clubs, it's all an offshoot of your father's work. Not that I haven't enjoyed it, but if given the chance at a redo, I'd have a career of my own. Doing what, I don't know. All I know is that I'm suddenly some-one who can help bring justice and it's not because it's expected of me. So buck up and do this for your mother."

Game over. She'd turned the entire thing around on him, playing up the guilt because she knew, when it came to her, he rarely said no. Damn. How the hell did she always do this? He ticked through the conversation, then burst out laughing.

"What's funny?"

He grabbed his cup, rose from his chair and kissed her on the cheek. "Nothing. You're brilliant. You've totally manipulated me into doing this. And I let you. Being around lawyers has rubbed off on you."

"You'll do it?"

"I'll talk to the artist. Then I'm done. I'm not an investigator and have no interest in being one. I have a law practice to open."

Mom pushed up from the table and held her index fingers up. "That's fine. Talk her into at least doing the reconstruction. You're better at that sort of thing than I am. Once you convince her, I'll handle it from there."

"I'm sure you will, Mom. I'm sure you will."

"And, by the way, dinner is at seven-thirty tonight. Zac and Emma will be here and Russ and Penny."

She ran her gaze over his clothes, starting at his long-sleeved henley. He knew she hated the Levi's jeans and boots, but he wasn't five anymore and didn't need his mother dressing him. "Don't start, Mom."

"Between the clothes and that facial hair, I have to ask that you not come to the table dressed like you escaped from prison."

Facial hair. She acted as if he had a hobo beard rather than the close-cropped one he favored. He snatched his favorite leather jacket, the one with the intricate stitching on the shoulders, off the back of his chair, and Mom's lips peeled back. "Mom, this is a two-thousand-dollar jacket. Besides, my *tux* is at the dry cleaner's."

"Don't be fresh."

More than done with this conversation, he shrugged into his coat. "I've gotta go. You've convinced me to talk to this artist. I love you, but quit while you're ahead."

Chapter Three

Morning sun shifted, the light angling sideways instead of straight into Amanda's studio, and she stepped back from the sculpture. She'd been messing with the lips of a cell-phone manufacturer's CEO, bending the clay, tweaking and retweaking for two hours, and she still couldn't get the mouth right. And worse, she couldn't figure out why. As much as it irritated her, drove her to near madness, it didn't matter. She'd keep at it. No matter how long it took. After the botched nose on the fireman, resulting in a shake-up of her confidence, she'd get these lips perfect.

The changing sunlight through the loft's oversize windows didn't help, so she adjusted the six-foot lamp behind her, directing the light in a more favorable position. Light, light and more light helped keep her focused for the sometimes tedious hours spent in front of a sculpture. Changing shadows meant time slipping from her greedy hands. She glanced at the clock. Eleven thirty. She'd been at it six hours, two of them lost on bum lips.

"Okay, girlfriend. You need to get it together here. Forget the nose. It's one nose. It shouldn't be a career-ending mistake."

Intellectually, she knew it. Emotionally, that faulty nose might do her in.

The studio phone rang, filling the quiet space with its annoying blinging sound. Typically, she'd ignore the phone until her exhausted and sore fingers gave out for the day. But now, with the rotten lips, it was probably a good time to take a break. Grab a quick lunch and refocus. She scooted to her desk in the corner and snatched up the handset.

"Good morning. This is Amanda."

"Good morning, Amanda. My name is David Hennings. You met my mother at an event last night."

And, hello, sexy voice of my dreams. Wow. The low-pitched resonance of that voice poured over her. With her dating history, he was probably five inches shorter than her and a total mama's boy. "Hello, Mr. Hennings. I did meet your mother last night. She's a lovely dinner companion."

For whatever reason, he laughed at that, the sound just as yummy as his voice.

"That she is," he said. "She told me she mentioned I was moving into a new place."

Seriously, he didn't sound short. Or like a mama's boy. If that even made sense because how could anyone know what someone looked like by the way he spoke? She had a vision, though. A good one, an exceptional one, of a tall man, fair haired and blue-eyed like his mother. And he'd wear suits every day. Slick, Italian suits that alerted the world to his blue-blood status. Yes indeed, she had a vision.

"She mentioned you'd be working with Lexi, who is a friend, by the way. Would you like to set up an appointment and we can discuss what you might need?"

"Definitely. I just spoke with Lexi. I could swing by. If you're available."

"Now?"

"If that works. Otherwise, we could look at tomorrow."

Apparently Mrs. Hennings was in a hurry. Amanda swung back to her sculpture and the stubborn lips. A break might help. Discussing new projects always seemed to cleanse the palate, help her look at existing work with fresh perspective and excitement. But she wasn't exactly dressed to meet a new client. Knowing she had a full day of sculpting ahead, she'd yanked her hair into a ponytail and slipped on her baggiest of baggy jeans and a "Make Love, Not War" T-shirt a friend had given her as a joke. The hair she could deal with by removing her hair band. The clothes? Not so much.

"Mr. Hennings, that would be fine. But I have to warn you, I'm working on a sculpture today and when I sculpt I dress comfortably. I didn't expect to have a meeting."

"Don't worry about it. I'm in jeans. My mother is on a mission, Amanda, and if you know my mother at all, you know that if I tell her I didn't meet with you because of what you were wearing, she'll skin me."

"So you're saying you're afraid of your mother."

"I'm not *afraid* of my mother. I'm *terrified of her*."

For the first time all day, considering the lips, Amanda laughed. A good, warm one that made her toes curl. Any argument she'd had to avoid meeting with him today vanished when he'd dropped that line about his mother. Simply put, she loved a grown man who understood his mother's power. How that grown man handled that power was a different story. Heaven knew she'd dated some weaklings, men who not only were afraid of their mothers, but also let them dictate how their lives should go. That, on a personal level, Amanda couldn't deal with. On a professional level, she didn't necessarily care as long as her fee got paid.

Besides, she liked David Hennings. She liked the

sound of his voice even more. Call it curiosity, a mild interest in meeting a man with a voice like velvet against skin, but she wanted to check him out.

"Okay, Mr. Hennings. You can come by now."

"Great. I'll see you soon. And it's David."

INSIDE THE STAIRWELL of the hundred-year-old building on the city's West Side, David climbed the last few steps leading to the landing of Amanda's second-floor studio. He loved these old structures with the Portland stone and brick. The iconic columns on the facade urged the history major in him to research the place. Check the city records, see what information he could find on who'd built it, who'd lived here or which companies had run their wares through its doors.

Structures like this had a charm all their own that couldn't be duplicated with modern wizardry. Old buildings, this building, had a life, a past to be researched and appreciated.

Or maybe he just wanted to believe that.

He rapped on the door. No hollow wood there. By the scarred look and feel of its heavy weight under his knuckles, it might be the original door. How amazing would *that* be?

The door swung open and a woman with lush curves a guy his size could wrap himself around greeted him. She wore jeans and a graphic T-shirt announcing he should make love, not war—*gladly, sweetheart*—and her honey-blond hair fell around her shoulders, curling at the ends. The whole look brought thoughts of lazy Sunday mornings, hot coffee and a few extracurricular activities, in a bed and out, David could think of.

To say the least, she affected him.

And she hadn't even opened her mouth. *Please don't be an airhead.*

"David?"

Yep. That was the voice from earlier. Soft and sweet and stirring up all kinds of images right along with Sunday mornings and coffee. With any luck, more than the coffee would be hot.

Hokay. Mission Pam Hennings getting derailed by wicked thoughts. Time to get serious.

"Hi. Amanda?"

"Yes." She held her hand out. "Amanda LeBlanc."

David grasped her hand and glanced down at her long, elegant fingers folding over his. Her silky skin absorbed his much larger hand, and he might like to stay this way awhile. Nice hands. Soft hands. He'd imagined a sculptor's hands to be work-hardened and rough. Not that she swung an ax all day, but he'd expected…different.

"Um." She pointed at their still joined hands. "I kinda need that hand back."

Epic fail, Dave. He grinned and regrettably slid his hand away. "Don't take this the wrong way, but where have you been all my life?"

As recoveries went, it wouldn't be listed among the top hundred in brilliance, but a man had to work with what he had. Still, her lips, those extraordinary, shapely lips, twisted until she finally gave up and awarded him with a smile.

"Good one," she said. "Come inside and we'll talk about your project."

Right to business. Couldn't blame her. She didn't know him and he'd not only barged in on her day, but also hit on her. He stepped into the loft and let out a low whistle. A few walls had obviously been knocked out because her studio took up half of the entire floor. He scanned the room, his eyes darting over the open ceiling, the gleaming white walls, the easels and canvases in one corner. A large table covered with tools and brushes separated one area from a second space, where a bust was mounted on an adjustable stand.

She closed the door behind him. "I'd ask you to excuse the mess, but since it always looks like this, I won't bother."

"It's a studio. I'm not sure it's supposed to be neat."

"We can talk over here." She motioned him to a round table for four by the windows.

"This is a great space. Fantastic light. Do you know anything about the building?"

Her eyebrows dipped. "As in who owns it?"

"No. Sorry. I'm a history buff. Majored in it in college. The columns out front make me think early 1900s architecture."

"Ah. A man after my own heart. Believe it or not, I'm the only tenant right now. People just don't see the beauty. According to city records, it was constructed in 1908. I'm not sure my landlord has a clue what a gem he has. When I toured the building he told me he wanted to paint the front of it."

David opened his mouth, but nothing came out.

"I know," she said. "I had to give him the number of a company that specializes in stone cleaning and repair before he stripped the historical value out of the place."

"No kidding."

Amanda took the chair by the window, where a legal pad and pencil waited to be put to use. David slid his jacket off, set it on the chair next to his and sat across from her. Damn, the woman was gorgeous. All big brown eyes and soft cheeks to go with the healthy curves.

"Is that jacket a Belstaff?" she asked.

And, oh, oh, oh, she knew motorcycles. Or at least biker jackets. This expedition of his mother's might make his day.

"It is. You like motorcycles?"

"My dad does. What do you ride?"

"A Ducati. Diavel Carbon." He smiled. "It's a *beast*."

"It should be with a name like Diavel. You know what it means, right?"

He sure did. "*Diavolo*. Italian for devil."

She grinned. "And are you? A devil?"

"My mother would say I am. *I* think I'm a history nerd with a thing for motorcycles."

"Huh," she said.

"What?"

"Nothing. You're just not what I expected."

Now, this sounded good. Maybe. "You know I have to ask…"

"I expected someone who looks like your mother. Tall, blond hair, Italian suit. Instead I got dark with an Italian motorcycle."

He bit his bottom lip, then ran his teeth over it. "If my brother had knocked on your door, you'd have nailed it." He shrugged. "But hey, you got the tall part right."

"That's something, I guess."

She picked up her pencil and tossed her hair over her shoulder and David's pulse went berserk. Damn, this woman was beautiful. And not in the normal way. This was more corn-fed, casual beauty that she probably had no idea she possessed.

She angled her notepad in front of her. "Anyway, tell me about this project. What kind of paintings are you looking for?"

Nudes.

Of her.

His mother would castrate him. He cleared his throat and got *that* vision out of his head. The naked Amanda, not the castration. But the castration was no picnic, either.

But here was where this scenario got sticky because his sneaky mother, God bless her, had taken Amanda's card under the guise of providing him with art for his condo. Well, he'd get the art anyway because he would not waste this woman's time under false pretenses. "I'm not sure. I was thinking maybe we could work with Lexi on that. Something bold, deep colors. I don't know. It's not my thing. That's why I have Lexi."

"She's good at it, that's for sure. I can call her. Then I'll pull some paintings I think will work. If you don't like them, maybe I can create something specific for you."

Which, lucky him, would give him another reason to show up and maybe convince the lovely Amanda LeBlanc to have dinner with him. "That'll work. I have another project that my mother is interested in."

Amanda's eyebrows hitched up. No surprise there. His mother was notorious for spending big bucks on decorating. And landing her as a client would open a lot of doors when it came to an artist's career.

"What does she have in mind?"

"A sculpture."

"Oh, my specialty. Who will the sculpture be of?"

Here we go. "We don't know."

She laughed. "That's a new one. All right. I'll play. How do we find out who this sculpture will be of?"

Okay. So apparently his mother hadn't said anything— at all—to Amanda about her interest in the cold case discussed at the fund-raiser the night before. She'd totally set him up, and he'd give her an earful about that. When he showed up wearing jeans and *facial hair* at dinner.

That'd teach her. "Did my mother say anything to you about my father's law firm and their side work?"

"No."

Thanks, Mom. This right here might be one of the reasons he'd moved to Boston four years ago. Keeping up with the Hennings family shenanigans and the constant arguing and petty competition with Penny made his brain hurt. So he'd taken off. Got himself breathing room halfway across the country. *Welcome home, kid.*

"My dad is the founding partner of Hennings & Solomon."

"David, everyone in this city knows who your dad is."

True. "Right. Last fall my mom convinced him to have one of the firm's investigators work on a pro bono case. A cold case."

Amanda sat forward and waved her pencil. "I read about that. It involved a US Marshal or something."

"That's the one. His mother was murdered and the case, up to that point, was unsolved. The firm's investigator looked into it, and between her and the victim's son, they solved the case."

"Yes! I remember reading about it. Fascinating."

Glad you think so. That would only help when he ambushed her with doing this skull reconstruction his mother was so bent on. "Then my mother found another case she wanted to help solve."

"Your mother is a busy woman."

Honey, you have no idea. "She is. And her instincts are spot-on because the firm managed to help solve that one, too."

"How wonderful for her. And the firm's investigator must be excellent at what she does."

"She is. But she's had help. Cases like this take work

and she comes from a family of detectives with major contacts."

Amanda sat up straighter, pencil still at the ready, but her body language—stiff shoulders, pressed lips—went from curious to defensive. The temperature in the room might have plummeted to negative numbers.

This was it. Headfirst. Right here. "My mother overheard your conversation with the detective last night. The one with the unidentified skull."

She dropped her pencil and pushed the pad away. She held her hands up and sucked in her cheeks, the look hard and unyielding, transforming her from the lush sex kitten he wanted his hands on to a woman set for battle.

Where the hell *had* she been all his life?

"No," she said.

"I'm afraid my mother has you on her radar. And you're locked on."

"She'll have to unlock me, then. I explained to the detective last night that I couldn't do the sculpture. I have limited, insanely limited, experience with forensic sculptures. I've taken a couple of workshops, but I've never attempted a forensic reconstruction. I'm simply not qualified."

"If you've never tried, how do you know you can't do it?"

She set her palms flat on the table, the tips of her fingers burrowing into the wood and turning pink. "David, I'm sorry. Tell your mother I appreciate her following up on this, but my answer is no. It would be a waste of everyone's time. The painting for your new home, I'd be happy to do."

"Great. But indulge me on the reconstruction for a second."

Amanda huffed out a breath, half laughing but not really. In a way, he felt bad for her. He knew exactly how pushy the Hennings bunch could be. "Trust me," he said. "I feel your pain."

"Are you a lawyer like the rest of your family?"

"I am."

"Knew it. You have that lawyer tenacity."

He grinned. "I'm civil law. Everyone else is on the criminal side. But since I have that lawyer tenacity, I'd like to make you a deal."

"No."

Time to try a different approach because he wanted a dinner date with this woman and he liked sparring with her. Even if she didn't know either of those things.

Yet.

He sat forward, angled his head toward the sculpture across the room and pointed. "Looking at that, I'd say you're a talented woman."

"Thank you. And nice try."

She folded her arms, visually ripping holes into his body, and the twisted side of him, the strategizer, loved it. "You're welcome. What we have here is a detective trying to identify a body. A body deserving of a proper burial. Someone whose family is probably wondering what happened to their loved one."

"David—"

"Even if you don't think you have the experience, what would it hurt to try? I mean, this is fairly specialized work. I can't imagine there are a ton of forensic sculptors in this city."

"It would be a waste of everyone's time."

"I'll pay you."

Her head dipped. "You'll pay me to attempt a sculpture that may or may not serve a purpose?"

Apparently so. And that was news to him, too, but

he'd gotten on a roll, so why not? Cost of doing business when it came to keeping his mother off his back. "Yes. The worst-case scenario is that no one will identify the person. Best case is your sculpture helps the police figure out what happened, brings someone home and puts their family out of misery. And you'll get paid. I don't see the downside."

IF HE WANTED a downside, she could give him one. One so huge that if this project failed, and it could fail in any number of ways, she might find herself emotionally debilitated for years. Having an acute sense of her own emotional awareness, Amanda chose to avoid situations involving someone else's future. She'd learned that lesson from her now-deceased mother.

She drew in a breath and thought about the bright spring morning ten years ago when her mother had swallowed a bottle of pills. Amanda reminded herself—as if it ever went away—what it had felt like to touch Mom's lifeless body. Before that day, she'd never known just how cold a body could get.

Right now that memory kept her focused on convincing the extremely handsome and determined man across from her just how stubborn she could be. From the moment she'd opened the studio door, David Hennings had surprised her. Not only did he not look a thing like his mother, but he also didn't dress like any blue blood she'd ever met. If the chiseled face, sexy dark beard and enormous shoulders weren't enough, the man rode a big, bad motorcycle known to be one of the fastest production bikes out there. That beauty did zero to sixty in less than three seconds, and something told her David Hennings loved to make it scream.

Mentally, she fanned herself. Cooled her own firing

engines because…well…*wow. Stay strong, girlfriend.* She'd always had a thing for a man on a motorcycle. She sat back, casually crossed her legs and wished she weren't wearing ratty jeans. "David, trust me—there's a downside to this kind of work. People are sent to prison based on an artist's sketch. I don't want that responsibility." She waved her hand around the studio. "I want to paint and sculpt for my clients' enjoyment."

He nodded, but he obviously wasn't done yet. She saw it in the way he stared at her, his dark blue eyes so serious but somehow playful, as well. Whatever this was, he was enjoying it.

And between his height and his shoulders, he filled her sight line. Amazing that a man this imposing could come from a woman as petite as Mrs. Hennings. Then again, he'd clearly inherited his media-darling father's big-chested build. A few wisps of his collar-length hair, such a deep brown it bordered on black, fell across his forehead and he pushed them back, resting his long fingers against his head for a second, almost demanding those hairs stay put. Amanda's girlie parts didn't just tingle, they damn near sizzled.

Whew.

The object of her indecent thoughts gestured to the piece she'd worked on that morning. "May I?"

"Of course."

He took his time getting to the sculpture, his gaze on it as he moved, and Amanda's skin caught fire. Prowling, sexual energy streamed from him as he contemplated her work, head cocked one way and then the other, that strong jaw so perfect she'd love to sculpt it.

And her without a fan.

"What do you think?" she asked.

"I think your work is exceptional. And I'm not saying that because I want something from you." He smiled. "Certain lines I won't cross, and doling out high praise when it's not warranted is one of them."

"Thank you. I take it you like art?"

He shrugged. "I like to study things. To research them. Like this building. I saw it and had to know its history."

"All right, what do you see in that sculpture?"

"The mouth." He went back to the photo on the stand. "It's not quite there yet."

Amazing. "I worked on the lips all morning. Something isn't right."

Now he looked back at her, a full-on smile exploding across his face, and Amanda's lungs froze. Just stopped working. To heck with Michelangelo, Amanda LeBlanc now had a David of her very own.

"I have another deal for you."

Her lungs released and she eased out a breath. "You're full of deals today."

"I'm a lawyer. It's what I do."

"Fine. What's your deal?"

"I'll tell you what the problem is with your sculpture if you go with me to see this detective."

Moving closer, she kept her gaze on him and the not-too-smug curve of his mouth. "You know what's wrong with the lips?"

"I believe I do."

As a trained artist, one with a master's in fine arts, she'd spent hours trying to figure it out, and now the history major thought he knew. Oh, this was so tempting. She'd love to prove him wrong and knock some of that arrogance right out of him. But, darn. The way he carried that confidence, that supreme knowing made her stomach pinch.

"What's wrong, Amanda? Cat got your tongue?"

And *ohmygod*, he was *such* a weasel. A playful weasel, but still. She snorted. "Please. The cat having my tongue has never been an issue. Perhaps I'm merely stunned by your gigantic ego."

"Oh, harsh." He splayed his hand and his beautifully long fingers over his chest, but his face gave him away, all those sharp angles softly curving when he smiled. "You wound me."

Such a weasel. From her worktable, she grabbed her flat wooden tool. "Okay, hotshot. Let's see what you've got."

"If I tell you and it works, you go with me to see that detective. That's the deal."

"Yes. If it works, I'll go with you."

Silly, silly girl. All this to prove him wrong. Something told her, if he nailed this, she might never hear the end of it.

He smiled at her, spun to the sculpture and, without touching it, pointed to the right corner of the mouth. "It's not the lips so much but the small depression that should be right there."

What now? Lunging for the photo, she analyzed the corner of the CEO's mouth. Dammit. Right there. Well, not *right* there. The dimple was so slight it couldn't even be called a dimple. Her issue hadn't been the lips at all, but the mouth in general. And, oh, she could rail about how David had tricked her, about how she specifically meant the lips and the deal would be negated.

But she should have caught that. Even the tiniest of details, as they'd both just learned, could ruin a project.

"David Hennings, I don't know whether to kill you or kiss you."

His hand shot up. "Can I vote?"

She cracked up. "No. But darn it, I can't believe I didn't catch that."

"You were looking too hard. Happens to me sometimes when I'm working cases. I'll be searching for precedents and—bam—someone else reads my notes and in five minutes knows exactly what I need. It's irritating as hell."

"It sure is."

"That being said…"

He strode back to where they'd been sitting, his smile growing wider by the second. *So smug.*

And she'd just handed him that victory.

He slid his phone from the side pocket of his jacket and held it up for her to see. "What time shall I tell the detective we'll be there?"

DETECTIVE LARRY MCCALL ushered Amanda and David into a small conference room at Area North headquarters. The old building didn't have the charm her building had, but with a few fixes and a splash of fresh paint the dreary and dull white walls wouldn't feel so confining. Then again, Amanda supposed a police station wasn't meant to be paradise.

Inside the room, a veneer table large enough for six had been jammed into the corner. Probably the only way it would fit. Five chairs—what happened to the sixth?— were haphazardly pushed in, a couple almost sideways. Maybe the last meeting had ended in a rush.

Amanda took the chair Detective McCall held for her while David remained standing, casually leaning against the wall directly across from her. "Thank you," she said.

"No," the detective said. "Thank you for coming in."

"Detective, please, let's not get ahead of ourselves. As I said—"

McCall waved her off. "Yeah, I know. You're not a forensic artist and you're only having a look. I get it. Still, I appreciate whatever you can do."

He slapped a file onto the table, the *fwap* reverberating in her head, making her ears ring. *What am I doing?* She shouldn't be here. She'd spent years running from the lure of this kind of work. Years. And for good reason. As talented as her mother had been, her work with law enforcement had been the end of the fairy tale. For Amanda. For her father. And most of all, for her mother.

David shifted, drawing her attention, and she brought her gaze to his. He cocked his head—he did that a lot—and stared at her face while she worked on arranging her features into neutral. *No clues here.* Still, he narrowed his eyes and she knew he'd sensed something. Those haunting dark blue eyes of his burned right through her.

The file McCall had slapped on the table was open in front of her and she pulled her gaze from David, needing to be free of whatever psychoanalysis he performed on her. In front of her was a two-dimensional facial reconstruction—a detailed sketch—of a woman with shoulder-length dark hair flipped up at the ends. Big eyes. *So young.* The woman appeared to be late teens, perhaps early twenties. If so, the hair was wrong. No teenager would wear her hair in that style.

Not my call.

Keeping her hands in her lap, Amanda leaned forward. The drawing had been done on bristol paper, its surface rough and able to tolerate abundant erasures.

She glanced at McCall. "Was this done from the skull itself?"

"Uh, no." He reached over, shuffled through some pages in the file and pulled out photos of the skull. "These. Why?"

"Photos can distort the skull. If the lighting is wrong, the artist can misinterpret something."

Which could have been her problem with the photo of the firefighter.

"No foolin'?"

Amanda sat back, still refusing to touch the pages. If she did, they'd somehow bond her. "It can happen. The hair is long. Was there hair found near the skull?"

"Yeah. A few strands. We have it in evidence."

Okay. Well, she knew that was right at least. But truly, if they wanted an accurate image, the artist should have been given access to the skull.

"Did you have any hits at all on the drawing?"

"Not a one."

David finally moved from his spot against the wall and looked over her shoulder at the photo. His presence behind her, looming and steady, sent her body mixed messages. Messages that made her think he could handle anything. That the sheer size of him wouldn't relent. Ever.

Her gaze still on the composite, Amanda cleared her throat. "No missing-person reports?"

"Nothing that fits the timeline. Or her age."

"I'm assuming an anthropologist has studied the bones and given an age estimation?"

"Yeah. His notes are in there. He thinks she was early twenties. White."

Amanda dug through the stack of papers, located the anthropologist's notes and began her review, alternately checking the photos of the skull until she'd read the entire report.

David moved back to his spot against the wall, this time crossing his legs at the ankles and sliding his hands into the front pockets of his jeans. "What do you think?"

"About?"

He shrugged. "Anything. The photo, the file."

"The drawing is good. At least from what I can tell. One thing that's bothering me is that the artist didn't have a chance to study the skull. If I'd been assigned this, I would have requested to see the actual skull."

"What would that have done?"

"Sometimes photography distorts images. As I mentioned, the lighting could throw something off. Plus, I'd want to check tissue-depth data and get a frontal and lateral view of the actual skull. Looking at these photos, it's hard to tell how big it is. All of that plays in to the drawing."

And might be why they didn't get any hits on this poor woman. The artist, although quite good, could have missed something simply because he—or she—was not given the actual skull to sketch from. This victim was buried in a field, tossed away like trash, and the drawing might not even be accurate.

Which meant a family somewhere was still wondering where their loved one could be. And that old yearning for her mother kicked in.

At least she knew where her mother was.

She glanced at the drawing again, and McCall jumped all over her. "What if I could get you the skull? I cleared you with the brass already. They're on board with any help you can offer."

Oh, no. She stacked the papers, setting the anthropologist's report on top of the drawing and the photos of the skull so she didn't have to see them. Didn't have to feel the pull of a dead woman begging for justice.

She bit her bottom lip, really digging in because— *what am I doing?*—as hard as she tried to bury the image of that young woman, it was there, flashing in her mind.

"Amanda?"

David's voice. He was still leaning against the wall, once again studying her, trying to read her. Such a lawyer. Damn him for bringing her here. And damn her for allowing him to do it. For making that stupid bet.

She shoved the folder toward Detective McCall. "If I can see the skull itself, I'll do another drawing so you can compare it to what the other artist did. Having the actual skull might make a difference. That's as far as I'll go, Detective."

McCall bobbed his head, smiling as if he'd won the lottery. "No problem. I'll call the lab, tell 'em you'll be over. Anything you can do is great. We—uh—can't pay you, though. You know that, right?"

Now she looked back at David, grinning at him, returning the smugness he'd hit her with earlier. "Detective, it's your lucky day because Mr. Hennings has agreed to pay my fee. So, as soon as you arrange for me to see that skull, I'll get to work and hopefully, we'll find out where this woman belongs."

WANTING TO BE done with the entire situation, Amanda had agreed to go right over to the lab. Like Pamela Hennings, the detective was on a mission. Which meant David had had to drive her home to pick up her tools.

She'd offered to make the trip to the lab herself, but he'd claimed the least he could do was take her and then pick her up again when she'd completed her work.

Considering her nerves and angst over seeing the skull, Amanda didn't argue. Getting behind a wheel while distracted would do her no good.

And here they were. The forensic anthropologist, Paul something—she'd missed his last name thanks to the ringing in her ears—from the county's forensic lab set the skull with its vacant eyes staring straight up at her on the cork ring. She clasped her fingers together, squeezing hard enough that her knuckles protested, and snapped her mind back to her task rather than her nerves.

Dull beige walls and glaring overhead lights added to the sterile, stark atmosphere of the lab and sent a fierce chill snaking from her feet right up into her torso.

She forced her thoughts to the gloved hands positioning the skull inside the ring. Paul tilted it up another half inch so it would rest against the back of the ring, his hands gentle—reverent even—as he completed his task. This person, whose only remains were the skull in front of them, belonged somewhere.

Give her a name. Whether Amanda could complete that task would be determined, and she'd resist pressuring herself. For now, she'd be an artist, studying a subject, keeping her emotional distance, but doing her best to re-create a drawing that might help identify the victim.

Amanda squeezed the pencil in her hand, then relaxed her grip before she broke the thing. "Tell me about her."

"She's in remarkably good shape considering the elements. Based on the teeth and shape of the head, we're estimating her age at early twenties. Maybe late teens. We made a cast of the skull in case of reconstruction, but there's never been one done. Budgeting issues."

"So the cast is already made?"

Ugh. Amanda closed her eyes, thought of her mother and let out a frustrated laugh. It would be so like her mom to throw this project in her path, urging her to press on because, yes, they had a cast already made and she could take possession of it. To at least try the reconstruction. *Nice, Mom.*

"Yes," Paul said. "It's been sitting here waiting for someone to work on her."

Amanda brought her attention back to the skull on the

table. Detective McCall had told her the anthropologist had determined the victim was a white female, and the flatness of the face and the long, thin nasal openings appeared to represent that.

"She's a Caucasoid," Amanda said.

"Yes." He pointed to an area at the back of the skull. "In terms of injuries, there's a small, depressed spot here. Looks like she was hit with something small, but it was a forceful impact. From the shape of the wound, it could have been a hammer. It fractured her skull."

"Poor thing."

"Whoever buried her didn't dig far enough. That's why the dog dug up the skull. We never found the rest of the bones. Animals may have gotten to them and dragged them to another spot. That field is too big to dig up the entire thing looking for her." He held his hand out. "This is what we have."

Amanda's stomach twisted. "If they'd buried her deeper, she might never have been found."

"Probably not."

"I'll do another sketch. See if it's any different than the last one. I brought everything I need." She pointed her pencil at the table. "Can I work here?"

"That's fine. Holler if you need me."

"I will. Thanks."

Paul wandered off to a lab table with a giant microscope on the far side of the room. From the looks of all the equipment stacked on shelves and the shiny tables, he had plenty to do.

She dug her iPod from her purse, shoved the earbuds in place and scrolled her music library. For this, she knew exactly what she needed. A nice classical mix. She poked at the desired playlist, aptly named DESPERATE, and got down to business.

From her briefcase, she pulled a small stack of tracing paper, pencils and her copy of the tissue-depth table for Caucasoids. In the file Paul had left her, she located the life-size frontal and lateral photographs of the skull, set them side by side on her drawing boards and taped the corners. Over the frontal photograph, she placed tracing paper and began outlining the face while Chopin's Nocturne No. 2 softly streamed through her earbuds.

Song after song played as she carefully outlined, corrected and outlined again, taking her time, double-checking each element until it was time to call Paul over to help with tissue-depth markers. Then she'd begin filling in the face, adding the contours of the jaw and cheeks and then the eyebrows and hairline. The tiny details she could add later, but for now she focused on a blueprint to work with. Little by little, each element brought some new aspect to the face, giving it lifelike qualities.

The hair. Detective McCall had told her they'd found a few long, dark hairs with the body. How long, she wasn't sure, but she'd try shoulder length. After outlining the overall shape of the hair and filling in the length based on the hair found at the scene, she added subshapes—loose waves in the front—and then blended dark and light tones for contrast.

Chopin shifted to Beethoven again. Could that be? More than two hours' worth of a playlist? And she still had to fill in the details on the frontal eye–nose area. She stopped shading and glanced around. Paul had moved to a desk in the corner of the lab, clearly unconcerned about the approaching end of the workday.

Amanda sat back and stretched her shoulders as a beautiful young woman with sharp cheekbones and a small button nose stared back at her.

A woman with a hole in the back of her skull.

Stomach knotted, Amanda closed her eyes, forcing herself to detach. To not get sucked into the mind-ravaging warfare this case would create. Her mother had done this work on a regular basis, felt this pull of longing and heartbreak. Amanda supposed a person eventually got used to it. After all, the cause was noble, if not emotionally eviscerating.

She opened her eyes to someone whose family had yet to know her fate. Amanda thought back to those first brutal days without her mom, to the shock and anger and bone-shattering ache that came with sudden and tragic loss.

To this day, she didn't fully understand—probably never would—how her mom had thought suicide was the only option. Obviously, the emotional place her mother had reached was too dark, too painful to find her way free. Her work as a forensic artist probably hadn't helped, but Amanda would never truly know why her mom had done what she did.

At least Amanda had a place to visit. A place to sit and talk and grieve.

A proper grave site.

She ran her fingertips over the edge of the paper she'd sketched on. This woman's family had no answers. Maybe they assumed she was dead. Maybe not. Maybe down deep they held on to hope that she'd walk back into their lives.

And that tore into Amanda like a rusty chain saw. At least she knew her mother was gone.

"I'll bring you home," she said.

Chapter Four

While David stood beside her at the lab table, Amanda stored her drawing boards, wondering what kind of coward buried a woman and walked away, leaving her body to be ravaged by animals and the elements.

She didn't know. Didn't care to. All she knew was sitting in that lab, staring at the skull, sketching based on estimations of tissue depth, she'd experienced a buzz, the high of having the ability to change the course of an investigation—something her mother used to talk about. Amanda had never experienced it. Never quite understood the lure of forensic work. As a kid, she'd thought it all seemed…morbid…and she hadn't grasped what her mother found so intriguing.

Until today.

She thought about her workbench back in the studio where a forensic workshop registration—the one she kept putting off—was weighted down by a giant conch shell she'd found on a trip to Florida when she was nine. A shell her mother had uncovered while wading in the surf.

I know, Mom. I know. Every day she'd been without her mother, she'd never doubted her presence.

Beside her, David stepped closer and she glanced up, their gazes locking because when he pinned those haunting dark blue eyes on her, she couldn't resist the pull of them reaching right in and paralyzing her.

Something she didn't want to feel. With anyone.

"Everything okay?"

"Fine."

Breaking eye contact, she studied the intricate stitching on the shoulder of his jacket and the way the seam fell at exactly the right spot, the cut so perfect for his big body that she realized it might be nice, sometime soon, to have sex.

And wow. What a mess her mind was today. She couldn't deny there was a certain heat between them. From the time she'd opened her front door, she'd felt it. That simmer.

"This project," she said, keeping her voice low so she wouldn't be overheard by Paul, who patiently waited for them to get packed up. "It's complicated."

Receiving her message that she didn't want Paul eavesdropping, David dipped his head lower. "The sketching?"

No. *You.* "It's more than that."

Because with him she felt things, tingly things that made her system hum, gave her a little high. If only she liked that high. Highs and lows, in her experience, shattered lives. But it had been so long since she was beyond her personal safe zone. Since she allowed herself to immediately feel a certain way about a man. About this man. Feelings like that messed with her emotions, brought her to places that terrified her. For ten years she'd worked to not turn into a person tortured by her own emotions.

But David kept surprising her. In a good way. In a way that made something warm and gooey chase away the cold, empty heartbreak she'd felt in the lab. That alone was worth…she didn't know. She'd simply never met anyone who affected her this way. And so quickly.

Needing to get her mind right, she shook her head and stored her iPod in her bag while the quiet in the lab made her arms itch. Too quiet.

"When I was nine," she said, "my mom found a conch shell on the beach in Florida. I have it on my workbench where I can see it every day. It's a paperweight for important things. Right now one of those things is a registration form for a forensic workshop I've been thinking about taking. Pretty high-level stuff. I keep putting off registering."

"Why?"

She gave up on packing her things and faced him. "My mother was a forensic artist."

His eyebrows lifted. "She doesn't do it anymore?"

"She died. Ten years ago. Killed herself."

Wow, Amanda. Totally on a roll here. That miserable fact had only been spoken a handful of times and each time to people who'd proved their loyalty. People she could trust. Apparently, David was now one of those people.

"I can't imagine that. I'm sorry." He stood, unmoving, his face completely neutral, no judgment or horror, just a mild curiosity over whether she'd continue.

"Thank you. But I'm only telling you so you understand. She did a drawing once that helped convict a man of murder. He went to prison for a few years and was later exonerated. She never forgave herself."

His head snapped back and Amanda held up her hand. "She didn't kill herself over it, but it didn't help. My mother always battled depression. She may have been bipolar. I'm not sure. All I know is that there were tremendous highs followed by days she couldn't get out of bed. Work was her savior. She loved making a difference. After that man was exonerated she never did another sketch. Never. I think the loss of her work sent her into a spiral she couldn't come out of."

"And now we're asking you to do a reconstruction."

"Yes."

David cracked his neck, finally showing some indication of his thoughts. "If I'd known, I wouldn't have pressured you."

"I'll do the sculpture," she said.

For a moment he stood in his spot, his face deadpan, not even a flinch as dead air clogged the space between them. "I'm... Wow. What made you change your mind?"

So many things. *My mother. An unidentified dead woman.* She pointed at the image she'd created still sitting on the lab table. "Look at her. She was a beautiful girl. At least from my interpretation."

He reached for the sketch, then stopped, his hand in midair. "May I?"

"Sure."

"Your work is amazing."

He set the image back on the table and angled back to her. "Are you okay?"

"I am. I thought doing the work my mother loved would be this big dramatic scene where I'd be doomed by my own emotional sludge. Turns out, it wasn't so bad. If anything, I got a taste of what my mom went through each time. It's odd, but it was like I had a piece of her right there with me, and that made me come alive a little bit." Oh, what a thing to say to a man she barely knew. "I'm just babbling."

"You're not. I get it." He winced. "Ew. Sorry. No, I don't get it. Not really. What I should have said was I can see where, in a weird way, you'd connect with the work."

All she could do was nod. Talking about this, letting

him dissect her and examine her motivations, wouldn't help her stay detached.

From the work or him.

"If they'll give me the cast of the skull, I'll try it. The reconstruction will be 3-D and have much more detail than my sketch."

Appropriate or not, and definitely not caring that Paul sat just across the room, she stepped closer, slid her hand under David's jacket around his waist and went up on tiptoes to hug him. "Thank you for being a pushy Hennings. After spending the afternoon in the lab, I believe my mother is letting me know it's time I use my talent for more than what I've been doing."

He backed away from the hug and hit her with one of his amazing smiles, not lightning quick but a slow-moving and devastating one that creeped across his face and kicked off a tingle low in her belly.

"Well, we Hennings people like to do our civic duty. How about as a thank you for saving me from my mother's wrath, I buy you dinner one night this week? I can't do it tonight because I'm expected at my mother's."

"You don't have to feed me."

"Yeah, I do. You're doing this for us despite what you've been through. Besides, what I really want is a date with you, so a dinner kills two birds with one stone. As they say."

So slick, this one. Total charmer. And such trouble. But trouble, right now, might be nice. "I think I'd like that."

"Just pull up in front and drop me off," Amanda said as David turned the corner leading to her building.

He double-parked and turned off the engine. "I'll walk you to the door."

"David—"

But he'd already hopped out to get the door for her, which, the girlie-girl buried deep inside admitted, gave her a little thrill.

The door flew open and he waved her out, adding a little bow that made her laugh. How she loved a man who could make her laugh.

"Do you need help getting upstairs?"

"No." She retrieved her briefcase and tote from the backseat. "I'm all set. Thank you, though."

"I'll walk you to the door."

Early-evening darkness had fallen and the streetlamps gave her building a creepy glow. Having been gone all day, she'd neglected to leave any interior lights on. As she approached, she spotted something white stuck to the front door of the building. Vendors were constantly leaving bagged flyers hanging on the door handle, but no one had ever fixed anything to the door. The nerve.

Using the flashlight on her phone, she read the notice—what the heck?—marked City of Chicago, Building Department. Below the letterhead in thick, bold letters the sign left no doubt of the city's request. OFF-LIMITS. DO NOT ENTER.

She tilted her head, pondering this not-so-minor development. It had to be a joke. She glanced back at David a few steps behind her, thinking maybe he'd have... Nah. He hardly knew her well enough to pull this kind of prank. One she wouldn't think funny.

At all.

"What's up?" David asked. "Did you forget something?"

"I..." Stumped, she held her hand to the door. "I don't know. There's a sign from the city telling me not to enter."

Has to be a joke. Right? Because if it wasn't, she had big problems. But why would her building be sealed?

Something odd squeezed her stomach, shooting tension right into her chest. Without access to the building, she'd be locked out of her studio and home. Out of her life.

Frowning, David looked up at the door. "Why?"

As if she knew. She shone the flashlight on the paragraph below the big block letters and scanned it while the pressure in her head skyrocketed and a sharp throb settled behind her eyes. "It says the building must remain vacant until further notice. Are they *kidding* me? My entire life is in this building."

"They must have the wrong location. Plus, they haven't barricaded or padlocked the door."

"What does that mean?"

"It means the building isn't going to collapse. If it was they'd block the entrances. The city can't afford to barricade every door and window on every building. If the problem is due to contaminants and the building won't collapse, they do signage. Which they've done, so don't panic. Call your landlord and find out what's happening."

Yes. The landlord. The city had to have contacted him. Quickly, she scrolled through her contacts and found the number. "I've been trying to convince him to apply for landmark status on this building. And they want to *condemn* it?"

The phone rang a third time and Amanda grunted. "He never answers when I call." She left a voice mail explaining the situation, then disconnected. "I'm calling the building department."

"You can try, but it's after five. They're probably gone for the day."

She'd try anyway. Couldn't hurt. Not wanting to deal with searching for the number on her phone, she dialed information and was connected to the city's building department, where—yes—she received a recorded message telling her the office was indeed closed.

Terrific. She tapped the screen and scrunched her eyes closed. *Stay calm. Just a mix-up.*

Opening her eyes, she once again read the sign as her thoughts raced. *Work. Clothes. Checkbook.* Her damned allergy medicine. Everything was inside.

Forget calm.

Forget not panicking.

All at once, her body buzzed and throbbed and itched and all this emotional garbage was so not good for her, the woman who kept her life in a constant state of neither ups nor downs. Well, this was one heck of a down. "I don't know what to do. My clothes are all in there!" She flapped her arms. "My *work* is in there."

"Hang tight." David retreated a few steps and stared up at the darkened building, obviously formulating some kind of plan. "There's a back door, right?"

"Yes."

"We're going in the back."

"The sign says…"

"Yeah, but you just said you don't have any clothes. We'll sneak in the back door, hope we don't get caught and you pack up whatever you need for a few days until this gets hashed out."

Without the studio, she couldn't work. Without work, she couldn't earn. Her draining checkbook—the one inside the no-access building—filled her mind. "I lease a storage unit, but there's not enough room for me to work in there. I have a sculpture to finish!"

David slid the tote and her briefcase off her shoulders, walked back to his SUV and stowed them. "I've got this. My condo is still being renovated. You can use one of the bedrooms that's not being worked on. I'll put you in the guest room."

Amanda's head dipped forward. "You're letting me turn your condo into a studio?"

"Why not? The place is empty. You might as well use it until I can move in." He waved his hand at the building. "This'll get straightened out in a few days and you can move back here. No problem." He inched closer and grabbed both her hands. "We've got this. We'll load as much as we can and take it over to the condo."

The idea might not be a bad one. It might, in fact, be a short-term solution. "We can use my car also."

"Good. Then we'll get you set up in a hotel for the night. Is that a plan?"

"David Hennings, I could love you."

He threw his hands up, grinning at her. "Let's not get crazy now or you might be stuck with me."

At the moment, as she thought about every minute she'd spent with this man since he'd walked into her studio earlier that day, being stuck with him might not be a bad thing. She grabbed hold of his jacket, the leather Belstaff she loved so much, and dragged him closer. Going up on tiptoes, she kissed him. And it wasn't one those tentative let's-test-this kisses where they sort of eased into it. This one left nothing on the table. Tongues were involved.

And *she'd* started it. Total insanity.

But he certainly wasn't rejecting her. He made it worth her while by wrapping his arm around her and pulling her right up against him. A few seconds later a bulge at his crotch area announced itself in a truly obvious way, and her heart slammed. What he wanted couldn't have been clearer. No doubt. At all.

"Dude," a guy passing by said. "Lucky dog."

David pulled back and his amazing lips tilted into a wicked grin. "Dude," he said, "don't I know it?"

DAVID SET THE last box of supplies they'd taken from Amanda's in his extra bedroom and did a quick survey of the place. The walls were still unpainted and the dry-wall dust left a weird coating on the floors. For what she needed, it would do. If the dust didn't give her an asthma attack. "We'll run out tonight and get you a couple of tables to set up. It won't be perfect, but this is triage."

"Yes. Triage. I'm hoping whatever the mix-up is will be taken care of tomorrow and I can move back home."

Having dealt with bureaucratic red tape, David wasn't feeling hopeful. Miracles could happen, he supposed.

She checked her watch. "It's only six. I can still hit the office supply store for the tables. You said you have dinner at your mom's tonight. Go. You don't have to do this with me."

Whatever he expected her to say, that wasn't it. And yeah, part of him was insulted that she thought he'd leave her to handle this mess on her own. He propped his hands on his hips and shook his head. "My mother raised me better than that. We'll go get the tables and then I'll head out. I'll still be on time."

If he did ninety on the Eisenhower and didn't shower before dinner.

"Whoa," she said. "Don't be mad. Please."

"I'm not mad." He held up a hand. "Wait. Yeah. Maybe I am. I don't know what kind of men you've had in your life, but I'm not about to leave you alone with this."

"I'm sorry. I didn't mean…" She closed her eyes, shook her head. "I'm sorry. I'm not used to the help. I just don't want to be a problem."

"You're not. Let's get you tables. On the way, I'll make

some calls. See if any of my contacts know anyone in the city's building department. If that doesn't work, I'll pull out the big guns."

"The big guns?"

"My mother."

Amanda laughed. At least something made her laugh.

"Don't laugh. Do you know how many people in this town owe my mother a favor? She's sat on the board of every major charity. The mayor takes her calls on a regular basis. Favors don't come cheap, though. She'll help us, but if she does, she'll owe someone and I don't like putting her in that position. I could also ask my sister for help. She'll *love* that."

Wait, had he *ever* asked Penny for help? Most likely he hadn't. It would have become a weapon between them. The fact that their relationship had reached that point didn't say anything good about either of them.

"Why?"

"We…uh…don't get along. We're basically oil and water."

Because of the lack of chairs, Amanda leaned against the wall. "She must have had a hand in it."

"We should be ashamed of ourselves."

"You're siblings. There's bound to be some infighting."

"What about you? Brothers or sisters?"

"Two stepbrothers," she said. "My dad remarried five years ago."

"Was that hard?"

She scooped her water bottle from her giant purse and swigged. "No. And I wonder about that. Shouldn't it have been rough for me to see my father happy with someone else?"

"From what you've said—and I mean no disrespect

here—life with your mom wasn't easy. You know it, and your dad would definitely have known it. What's wrong with wanting someone you love to be happy?"

"I guess. In the beginning I was afraid it meant something. That somehow I was wrong for wanting my father to have a quiet—and stable—life."

"I'll tell ya, you worry a lot."

"I do. I'm always thinking. It's maddening."

He wandered over to her. "I can help with that."

She rolled her eyes but laughed. God, he loved to make her laugh. It was like every exceptional thing that had ever happened to him in one giant sound.

"I'm serious," he said. "I think a lot, too, but not like you. I don't worry like you do. It's gonna be what it's gonna be. Me worrying about it won't help. It's paying interest on a debt I don't owe. Who needs that?"

She cocked her head. Considered that. "That's a good way to think about it. Thank you."

"Amanda LeBlanc, you need fun in your life."

"I have fun in my life."

"Not my kind of fun. The kind of fun that has you on the back of a motorcycle tearing down country roads. Girl, you need to let go once in a while. Preferably with me."

"Promises, promises."

"Just take a chance. You'll see." He tugged on the end of her hair. "Now we need to go before I'm late for dinner and my mother murders me."

Chapter Five

Some things in life were out of David's control. Rainy days, crabby clients, the plague.

Family dinners.

He paused at the base of the stairs and listened to the chatter coming from the dining room. *The gang's all here.* Of course, he was late.

Blame it on his mother, who'd hooked him into this cold-case business. Even though Amanda LeBlanc had turned out to be beautiful—and alluring, smart, talented and *sexy* as hell—he'd still spent the better part of his day working on his mom's project.

"Where's *David*?" he heard Penny ask from the other room.

His sister had a snarky tone that hit his ears like nails fired from a gun and he bit down, already trying to control his rising temper. *Breathe, dude.* He inhaled, held his breath for a few seconds and then slowly let it out.

"Upstairs," Zac said. "He walked in with us. He's getting cleaned up."

"He's late for dinner and he didn't even need to drive anywhere?"

Holy hell, his sister made him nuts. From the time she was seven years old and wrapping everyone around her finger, getting him and Zac in trouble all the time, he'd learned to accept her power over this family. But sometimes it ate him raw. Time to break this up. He swung around the staircase and marched into the dining room, where his dad was just landing in his normal spot at the head of the table. His mom would sit at the opposite end by the windows, and David would sit to her right. From there, he wasn't sure. With Zac and Penny having significant others now, the seating arrangements could have changed. Another reminder of how long he'd been away. Penny stood at the sideboard pouring a glass of wine and Russ stood next to her.

"I'm right here," David said. "Sorry I'm late."

"Hey," Zac said, holding a chair for Emma, who looked pretty in one of those wrap dresses that were suddenly back in style. "No prob. I told them you were late getting back."

David looked over at Penny, who had her big blue eyes pinned to him. "I heard," he said.

"Oh, puh-lease. All I said was you were late and didn't have to drive anywhere. That's it."

She jammed the stopper on the wine decanter with enough force the thing should have splintered. But, as usual, no one said anything about the dramatics.

He'd be the bigger person and not take the Penny bait. Regardless of whose fault it was, their every argument started this way. One of them said something that, on the surface, seemed harmless but underneath held enough venom to kill an elephant. He wasn't going there. He'd promised Mom—and himself—he'd find a way to mend things with his sister.

He walked over and shook hands with Penny's boyfriend. "Russ, good to see you."

"Hey, Dave."

The FBI agent, still in his suit from work, his dark

hair neatly groomed, stayed cool. He'd been that way the first time they'd met in person the week prior. Not surprising, considering that Penny had probably filled him in on their constant arguing. It didn't matter. As he should be, Russ was Team Penny, and David respected that. Loyalty in a relationship, at least in David's mind, could make or break things.

He turned to Penny and touched her arm. "I don't want to fight with you."

Hitting him with direct suspicion, she narrowed those piercing blue eyes, but he stayed quiet, refusing to start a war.

Finally, she nodded. "Me, neither. Mom is really excited about this dinner. Let's not ruin it."

"A truce," Russ said. "Someone alert the media."

Zac took his seat next to Emma. "Nice."

Russ laughed. "You think I'm kidding?"

Penny flapped her hands. "Okay, *Russell*. Knock it off."

Waiting to see where Penny and Russ would land, David stood behind his chair. Russ moved to the opposite side, next to Emma and facing Penny. That meant David would be in his normal spot by Mom with Penny on his opposite side.

"Hey, Dad," he said.

"Son, how was your day?"

Ha. That was a loaded question. "Busy."

The table was packed with food, his favorite roast, a ham—because apparently the roast wasn't enough—a huge dish of twice-baked potatoes, salad and some kind of vegetable dish. Never a fan of vegetables, he'd try it, but chances were it wouldn't work for him. The aroma of the meat mixed with spices from the vegetables, and his stomach rumbled. No lunch. He'd forgotten. What with the hotness of Amanda LeBlanc distracting him.

He took his seat and dropped his napkin into his lap.

"Hellooo, my darlings." Mom swung into the room, her hair tucked behind her ears and a fresh face of makeup. "How are we all tonight?"

A variety of responses sounded as his mother worked her way around the table, bending low to kiss each of them on the cheek. At least until she got to David, who was still dressed, as she'd put it that morning, like a prison escapee.

It wouldn't make her happy, but he'd already gotten home late, and another fifteen minutes to shower and change would have thrown off her carefully crafted schedule.

"Oh, David," his mother said. "Really?"

Dad held his hands up. "Already? What is it?"

"She's mad I'm wearing jeans."

Mom smacked his shoulder and moved to her seat. "I'm not *mad.*"

"Yeah, you are. And I'm sorry. I was running around working on your project all afternoon. My choice was to shower, change and let the food get cold or just wash up quick. I chose to not ruin your meal."

"You were doomed either way," Zac said.

"Amen, brother."

Penny passed the dinner rolls without snagging one. "What project?"

"Well," Mom said, "I hope it's good news."

David took two rolls and passed the basket to Mom. "Eh. Halfway. I got her to talk to the detective. She spent all afternoon working on a new drawing. You're going to owe her big for that alone, but she's agreed to do your reconstruction. And, oh yeah, while she was at the lab viewing the skull, the building she lives and works out of got condemned."

Clothing issue already forgotten, Mom's jaw dropped. *"Condemned?"*

"It has to be a mistake. The place, for as old as it is, is in great shape. Anyway, I set her up in my condo so she has a place to work. She's staying in a hotel until it gets sorted out."

"What project?" Penny repeated.

Mom passed the basket of rolls on. "David is helping me on another cold case."

From the other end of the table, Dad coughed up whatever he was drinking. Russ shot out of his chair and slapped Dad's back a few times.

"Are you all right, dear?" Mom asked, perfectly calm, and David had to laugh.

Dad didn't look all right. Not with the red cheeks that probably had nothing to do with the coughing fit. "I'm fine. Is this the cold case you and Irene eavesdropped on last night? You're not volunteering us again, are you?"

"No. Of course not. I spoke to Irene this morning. They're willing to help. So David is handling it this time."

What now? David stabbed his fork into a couple of slices of roast and then grabbed some ham. "Uh, no, I'm not. I told you I'd do this one thing. That's it. From here on out it's someone else's deal. I'm not an investigator and I'm damned sure not a criminal attorney."

The minute—no, second, *milli*second—it left his mouth, he regretted it. Replaying it in his mind, he knew it sounded bad. As if he was once again singling himself out from his family. Penny had never been one to let that go. And then Dad and Zac would take her side and Mom would try to stay neutral, but that never worked because staying neutral meant she wasn't on either side. Which made David the one standing alone, irritated and feeling childish.

But he'd nix it straight away. "I didn't mean—"

"Yes, *David*," Penny drawled, "we're aware that you chose civil law. What's the matter? Bored? Coming to the dark side?"

"Penny," Russ said, his voice tinged with warning.

David breathed in and held his hand up. "It's okay. That sounded bad. I was about to say I didn't mean it the way it sounded."

Penny sawed at the roast on her plate. "Well, that'd be a first, wouldn't it?"

So much for the truce. His plan for making nice with his sister had been an epic fail. But this was years of damage done by the two of them and he'd take his share of the responsibility. He'd had his own demons to battle—petty jealousy, for one. Penny was not only the baby, but also the only girl, so she basically got away with murder. She'd also become the golden child their father could groom into taking over the firm. A role David had rejected and shouldn't have been bothered by, but he'd allowed it to intensify his resentment of his sister. At least until recently when he'd realized it wasn't Penny's role at the firm he envied, but their father's approval.

And now it needed to stop.

David stood, tossed his napkin onto the table and tugged his sister's jacket sleeve. "Come with me."

"No."

"We need to talk."

"I'm eating."

"I know. We need to talk. Now."

"No, David. I'm hungry and this food will get cold."

Russ jerked his head sideways. "Penny."

Points to him for trying to get his girlfriend to co-operate.

"Whatever it is, David, we can talk here."

Great. She wanted to do it in front of everyone. Whatever. "Fine. We'll talk here. I'm home now. Okay? Moved all the way back here from Boston because guess what? It would be nice to feel like a part of this family."

"And whose fault—"

"My fault. But you helped me out the door. I'll own my part, but you're not exactly easy. Now, though? I'm tired of fighting. I want my sister back. But you, you're like a...a panther...ready to pounce on every damned thing I say and it wears me the hell out. Every time we're together I have to mentally psyche myself up for it. Let's forget the stupidity and figure out how to get along."

Any chatter going on stopped. Zac sighed, grabbed a roll out of the basket in front of him, tore it in two and handed half to Emma. "Eat. You'll need your strength."

And Emma, God bless her, laughed.

Apparently horrified over her outburst, she slapped her hand over her mouth, forgetting, of course, about the roll, and wound up bouncing it off her nose.

Everyone, including David, cracked up. Who knew sweet, levelheaded Emma had comedic timing?

"Mrs. Hennings," she said, "I'm so sorry."

But Mom laughed right along with them. "Oh, Emma, not at all. Thank you for the diversion." She swung her finger between David and Penny. "Please compromise. David, let her eat and then the two of you can go in the study and work this out. Kill each other if you must, but do not ruin my meal."

"Wow, Mom," Zac said.

"You." She poked her finger at him. "Hush."

David took his seat again, flattened his napkin in his

lap and started shoveling food because Emma wasn't the only one who'd need strength.

"Can we talk about this cold case?" Dad asked. "Is it that skull you told me about last night?"

Mom set her fork down and sat back in her chair. "Yes. The skull. You said your investigators were busy and David is bored. He agreed to do it."

Swallowing the mound of food in his mouth, David turned to his father. "Now, *that's* funny. I told her I'd talk to the sculptor. That's all."

His mother. Unbelievable. David slammed the full glass of water in front of him. As soon as dessert was cleared and he had his chat with Penny, he was going to bed. Crazy, exhausting day.

Penny gripped his sleeve and he glanced down. Still hanging on, she leaned over. "I'm sorry. I don't want to fight anymore, either. I'll try. I promise."

"Thank you. By the way—" he leaned closer, bumping her shoulder "—I love you. I haven't said that enough. You drive me nuts, but I do love you."

"Huh. You really are full of surprises tonight."

"Penny," Russ said.

But his sister kept her gaze focused on David and smiled up at him. "I love you, too. And I'm glad you're back. Even if you drive me nuts, too."

AT TEN THE next morning, accompanied by Detective McCall and David, Amanda again entered the county forensic lab, but unlike the day before, she knew what to expect from this particular visit. Yesterday, she'd been determined to draw the sketch and be done with her end of this bargain. At least until she'd set eyes on the actual skull. She'd seen human skulls before in classes and workshops, but in those instances, the experience was more clinical. An artist studying a subject. This time, when she looked at the skull, studied the wound on the back of it, she imagined a young woman, someone younger than herself, getting her head bashed.

And that, she almost couldn't stand. Her death had most likely been fast, but no one should suffer the violence surrounding it. Particularly a twenty-year-old woman.

Paul, the forensic anthropologist she'd met yesterday, glanced over, spotted them and set aside some bones he'd been working with. His lips lifted into a small smile. "Good to see you back."

Amanda nodded. "Hi, Paul." She turned to David. "This is David Hennings, and I think you know Detective McCall."

The men exchanged hellos as Paul led them to the metal table Amanda had worked at the day before. On top sat a box with a manila folder next to it. Amanda assumed that would be the required documentation and copies of any pertinent information she would need to sign for.

Detective McCall walked to the opposite side and shuffled through the folder. "It's all here?"

"Far as I know." Paul faced Amanda. "We gave you copies of photos of where the body was found, the detective's notes, the anthropologist's report and the dentist's report. We just need you to sign everything out."

McCall handed one of the sheets over and Amanda perused it. At the very top it read Forensic Art Activity Report and below that was written the name of the law-enforcement division she'd be working with. In this case, Special Crimes. Whatever that meant. Below that were boxes asking for administrative details of the case, the date, who requested the work to be done, the case number and so on. The next larger section pertained to the examination and analysis portion of the investigation. That section requested everything from the race and sex of the victim to the clothing and accessories that may have accompanied the body. Sadly, in this case, Amanda would only be taking the skull cast and copies from the case file.

She read through the file quickly, then glanced at the box where the plaster cast waited for her to take possession. *What am I doing?* Last night she'd been so sure this was the right decision, but once she signed this paperwork she was in it. Knee-deep, which was terrifying. Sure, she could always back out, tell the detective she'd tried but couldn't do it. She wasn't on their payroll and wouldn't be taking taxpayer dollars, but she'd given her word. If she backed out, she'd disappoint all parties.

And commitment meant something.

I'm stuck. She let out a small breath and glanced at the box again. Beside her, David angled toward her and she could feel that penetrating gaze reading her.

"Uh, fellas," he said, "wanna give us a minute?"

Thank you.

After a short pause, McCall nodded. "No problem."

Amanda waited for Paul and the detective to reach the far side of the room where Paul had been working when they'd first arrived.

She set the pen on the table and David puckered his lips slightly before shifting an inch closer and nudging her with his elbow. "Second thoughts?"

"Nerves."

"You're about to take possession of a skull with the intent of reconstructing it and helping identify a murder victim. I'd say feeling nervous is reasonable."

To him maybe. To her it brought every fear, all those years of wondering what her mother's life had been like, the emotional toll, bubbling up. Since her mother's death, she'd fought the negativity, fought the desire to try forensic work, fought the urge to make a difference because somewhere down deep, she knew, it would be all-consuming. The highs and lows that came with this type of work would be constant. All-consuming meant winding up like her mother.

That, she would not do.

"Look," he said, "if you don't want to do this, we'll walk out of here. Personally, I think you're intrigued by this project. You did the sketch hoping that would be enough. Then you saw the sketch and decided to do the reconstruction. At each juncture you've tried to talk yourself out of this. Maybe that's your pattern, this going back and forth. I don't know. Doesn't really matter. But if you leave without that skull, you'll always wonder. And that's a rotten way to live."

She tapped her fingers against the table, considering the options. What if she pulled it off? What if she took this skull back to her studio—well, David's condo, which was her makeshift studio—completed the reconstruction and was able to help them identify the woman?

Really, that should be her only thought right now. Rather than worrying about her own emotional stability, she should focus on the victim. On bringing this woman home and giving her family answers.

She picked up the pen, rolled it between her fingers—*do it*—and scribbled her name on the form. Then she shoved it as far across the table as she could, hoping it would keep her from changing her mind and ripping the thing up.

David laughed. "You're cute, Amanda."

McCall and Paul wandered back over. Paul took possession of the form—*it's done now*—and slid the box in front of her.

"We packed it good to protect it." He tapped the top of the box. "It's only a cast, but she's been here a while. Take good care of her."

Amanda grasped the box, her fingers wrapping around the edges as she slid it toward her. "I will. She'll be safe with me."

Chapter Six

At the condo, David placed the box containing the skull cast on one of the folding tables they'd set up the night before. He wasn't sure where Amanda would want it positioned but figured his best option was to let her deal with it in her own way. Give her some space.

Later.

Right now he'd like to take her to lunch, maybe get her mind off the fact that the city still hadn't returned her landlord's calls.

David had pretty much decided to give the landlord until the end of the day to make something happen. After that, he'd work his own contacts to speed things up.

"I have an idea," he said.

"What's that?"

"I have a buddy. Brian Dyce. His mom was at the fund-raiser you attended the other night."

"She sat at my table. Lovely woman. You're friends with her son?"

"We went to grammar school together. That was before his parents started the youth center and his father became a bigwig. If you have time, I'll take you to lunch now and then we could swing by the center. Show them your sketch. It's a long shot, but they know people at the area shelters. Maybe someone will recognize the woman."

Amanda poked him in the chest. "I like it. Good thinking."

"Eh. I can't take all the credit. My mother said she paved the way."

He cocked his arm out and she glanced down, a slow smile drifting across her face. After that poke to the chest, he didn't think linking her arm with his would be a hardship. Except waiting for her to respond could be a slow, paralyzing rejection and he couldn't seem to move his arm.

When she finally grabbed hold, his stomach unclenched enough that he might actually be able to put food in it.

It'd been months—many—since he'd walked arm in arm with a woman. In Boston, he'd kept to himself, dating occasionally but not anyone steady. Mostly, dating was about sex and getting it and he had a knack for finding just the right women. Ones who, like him, wanted a good time and would treat the person well when they were together. All in all, not a bad life. No strings, no responsibilities, no hassles.

Now, with Amanda's arm tucked in his, it made him think the life he'd left in Boston wasn't so great. It had worked then. Got him through. Being home, though, seeing his younger sister and brother in relationships and on their way to settling down made him the only one without a significant other at the dinner table, and he wasn't sure he liked that.

"Phew," he cracked. "Scared me there."

"I can't imagine anything scares you."

"A lot of things scare me," he said. "I'm not about to admit them, though."

"Except your mother."

He laughed. "Yeah. That one I'll own. *Everyone* is afraid of her."

"I like you, David Hennings."

Good to know. Because he liked her, too.

MRS. DYCE CHARGED into the lobby of the youth center, her conservative heels clicking against the tile and her face lit up like a kid's at Christmas. She wrapped David in a hug that should have broken his spine. The woman was a good seven inches smaller than him, but she had one hell of a grip.

"It's so wonderful to see you." She released him but still held on to his arms. "Have you seen Brian? He stopped over the other night and mentioned he'd called you."

In the years David had been acquainted with this family, certain things never changed. Mrs. Dyce's energy for one. Still rail thin, she moved quickly, all the time, and she never said just one thing. It was always a rush of thoughts that flew. Some would call her impulsive, but that, in his opinion, didn't fit. She had stamina and a brain that operated on rapid-fire 100 percent of the time.

"Yep. Getting together next weekend. We got caught up on the phone, though."

"Good."

She stepped back and held her hand to Amanda. "How nice to see you again, Amanda. Welcome. Come back to my office and we'll talk."

He gestured Amanda ahead of him and followed her down the long hallway lined with doors on each side. The walls had been painted a sandy beige rather than the stark white they'd been the last time David visited. The beige was better. Warmer. More welcoming.

Ahead of him, Amanda's head swung back and forth

as she took in the various artwork along the way. Nothing fancy or overdone, but enough to give the corridor some life.

Near the end of the hallway, Mrs. Dyce hung a right into her office and waved them to the guest chairs in front of her desk. She tucked her hair—was it more red than the last time he'd seen her?—behind her ears and took a seat behind the desk. Like his mother, she was high profile in the city and often wound up in the local media. With that came pressure to look a certain way, and Mrs. Dyce took that seriously. She'd definitely had a face-lift recently, because her skin was as smooth as a baby's bottom, and at her age, that just wasn't possible. But she looked healthy and elegant and camera ready.

She closed an open file on her desk and set it aside, giving them her complete attention. "Tell me why you're here." She leveled one of her playful smiles on him. "Other than you missed me dragging you around by your ear."

Amanda slid him a pointed look. Together, these two women would be a handful. Add them to the list of things he feared. He smacked his hands together. "Anyway..."

Mrs. Dyce laughed. "Yes. *Anyway.*"

David held up the large envelope containing extra copies of the sketch. "I think my mom mentioned Amanda is helping the police on a cold case."

"It came up when I spoke to her yesterday. Something about an unidentified skull."

"Yes, ma'am. Amanda has completed a composite image of what the victim might look like. She's also doing a reconstruction."

If Mrs. Dyce's eyebrows could move, they would have, but the overall effect was her eyes widening. "A *recon-*

struction." She drew out the word. "As in you'll re-create the face?"

Amanda nodded. "Yes, ma'am."

"Fascinating. How wonderful."

David pushed one of the copies of the sketch across the table. "This is Amanda's rendering of what the person may have looked like. Do you think you could show it to Mr. Dyce or some of your contacts at the shelters? Maybe someone saw her. It's a long shot, but…"

She kept her eyes on David as she leaned forward to glance at the sketch. "Absolutely. But five years is a long time, David. Thousands of people go through city shelters. I know just from the number of kids I see here every day how hard it is to remember everyone."

"But it's worth a try, right?"

"It's always worth a try. Who knows? With everyone Mr. Dyce knows and my contacts, maybe someone will recognize her." She picked up the sketch and studied it for a minute, and her lips parted slightly. She looked back at Amanda. "You drew this? It's quite good."

"I did. I had the skull to work from. It won't be exact, but I'm hoping it's close. The real details will come when I do the reconstruction. I like to think of the sketch as the blueprint."

"Well, it's an amazing blueprint. I'd love to see some of your work. Maybe we could set something up?"

"I'd like that." She dug in her purse for a card and handed it over. "Call me anytime. I could bring you some things to look at."

"Wonderful."

Seeing as they'd done what they came to do—and even got Amanda a potential client as a bonus—David stood. "We won't keep you."

He held his hand out, helping Amanda from the chair,

and the normalcy of it, the feel of her skin against his—he liked it. So he held on, linking his fingers with hers.

Taking note of the gesture, Mrs. Dyce gave him a wry smile. "Mr. Dyce will be sorry he missed you. He's out at a meeting."

"Tell him congratulations on the presidential appointment. What an honor after all the work you have done."

In Chicago, the Dyce name was known for raising awareness of gang and gun violence. When they organized rallies, thousands flooded the streets to hear Mr. Dyce speak. And now those years of work had made him a household name in Washington and grabbed the attention of the president.

"I will. He's thrilled. And anxious to make a difference not just here, but across the country."

David grinned. "Spoken like a true politician's wife."

"Young man, I can still drag you around by your ear."

He leaned down and pecked her on the cheek. "I know. Forgive me."

"It's good to see you. Don't be a stranger." She waved them out. "Get out of here, you two. Go make a difference."

SITTING IN THE front passenger seat of David's SUV, Amanda studied his condo building, a four-story brick structure that, if she guessed correctly, dated back to the early 1900s. Given David's reaction to the building she lived in—the condemned one—his choice of home came as no surprise. The man had a thing for history and classic architecture. This building's aged brick and avant-garde rounded edges reflected both.

"I love your building," she said. "I didn't get a chance to tell you that last night."

His beautiful mouth with those totally kissable full

lips twisted into a smile. "Thanks. Before I even saw the inside, I wanted to live here. It's a total throwback."

"That's how I felt about my place."

"Speaking of which—"

"No news from my landlord."

David shook his head. "If you don't hear anything by the end of the day, I'll get on it. See if I can scare up any info. For now," he held a key up, "here's my extra key for you. Come and go as you please."

Her fingers brushed his as she wrapped her hand around the dangling key and his sultry dark blue eyes bore right into her, leaving her body tense but a little gooey all at the same time.

Where should she take this?

Easily she could invite him inside and they could pull up a couple of the folding chairs they'd bought the night before and talk. And…um…other things.

She bit her bottom lip and thought about those other things and her cheeks fired.

"Damn, you're gorgeous," he said.

"Thank you. But, so help me, David, if you come inside I won't get any work done."

At that, he laughed. He leaned over and brushed his fingers down the side of her face, slowly moving over the curve of her cheek, along her jaw, to her mouth, where he ran the pad of his thumb over her lips. "If that's meant to scare me off, it's not working."

She dipped her head and rubbed her cheek along his fingertips. "It is your condo. I have no right to tell you when you can be here."

But his being there, with the energy between them, would lead to things. Things she wasn't ready for. The man unnerved her and it felt like too much too soon. No matter what, too much too soon was never good. *Safe zone*. That was where she needed to stay. No highs or lows. Particularly now with her home and studio situation leaving her life in flux.

Now she'd send him on his way. Even if her hormones didn't like it.

"I'm not staying," he said. "In case you were wondering. I have a contractor waiting on me at my office."

She pushed the door open but didn't move. A gust of wind blew her hair into her face and she shoved it back. "Okay."

"Unless you want me to."

"That's the problem."

"What?"

She sighed and rested her head back against the seat. "I really sort of stink at relationships. I like you. There's a vibe that makes me want you close. I'm a girl used to being on her own, so I'm confused by it."

He pulled a face, flopping his lower lip out. "We're getting acquainted. Just let it happen. Why do you have to feel a certain way right now?"

"Because loss isn't easy for me." And once again, diarrhea of the mouth around him. *Loss isn't easy?* Goodness, if that didn't send the man running, she might have to marry him. "I'm…"

He held up his hands. "You're careful. I get it."

"But?"

"If you never took a chance on anyone or anything, what fun is that? Are you going to live your life in neutral?"

Another blast of wind whipped through the open door and she shivered. At the cold and his colossal nerve. "I don't live my life in neutral."

"When was the last time you went on a date?"

"Two weeks ago."

His head dipped forward. "Really?"

Take that, fella. "Yes. I date. I happen to be an attractive woman."

"Believe me, I know. Let me rephrase."

"Says the lawyer."

A fast smile lit his face. "And she's quick on her feet, too. When's the last time you had a relationship? Not just casual."

Easy question. There had only been a handful of guys she deemed relationship material. Each of them heartbreaking and enough to make her not want to play in that sandbox. "Three years. And I've been happy."

"But you just told me you're not sure how you feel. I think whatever you're feeling now is different in some way. It's not the status quo for you. Unless you make a habit of telling men you want them close. In which case, most men would willingly oblige and you'd have a revolving door."

For sure, the man had a sharp tongue. And she now had a taste of what life must be like between him and his sister. "Did you really just say that to me?"

"Yeah. I did. Not that I believe it. My point is whatever this is between us, it's not the norm for you. You told me that. It's not for me, either. Last girlfriend I had drove me insane. That was a year ago and I've been fine on my own. But now?" He shrugged. "I like being around you. Why can't we let things roll? See where it goes?"

"Because then I'd have to trust that you won't break my heart. That the highs won't be too high and the lows too low."

Again he ran his fingers under her chin, this time tipping her head back. "Your theory is if you go through life without heartbreak you won't suffer the lows. What about never having the highs, either? If you ask me, going through life in neutral kinda stinks."

Sure it did. She cocked her head, away from his fingers, and he took the hint, dropping his hand.

"David, my mom had highs and lows all the time. It was horrible. For her and for us. There was no middle ground. No *neutral*. I don't need that stress. I'm okay with my life. I'm not unhappy. I'm not lonely. I take care of myself. Independently." She waved her hand. "Neutral, as you put it, isn't so bad."

"But what if there's something better than neutral?"

"Is that what you think this is?"

He shrugged. "Don't know. But what if it can be? I wouldn't want you constantly keeping me at a distance because you're afraid of getting hurt. Sitting here, I know before I even leave that I want to see you tomorrow. I like that kind of fire. I want to run headfirst into it. You'd have to want to do it with me, though."

She gazed up at him, her eyes locked on his, the intensity ripping her body in two. Why did everything he said make sense when it was the dead last thing she wanted? This was the battle. To stay steady and not be like her mother. Not allow her emotions to dictate her actions.

But, heaven help her, she wanted to kiss this man in the worst way. Taste his lips, draw his breath, feel his skin against hers.

"Come on, Amanda, let loose a little."

"I hate you, David Hennings."

"I know."

Moving quickly, he leaned over the console and kissed her.

She reached up, squeezed the soft leather of his jacket and breathed in his musky and ultra-male scent while he drove his free hand through her hair and went crazy on her lips, nipping and licking. She moaned softly, the sound low in her throat sparking her brain to overload.

So hot. So…so…astonishing.

Slow it down. That was what she needed. She slid her hand back down his shoulder, softened the kiss and dropped short, quick pecks on his lips, most definitely putting the brakes on.

He eased back, dotted kisses along her jaw and grinned. "Well, that was…electrifying. You may have noticed."

"I did notice. Too much so for sitting in your car in the middle of the day."

He shrugged. "I didn't mind so much. Any time you want to try again, I'm ready, willing and very able."

Coming from the family he did, he had clearly never had a problem with confidence. And without a doubt, he excelled at the art of kissing.

"David, I don't know quite what to do with you."

"I can make a few suggestions."

She snorted. "You are *such* a man."

"Thank you."

Finally, she laughed, the angst from a second ago peeling away. She waggled her fingers between them. "You're good at this, aren't you?"

"Uh…"

"Not the kissing."

"Ouch."

"No! You're definitely good at that, too. Trust me."

Feigning effort, he wiped his brow. "Phew."

She grabbed the edge of his unzipped jacket and balled it in her hand. "I was talking about defusing tension. I was embarrassed and you took care of it. Lickety-split, bam."

He pulled her close again and kissed her. Softly this

time, barely a brush of their lips. Too easy. Natural. And something she wanted more of.

Often.

"I need to go," he said. "My contractor is waiting on me. Think about what I said. I plan on sweeping you off your feet."

Chapter Seven

Midmorning the following day, David stood in the middle of his empty living room while Lexi waxed poetic about the subtleties of the dark brown paint sample she'd sloshed onto his wall. It had some fancy name, but really, all he saw was brown.

"Lexi, it's brown."

"It's not brown. This is more than brown. It has flecks of silver in it. This screams sophisticated. It would be perfect with those steel tables I showed you."

"Amanda!" David called. A minute later she poked her head out of the bedroom where she'd set up her temporary studio. She must have had a rough night because she appeared pale, more drawn than yesterday, and it only accentuated the dark rings under her eyes. "What do you think of this brown?"

"I like it."

"Why?"

"It's masculine and neutral at the same time. Purple, orange and yellow would work well with it. Red also."

Huh. What the hell did he know? "Okay. Thanks."

Before Amanda disappeared again, Lexi held up her hand. "What's happening with your building?"

"Not sure yet. My landlord is working on it."

David cocked his head sideways, still studying the

brown. "My sister found us someone in the building department. I'm waiting for a call back from the guy." He waved at the brown sample. "This is fine, I guess."

"If you don't like it, we can try something else. But I think when you see the entire room with it, you'll love it. Plus, your mom suggested it."

"Oh, then by all means, let's go with it."

Because it would be so much easier than dealing with his mother questioning why he didn't like the color she'd picked.

Lexi laughed. "She'll be thrilled. I'm heading over there now. She's redoing your father's study."

"I heard. The old man isn't too happy about it. He likes his study. But he, too, has learned which battles to fight."

"I love smart men," she said.

On her way out, Lexi stuck her head in and said goodbye to Amanda, who looked amazingly good in David's extra bedroom. He wouldn't get too comfortable with that, though. As soon as the mess with her building was situated, she'd be back in her own space.

After Lexi cleared out, he leaned against the doorframe and watched Amanda press some sort of narrow rubber markers into the strips of clay she'd placed on the skull cast. At some point, she'd mounted the skull on a stand and had added eyes—brown—to the sockets and lined them with clay to hold them in place. Already, the skull had begun to take on life, and something pinged in David's chest. All this time they'd been talking about the skull as an object, a project, but now, seeing it in this form, even before Amanda had reconstructed the face, it had become an actual person.

A victim.

Curious about what she was doing, he took one step into the room. "What are those?"

"Tissue-depth markers. They tell me how thick the skin in each area of the face should be. It's based on tables developed by a forensic anthropologist. Once I have all the markers placed, I'll start adding clay until I reach the right thickness. I'm basically rebuilding her face."

"Now, that's cool. Why brown eyes?"

"I guessed. The hair they found was dark. That doesn't always mean dark eyes, but I went with my instincts."

Seemed reasonable. He moved farther into the room, circled behind her and studied her work. "It's fascinating. Watching it take shape."

"It is, isn't it? It's like seeing a five-thousand-piece puzzle come together." She attached another marker. "I spoke to Detective McCall earlier. They released my sketch to the local media and a couple of national news outlets. He's hoping for leads."

"What do you think?"

"I suppose he needs to try, but the 3-D reconstruction will have much more detail when it's complete. We're more likely to get hits on that versus the sketch."

He scooted closer, dipped his head and kissed her on the shoulder. "Are you ready for a break?"

"No."

Come on. Really? Times like this, being a stubborn Hennings came in handy. "We could make out."

Before he could dot kisses along her shoulder, she sidestepped, leaving him standing there, bent over, lips puckered.

"Are we sixteen? Go away. I have work to do. Work you're paying me for, I might add."

Excellent point. "Have we discussed your fee? Wait. Don't answer. It doesn't matter. I'll pay overtime."

She clucked her tongue. "You *are* a devil. Now go.

Take a ride on that motorcycle of yours or something. Just get out."

Tough nut, this one. "You're throwing me out?"

"I am." Her cell phone rang and she leaned over to check the screen. "Oh, my landlord." She set the rubber markers on the table and scooped up the phone. "Hi, Mr. Landry."

David wandered back to the doorway and leaned against the frame while he inspected the crown molding in the hallway.

"Are you kidding?" Amanda said, her voice squeaking.

He swung back to her. Whatever it was, it didn't sound good.

"That's ridiculous." She shook her head and then rubbed her free hand up her forehead. "Okay... Thank you."

She disconnected and set the phone down.

"Bad news?"

"He spoke with the building inspector. They're saying the building has a mold infestation."

"You don't believe it?"

"Not for a second. Have I mentioned I'm highly allergic to mold? I mean, dangerously allergic. I carry medication with me everywhere I go."

Whoa. David was no doctor, but being a civil lawyer, he'd done his share of medical research. "If there was an infestation, you'd have been hospitalized by now."

"After all the time I've spent in that building, by now I'd be dead."

AMANDA SET BOTH of her hands on top of her head and squeezed. So maddening. And exhausting. Between the stress of being thrown out of her home and studio and having to sleep in a hotel—never an easy task anyway—she hadn't managed much sleep the night before.

This news only stretched her already thin patience and left her more exhausted. "I can't even believe this. There is no mold in that building. All this is doing is keeping me from my work."

Holding up one finger, David waggled it. "You know what? Let's go see your friend McCall. You're working on a case he's invested in. If we tell him you're hindered by this problem with the city, maybe he can shake something loose. Get you back home." He clapped his hands together. "Saddle up, sweet cheeks. We're moving out."

Amanda glanced down at her paint-stained T-shirt and ripped jeans. Her working clothes. "Okay. I need to stop at the hotel first, though."

That got her a frustrated grunt. "Why?"

Had the man suddenly gone blind? She couldn't walk into a police station dressed like this. "David, look at me. I need to change. It'll take two minutes."

"Right. Sorry. We'll swing by there on the way. While you're changing, I'll track down McCall. We have to take your car unless you want a ride on my bike."

"Not now. Later, though. It'll be fun after all this mess."

At the hotel, Amanda left David in the lobby to phone Detective McCall and let him know they were coming for a chat. At her room, she slid her key in the door and waited for the little green light to give her access, but… red.

She checked the key, made sure the arrow was pointing the right way and tried again. Red light. *Deep breath.* They'd given her two keys. Maybe she'd used the other one to get into the room last night. She dug into her purse, found the second key, lined it up and slid it home. Red lights blinked back at her.

"This is totally insane." For kicks, she flipped the key over and tried the other way. Nothing. "Ugh!"

Three doors down, a housekeeper, a young girl, maybe early twenties, who could have been a college student, stepped into the hall to retrieve something from her cart and spotted her. "Something wrong, ma'am?"

"My keys won't work. I'm trying to get into my room. Would you be able to open the door?"

"Oh, I'm sorry. We're not allowed. For security reasons. I could call someone, but if there's a problem with the key, you'll have to go down and get another one anyway."

Frustration pooled dead smack at the base of Amanda's skull and she tipped her head to stretch the muscles. At this rate, with all that pressure building, her head might pop right off her shoulders. Boom. Gone. But yelling at the housekeeper wouldn't help. First, it wasn't her style and second, it wasn't this woman's fault the keys didn't work. "No. It's fine. I'll go downstairs. Thank you."

She charged into the lobby, where David leaned against one of the giant marble columns and talked on his phone. He spotted her still in her work clothes and swung his free arm out in a *what the hell?* gesture. At any other time, if her head wasn't about to explode, she'd have laughed. She held up the key as she marched by him. "Key isn't working."

"I gotta go," he said into the phone. He poked at the screen and shoved the phone in his jacket pocket. "It worked last night."

"Yes, it did."

The cheery desk clerk spotted Amanda and smiled. "Good morning. How can I help you?"

The woman's eyes tracked right, over Amanda's shoul-

der, and zoomed in on something. Amanda turned and—
yep—David strode up behind her, clearly the focus of the
desk clerk's attention. He had that way about him. The
broad-shouldered build, the dark hair, the close-trimmed,
sexy beard. The biker jacket. He screamed bad boy.

In a blue-blood way.

Amanda turned back to the desk clerk, Bethenny—
according to her name tag—grateful the girl wasn't fan-
ning herself. She set the keys on the desk. "My keys
aren't working."

"I'm so sorry. What room?"

"Five forty-six."

Bethenny tapped on her keyboard. "Can I see your
ID, please?"

"Of course."

Security check complete, Bethenny went back to the
computer monitor. "Oh," she said. "There was a problem
with your credit card."

Ha! Perfect. "What problem?"

"It doesn't say. We were notified this morning of the
issue."

"Are my clothes still in the room?"

"Yes, ma'am. We just need to get another credit card
from you and I can reissue keys. Do you have another
card you would like to use?"

David leaned one elbow on the desk. "What happened?"

Amanda slid her debit card out of her wallet, which
was still sitting on the counter from when she'd pulled
out her ID. "My credit card was declined, which is crazy
because I pay it in full every month."

Every month. Without fail because she guarded her
credit rating like the Secret Service on the president.
Being so diligent about her credit, she didn't even have a

second card to use. In her opinion, more than one credit card led to multiple accounts stacked with debt.

David reached into his jacket pocket. "I've got one."

No! She'd sooner sleep on the street than use his credit card. "Don't you dare." Even to herself, she sounded sharper than she'd like and she breathed in, set her mind on solving the problem. "I appreciate what you're trying to do, but I'll use my debit card."

She held the card out, but the desk clerk was busy cooing at David, and Amanda rolled her eyes. Could she not get a break today? *Whap!* She slapped the card on the counter, shocking the clerk to attention.

Amanda tapped the card. "This should do it."

David offered up one of his sexy grins, apparently enjoying the clerk's attention. Men. Put a young, pretty woman in front of them and their brains melted. Total lava flow. Bethenny swiped the card and waited. And waited.

Oh, come on!

"Um," she said, "I'm sorry. It's been declined."

Before she even had time to argue—or die of humiliation—David slapped his wallet on the desk. "This is stupid. Just take my card."

"No." Amanda set her hand over his. "Thank you. But no. Obviously there's a problem. I'll call the credit card company and the bank and get it straightened out."

And forget about this experience. In fact, she'd pack her things and leave this hotel. With the number of hotels in Chicago, she didn't need to walk through the lobby again and be reminded of this event.

For two days she'd been dealing with eviction from her studio and her home, her entire life really, and now this? The level of fatigue assaulting her body, the sheer force of it, brought her back to the days following her mother's death. And that was a state of being she didn't want to reflect on.

The clerk pretended to be busy with something on the computer and, yes, her not looking at Amanda and making her feel like some down-and-out slug would certainly ease the embarrassment. "I'd like to get my things, please. I'll need someone to unlock the room so I can move."

"Amanda," David said.

She reached across and squeezed his arm to shut him up. What she didn't need right now was a discussion. Or his opinion. "I'll find another hotel when I get this straightened out. I really just want to leave here."

Getting the message—how could he miss it?—he turned to the perky clerk still ogling him. "Let's get her room unlocked so she can pack."

"Of course."

Sure. The Greek god asked and the woman leaped to action. Amanda locked her jaw closed. They had a situation here and the clerk's only interest was flirting with David. What if he were Amanda's husband, for crying out loud?

Having bigger issues to resolve, she planned on keeping silent. Truly did. At least until the clerk shot David another look coupled with a smile. That, after the embarrassing situation that had just occurred, was outrageously unprofessional. Rude. And it snapped Amanda's last surviving nerve.

Now I'm done.

"Excuse me, Bethenny. You have no idea who this man is to me. If I told you he was my husband, would you stop flirting with him?"

"Whoa," David said.

"Oh, just forget it." She swiped her wallet off the

counter and stuffed it into her purse. "Please send some-one up to unlock the room."

DAVID WAITED IN the hallway outside Amanda's hotel room while she packed and took the opportunity to change her clothes. He figured that was the safest place because he'd rather amputate his own leg than risk waiting in the lobby with the desk clerk and having Amanda wonder if he was being a slimeball.

Nope. As hot as that chick was, he had no interest. Zippo. Nada. And Amanda needed to know that.

The door came open and she stepped into the hallway wheeling her luggage, minus black slacks and a fitted white sweater that even under her jacket did amazing things to him. He reached for the bag, his hand closing over hers on the handle. "I've got it."

"Thank you," she said, her voice that normal Amanda calm.

Unlike a few minutes ago when her temper had got-ten to her and revealed a spicy side. Twisted moron that he was, he liked seeing her riled. Letting loose. Unfor-tunately, it had come from him upsetting her, and *that* he didn't want.

The door shut behind them and they headed to the elevator. "I'm sorry about before."

She kept walking, maybe even picking up speed, but she said, "Ugh. Seriously humiliating. I popped off. I was frustrated and couldn't seem to get her attention."

They stopped at the elevator and David smacked the button while she pressed the heels of her hands into her forehead. He should say something. Definitely. Some-thing that wouldn't make it worse. With his track record, that might be a challenge.

He touched her arm. "You know I had no interest in that woman, right?"

"It's me. It's not your fault you look the way you do. You were standing there. She was the one ignoring a guest. I don't know what women think sometimes. I mean, she couldn't have known if you were a relative or a boyfriend. It was just a bad ending to a bad situation. Let's move on so I can get to the bank. After that, I'll call my credit card company." She jerked her hands out, fingers stiff and spread wide. "I have no access to my money right now. Nothing."

He'd love to tell her the credit card and bank situation were weird coincidences. Would love to. Except, being naive had never been an issue for him. Couple the credit-card fiasco with the mysterious mold infestation, and it seemed to him someone had taken an interest in messing with her. In a bad way.

"David, I'm the only one leasing space in that building. And now my finances are a mess. What are the chances someone is trying to get me out?"

Considering it, he rubbed his hand over the back of his neck. "I don't know. Who would want you out of your home and studio? All of this happened in the last two days. Nothing before that? Harassing calls, weird encounters, anything?"

"No. Well, aside from you showing up at my door."

The words came at him slowly, like tiny pebbles being tossed his way, lightly stinging his skin. *You showing up at my door.* The corners of Amanda's lips tilted down and her eyes narrowed.

Bingo.

They both started babbling, talking over each other about coincidences and the skull and the chances.

Amanda held up her hand.

"Sorry," he said.

"It's all right. We're both thinking the same thing. Could this be about the skull?"

"I sure hope not, but if that's the anomaly, it's a pretty decent guess. Who knows you're working on the reconstruction?"

The elevator dinged and the doors slid open to an empty car. Perfect. They could keep talking.

"Your mother knows," she said. "You, your family and their contacts, the detectives, the lab guy, Lexi and whoever they've told."

"I think we need to get with McCall. Everyone else is someone we trust. But McCall. He could have told any number of people."

If the building situation and her assets being frozen happened because of her working on the sculpture, a project he'd pushed her hard on, they had serious issues beyond her current state of affairs. They'd inadvertently poked a sleeping bear.

He watched the numbers on the elevator flash off as they descended and he tapped the handle of her suitcase. If this was his fault, he'd go insane. Seriously, unreasonably, certifiably nuts. The guilt alone would kill him.

"We'll go to the bank first," he said. "Get that straightened out."

"Then I'll call my credit card company. By then we'll have quite the story for Detective McCall. I'll find another hotel tonight."

"Uh, no."

"Pardon?"

"I don't like all this nonsense around you. Hotels are miserable to sleep in anyway."

She gave him the eye-rolling, idiot-on-board look.

"Have you forgotten I can't go home? Where am I supposed to sleep?"

Lucky for her, the idiot-on-board had a plan. "You'll come to my mother's. She's got a guest room with a sitting area. You won't even have to leave the room if you don't want. But I'd feel better knowing you were there and not alone in some hotel."

"I'm fine being alone."

"I know you are, but until we get you back in your place, you'll work out of my condo and stay at my mother's." The elevator doors slid open. "Ladies first."

She stepped off and came to a stop facing him. "It sounds like you're ordering me around."

Of course he was. He also didn't care. He wanted her under his mother's roof. Period. In case anything else went wrong. And the way things were going, Amanda was on a hot streak.

He reached under her chin and drummed his fingers. "I don't like to think of it as ordering you around. I like to think of it as taking care of a smart, independent woman."

She laughed. "Oh, you're good."

He leaned in and got right next to her ear, more than willing to show her how good he could be. No problem there. But, for now, he'd behave. "Humor me. My mother will feed you well and you'll get a good night's sleep. If my condo had furniture, I'd have you stay there." He waggled his eyebrows. "With me. Since that's not an option, my mom's is the next best thing."

Eyes welling up again, she blinked a couple times. Now he'd made her cry. What the hell did he say that had brought *that* on? Rough day all around. He pulled her close, wrapped his arms around her and ran his hand over the back of her head. "I didn't mean to upset you."

"You didn't. It's… Thank you. I could call my dad, but

they don't have an extra room. Neither does Lexi. She's got a one-bedroom cottage and the last thing I need is her detective boyfriend asking questions. I'd have to try and explain all this and I don't have the energy for it. How do I explain something I don't even understand? And you're right here, giving me a place to work and sleep, and I can't believe it. After all this time of being alone, you came into my life at the exact time I needed someone."

So, okay. *Major points, Davie boy.* But this wasn't about the points—at least not totally. This was doing the right thing for a friend—hopefully more—who needed help.

He kissed the top of her head, letting his lips linger for a second against the softness of her hair. "Just do me a favor and remember this conversation when you're mad at me."

Amanda marched into her bank, head held high, mind centered on not losing that last bit of control she'd locked down. Currently homeless and without a studio, and now, on top of it all, no way to access her money. Someone had some explaining to do.

A few customers waited in line for tellers, but she and David veered left to the five desks occupied by the personal bankers. One of whom would be lucky enough to have a mega-irritated, borderline about-to-turn-psychotic customer plop down in front of him.

The bank's ancient marble columns and floors reminded her of all the reasons she'd fallen in love with her building. The one she'd been thrown out of and—oh, her blood pumped just thinking about it. *Forget that.* One issue at a time.

"Good morning," one of the bankers called from her

desk, where two open chairs sat ready for the next customer.

"I'll wait here," David said.

At this point, her life was an open book to this man, but she appreciated his willingness to offer privacy. She gripped his arm. "Thank you. For all your help."

"Give a holler if you need me." He tugged on her hair. "Send up a flare or something."

She spun back to the banker, a woman in her thirties with glossy red hair and creamy skin. A few freckles dotted her nose, and artist Amanda imagined that if the woman spent any time in the sun, those freckles would multiply. The nameplate on the desk revealed the woman to be Elizabeth Nelson. Personal Banker.

Perfect.

Amanda set her purse on the floor and took one of the vacant seats across from Ms. Nelson. "Good morning. I'm Amanda LeBlanc. I have several accounts here and there seems to be an issue with them."

"I'm sorry about that. What's the problem?"

"My debit card isn't working."

"Well, let's see if we can clear that up."

After proving her identity, Amanda sat quietly while Ms. Nelson tippity-tapped on her keyboard.

Frowning, she leaned forward a few inches and studied her screen. No frowning. *Nuh-uh.* Frowning was decidedly not good. From Amanda's vantage point, all she saw were grid lines and one highlighted field.

"I see the problem," Ms. Nelson said, "but I'll need to check with my manager on something. Excuse me one moment."

Without waiting for Amanda to reply, the banker popped out of her chair and hurried to an office in the far corner of the building. Amanda shifted sideways and made eye contact with David, who abandoned his post against one of the columns and wandered over. "What's up?"

"I don't know. She said she saw the problem and then ran off to talk to her boss."

"Ms. LeBlanc?"

The two of them glanced up.

"Hello," Ms. Nelson said to David.

"Hi." He reached to shake her hand. "David Hennings. I'm a friend of Amanda's."

Ms. Nelson remained standing behind her chair. As in making no attempt to sit. Another not-so-good sign along with the nothingness pasted on her face. Not a smile, not a grimace, nothing to indicate…well…anything.

"Ms. LeBlanc, if you would follow me. The branch manager would like to speak with you."

"Is everything all right?"

She held her hand toward the office. "Right this way."

Okay. None of this felt right and Amanda's pulse kicked up. Pressure exploded behind her right eye and she squeezed her eyes closed for a second. Just one second to center herself. *Just get through it.* Whatever this was, she'd get through it. But, damn, she despised emotional warfare.

She rose from her chair and once again made eye contact with David, who cocked his head in question. She'd love to give him an explanation, but she was just as confused. With her current state of unease, it might not be a bad idea to have a second set of eyes and ears with her. A lawyer to boot.

She paddled her hand. "Come with me. Please."

As he fell in step beside her, his long legs and big shoulders moved with such confidence that her panic, that streaming anxiety from seconds ago, vanished. David would help her. Whatever this was, he'd help her.

"We've got this," he said.

A girl had to love a lawyer. At least when he was on her side.

Once inside the branch manager's office, Ms. Nelson closed the door and left. *Oh, boy.*

"Ms. LeBlanc. I'm Mariette Clarke."

Unlike Ms. Nelson, Mariette Clarke was an older woman, maybe mid-fifties. She wore her navy suit jacket buttoned and her hair in a tight bun that created an instant face-lift. Simply put, she looked like a prison warden.

The two women shook hands and Amanda introduced David as Ms. Clarke motioned them to chairs. "Have a seat."

Far from in the mood for small talk, Amanda got right to it. "Thank you. Forgive me for cutting to the chase here, but what's the problem with my accounts? I have both my business and personal accounts with this bank and I can't access either."

"Yes. I apologize for that. Unfortunately, I'm not able to release any funds to you."

Amanda took a deep breath, then let it out slowly. She would not, not, not lose control. But that about-to-turn-psycho person inside her might be on the brink. "Why?"

"Your accounts have been frozen. We received an order this morning."

An order... What? Amanda shook her head, letting the words sink in.

David reached over and squeezed her hand before she could say anything. "And the order came from?"

"Cook County."

He stood. That fast. Just up and out of his chair.

"Thank you," he said. "Let's go, Amanda."

"What? Wait."

"The bank received a restraining order," he said. "Apparently from the Cook County State's Attorney's Office. They are legally bound by it. They cannot release any funds to you."

Ms. Clarke nodded and Amanda gritted her teeth, barely hanging on to that last bit of control. The last couple of days had been a maze with brick walls in every direction.

Clearly in a rush, David held the office door open and waved her through.

"I'm sorry," she said, moving quickly to keep pace with him. "But I'm not sure I understand. Someone from the State's Attorney's Office froze my accounts?"

"It appears so."

Outside the bank, stinging wind clawed at her face and she hunched against it. Her eyes watered, whether from the wind or the ungluing of her life, she didn't care. Hanging on to her emotions, maintaining that brutal control she always fought for, mixed with the lack of sleep last night, left her wrung out. She wiped at her eyes, inhaling and exhaling a few times to let that good, clean oxygen clear her mind. *I can do this.*

At the corner, they stopped to wait for the red light and she faced David. "Why would they freeze my accounts?"

"I don't know. But my brother is an ASA for Cook County. We'll call him and get answers."

Two blocks from Zac's office, David and Amanda entered a café and grabbed an empty table toward the back. The surrounding tables were all unoccupied and would give them some privacy. Thanks to the aroma of fresh coffee and baked goods, David craved a caffeine-laced sugar buzz.

A handful of customers were busy yapping with their friends or messing with electronic devices and barely noticed them. Zac had made a good choice with this place.

Upon leaving the bank, David had called and given his brother the Amanda's-life highlights and he must have made a call or two, because he suddenly had info for them. And by arranging to meet at the café rather than his office, it was clear he didn't want his coworkers to see him delivering that info.

The bells on the door jangled and Zac entered, suit in perfect order, his blond hair equally neat, and David was reminded of their differences. *I have to be adopted.*

Sharp-dressed Zac was the epitome of blue-blood offspring. His overall fair-haired appearance gave him an air of confidence—superiority, really—which he exploited in every way possible. Whether in a courtroom or socially, Zac knew how to work people and he wasn't ashamed to throw around the Hennings name if it got him somewhere. David? He'd done his best to avoid references to the family name. Whereas David looked like a regular Joe in his jeans and biker boots, his little brother screamed wealth and privilege.

Zac perused the place, but with the lack of crowd, they weren't hard to spot.

"Hey," he said, backhanding David on the shoulder.

David stood and shook his brother's hand. "Thanks for coming. This is Amanda."

Zac hit her with the famous Hennings grin, and David damn near puked. He supposed he shouldn't comment or crack wise because as much as he avoided throwing the family name around, he had no problem whipping out his own version of that smile when necessary. At this point, it was a tool in their arsenal. A tool that rarely failed.

"Thank you for seeing us," Amanda said.

"Sure. If my brother is involved, I'm happy to help."

"Yada, yada," David said. "What do you have?"

Zac took the chair between them and leaned forward on his elbows. "Not much. It's a little sideways."

Everything was these days. David held his hand palm up. "Meaning?"

"I talked to the prosecutor who wrote it up."

"And?"

Zac swung to Amanda. "You need to hire an attorney."

Not what David wanted to hear. Hiring an attorney meant the government's case had teeth. What they needed to know was how sharp those teeth were. And if they were real. Because the spooked looked on Amanda's face and the sudden dismemberment of her life led him to believe someone had targeted her. He didn't know her well. At all. But he liked to think his judgment was sound when it came to people and their character, and nothing about her set off his thief meter. He leaned toward her and held out his hand. "Give me a dollar."

"What?"

"My brother has told you to hire an attorney. For the time being, that's me. Give me a dollar and you've retained me."

"Oh, my God. What's happening?"

Zac jerked his chin. "Give him a dollar."

Amanda dug out her wallet and combed through the bills. "I don't have a dollar."

She slapped a five into his hand.

"That works." He went back to Zac. "What have you got?"

"They think she violated UDAP."

UDAP. What the hell? "How?"

"What's UDAP?" Amanda asked.

Zac took that one. "It's a consumer protection law,

part of the FTC Act. Have you ever been involved in a check-cashing business?"

"No."

"Know anyone who has?"

"Don't answer that yet." David kept his eyes on Zac. "What do they think she did?"

Whatever this was, Zac had at least some details, and as much as he trusted his brother, he still worked for the state's attorney, who'd just seized Amanda's assets.

"From what I saw, they think she's involved with a company that buys debts owed to payday-loan places. They allegedly call consumers and tell them they owe an amount higher than the original loan. Someone thinks you helped bankroll a check-cashing company where he cashed a couple of checks. Then, months later, he gets a call from some company saying he didn't pay back the loan and he'd be going to jail if he didn't make it snappy. It's all bogus. The SA went into an ex parte hearing this morning."

Amanda's head dipped. "Ex what?"

"Parte," David said. "It means they don't have to give you notice. It's usually for temporary orders until a formal hearing happens. In this case, they want to make sure you can't start moving money."

Of the list of offenses David had guessed—mail fraud, kiting checks—a loan scam hadn't even come close to the top. And he knew, as sure as he was sitting there, this was garbage. Had it been just the UDAP violation, he might have been able to stretch his imagination and at least consider the possibility. As a wills and trusts attorney, he saw all kinds of financial shenanigans. All these weird occurrences combined? No way. Someone was methodically dismantling Amanda's life.

"No." She jammed her finger into the table. "Nuh-uh. That's not me. I've never been in one of those loan places, let alone funded one. How can they just tie up my money?"

David patted air. "This is nonsense. But yes, they can do it. Asset forfeiture allows prosecutors to freeze accounts they believe are part of alleged criminal activity." He set his hand on her shoulder and squeezed before going back to Zac. "Whose name is in the court filings?"

"Simeon Davis," Zac said to Amanda. "Do you know him? Maybe he's a past client or someone you interacted with."

"Or," David added, "someone who might have a beef with you?"

For a few seconds, she stared down at the table, gripping the edge, popping her knuckles with the effort. After a minute, she met David's gaze straight on. "I don't think so. The name isn't familiar."

"But you're not sure."

"David, I've interacted with a lot of people over the years. He could be the guy who works where I buy my art supplies. I know he's not a client or someone I do business with on a regular basis."

He sat back and rested his hands on his thighs. Annoying her wouldn't help them. "All right. Don't get mad."

"I'm not mad. I'm being honest."

Zac's phone beeped and he rose from his chair. "Listen, kids, I gotta get back. Obviously, this conversation stays between us."

"No doubt," David said. "You haven't told us anything I couldn't find out on my own anyway. You saved me time, though. Thanks."

Amanda stood and held out her hand. "Thank you, Zac."

He glanced down at her hand, and the side of his mouth twisted. "Hell with that."

And then, little brother, being a total wise guy, leaned in and hugged Amanda, the whole time his eyes on David, challenging the bonds of brotherly affection.

"I know what you're doing," David said.

"I'm sure you do, Dave. I'm sure you do."

After mauling her, Zac gave David their version of the shoulder-slap-chest-bump man hug. David had his issues with Penny, but he and Zac? They were solid. Always had been.

"I'll see you tonight," he said. "I told Mom I'd swing by. She's got some invitation samples for Emma to look at."

"Yeah, well, good luck with that."

"I hear you, brother. Later."

Amanda slid back into her seat and waited for David to do the same. "I like him," she said.

"You should. He's the best."

"So, no sibling rivalry with him? Only Penny."

"He's the mediator." He shrugged. "From the time we were kids, it's been that way. But we're not talking about that now. Now we head to my condo and do research. Let's find Simeon Davis and see why he's accusing you of fraud."

DAVID NABBED A parking space in front of his building and as soon as he'd cut the engine, his cell phone rang. At least someone's phone had activity; Amanda's had remained annoyingly silent. Nothing from her landlord on her building or her call in to Detective McCall. And now, with this Simeon Davis development, she'd tried again but was told the detective was on a homicide call. Who knew when he'd get back to her?

"Is it McCall?"

He shook his head. "No. My contractor. Finally. Been chasing him about my office for two days." He hit the button before the call went to voice mail. "Hang on," he said into the phone.

He slid her car key from the ignition then dug into his pocket and handed her his key ring. A simple, worn leather braid with—one, two, three—four keys on it. Her best guess? One for his office, one for his parents' home, one for the condo and one for his car. No clutter of unnecessary keys for this man. He was nothing if not efficient.

"The signal in the building sucks," he said. "Go on in while I take this. Be there in two minutes."

Gladly. The few minutes alone would allow her to make a cup of tea and wrap her head around the current state of her life.

She strode up the walkway to David's private entrance. The units on the upper floors had interior entrances via a doorway that led to a stairwell, but the two units on the ground floor had direct access from the front and rear. Another perk of the building.

With no idea which key fit the door, she tried the first one—no good—then the next one, and hit on the door key. Soon, she imagined, he'd move his condo key to the end, as that would be the one used most often. But that could be the way her brain worked. She and David, though, were like-minded in some ways. This might be one of them.

She unlocked the door, pushed it open and stepped inside. The living room light fixtures had yet to be installed and the afternoon sun offered minimal help in illuminating the room. For now, she'd put the stove light on and hope it threw some secondary light over the breakfast bar into the conjoined dining and living areas.

They'd also have to put a shade or curtain on the glass door at the end of the hallway or people would be peeping in. Frankly, the door was a break-in waiting to happen. All someone needed to do was cut—or punch—a hole in the glass, reach in and flip the lock.

And, holy smokes…

The lock. More specifically the knob on the lock. Before they left, David had checked it. She'd watched him lock it, leaving the oblong knob in a vertical position. Vertical equaled locked.

So why was the knob horizontal?

Lexi. She had a key. Maybe she'd come back after they'd left and forgotten to lock it again. From where Amanda stood, the door appeared unharmed, so it must have been Lexi. Or maybe someone else David had given a key to. That had to be it. Amanda breathed out. Stress had morphed into crazy-making hypervigilance. This was what happened when she left her safe zone. Emotional upheaval obviously made her paranoid. Unsteady.

Need my plain, boring life back.

For now, she'd relock the door and mention it to David. Anyone with a key needed to make sure they locked up before leaving. Three steps in, something clinked—*guest bedroom*—and Amanda halted.

Paranoia?

Clink.

And then a scrape. Like someone dragging something. And that was definitely not paranoia. Unless paranoia clinked *and* scraped.

Whatever or whoever was in there must have been moving the table or sculpture stand she'd set up.

Could be a worker. She didn't know who he had in and out of here. But he'd also told her they wouldn't be working in that bedroom while she was in there. He had, in fact, told everyone to stay out.

A slow tingling crawled up her arms. *Get out*. As silly and cowardly as she'd feel, she'd go outside and get David and the two of them would come back in. Cowardice aside, a smart woman didn't confront an unknown person. She lifted her foot, ready to turn back, when a man, a big man with linebacker shoulders, exited the room. Veins exploding, her entire system came to a state of alert. Her focus narrowed, zoomed right in on the profile of a man wearing a blue hoodie. In his hand he held…*no*…the skull. As if he sensed her, his head came around—beard. Not full. More stubbly. The man's eyes widened. He hadn't expected anyone else to be there.

That made two of them.

The tingling on her arms changed to a full stab, and the chemical odor in the room intensified, burning her nose and throat.

Skull.

She stepped forward and the man put his arm out. "I don't want to hurt you."

"Take whatever you want. Not the skull. Please."

She took another step, but he backed away. "Don't," he said, stretching the one-syllable word to two.

Nervous. She should run. Just let him escape. The sheer size of him terrified her. But that skull—the PD had left it in her care. It was their property, but they'd entrusted her with it. She'd promised… "Just…please… leave it."

She moved closer and held out her arms and then something in her head snapped, something feral and desperate and protective and she lunged—big mistake. The man reared back, swinging sideways, pulling the skull from her reach, but her fingers grazed his meaty hand.

"No," she said, struggling to grab hold.

The man yanked free, spun back and, with his free arm, launched her. Shoved her with enough force that she flew backward as if she weighed nothing. *Crack.* She hit the floor, hard, her tailbone taking the direct hit.

Pain roared into her back and down her legs and she closed her eyes for a split second. One tiny second to recover because—*God*—that hurt. *Where is he? Where is he?*

She opened her eyes, ready to fight off another attack, but the man had gone the other way. Back door.

"No!"

Amanda scrambled to her feet just as David came in the front. "Get him!"

He ran toward her. "What happened? Are you hurt?"

"He stole the skull. Back door. He went left. Blue hoodie!"

Being closer to the front, David tore out that door and Amanda followed him, limping a little, as he charged around the side of the building.

"Stay inside!" he hollered. "Lock yourself in!"

he summoned all his strength, flat on his back. His arm? Sure to crack along the edge of the grass curb, the impact and probably power burn a concussion ...

Chapter Eight

David flew around the corner of the building, eyes scanning left and right. There. Blue sweatshirt. A big guy lumbering down the sidewalk. Out of shape. David picked up speed. Easily, he'd catch him.

Parked cars lined the street, and the man ran by them, heading to the corner, where, dammit, an ancient Chevy with a missing rear hubcap sat parked, puffs of smoke coming from the tailpipe.

David kicked his sprint up in case he could tackle the guy before he got to that car.

A biker shot out of an alley and the big guy swerved. Too late. He crashed into the rider and—yow—the rider went one way and the bike the other, both landing directly in David's path. He veered left, intending to leap right over the bike and maybe, maybe, catch the runner. As long as the rider stayed out of his way.

The biker hopped to his feet.

Of course he did.

David leaped and—*oh, man*—sucked a huge breath and readied his body for impact, twisting slightly to avoid a direct hit to the chest. Bam. Their shoulders collided.

"Oof!" the biker said. "Dammit! Watch where the hell you're going."

A sharp pain ripped into David's chest and neck and

he plummeted, hitting the sidewalk flat on his back. His head bounced off the ground, the edge of the grass easing the impact and probably saving him a concussion. Still, his vision blurred and he squeezed his eyes shut, then opened them quickly and refocused.

"What the hell?" the rider said "He could have killed me!"

That might be extreme, but the guy could have seriously gotten his bell rung. Shaking off the impact, David rolled to his side and spotted the idling car pulling into traffic. Missed him. The stream of swearwords from his mouth would have lit up his mother for sure.

"Who was that guy?" the rider asked.

"No idea. He broke into my condo. Are you all right?"

The man stretched his right leg. "Tweaked my knee. I think it's okay."

David rolled to his feet, brushed the dirt off his jacket and took inventory of his clothing. The knee of his jeans was blown out and his jacket sleeve was scuffed, but everything else was intact. The goose egg on the back of his head would hurt later, though. He grabbed the bike and held it upright while the rider got to his feet.

"You sure you're okay? Don't need an ambulance?"

"Nah. I'm good. Wouldn't be the first time I got tossed off this thing. I live around the corner. I'll walk it the rest of the way."

David glanced behind him, making sure Amanda hadn't followed.

And hello…

On the ground right behind him, where the suspect had leaped out of the way to avoid the biker, sat a set of keys. David pointed. "Those yours?"

"Nah, man." He gestured to a small pouch attached to the bike's seat. "Mine are in my pouch. I think they fell out of the guy's pocket. I heard something clink but figured it was something on the bike."

"You got any tissues in there or anything?"

"Yeah." The rider dragged a napkin, one of those cheap ones fast-food places offered, out of the pouch and handed it over.

Using the napkin, David clasped the edge of the plastic key ring and wrapped the keys in the napkin. When he got back to the condo, he'd find a baggie or something to put them in and then decide what to do with them. For sure, they'd check them for prints. It was just a matter of who would do the checking—Hennings & Solomon's private lab or the PD's lab.

He cut through the alley on his way back to the condo. With the darkening sky, he hoped he wouldn't scare the life out of Amanda by banging on the back door. Assuming she'd locked herself in.

She'd better have locked herself in.

He jogged up to the door where the overhead light lit the immediate area, including just inside the door. But his view didn't stop there. He could see clear into the shadowed hallway thanks to the stove light. He needed to get something to cover this window. Something he should have thought about way before now, but the place had been empty. Who'd rob an empty condo?

Someone looking for a skull maybe.

And yep. Back door locked. Good girl. He knocked lightly. "It's me," he said, his voice loud but not yelling.

Would she even hear him? Her head poked out of the room where she'd set up her makeshift studio and he waved. She rushed to the door, unlocked it and didn't give him three seconds to get inside before launching herself at him. A hug from her he'd take any day and he wrapped her up and held tight while patting her lower back.

"Honey, let me get inside so we can lock up again."

She backed up a few steps, apparently too terrified to let go, and that made him want to tear something apart.

Reality was, he'd convinced her to do this reconstruction and right after that her life went to hell. And now someone had stolen the damned skull.

"He bolted," David said. "Got into a car and took off."

She backed away and gave him a once-over. "Your pants are ripped. And your jacket! What happened?"

"He took out a guy on a bike. The rider wasn't too happy when I plowed into him."

"Are you hurt?"

She ran her hands over his arms, squeezing as she went, checking for injuries. The fussing was nice, but if he had a broken bone he'd feel it. He pointed at the back of his head. "Got a bump. No big deal."

"Let me see you." She walked around him, her hand traveling across his shoulders and gently moving into his hair so she could feel the lump. Suddenly he wasn't thinking about hoodie-wearing bad guys.

"I'm fine. You looked like you were getting up when I came in. Did he hit you?"

"No." She waved toward the end of the hallway. "He pushed me over. He said he didn't want to hurt me. And he sounded nervous. I think he just wanted to get me out of the way, but I panicked."

David stepped closer, wrapped his arms around her and cradled the back of her head. "I'm sorry this is happening. Did he take anything else?"

"No. Just the skull."

"Which means he found what he was looking for. And if nothing else, we know, without question, someone doesn't want you finishing that reconstruction."

As MUCH AS Amanda wanted to disagree with David's assessment, reality had made it clear that her willingness to do the reconstruction had caused her life to implode.

"I know. There's no way the timing on these mishaps is a coincidence. I'll try McCall again."

She strode to the end of the hallway, where her purse still sat on the floor after her fall. "I checked the locks. They're all intact."

"He must have picked it. Doesn't surprise me with how cheap that lock is. And it serves me right for putting off installing the new ones. Wait."

He patted his jacket pocket, then pulled out a folded napkin. "What's that?"

"This, my love, is a set of keys I think your assailant dropped." He started for the back door. "Wouldn't it be interesting if one of these keys fit my door?"

Without waiting for a response and keeping the napkin wrapped around the end of the key, he shoved one into the lock and jiggled it. Nothing. He moved on while Amanda wrapped her hand around the two middle fingers of her other hand and squeezed. The pressure from her ring sent a piercing stick straight to the base of her finger and she loosened her hold. Damned nerves. Totally fried.

After trying all the keys, David turned back to her. "They don't fit."

"Well, good. Because that would have been another flipping mystery to solve. We need to tell McCall. I'll get a hold of him."

David blew out a breath and propped his hands on his hips. "Hang on."

Hang on? For what? "Why?"

"Let's think about this. Your building was condemned and then your accounts were frozen."

"And?"

"Think about it. The city's building department issued the vacate order on your building." David held his finger up. "And your accounts were frozen after the bank was issued an order from the Cook County State's Attorney. Where's the connection?"

Following his logic, Amanda thought about the administrative offices within city government. "Holy cow. The city. Could someone at the PD be behind this?"

"It could be. I mean, they would definitely have connections with the SA's office. The building department? Eh. Possibly."

"But…"

"What?"

She held her hand up, then let it drop. "I don't know. I'm just…confused. Why would McCall ask for my help if he was behind all this?"

"It might not be him. Maybe it's someone he works with."

"How do we figure that out?"

David grinned. "Hennings & Solomon has investigators. Good ones. They know everyone in Chicago. Plus, Penny's boyfriend is FBI. Between them, we're aces."

"Wow."

"Yep. And based on the conversation we just had, I think we should turn the keys over to McCall but, as a backup, *borrow* one of them and send it to the lab my dad's firm uses. They'll check them for prints. So will the police. Hopefully, we'll get a similar result."

"Oh, David. McCall won't be happy if we do that."

"I know. Wouldn't be the first time someone was mad at me. I'm good with it. But this involves you also. We're a team. If you're not comfortable, we'll give McCall everything."

Not in her lifetime would she be comfortable with

this. Any of it. For three days she'd been in hell. And now David wanted her to knowingly annoy a homicide detective she was supposedly helping solve a murder.

Before her life had fallen apart, she'd have gladly turned the keys over to McCall. Now? With all this craziness, the only one she trusted was David. And he had a plan that sounded, in an off way, reasonable.

She met his gaze, and those alluring eyes of his sucked her in. The man had no fear. None. Maybe she could learn a thing or two from him. Considering that she'd spent the past ten years trying to live her life in neutral. She shook her head.

"I don't like it," she said. "But do it anyway."

He jerked his head. "Good. I'll take the heat on it. No problem there."

Then he plastered a kiss on her. A good, solid smack, more fun than steamy, but a little bit of tongue was involved and she gripped his jacket, holding him in place for a few seconds before releasing him.

"Nice," he said. "We'll do more of that later."

"Excellent. And thank you."

"For what?"

"Everything. If I had to deal with this alone, I'd have had a nervous breakdown."

IGNORING HIS POUNDING headache, David snagged his cell phone from his back pocket and scrolled to Penny's name on his phone. And God help her if she gave him any attitude. In the mood he was in, it'd be war. He tapped the screen and hit the speaker button. "This should be good."

Amanda stood a few feet from him, her back flat against the stark white wall that basically served as a canvas showing off her supple curves. Her hips and the idea of them under him might drive him insane.

"Who are you calling?" she asked.

"My sister."

"Ah."

Penny picked up. "Hi."

She sounded decently cheery, which would only help his cause. "Hey. I'm about to make your night."

"Really?" she said, her voice laced with that special brand of skeptical sarcasm only Penny could pull off.

"Yep. I'm calling to ask for your help."

He grinned at Amanda, actually enjoying the banter with Penny. For a change, he wasn't wondering the myriad of ways she'd make his blood boil. Particularly when he was trying not to lose his temper around her. Most conversations with his sister were a lesson in self-control, forcing himself not to blow his stack when she made snide comments about him running away from his family and the firm. She always claimed to be joking, but down deep, he wondered. He couldn't blame her entirely. He'd done his share of needling over the years.

But now, finally, they'd each agreed to play nice, and like a plug pulled from a drain, the pressure was off.

"Let me call *The Banner*," Penny cracked. "We could probably get page one for this."

"Good one, Pen."

"Thank you, David."

"You're welcome. But I do need your help on something."

"What's up?"

He spent the next five minutes filling Penny in while his ever-diligent defense attorney sister peppered him with questions. As he spoke, he reached his free arm out for Amanda, who pushed off the wall and let him pull her to his side. Whether from being still pumped up from the intruder or simply adrenaline, his chest pinged.

He'd been on his own for so long he hadn't realized, or much cared, whether he had companionship. Before, having someone around meant being smothered, losing his privacy and downtime. Forgoing solitary day trips on his bike.

Having to fill the silence when he'd rather not.

With Amanda, something had changed. When she wasn't close, he wanted her there.

And didn't mind feeling that way.

"Wow, David," Penny said, "you've been busy."

"Ya think?"

"Call the detective. What's his name… McCall?"

"We tried him earlier. He's working a homicide. Pen, not a lot of people knew Amanda had that skull. And it seems convenient that as soon as she agreed to do the reconstruction, her life came apart."

"You think someone at the PD might be involved."

"Don't know. But I wouldn't mind seeing if we can locate the guy who stole the skull before I bring in the cops. For all we know he's this Simeon Davis accusing her of fraud. That's why I'm thinking we keep one of the keys and test it ourselves."

This was met with silence. Clearly his sister didn't agree. Couldn't blame her. As a lawyer, he knew better. "Say it, Pen."

"Don't yell at me."

"I won't."

"I feel like you should at least call the detective and report the break-in. Besides, we have to tell them the skull cast is gone."

We. Not you. *Aces.*

Beside him, Amanda winced, probably at the idea of the skull being gone. He slid his arm over her shoulder. "They'll have to make her another cast. But it's getting close to five now. The lab guy is probably gone for the day."

Penny laughed. "You are great at talking yourself into things."

"I know. It's a beautiful thing."

"Yes, but a crime has been committed and you know it. Let's not muddy this up. Call McCall, report it and turn over those keys. We can still work it from our end and you'll have covered your butt with the detective."

This was what he'd missed in Boston. His sister could be a hassle, but she wasn't afraid to jump into the fray. "I will. But can we send one of the keys to the firm's lab? Pen, I don't know who we can trust. As soon as Amanda signed on for the reconstruction, someone went project demolition on her life. And that's bugging me." He glanced down at Amanda.

"What?" Amanda said.

"Did you notice if the guy had gloves on?"

She pursed her lips. Thought about it. "No. When I tried to get the skull from him, I felt his skin."

"Okay," Penny said. "I heard that. So the PD will get some prints taken in there, as well."

"Yeah. Can we use the firm's lab for the keys?"

"You said one key, David. Not the whole set."

Got her. *Yes.* He grinned. "One key. Yes."

"This makes me incredibly nervous and you know why. If we go to trial, the chain of custody alone could get those keys thrown out. Then what?"

"I know. But Amanda can identify him. We'd still have enough to make a case. There's also the car. He got into a beat-up Chevy. An Impala, I think. It had to be thirty years old."

His mind went wild. Not many people drove a Chevy from thirty years ago. They could put together a list. All he'd have to do is jump on the internet and search images of Chevy Impalas from the eighties. Maybe narrow it to a specific year. "If I can figure out what year that car was, can one of the firm's investigators hunt it down? Maybe through DMV?"

"Maybe. Run that key over here and I'll have Jenna take it to the lab."

"Thank you."

"You're welcome. But if we get in trouble for this, it's your fault."

At that, he laughed. Couldn't help it. Some things never changed. "Sure. Whatever. My fault. Thanks."

His sister disconnected and David shoved his phone back into his pocket. "Wow."

"What is it?"

"Penny and I just had a conversation. No screaming. No calling each other names. No irritation. I'm…" He breathed in, then rested his head back against the wall. "I don't know. Stunned? Happy? Relieved?"

Amanda gripped his shirt. "It could be all three."

He dropped his arm over her shoulder, drew her back against his side and kissed the top of her head. Whatever he felt at that moment, it was…good. And he hadn't been able to say that about his relationship with his sister in a long time.

How LONG DID homicide scenes take to process? That was Amanda's question because Detective McCall was still unavailable.

Something that made David happier than it should

have, but Amanda chalked it up to being another twisted experience in a series of twisted experiences.

Two hours had passed while waiting on the detective, and Amanda sat in the kitchen of the Hennings' mansion marveling at the brute size of it. Stylish cabinets and stainless steel surrounded her. The entire space was spotless but not a museum. Strategically placed fresh flowers and family photos gave the room a bright warmth and she envisioned a gathering place for family parties and laughter and meals. During childhood—even now—she would have spread her drawings out on the stone countertops and settled in for a few hours.

Mrs. Hennings set a mug of steaming chamomile tea in front of her and sat in the adjacent seat, her crystal-blue eyes on her. Looking into those eyes, Amanda understood why people caved when Pamela Hennings made a request. There was an intensity there but at the same time a softening twinkle. Dangerous eyes.

Right about now, David could come back from wherever he'd disappeared to.

Amanda sipped her tea. "I imagine your children didn't get away with much when they were kids."

"You'd be correct."

"I figured. You have a look about you. Sort of an 'I can kill you, but I'll use a feather so it won't hurt as much' vibe."

That made Mrs. Hennings laugh and Amanda smiled, enjoying the company of an older woman. A woman roughly the age her mother would have been.

"My children were a handful. All good kids, but they were born litigators. The color on a carton of milk could start a debate in this house." She sat back and crossed her legs, resting her hands in her lap. "Are you sure you weren't hurt tonight?"

"I'm fine, ma'am. Thank you. I think it scared me more than anything."

"As it should. I'm glad you're here. My guest room is in need of a visitor. And David doesn't count. He still likes to sleep in his old room, which I love about him. And it leaves the guest room for you. Please stay as long as you'd like. I enjoy company."

"Thank you. I'm hoping the building inspector will clear my place in the next day or so."

"Such craziness."

"Ladies," David said, striding in from the doorway leading to the main hall.

Mrs. Hennings checked over her shoulder. "There you are. Where have you been?"

No kidding. He bent low, kissed his mom on the cheek, then ran his hand across the back of Amanda's chair, all seemingly in one smooth motion before taking the seat on the other side of her. "On the phone with Penny. And Jenna. She's running down anyone in the area who owns an eighties-era Chevy Impala. It'll be a start until we hear back from McCall." He turned to Amanda. "You've got to be beat."

Completely. But fearing she'd sound rude if she admitted it, she shook her head. "I'm fine. Your mom makes a great cup of tea." She fiddled with the mug, running her fingertips over the handle, an obviously handcrafted letter *H*.

His mother eyed him. "You should rethink calling the police about the break-in."

"Mom, you'll be happy to know I did call the police. Not my fault the detective is busy." He grinned. "And before you yell at me for being a smart mouth, I have a plan here. I don't trust anyone right now, and since McCall is the detective on this case, I want him to handle the break-in and he's busy. I've already told all the workers to stay out of there. The crime scene will be intact for McCall. And it buys us time to do some investigating on our own. Got it all figured out."

"Apparently so. My darling, I hope you know what you're doing."

That made two of them.

Mrs. Hennings patted her lap and stood. "I'm heading upstairs to drag your father from his office. I'll see you both in the morning."

"Good night, Mom. Thanks for the help."

"Of course." She turned to Amanda. "It's the least I can do. If I'd known getting you involved would create this mess, I'd never have done it. For that, I'm sorry."

"Please don't apologize. I'm doing the reconstruction for my own reasons. She needs to be identified. This other business is ugly, but the goal is still to bring that woman home."

Mrs. Hennings squeezed her shoulder. "You're a special person. I hope you know that."

Did attempting a reconstruction make her special? Maybe. Or maybe she was someone who'd lost a loved one to tragedy and couldn't imagine not knowing where that person was or how she had died. The loss alone devastated a family, ripped worlds apart and tore foundations away. In seconds life changed. Forever.

Now someone wanted to stop her from helping to identify this person and Amanda couldn't have that. A week ago, a few days ago, she'd have resisted the case, instead preferring to stay in her neutral zone—as David called it—but now, with what had gone on in her life, she needed to fight back. To not let her life fall apart on her. To take control again and help bring a dead woman home.

For the first time, staying in neutral, denying the highs

and self-protecting from the lows wouldn't cut it. No matter the cost.

"Thank you, ma'am."

She wrapped her fingers around the mug, letting the warmth seep into her hands and chase away the heaviness of the past few days.

David shoved his chair back. "Come with me. I'll show you the guest room. Bring your tea with you."

He led her to the third floor, where the circular staircase ended at a large landing that opened to a hallway painted a muted gray lined with doors on each side.

At the third entrance on the right, David threw open the door and flipped the lights on. The guest room had to be seven hundred square feet. It looked more like a studio apartment than a bedroom. On one wall sat a fireplace with two chairs and ottomans. A small love seat completed the area, giving it a cozy feel. The walls had been painted a deep beige and the walnut floors were covered with area rugs. Splashes of reds, purples, yellows throughout the room reminded Amanda of Lexi's work and she wondered if her friend had been the designer.

"The bed is a king," David said. He pointed to a closed door on the far side of the room. "And the bathroom is through there."

"Thank you. Where's your room?"

Ouch, that sounded bad. Seriously bad. She pressed her fingers to her lips, hiding a smile. "I didn't mean that the way it sounded."

"Then I'd say that was a shame."

He stepped closer, brought one hand up and rested it on her neck as he stroked her jaw with his thumb. Tiny explosions trailed from her hips into her chest straight to her firing cheeks. Something about this man's hands on her made her jittery and happy and...safe.

"You're beautiful, Amanda. Smart and funny, too. When we're done with this mess, I want to spend time with you. If that's okay."

Definitely okay. And if her comfort level with him was any indication, it would be something she'd enjoy. "I'd like that. It's important to me that I finish this reconstruction. Someone doesn't want her identified. She needs her name back. And I want to help with that."

"Does that scare you?"

"It does. For years I've played it safe, not wanting to risk emotional upheaval. The last couple of days? I mean, talk about emotional. I'm sad about it and worried, but I don't feel hopeless. I don't feel like I'll turn into my mother and fall into despair that has no escape. I think that's because you're helping me through it."

He kissed her. Softly. His lips brushing hers in easy strokes, lingering. She closed her eyes, put thoughts of the bed right behind them out of her mind because it would be so easy to fall into it and take comfort from hunky David Hennings. The little explosions happened again and she rested her hand on his waist.

Regrettably, he eased back, smiling down at her. "I need to go. Otherwise, I won't. I know you're tired and if tomorrow goes like I think it will, it'll be just as active. If you need me, I'm right next door."

And, oh, the torture of that. "I'll keep that in mind."

Chapter Nine

Amanda lay in the king-size bed and stared at the ceiling. A sliver of moonlight squeaked between the curtains on the French doors and gave the darkened room an eerie bluish tint. Still, creepy tint and all, any anxiety she'd had about what she'd been through these past days drifted off the second David had driven through the front gates into the safety of his parents' estate.

These people were loaded—L-O-A-D-E-D—and this kind of wealth, the privilege of a lifestyle with no financial worries, was beyond anything Amanda had ever known. Her life, even as a child, had been spent watching pennies, managing money, securing a future. No extravagant spending. No useless toys. Even now, when she made enough to afford a few luxuries, she bought things she needed or wanted, within reason, but the majority of her disposable income went into investments.

She rolled to her side and stared at the doors and the light refusing to be shut out. When she'd come to bed, she hadn't bothered to look outside and she now wondered about the view from three stories up. Fifteen miles outside the city, the property spanned at least a few acres between neighboring homes, leaving Amanda thrilled that this much open space could be found so close to downtown. Of course she'd known, had even driven around the area looking for inspiration, but now that she'd experienced it during a time when she desperately needed to de-stress, the quiet meant so much more.

Giving up on sleep, she tossed the covers back and strode to the balcony doors wearing only her long-sleeved nightshirt and fluffy socks she liked to sleep in. She checked the doors for security sensors. Not seeing any, she flipped the lock, squeezed her eyes closed—please don't let there be an alarm on—and slowly pulled the door. It slid open easily, no sticking like the ones in her building, but that wasn't a surprise. She imagined Mrs. Hennings inspected every detail on a continual basis.

A light wind blew, sending a chill over her cheeks and bare legs, but she stood staring out at one tiny light shining in the distance between a clump of trees. She inhaled, enjoying the lack of frenetic energy. In her building, city life offered traffic noises, sirens and planes overhead. She loved it but found this new and inviting. A mini-vacation.

"Amanda?"

At the sound of David's voice, her body stiffened, each muscle locking. He sat on the balcony in what looked like an iron chair, that eerie moonlight throwing enough light for her to spy him in a sweatshirt over a pair of plaid lounge pants. His rumpled hair, that gorgeous ebony hair, poked in all directions and curled lightly around his ears. The man was beautiful in a completely male and rugged way. No soft angles for him. Anywhere.

She stepped out, gently closing the door behind her. "You're awake?"

"Couldn't sleep." He tilted his head up to the sky, where a bazillion stars winked at them. "I like to sit out here."

She moved closer, then leaned against the iron rail

that spanned the full length of the home. "I can't sleep, either. My mind won't stop. It's so peaceful out here."

"It sure is."

"It's also freezing. How long have you been sitting there?"

"Maybe half an hour. I was about to go in." He grinned up at her. "And lucky me, you came outside."

She glanced back at the door behind her. The one that led to a lovely sitting area with a stocked wet bar and a gas fireplace. But asking him to come inside meant inviting him into a bedroom, one that was temporarily hers, and she wasn't naive enough to believe that setting wouldn't spark a fire.

Then again, it *had* been a while since she'd experienced fire.

She gestured to the door. "I'd like to invite you in."

"But?"

"There's energy between us and I don't want to move too fast. I'm…nervous."

He stood, his long body gracefully lifting from the chair, and the girlie parts went wild.

He wandered to her, set his hands on her shoulders and unleashed a crooked smile. "With the way I feel about you, you should be nervous."

And, oh, that was a great line. At least to her. She so adored a man who knew what he wanted. He had to be a Scorpio. Had to be. He possessed a detached cool, but she imagined an inferno under his skin. One she all of a sudden wanted to reveal because he was never quite what she expected.

And wasn't that the thing she feared most? The not knowing? But with him, not knowing didn't torment her. Didn't knock her off her axis.

"How about," he said, "I promise not to hit on you?"

That made her laugh, a good, solid laugh that came right from her belly and felt so good after her crazy couple of days. "How very gracious of you."

"I'm trying here. Let's go inside. I won't even sit on the couch with you. I'll sit in the chair and you can take the couch. Or we'll slide the two chairs in front of the fireplace. I've never done that and it sounds kinda cool."

That it did. She backed out of his grasp toward the door. "I like that idea. Talking would be nice. Getting to know you would be nice."

"Oh, hey, I didn't say anything about talking."

DAVID FOLLOWED AMANDA into his mother's guest room. His *mother's* guest room. He'd just keep reminding himself of that fact because—yeah—his parents' bedroom was just below them and he'd never had sex in their house. Not even as a horny teenager. Never. His mother knew everything. She didn't even need cameras. Her intuition told her all she needed to know. Pure psychic ability.

Amanda closed the door behind him and as he headed toward the sitting area, he glanced at the bed, covers on the right side thrown back. A right-side sleeper. Interesting. He favored the left. How convenient.

"Have a seat," she said. "Or should you be telling me that, since it's your home?"

"Technically, it's not my home. I'm a squatter until the condo is ready."

Before sitting, he went to the fireplace and flipped the switch on the wall. The flames ignited, softly illuminating the room. In a few minutes the heat would be too much and he'd shut it off. Couple that with the heat between him and Amanda, and he might be toast. Charred good.

He glanced at the bed again on his way to the chair he'd promised he'd sit in, and a vision of her spread across it, bare-butt naked, popped into his head. Hey, he was a man and men had impure thoughts. Sue him. Or sue his penis because that bad boy was definitely coming to life.

Grunting, he dropped into the chair and rested his head back. High-backed chairs were underrated. He hated those low ones he couldn't lean his head against. These chairs? Perfect.

"It's a great place to squat. It must have been nice growing up here. I'd have loved all this open space."

"We didn't move here until I was fifteen. We lived downtown before that. The place was barely bigger than a bungalow and Zac and I shared a bedroom. Coming here was a major shock." He laughed and shook his head. "For the first month Penny was terrified. She was used to her small room and us all being within spitting distance. Being in a room three times the size of her old one spooked her."

"Really? You'd think she'd have loved it."

"Nah. She'd sneak into either Zac's room or mine and sleep on the floor. I don't know how he did it, but eventually my dad convinced her she'd be safe in her room. Sometimes I miss our old house."

"Why?"

"I don't know." *Liar.* He knew exactly why. Realized it years ago, but had never, not once, admitted it to anyone. "Life was simpler then. My dad's career took off the year before they built this house. One case and his career exploded. After that, things changed. He had more responsibilities, my mom had functions and everyone seemed to be running all over. I missed the nights where everyone was home. Penny and I had always fought. She was my pain-in-the-butt little sister, but after that one case, it got worse."

"Do you remember the case?"

He'd never forget it. "The Deville case. A supposedly impossible murder case to win. But my father loves the unwinnable ones. I chose civil over criminal law because of the Devilles."

"Why? Was the person guilty?"

"I think so. And my dad got an NG—not guilty."

"Oh, my God."

"Yeah. The kid who was on trial was nineteen. He was accused of murdering his parents. The night of the murder he was pulled over. The cop suspected he was high and asked if he could search the car. The kid was stoned, so he agreed. While searching the trunk, the cop found a bag. Inside the bag was a bloody knife."

"The murder weapon?"

"No doubt. And my dad got it thrown out."

Amanda sucked in a huge breath. He knew how she felt. Horrified, awed and confused. All at the same time. Welcome to the world of Gerald Hennings and family.

"How did he do that?"

"The cop asked to search the car, not the contents of the car. My dad argued that the kid's consent didn't include searching the bag. The bag was content and therefore outside the scope of consent. The trial court agreed. It went to the appeals courts and they also agreed. If I'd been the prosecutor, I'd have taken it to the Supreme Court. Any reasonable person would believe consent included the items inside the vehicle. Anyway, when the knife got suppressed, the state's case fell apart. Whatever was left of their case, my dad carved to pieces. He's brilliant at what he does."

"But a murderer went free."

"Probably. I was too young to get it at the time, but when I was in high school, thinking about law school, I studied my dad's cases. And that one bugged me. I asked him if he thought the kid was guilty and if so, why he took the case."

"What did he say?"

"He said people were entitled to have their rights protected. His job was to do that. His job wasn't to decide guilt or innocence or which rights should be protected and when. He didn't have that luxury. The cop didn't have permission to search the bag. The kid's rights were violated. Period."

"In an odd way, it makes sense."

"Intellectually speaking, yes, it does. But because of that, a murderer is walking around. And he inherited his parents' estate. A very large one."

"Wow."

"Yep. My dad and Penny love the war of defense work. It's an intellectual battle for them. Me? I'm an intellectual, but I can't stomach murderers walking. My father still doesn't understand that about me. And it took a long time for him to accept that I wouldn't be his right hand at the firm." He snorted. "And then Zac decided to be a prosecutor and I thought my father would go insane."

"That left Penny."

"She was all in. Still is. She loves it. Thrives on it, actually."

"Does that bother you?"

"Immensely." He winced. *Damn, Dave, way to sound like a jerk.* "Hang on. No. I spoke too fast. Her thriving at the firm doesn't bother me. Her working for my dad became a pawn in our battle and I hate that. She throws shade because I'm not a criminal attorney. It translates to me disappointing my dad when she didn't."

"That's a little harsh. Have you talked to her about it? Called her out?"

"Not reasonably. Usually we're screaming at each other. All I know is I need it to stop." He glanced around the room, took it in. "I'd like us to go back to being the family we were before this house. Before the Deville case put me on a different path. That's why I came home. I'm sick of being on my own and I want my sister back."

Amanda nodded. "I hope you get that. I'd hate for the two of you to not work this out. Things in life can change quickly. And forever."

"Like with your mom?"

She nodded. "I'll never recover from that. And I'll always have regrets." She sat forward and set her hand on his knee. "Don't have regrets. It's horrible."

He stared down at her hand on his knee, and the air in the room got thick, unbreathable. But he kept his gaze glued to her hand. If he looked up, into her eyes, he'd break that promise of not hitting on her. Because all he wanted right now was to hit on her. To kiss her. To get her into that giant bed behind them and show her all the things he'd like to do to her. On an ongoing basis.

"Amanda?"

"Yes?"

"If you don't move that hand, I'm throwing my promise out." He smiled. "I'll suppress it. Somehow I'll argue that you've violated my constitutional rights."

Wisely, she snatched her hand back, but she laughed at his corny joke while doing it. "You're a good man, David. I don't know what I'd have done without you these last couple of days."

"It's what we Hennings people do." And that meant keeping his word by walking back to his room because Amanda LeBlanc wasn't ready for him. Not yet at least.

He stood and lightly clapped his hands together. "Now I'm leaving."

She nodded, then stood. Coming closer, then going up on her tiptoes, she kissed him. A peck. Barely a peck. But enough to send the message that maybe, just maybe, next time she wouldn't be so nervous about inviting him into her room.

AMANDA WANDERED INTO the kitchen just after 7:00 a.m., her eyes a little puffy—totally his fault, thank you very much—but she looked amazing in a pair of skintight dark-washed jeans and a lightweight sweater that clung to every place he'd dreamed of touching the night before.

She eyed his steaming mug of coffee and he held it out. "Want it?"

"No, thank you. Tea maybe."

He'd like to take a chance on pulling her onto his lap, see how she'd respond, but chances were his mother would show up any second.

But those jeans…

To heck with it. As soon as she got within arm's length, he hooked his finger into her belt loop and guided her to his lap, where, yes, he had a boner. A good healthy one just from thinking about touching her.

That should have been cause for embarrassment, but… nah. It wouldn't kill her to know he wanted her. He'd probably made that fairly clear already.

She ran her hand over the side of his face and down his beard, where the friction did nothing to alleviate his current state. "This is nice."

"Not a bad way to start the day, if you ask me. What's your schedule today?"

"In spite of the chaos, I have a business to run. I need

to head over to my storage facility and pick out a painting for Mrs. Dyce's youth center."

"She called you?"

"She did. Yesterday. I think I have something she'll like. I told her I'd run it by there tomorrow. Wanna come with me to the storage unit? You might be able to tell if she'll like what I pick out."

"Absolutely." He patted the upper part of her rear. "I'll get you that cup of tea."

She hopped off his lap and followed him to the cabinet where his mom stored all the makings for tea. She had all kinds of stuff in there. Stuff he had no clue what to do with. All he knew was none of it resembled tea bags.

"What's wrong with plain old tea bags?"

Amanda laughed. "Nothing. Some people, like me, do it themselves. I'll take care of it."

Even better. "Go to it. Use whatever you need. I gotta run. I'm meeting Penny's investigator."

"Jenna, right? She's the sister of Lexi's boyfriend."

"That's right. She found three people in Cook County who own a blue Chevy Impala from the eighties. We're gonna scope it out. See if we can find the right car."

"You'll recognize it?"

"I think so. The one from yesterday was missing a rear hubcap. You stay here until I get back. Shouldn't be long."

She stopped messing with the tea and faced him. "Uh, no."

"What no?"

"I'm not staying here and doing nothing, David. Not when I have things to do. Either I'll go with you or you drop me at the condo so I can pick up my car. While you're with Jenna, I'll run to the storage unit and pick up the painting."

His brain might not have kicked into high gear yet, but

hadn't they just, as in thirty seconds ago, decided he'd go with her to the storage unit? "I'll help you with the painting. Don't worry about it."

Whatever he'd said fired her up because her beautiful brown eyes nearly severed his cojones.

"Listen," she said. "I get what you're doing here. And I love that you want to take care of me."

"But?"

"No but. Let's say *and*. I love that you want to take care of me *and* you need to know that I thrive on routine. None of which I've had in the last few days. Part of my routine is going to my storage unit when necessary."

He leaned into the counter and folded his arms. "I understand that. Except, as you said, none of this has been routine. Don't you think it would be wise to take precautions? Like maybe not going places alone?"

"Well...yes...but..."

He shrugged. "What?"

"I don't want you ordering me around."

Ordering. Her. Around.

It took everything he had, every ounce, every gram, for crying out loud, not to blow his stack. Was she serious with that? He'd spent days trying to help her, and this was what he got?

Here we go. The old David, Boston David, would have lost it and started yelling. This David, the new, improved one, was damned sure not going to do that. Not in front of her anyway. As soon as he got someplace private, he'd let loose. No harm in that.

For now, he laughed, ran his hands over his face and sighed. And here he thought making nice with Penny would be hard.

"What's funny?"

"Nothing. Believe me. Nothing." He blew out a breath,

folded his arms again, thought better of the body language *that* conveyed and dropped them. *Concentrate.* This conversation would require a balancing act. One slip and he'd fall right off the edge. Destroy the great start to the day. "Amanda, I'm not trying to order you around. Honestly. Maybe I got ahead of myself. I saw the text from Jenna and figured we could jump on finding this car. Then when McCall gets back to you, if we have something to pass along, maybe we can have him run it down. That's all I'm saying."

He wanted to add that if she felt going to her storage unit was more important, by all means, they should absolutely do that. And then he'd find the sharpest knife in this kitchen and plunge it into his own heart.

With his rotten luck, he'd survive.

"I know you think it's dumb. I can see that. But I've spent my life figuring out how to stay emotionally healthy. Part of that is taking care of myself, not depending on anyone or anything to make me happy. It's been years of learning how to not turn into my mother. Part of that is sticking to a routine. You can't come in and decide you're taking over. That's all *I'm* saying."

She turned back to the container with the tea, shoveled some into a glass pot, then slapped the spoon down. He wouldn't call it a slam, but it wasn't gentle, either.

And, holy hell, that snit was hot. Sick, he knew, but calm, cool Amanda had a temper buried inside her. Good to see.

He held up his hands. He didn't completely understand what they were fighting about—nothing new in his life— because all he was doing was trying to keep her safe, but at least she was honest.

"I apologize," he said. "I didn't mean to take over. I jumped on an opportunity to get something done. I do that. So, how about we hunt down this car with Jenna and then go to your storage unit? We'll do it together."

When she didn't respond, he moved closer, set his hands on her shoulders and kissed the back of her head. "I'm sorry."

Under his hands, the tension in her shoulders eased.

She dropped her head an inch. "Thank you. I'm not easy, David. I'll probably make you crazy before this is over. But I know what I need."

"Well," he said, "I guess we're perfect for each other because I'm not easy, either. We'll figure it out." He snorted. "Just have patience."

She tipped back a bit, rested her head against his chest and pulled his arms around the front of her. "I will. You, too. After I make my tea, we'll go find that car."

"THAT'S IT," DAVID SAID.

He pumped a fist and Amanda breathed in. For close to two hours they'd been cruising the city checking addresses where they might find a 1985 Chevy Impala with a missing hubcap. On the third try, they'd apparently found it, and Amanda's excitement over their success mixed with a creepy feeling of dread. What were they doing? After the break-in last night, they shouldn't be here. Detective McCall should be here.

David angled back to Jenna, who peered out the rear driver's side window. "That's the car."

The car sat wedged between two others in a line that spanned the short block. A car cruised by, constituting the only traffic. Narrow alleys separated the homes, and Amanda focused on the brick-faced bungalow in Jenna's path. A collapsing chain-link fence guarded the home. In this neighborhood bullets probably flew by that fence on a regular basis. The boarded-up home to its right might have been evidence of that. Just being here made the muscles in her neck bunch. Local gang shootings were a weekly—if not more often—occurrence and despite the quiet street, the energy pulsed and throbbed with an unspoken threat of an eruption.

Amanda scooted forward to see around David, and the morning sunshine coming through the windshield warmed the side of her face. "Are you sure?"

"Unless there are multiple 1985 blue Impalas with a missing left hubcap, yeah, I'm sure."

"Okay." Jenna pushed open her door. "Wait here. And turn so they can't see you."

Amanda spun around. This supermodel of a woman with her long, glossy hair, bombshell body and perfect face was getting out of this car alone? Was she insane? "Where are you going?"

This is bad. Bad, bad, bad.

"I'll knock on the door and see who answers. You two pay attention. You never know who'll open the door. It might be someone you recognize."

"It's too dangerous," Amanda said.

Halfway out of the car, Jenna glanced back. "This is nothing. Really. I've been in crack houses on my own. I'll be fine. Besides, neither of you can come with me. If it's the guy from last night, he'll never open the door. The only way to know is to get him to open up so we can see his face." She flashed a full-on smile. "I'm good at that."

"If you need something," David said, "hold your hand up and I'm right there. Got it? No screwing around, Jenna. Just give me the signal."

"Will do. Relax. It's all good."

With that, she slammed the door and made her way across the street in her skintight skirt and high-heeled boots. She might as well be the Queen of England living in the projects the way she stuck out.

"David, this is a rough neighborhood."

"Sure is." He reached across, set his hand on her thigh and squeezed. "She'll be fine. Two minutes and we're out of here."

They watched as Jenna knocked on the door. A minute later an older man, maybe about seventy, with gray hair and a long beard answered.

"Well, that's not the guy I saw in the house," she said. "Did you see the driver?"

"No."

Jenna spent a couple of minutes chatting with the man, smiling at him and nodding. No help signal came and Amanda sat back to watch her work. A minute later, a still-smiling Jenna typed something into her phone before waving goodbye to the older man.

Good. No chaos.

She hopped back into the car and buckled her seat belt. "Supersweet man."

David glanced in the rearview mirror. "What happened?"

"I told him I wanted to buy the Impala. That my boyfriend was a classic-car freak and would love to restore it."

After shifting the car into gear, David pulled away from the curb. "What'd he say?"

"The car is registered to him, but his grandson drives it most of the time and he doesn't want to sell it without checking with him."

Amanda turned back to her. "The grandson wasn't home?"

"Correct. The truly excellent news, though, is, being the kind woman I am, I offered to call his grandson and—" she waved her cell phone "—voilà, he gave me his number."

David stopped at a traffic light and smiled. "No wonder my sister loves you."

"Eh, what can I say?"

How about that she was completely awesome? If they could find the grandson, maybe the police could question him. "Can we track his cell phone?"

"Yes," David said. "Need a warrant, though. That's McCall's territory."

Which meant finally admitting to the detective that the skull had been stolen. The man would be furious with them, and rightfully so. They'd have to face it eventually, though. Might as well get it over with. She dug her phone from her purse. "I'll try him again."

The light turned green and David made a right, heading toward Lake Shore Drive, where Amanda would open her window and stick her face into the moist lake air that would wash away the cold dread that had swallowed her.

Not even lunchtime and she was completely drained. And she still had to face Detective McCall, which she sensed would not be an easy conversation.

Forgetting about the phone for a second, she rested her head back and stared at the car in front of them, letting her thoughts narrow to only the curve of the bumper and how it joined with the back quarter panel. Just a few seconds of distraction to get her thoughts in order. To shut out the stress of the past few days and catch her breath. That was all she needed.

"Everything all right?" David asked.

She picked up the phone again and scrolled her contacts. "Fine. Just thinking."

And summoning the nerve to make this phone call.

"Okay." He gestured to the phone. "McCall won't be happy we didn't report the break-in last night. Be prepared."

Chapter Ten

Standing in David's yet-to-be-finished kitchen, his beefy arms crossed, McCall had a look about him. One that bloated his face and made his eyes so hard he could snap concrete with them.

David had expected this. Detectives like McCall seemed to crave control. Probably because much of what their jobs entailed was so far *out* of their control. Understandable. In fact, if the roles were reversed, David would have been storming this condo and railing on them, well, as much as he could without compromising a crime scene.

"Let me get this straight," McCall said, his voice low and on the edge of containment. "You caught a guy in your house, stealing evidence, and you didn't consider that important enough to hunt me down?"

"We called you," Amanda blurted. "Whoever mans the desk told me you were out."

She stood beside David, shoulders back, gaze straight ahead, ready for whatever the detective could hit them with. A valiant attempt, but the excuse was lame and they all knew it.

"My foot! You should have said why you were calling and they'd have gotten to me." He pointed at David. "He's a *lawyer*. He knows better."

Yeah, I do.

Again he pointed at David, this time poking his beefy finger. "I'm not happy with you."

Got that message. Loud and clear. And they absolutely deserved his frustration, but if a do-over came David's way, he'd do things exactly the same way because they'd already gotten a jump on the car and its owner.

Giving McCall a dose of his own body language, David poked a finger back. "If you're done screaming, I'll tell you we left here right after the incident and no one has been back since. Your lab can still process the place."

McCall huffed. "At least you did somethin' right."

Having reached the level of nonsense he was willing to take, David pulled the baggie with the burglar's keys out of his jacket pocket. "These are the guy's keys. They fell out of his pocket when I was chasing him. Maybe we can get prints off them."

McCall snatched them out of David's hands. "Dammit. Did you touch them?"

"No. I used a napkin to pick them up. They've been in the bag since."

And the gates of hell will open up to me because I'm a liar.

"We could have had these processed already."

"Hey," David said, "I get it. You're upset. We screwed up. Move on, Detective, because we've got a skull missing and you whining about what we did or didn't do isn't getting us anywhere."

McCall gritted his teeth and sucked a huge breath through his nose. *Seriously trying the man's patience.*

"I should crack your skull, Hennings."

"Probably. But you won't because I'm bigger, younger and in better shape. Eventually, you'll tire out and I'll pummel you."

"Pfft."

McCall stepped forward, getting right in David's space. As if that would scare him. He stayed rooted in his spot, tilting his head down a bit. His height gave him an inch or two on the older man and he'd use that to whatever advantage he could. Even if it was only a mental advantage, he'd use it.

"Really?" Amanda said. "Are the two of you going to fight it out? *That* would do wonders for your crime scene."

Good one. David fought a grin. Call it more of a smirk. McCall huffed and shook his head before peeling off and ripping his phone from his belt holder.

Dodged one there.

Amanda's phone rang and she glanced at the screen. "My landlord. Maybe this is about my building." She pointed over her shoulder toward the living room. "I'll take this over there. Away from the *crime scene*."

"Good idea. We've already given this guy a heart attack today."

"I heard that," McCall said, shoving his phone back into his belt holder. "Lab guys are on the way. We're gonna have to fingerprint both of you to rule out your prints. You better hope we get a hit on this guy. And I'll talk to the lab about making another cast of the skull. My lieutenant is gonna blow an artery."

"Someone doesn't want her finishing that reconstruction. First her studio is condemned. Then her accounts are frozen. It's psychological torture. They're dismantling her life. And seems to me, everything happening is somehow related to city government."

"Please, Hennings. Stick to civil law, because no one from the city is doing this."

Stick. To. Civil. Law. David locked his jaw and fought the wave of anger that shot in all directions, making his legs and arms itch. No better hot button existed, and Mc-Call had hit it.

Dead-on.

Typically, that insult came from Penny, her go-to jab because she knew he couldn't resist it.

Until now. Now it wasn't about him and his need to escape the family legacy. This mess was about Amanda. As painful, as mind wrecking and body shredding as it was to keep his trap shut, he'd let McCall slide on this one.

David shrugged. "You got a better guess? The timing is too convenient. Who knows she took possession of that skull? Make a list. And check them out. That's all I'm asking."

"Great news," Amanda called from the living room.

They could use some of that. David glanced over the breakfast bar to Amanda still standing by the front windows. "What happened?"

"The building inspector didn't find any mold. They said it must have been a mix-up with the address." She held her hands up, her phone still clutched in one of them. "Tomorrow, I should be able to move back in to my studio."

One piece of good news. Sort of. Because jerk that he was, her moving back to her building meant leaving his mom's, leaving safety, leaving him. *Jerk.*

But he'd buck up here and give her a double fist pump. "*Yes.* One piece of your life restored."

"That's good," McCall said. "I'll look into the fraud case. I know a couple guys that work fraud. I'll see what they know. Meanwhile, I need statements from you about this break-in and that cell number for the driver of the Impala. Let's get on it and figure out what the hell is going on with this case."

CLOSER TO DINNERTIME than she'd expected, Amanda unlocked her storage unit and David slid the door up. Funny, that. She'd been handling that door on her own for three years and suddenly the man in her life—if that was what he even was—decided he'd be the one to do the lifting.

Sure. Why not? As long as she was safe in the knowledge she could do it, she'd let him play Tarzan.

He backed into the narrow hallway, letting her enter the unit first. Inside the twelve-hundred-square-foot space were one hundred and twenty-seven unframed paintings, all stored vertically with foam-covered boards to separate them and allow for air circulation. She'd learned early on that proper airflow prevented condensation and possible water damage.

"Huh," David said. "It's a mini studio."

"Sort of. It's climate controlled and cheap. I wanted space in my building, but the units are too expensive. This works out. It's a pain to schlep over here every time I need to pick up a painting, but it's twenty-four-hour access with security cameras. What did you think when I said storage facility?"

"I don't know. I was thinking a gallery or something."

A reasonable assumption, but economically impractical at this stage in her career. She made an adequate living, but she ruthlessly controlled her expenses. "That would be a small fortune. For now, this works." She grabbed a pair of white nylon gloves from the bag she'd hung on the wall. "The gloves I have will be too small for you, so no touching anything. If there's something you want to see, let me get it. Some of these aren't fully cured yet. It takes about six months for them to dry."

David saluted, earning himself a swat on the arm. She couldn't help being protective of her work. These pieces would make up her income for the next year or two, and care had to be taken.

"While we're here, I can show you some things for your place." She pointed to a set of paintings to the right. "I think the ones you'll like are in this group."

They might as well multitask while here. She'd pick up the painting for the Dyce Youth Center and let David peruse her stock. And since they hadn't heard anything from Jenna's lab about the prints on the key, they were in standby mode.

"I'll get the one for the youth center out first. We'll box it up and then I'll show you some I think you'll connect with."

"What can I do?"

She pointed to the tall, narrow boxes stacked against the wall just inside the doorway. "Grab me one of those boxes."

After wrapping the painting in glassine to protect it, she added Bubble Wrap—flat side facing the canvas—and taped the seams. David held the box while she slid the painting inside and sealed it, attaching a strip of plastic to the top to act as a handle.

David nodded. "Pretty slick, lady."

"I have it down. How about you take this one to the car so it's out of the way? While you're down there, I'll pull the ones for your place. And please make sure you lock the car."

Someone stealing a two-thousand-dollar painting would be the capper to the past few days.

"Yes, ma'am. Got it."

With him gone, she wandered through the unit, checking the labeled racks for the pieces she wanted to show him. After locating each one, she set them upright in an empty rack and continued her search for the next. By the time David returned, she'd found all five paintings.

"Look at you, all ready for me."

Something about the tone in his voice, the richness, caused a tingling hum inside her. Made her mind wander back to the night before when they'd sat in front of a fire, talking. Only talking. At the time, it seemed the right thing. Now? Her libido suddenly made it known she might be ready for David Hennings in other ways.

Ha. She'd never be ready for him.

She lifted the first painting from the rack and set it on the easel. "This first one has all the bold colors you like. It's more modern than I typically do, but I like the red slashes. If you don't like it, we can move to the next one."

"No. I like it. You guessed right."

"I knew it. Already I'm figuring you out."

"Ooh," he said. "That might not be good." He gestured to the painting. "What will this beauty cost me?"

"Three thousand," she said.

She'd give him credit for trying to mask it, but his eyes went a little wide. Even blue bloods sometimes balked at spending money on something they could only stare at. He'd pay thousands for a leather jacket but not a painting.

"*Hokay.* Don't take offense, because I know this piece is worth every cent, but my mother is killing me. I have never paid three grand for artwork. Hell, I'd be happy with posters in my house."

She snorted. "Posters. That's funny. Are you sure you're a Hennings?"

"Honey, I ask myself that every day." He gestured to the painting. "I'll take it. We'll consider it my first grown-up piece of art. My mother will be thrilled."

She smiled up at him. "Thank you. I love this piece.

I'm so glad you like it. I'll get it boxed up and we'll take it with us."

An alarm screamed in the hallway, the piercing wail bouncing off the cement walls. What on earth?

David's mouth tilted down. "Fire alarm?"

"I don't know. I hope not. Because if it is, the sprinklers might go off."

Sprinklers. No. It took a few seconds to fully register. She tilted her head back and scanned the ceiling because—please let there *not* be one in here. There.

"Oh, no."

Outside the unit, the alarm continued its droning whoo-whoo-whoo loud enough to make her ears throb. An icy panic gripped her shoulders.

Get out.

She spun, frantically grabbing paintings. No longer concerned with his lack of gloves, she shoved them at David. "Take these. We have to move them. There's a sprinkler. If they get wet, they're useless. Help me."

A spray of water rained down from the ceiling, and Amanda lunged for another canvas. *Ohmygod.* Her entire inventory was in this space. They'd never get them all out. Her chest locked, all the air from her lungs seizing.

"No!" She continued dragging paintings from the racks.

"The hallway has sprinklers, too."

"Then run," she said. "Please. Get them out."

Each with two paintings, they ran, water shooting down on them. With the amount of water coming down, there was no way they'd save everything. No way.

They burst through the side door of the building into the streaming sunlight. The manager stood in the parking lot staring up at the building, obviously searching for smoke.

"Fire?" David asked.

"I don't know," the man said. "You gotta stay out, though. The fire department is on the way."

Amanda set one of the paintings against the outside wall. She'd find a better place after she recovered what she could from inside. "Until I smell smoke," she said, "I'm going in."

She ran back, David following behind, the two of them sprinting as she thanked her own wisdom for her first-floor unit.

David scooped up two more paintings. "Can we throw something over them? Plastic or something? We don't have enough time to get them all out."

"Maybe the boxes."

Cardboard. They'd get soaked, as well. For half a second, she considered it. By the time she shoved the paintings inside the boxes, she could just as easily carry the pieces out of the building. She set the boxes on top of the racks.

Spraying water fell from the ceiling, drenching her skin, saturating everything in the unit. She shoved two more paintings at David and hauled another two out. They worked together, each trip seeming to take longer as puddles formed on the tile in the narrow hallway. Once her flat-soled shoes slid across the floor and David, his hands occupied with the paintings, body blocked her so she wouldn't fall over. The rubber on his boots kept him upright and once she was steady again he took off running.

Water continued to pound them—*no use*—and she choked up. *No.* Crying wouldn't help. She breathed in, setting her mind on the task at hand. Forcing herself to focus on her footsteps. On getting out.

Later, she'd worry about the loss. Now they'd save

what they could, which wouldn't be much. Even what they'd taken out was probably a dead loss. All her work.

Gone.

Forget focusing. The final element of her livelihood had been destroyed. Whoever was behind it all knew just how to make her suffer. A sob broke free as they burst through the door.

"Don't think," David said. "We'll figure it out later."

She nodded. *I'm not alone.*

David was here. Helping her. Sirens wailed as the first fire truck roared into the lot and whooshed to a stop. One of the men jumped from the truck and held his arms out to them.

"Sorry," he said. "No one goes in."

"There's no smoke. My paintings are in there. Please."

"Sorry, ma'am. I can't let you in there."

She spun to David, her eyes filling with tears, and he grabbed hold of her and hugged her while she sobbed into his chest. The anger and heartbreak poured out of her. Months and months and months of work, ruined.

"I'm so sorry," he said.

"All my work."

Her breath caught again and she backed away and slammed her hand against her chest because…this was not happening. Not happening. *All my work.* She swung her head back and forth and began pacing the parking lot, trying to take it all in. Her accounts had been frozen and now her inventory had been destroyed. *No money.* What would she live on?

Beside her, David fell into step. "Insurance. You have it, right?"

Insurance. She stopped pacing and glanced up at him and her chest unlocked.

He held his hands out. "I know the loss of the paintings is devastating, but financially, you'd be compensated."

"Ohmygod." She doubled over, breathed out, let loose a fresh batch of tears. *Please, with the crying.* "Yes. They're insured."

Each painting had been inventoried, priced accordingly and reported to her insurance company upon completion. The premiums damn near killed her, but she'd been diligent with her reporting. Playing it safe wasn't always a bad thing.

David eased his head back and stared up at the sky. "That's good. Smart girl."

The alarms went silent and Amanda bolted upright. Firefighters lingered in the lot, none of them rushing to be anywhere.

"No fire," she said.

"Doesn't look like it."

David wandered away, spoke to one of the firefighters and came back to her. "No fire. Someone pulled the alarm."

"At the exact time we were in there."

"Yeah."

"Whoever is doing this is systematically destroying my life."

"Unbelievable. Someone followed us here."

She turned back to the building, where the paintings they'd taken from the building sat propped against the facade. *Trash.* She knew. Too much water had fallen too quickly. Which only sparked a simmering rage inside her. This would not break her. She couldn't let it.

Never.

"Well, guess what?" She gestured to David's car, where he'd stored the painting for Mrs. Dyce. "I'm not leveled yet. I have one painting left. And the ones in my studio that aren't complete. I'll finish those and rebuild my inventory. Whoever is doing this will have to work a lot harder to break me."

Chapter Eleven

Eleven p.m. and Amanda hadn't managed to nod off. If she were in her apartment, she'd wander down to her studio and work until her body finally gave out. One of the perks of living and working in the same location.

Here, in the Hennings' guest room, she didn't have that luxury. Here, she'd be forced to play this twisted game of chicken her body insisted on.

From outside came a noise. Something scraping. Something that sounded like the iron chair she'd found David sitting in the night before.

And, oh boy, the idea of a replay of last night kicked up her pulse. Talking with him was easy. His brutal honesty, although overbearing at times, appealed to her. No pretenses, no games, no deception.

She tossed the covers off and once again in her nightshirt and fluffy socks headed for the door, pausing only to shove a brush through her hair. The man had already seen her in her jammies, but she could at least have tamed hair.

At the door, she hesitated. Getting used to these late-night chats wouldn't do her any good. The past four days had been intense and she'd relied on him too much. Tomorrow, with any luck, she'd go back home. Back to being alone. Back to working out problems on her own.

But that would be tomorrow.

She opened the door and a light wind met her. In typical Chicago fashion for wacky spring weather, the temperature tonight had gone up rather than down. She couldn't call it warm, but the chill definitely didn't pack the punch it had the night before.

Poking her head out, she peered left. David must have heard the door open and shifted in his seat. The same burst of moonlight from the night before illuminated him. Tonight, though, he wore a crew-neck sweatshirt and track pants and even in the darkness she saw him smiling.

"I was thinking about a ride on my bike," he said. "It's a good night for it, but I changed my mind."

"Why? Too cold?"

"No." He turned to her, meeting her gaze in the darkness. "I was hoping I'd see you out here."

Oh, the girlie parts loved it. Those babies sent her into full flutter. She stepped out and gently pulled the door closed. "I can't sleep."

He held his hand out and—yes—that would be nice. To just grab hold, as if it was the most natural thing to do. And why not? In the time they'd spent together, he knew more about her than some people she'd known for years.

At her hesitation, he cocked his head, clearly wondering if she'd reject him. If she'd warn him off as she'd done last night.

Not tonight.

Tonight, after a rotten week, she'd enjoy David's company.

Before he gave up on her, she grasped his hand and let him pull her close and lower her to his lap. "Gee," she said, "if I'd known this would happen, I'd have come out way sooner."

"And that would have made me a lucky man."

He reached sideways, grabbed something—a blanket—

off the chair to his left and spread it over them. "Your legs will freeze."

"Thank you. Aren't you cold sitting out here?"

He grinned. "Not anymore."

"Oh, the charm."

"I do try."

He tucked the blanket around her and she leaned in, resting against his chest as his hand moved up and down her back in a slow, caressing stroke. She tilted her head back and breathed. If she could freeze this moment, the pure relaxation, she'd do it. Just stay here forever, surrounded by darkness and chilly air and David Hennings in all his sexy glory.

This moment was made for the artist in her. Only, for once, she didn't want to paint it or sculpt it or sketch it. She simply wanted to experience it.

And that was new.

"I love sitting with you like this."

"Ditto that. And it feels damned naughty, considering that my folks are just below us."

Oh, stop it. "You had to bring that up?"

He dropped a kiss on her lips and she slid her hand over his chest, where even through the thick material of his sweatshirt, her fingers curved over cut muscle. David Hennings logged hours in the gym. No doubt. Seeing him naked, she was sure, would not be horrible.

"Amanda?"

"Yes?"

"If I wanted to move this into my room, what would you say?"

His mind-reading capabilities continued to amaze. "I'd say yes. I've had a miserable week and this is the first thing that's felt incredibly, undeniably right since this whole thing started."

The idiot grinned. "I do love the way you think."

He was so damned smug and confident and adorable that the explosions inside her happened again. If whatever this was didn't work out, it would hurt. She knew that. The man was a risk. A big one. But somehow he settled her, gave her a sense of calm even when her world was coming apart. Something she'd never experienced.

Ever.

With anyone.

He stood, easily lifting her as he went. "Hang on."

She tucked her legs and arms around him, grinning like an idiot herself because this was just too much fun. "I even get a ride."

"Oh, honey, you'll get a ride. Trust me on that one."

David's tone, the soft, sexy rumble against her ear, made her shiver as he carried her through the doorway, kissing her neck, running those amazing lips up and down, under the neckline of her nightshirt and grazing that sensitive spot on her collarbone. Her body responded. Loudly.

Still holding her, he used one hand to quietly close the door—probably so it didn't wake his parents. God, the man was strong. Considering that she wasn't exactly a lightweight. She grabbed his cheeks, ran her hands over his trimmed beard and suddenly she couldn't get enough.

She kissed him and drew herself closer in a relentless quest to eliminate any space between them. Their tongues collided, their breaths mingling until all of it became one intensely sparking fire that burned furiously. If she'd ever been kissed like this, she didn't remember it.

Still holding her, he backed her against the wall, pressing against her, not gently, either, and—*wow, that's wild*—his hands went crazy, touching her everywhere all at once while she tugged at his shirt because she wanted him. Now. Fast and hot and…*physical*. So not like her. The one who liked to play it safe all the time. But something about this man, his presence, gave her a feeling of protection and control and desire.

Safety.

With him, she'd be safe.

Using his hips to prop her against the wall, he tugged off his shirt and even in the dimly lit room, her eyes feasted on a patch of dark, swirling chest hair and the ripped muscles that spanned his shoulders and arms.

"My God, your body is unbelievable."

"Gym. Lots of it. Push-ups every night don't hurt."

He kissed her again and the bulge in his pants—hello, fella—left no doubt he wanted exactly what she did. He tasted like cinnamon and she yanked him closer until her breasts mashed against his skin and…perfection.

He tore his lips away and pressed them to her ear as he rocked his hips against hers. "Tell me what you want."

And, oh, that voice. The one she'd heard the first time through the phone line and immediately fantasized about it. She wanted so much. Safety, love and mindless, hot sex. All of it a jumble of emotions she didn't understand—this wanting to stay in her safe zone, yet break out of it. She wanted all of it. With him. Right now.

She gripped his shoulders, arched her back and closed her eyes, imagining that first moment… "I want *you*."

Always.

But he swung her around and carried her to the bed, where he tossed her on it, grinning down at her as if he could eat her alive, and none of it scared her. With the look on his face, it should have. David Hennings might undo her. In every way.

He dug a condom out of the bedside table and she bolted up, grabbed the waist of his pants and shoved them down, taking his briefs with them. His erection sprang free. The man was absolute perfection.

All hers.

At least for now.

"Amanda, who knew you were such a hellcat?" he teased.

Certainly not me. She slid her underwear and socks off and rested back on her elbows while she waited for him to deal with the condom. His extremely naked and hard body unleashed something primal—rough—inside her. "You bring it out in me. First time for everything, right?"

He liked that. His sexy, slow-moving smile told her so. And being who he was, she sensed the pride he took in that. The knowing that he'd reduced her to something wild and new.

Still standing, he moved to the edge of the bed, grabbed her behind the knees and yanked her closer.

So ready. *Please.* For once, she didn't want to play it safe. Didn't want boundaries or worries about giving too much. She wanted to take and give it all until there was nothing left. No worry, no hurt, no restraint. All of it.

And then he was inside her and the fast, hard invasion took her breath, making her gasp.

He stopped and she nearly screamed. "Does that hurt?"

"No. Amazing. Don't stop."

Instinctively, her hips moved with his, riding the crazy wave of lust, wanting more and more. At this rate, they'd probably send the mattress clear off the box spring, but—yes—this was what she needed.

He gripped her thighs tighter, his fingers digging in, holding her in place as he drove into her, over and over. He tilted his head back and closed his eyes and the look on his face, a cross between concentration and pleasure, made her ache to touch him. To smooth the lines between his eyebrows. Finally, he opened his eyes and met her gaze and she locked herself around him, waiting for the explosion, the ultimate release.

She rolled her hips and he groaned and the force of it, knowing she could do this to him as much as he did it to her, emboldened her, made her lovemaking a little rougher because she wanted to watch him fall apart. At her hands. This man who prided himself on taking charge. Just once, she wanted him weak.

She squeezed him tighter and his chest hitched. Suddenly, her body was a tight, perfect coil and she watched him watching her, their gazes in a fierce battle, that connection so powerful she wanted to hold on as long as she could, not let go, not let it end.

Can't. She rolled her head side to side, imagining the intensity of total release. Letting go. Allowing herself to be completely raw and bare and vulnerable.

Her mind exploded and she wanted to cry out, but held it because, yikes, his parents were right below them. The sound was a twisted, strangled grunt—how lovely—and David laughed at her attempts to hold back, but his reaction only intensified her orgasm. She closed her eyes but quickly opened them again, wanting to see that moment when he was hers. Completely.

He threw his head back, pumped his hips faster and she reached up and ran her hands along his arms, needing to touch him but unable to reach his body as he arched away. He met her gaze again, the intensity pure and electrifying and something she'd never known. This was passion. Hallelujah.

"Damn, Amanda."

He let out a burst of air and she held on as the orgasm ripped through him, his body buckling. He moved on top of her on the bed, propping himself on his elbows, their bodies still joined.

"Thank you." She kissed him lightly, ran her hands over his face, loving the prickles of his beard against her palms. "That is what I've always hoped it would be."

He nuzzled her neck, got right up to her ear. "That's because I'm crazy about you. And to think, we've got all night."

THE FOLLOWING MORNING, showered and ready to face the day, Amanda wandered into the kitchen and found David finishing a phone call. Jenna sat beside him, her long, dark hair falling over her shoulders. She wore a blazer with a white blouse and looked more like an upscale clothing catalog model rather than a private investigator. In front of her were a bottle of water and a plain manila folder that hopefully held something worthwhile.

David dropped his phone on the table. "Well, that was a bust."

He spotted her and slid his gaze to Jenna, then back to Amanda. "Morning," he said, downplaying the fact that she'd slid out of his bed and tiptoed back to her own room an hour ago.

"Good morning. What was a bust?"

"That was McCall."

Ah.

Jenna cracked open the bottle of water and took a drink. "What happened?"

Backing away from the table, he stood, motioned Amanda to his chair and then leaned against the large island, crossing his arms and settling his gaze on Jenna. He did that when he spoke to people. Focused his intense eyes on them, offering every bit of his attention.

"McCall pinged the grandson's phone yesterday. They picked him up, but he's not talking."

"That's not a surprise."

Amanda shifted in her chair and faced him. "What about the security video from the storage place?"

Upon leaving the storage facility, they'd notified McCall of the false alarm and he'd agreed to look into it by checking the security footage.

"That," David said, "might be promising. He's emailing me the video. They can see who pulled the alarm, but apparently the guy's face is hidden. He's not stupid—that's a definite. If nothing else, we can see if it's the same body type as the guy who broke into the condo. Maybe we can narrow both events to this one guy." He held his hand to Jenna. "What have you got, Jenna?"

She flipped the file open. "I'm still waiting on the lab report for the key. They had to bump us for another murder case. As soon as I hear from them, I'll let you know." She handed Amanda a few sheets of paper, then gave David what appeared to be copies of the same stack. "For now, let's talk about Simeon Davis. This is everything I found. He's clean as a whistle. Barely a parking ticket. Thirty-eight years old. He lives on the north side, makes sixty grand a year selling insurance, has a couple of teenage kids and a wife who works as a cleaning lady."

An insurance salesman. Amanda propped her chin in her hand and thought back over the years and the clients who'd come and gone. Nothing. If she'd worked with him, she didn't remember it.

David cocked his head. "What insurance company?"

"A local agency. TRU Associates. They work with all the big companies."

Both of them turned to Amanda, the question unspoken but delivered. "They don't handle my insurance. And I've never heard of them."

"Okay. There's a photo of him in the stack. Page three. Take a look."

Amanda shuffled through the pages until she found the grainy color photocopy of what looked like a driver's license photo. Simeon Davis was a white man with sandy-blond hair, a mustache and full cheeks that indicated he carried more extra weight than was probably healthy. He also had a prominent mole above his left eyebrow.

As a person who studied details, she would have remembered that mole. She thought back over her clients, vendors she worked with, friends of friends, but…nothing. No recall. The thick mustache could be throwing off her judgment. She held her finger across the mustache, trying to picture him without it.

"Anything?" David asked.

"No. If I've met this man, I don't remember it. And I have a fairly good memory. It's crazy." She flicked the photo. "I don't even know him and suddenly he's accusing me of fraud? I've never even been in a check-cashing place. I'm an artist. Everything I make goes into legitimate investments. I keep some spending money, but otherwise, I save it all."

Humiliation over having to talk about her finances in front of Jenna, a near stranger, burned in her throat. David was bad enough, but she'd gotten beyond that this week. Pretty much her life was an open book to this man and after last night and the rather *inventive* things they'd done, she didn't anticipate that changing. Sexually, the man had tapped into desires she'd never explored and that was…well…exciting.

But risky.

Dangerous.

Her face grew hot and she propped her elbows on the table, resting her forehead against her palms.

A large hand—David's—landed on her shoulder. She glanced up at him and he squatted next to her. "I promise you, we'll figure it out. Jenna will work on it until we do."

"And who's paying for *that*?"

David shot up and spun toward the doorway, where a woman, a younger, mini version of Mrs. Hennings, stood. With the resemblance to David's mother, this had to be Penny. A petite little thing—something Amanda hadn't expected considering David's size—she wore a lightweight camel coat over a winter white suit.

The second she stepped into the kitchen, the atmosphere turned frigid. Tension flew off David like erupting lava.

Penny avoided him and beelined for Amanda. "Hi, I'm Penny. You must be Amanda."

"Yes." Amanda reached to shake hands. "I'm sorry we've tied up your investigator."

She slid her gaze to David, who'd stepped back to his spot at the counter, his arms crossed, jaw locked. This wouldn't be fun.

"It's not your fault." Penny faced David. "We don't mind helping, but we have clients. *Paying* clients. At the end of the month, we need to account for Jenna's time."

Jenna smacked the file closed. "That's my cue. I'll leave you guys to discuss this. Because, honestly, I don't want to be in the middle of it. Just someone call me and tell me what I'm supposed to do."

"Thank you, Jenna," David said.

Jenna left and David glared at his sister. "That entrance was necessary?"

"I didn't make an entrance. I asked a question."

David scoffed. "Right."

"Oh, just stop it. We run a law firm. Now that you're about to open your own practice, you should understand we have certain accounting policies to adhere to. And you commandeering our investigator is a problem."

Commandeering? That might have been extreme. Amanda stayed seated, her gaze darting between the two of them. From what David had said, his relationship with Penny was rocky at best. And at the moment, Penny had a tone that was sure to set her brother off. Whatever his initial reaction was, he'd held it back. Amanda could see it in the way he locked his jaw and shoved his hands into the front pockets of his jeans. Good for him.

"I didn't *commandeer* her."

But Penny wasn't backing down. She threw her shoulders back, and for a small woman she had a ferocity about her. No wonder she was a litigator.

This could turn into a bloodbath. And given how hard David had been trying to avoid fighting with his sister, Amanda didn't want her situation to cause a family war. "Please don't argue."

"In a way," Penny said, "you did. I signed off on Jenna locating the car and working with the lab. Those were isolated things."

David waved his hands at her. "Don't start. You'll only annoy me and we know how that ends up."

"Quit waving your hands at me. I came over here to talk to you about this and now you're giving me attitude. Why doesn't *that* shock me?"

And, yes, Amanda could see why David got upset with Penny. That biting sarcasm could be grating.

David laughed. "And it begins…"

"I didn't sign off on her spending all of yesterday morning with you hunting down some car. I came to calmly address that and I find her here, when she's supposed to be working a case for me, and I hear you telling her to do more." She turned to Amanda. "Please don't misunderstand. We have no problem helping you. Not one bit. My mother started this and we feel responsible. But we need to manage Jenna's time correctly."

Managing their employee's time was a reasonable request, and had the message been delivered differently, David would probably agree. He could be bossy, but he listened when people had concerns. But his sister's tone had probably forced him to check out the minute she got snarky.

The best Amanda could do right now was try to defuse the situation. For no other reason than that David had confided in her about wanting to make things right with Penny. For him, she'd play mediator. "I understand. And I agree with you. We shouldn't take over your employee. I've been preoccupied and didn't think it through."

About to suggest that they come up with a time frame when they would need Jenna, she shifted to David and found his deep blue eyes pinned to her. Not in a good way, either. *Venom.* Her arms tingled and she sat up a little.

"And what?" he said. "It's *my* fault now?"

WASN'T THIS DANDY? Amanda taking Penny's side. Over the most idiotic thing. And what really chapped him was that he shouldn't lose it over this, shouldn't let his hang-ups over always being the odd man out get to him. He'd promised himself he'd work on getting along with Penny, to not let her bait him into arguments, because she knew, as well as he did, she had a knack for firing his temper.

He'd accepted the rules of the game years ago, accepted the mind-messing toll it took, accepted that he and Penny would always compete. Sometimes viciously. Those things he got. But what he didn't get was how, after he'd been idiot enough to confide in Amanda about his relationship with Penny, not to mention his insecurities over being the outsider of his family, she could side with his sister.

Against him.

He'd trusted her. And what did he get out of it? A night of great sex and her discounting everything he'd done for her in the past few days.

Damn, this ripped him.

"Whoa," she said, her eyes catching fire. "I didn't say it was your fault."

"Well, honey, it sure sounded like it."

"Oh, come on, David."

"Come on what? I've been running my tail off trying to help you, and my sister walks in and all of a sudden you two are allies."

Drama Queen Penny threw her hands up and huffed. "Every time. Every damned time I try to have a conversation with you and think we can get along, you throw a hissy fit."

"Are you insane?" Amanda said, talking over Penny and—damn—the wheels were coming off this truck fast. "I'm not taking anyone's side. But, God help me, I can see why you two have issues."

Ignoring Amanda, he went back to Penny. "You're the one who walks around here smarting off at everyone. Why Dad and Zac let you get away with it, I have no idea. You're not twelve anymore. Grow the hell up."

The corner of her mouth lifted, but it wasn't a smile. Far from it. What he had here was more of a resigned sadness with some smug thrown in.

"There's the brother I know. I wondered how long it would take."

"Oh, David," Amanda said. "You don't mean that."

No. He didn't. But, dang it, they'd gotten him riled up, never hard with Penny, and he'd lost his temper.

"Sure he does," Penny said. "Because despite all this garbage he's been feeding me about wanting to improve our relationship, my brother simply doesn't like me. He may love me, but he doesn't like or respect me."

He glanced behind him at the knife rack next to the stove, contemplated the handle on the carving knife, pictured it protruding from his chest. After he'd put it there. That would break his mother's heart. Bad plan. He turned back to his sister. "Now I don't like you? Do me a favor, don't tell me what I don't like."

"Whatever, David. But if you want to use the firm's investigators, you need to ask. That's all I came here to tell you."

Penny marched out and for a few seconds he considered chasing after her. Experience had taught him that wouldn't go well. For either of them. When they fought, it took a couple of hours for reason to grab hold again. So he'd wait. Maybe talk to her later.

"Well," Amanda said, "I see what you meant about you two."

He squeezed his eyes closed and ran the palms of his hands over his head because his rising blood pressure gave him a damned headache. "Yeah. That was classic Penny and David. A couple of dopes. But I needed you on my side."

"I am on your side."

Could have fooled him. "By agreeing with her?"

"I didn't agree with her. All I said—"

"Hold up. I've told you what life is like in this family. I'm the rebel. I don't think it's a lot to ask of you to support me."

She craned her neck forward, then let her head drop

half an inch. Incredulous. That was what she was. Clearly, he was speaking another language, because she didn't get it.

"David, I'm assuming you're keyed up right now because I *cannot* believe you're blaming me for this. All I said was I understood what she was saying."

"Yeah, but you don't know her. She'll use that as ammunition. And I'm sick of that. I'm sick of everything I say turning into a fight. So, if you and I are gonna work, you need to be Team David."

"And you don't think that's ridiculous?"

Hell no. Even if it was, that was reality. "It's how things work around here. In a house full of attorneys, either you win or you lose. I need to be able to count on you. If this is gonna work, you've gotta have my back. Whether I'm wrong or right we can talk about later, but when it comes to my sister, you're on my side."

She sat back, her shoulders slumping, her body nearly folding over, and whatever she intended to say, it wouldn't be good for him.

"Wow. If that's the way you operate, you people are brutal. Seriously, brutal. Whether you believe it or not, I am on your side. But there will be times when I don't agree with you. It doesn't mean I'm not supportive." She slid out of her chair. "That's a lesson both you and your sister need to learn. It's not about sides. It's about figuring out how to work together."

She pushed the chair in, then kept her grip on the top of it for a few seconds, and the raging pain at the base of his neck shot straight into his head. The next few seconds would be bad. He knew it.

She let go of the chair and faced him, her eyes not nearly as fiery as before. What he saw now was worse.

This droopy sadness might kill him. *Where's that carving knife?*

"You can call me when you learn that lesson because I can't have this. I've said all along I don't want the drama. Emotionally, it'll destroy me. And I know what that looks like. I won't risk it. Now I have a painting to deliver."

What the hell was she doing? They'd had a fight. After one argument she wanted to turn tail? Nuh-uh. Not happening. "That's it? End of discussion?"

By the time she got to the hallway, he was on her. "Amanda, hang on."

"No, David. One thing I won't do is *hang on*. You've made it clear what you need. I can choose not to give you what you need."

"I don't want you going alone."

"I don't really care what you want. I'll be back to pick up my things later. So, yes, I believe this *is* the end of it."

AMANDA CLIMBED INTO her car, her body going through the motions of starting the engine, shifting the car into gear, pressing the gas pedal and maneuvering down the winding driveway. If she concentrated on the task, focused on each individual element, she wouldn't come apart.

All along she'd been right. Living in neutral might not have been exciting, but it wasn't this, either. This agonizing stab of heartbreak. But this was what happened when people opened up, trusted others and allowed them in. Fell in love. Which, darn it, sounded stupid after only a few days, but if she could force herself to believe she had fallen in love, she wouldn't feel so crummy right now. She'd have an explanation other than her own stupidity.

She banged the steering wheel—boom, boom, boom.

Ow. That last one sent a shock of pain tearing right up her arm.

Her throat locked up, just a vicious clog of air that wouldn't let loose, and her eyes filled with tears. *Darn it.* She hated crying. But why not? Might as well cry it out.

The road ahead blurred. She swiped at her tears and eased the car to the side of the road, the tires crunching over gravel that lined the shoulder. From the floorboard in the backseat, the box with her painting—her only remaining completed work—shifted and she spun to check it.

It's fine. Everything would be fine. She'd give herself a couple of minutes to cry it out. To wail like an infant because she was alone and no one would know and she wouldn't have to be humiliated.

Maybe, for once, a good cry would do her good.

Except her phone rang. Of course. Lexi. Probably checking on her. She'd been giving Lexi daily updates on the goings-on, and besides David, Lexi was the only other person who knew the whole of it. With Lexi, there'd be no bringing her up to speed. This call she would most definitely answer. "Hi. Where are you?"

"My office. Why?"

"Can I come over? I need a friend."

"My goodness, Amanda, in all the time I've known you, I don't think I've ever heard you say that."

"That's because I never have."

DAVID STOOD IN his mother's kitchen, hands on hips as he stared out the back window. How long should he wait to call Amanda? If she were anything like him and Penny—and wasn't getting involved with a woman like his sister a thought that gave him stomach cramps?—she needed a cooling-off period. Chances were, as ornery as she'd looked when she'd walked out, she probably wouldn't answer his call.

What he should have done was gone after her. Even if she had said she didn't want him to. After the past few days, it wasn't safe for her to be out alone.

He kicked his foot out, just missing the doorframe because his mother would crucify him if he did any damage. There wasn't one damn thing to punch or pummel or pulverize, and all that frustration sizzled inside him like acid on skin.

"Oh, my," his mother said, entering the kitchen. "What now?"

Terrific. Add her to the pile. What else could be thrown at him today?

"Women," he said. "That's what. If I live to be a hundred, I'll never figure your gender out."

Mom laughed. Laughed. Seriously?

"Your *gender*? David, you make us sound like we live to torment you."

Yeah, well. *He* wouldn't be the one to say it.

He turned from the window. "Mom, you have to be straight with me and tell me I'm adopted. It would explain a lot. Because I sure as hell do not have the people skills I need to survive this family."

She cocked her head, narrowed her gaze in that all-knowing-mother way. "You're the spitting image of your father. Chances are, you're not adopted. Furthermore, I think your people skills are fine. But whatever is bothering you, sit down and tell your mother about it. I'll heat you up a brownie. That always helped when you were little."

Brownies. In the morning. Excellent.

From the cabinet next to the fridge, she pulled out a plastic container and a paper plate. "I made them yesterday and hid them. Between you and your father, they wouldn't have lasted an hour."

She popped the brownie into the microwave. "I suppose you want a glass of milk?"

Yep. His mother knew him. "I'll get it," he said.

She shooed him away. "Sit. You've had a long few days. And I don't get to mother the three of you anymore. I miss those days."

"I know you do. Damned kids always have to grow up."

And fight.

He dropped into the chair and rubbed the palms of his hands into his eye sockets. "Mom, I'm tired of arguing."

"My darling, you come from a family filled with litigators. I don't think the arguing will end soon. You have to do what I've done and learn to work around it."

Ha. Good one. "How?"

"Practice. Years of it. Don't get upset with me, but your way of dealing with the issues you have with Penny, and to a certain extent, your father, is to escape. You moved to Boston. And I don't blame you. You're entitled to live your life the way you choose. But I think you've realized you can only hide for so long. Now you're back. And I think you'll be much happier if you stop letting your sister frustrate you. I swear I could knock your heads together. The two of you can barely be in a room together without one of you picking at the other. One of you starts and the other always bites."

"She usually starts."

She rolled her eyes and scoffed. "Very mature. You do your share."

He grunted. But no argument materialized because yeah, he tended to strike, as he'd just done, in anticipation of Penny getting snarky with him. Dammit.

Mom set a giant glass of milk and a warm brownie in front of him. "You know, Zac loves brownies, too. He likes ice cream on his, though, while you like them plain."

"What about Penny?"

"No. She's gummy bears. Buy her a bag and she'll love you forever."

Gummy bears. How did he not know that? Shouldn't he have known that? Sure, he'd been living away for a few years, but still, he could have taken an interest in the things his sister liked. And not taking that interest, in his humble opinion, made him someone he didn't want to be.

He slouched back and shook his head. "I'm a jerk."

Mom set her hand on his shoulder and kissed the top of his head. "We're all jerks sometimes. Take your sister gummy bears and tell her you're done fighting and poking at her."

"I already did that at dinner the other night. Sort of."

"Well, make this one definitive. After that, it'll be up to her to do the same. The two of you can get along. You've just never figured out how to not antagonize. My suggestion? Go to lunch alone with her once a week. You'll probably find the two of you have a lot in common. I know I see it. You just don't know each other, David. And, God help me, it's wearing me out."

He shifted in his chair and stared up at his mother. "I'm sorry, Mom."

"I know you are. But fix it. Please."

"We will."

"And I saw Amanda leave here without you. You're on a roll, my boy. Whatever that was about, you need to fix that, too. I've got my eye on her for the next member of this family."

David cracked up. "Hey!"

Mom held her hands up as she left the room. "That's all I'm saying. Just fix it."

His mother made it sound so easy. As if years of he and Penny ripping at each other could be fixed with one conversation.

If it could, he'd be in great shape because not only would it eliminate the jealousy and competitiveness with Penny, but also it would score him points with Amanda.

And after the fight he'd just had with both of them— *way to multitask, Davey*—he needed both.

The plan on how to make that happen started with conversations with both of them. He slugged the last of the milk and his brownie, slouched back in his chair, stretched his legs and studied his boots while the low hum of the fridge knocked his blood pressure down a few hundred notches. A ride on his bike, a couple hours to check out and breathe, would do him good about now. What a damned start to the day.

But, as his mother had said, he could fix it.

He'd call Penny first. Then Amanda. But he knew his sister, and she hadn't had her two-point-five hours to cool down. If he tried her now, she'd still be in viper mode and that wouldn't play well.

He picked up his phone and tapped at the screen to call Amanda. It came as no surprise that the call went to voice mail. After four rings. Meaning, the lovely Amanda LeBlanc was PO'd at him and ignored his call. He'd let that ride for Penny's requisite two-point-five hours, too. Get them both after a cool-down period. But he'd leave her a message—an apology—and hope to hell she was the forgiving type.

He set his phone aside and flipped open the file Jenna had given him on Simeon Davis. The first page gave the basic who, what and when and David perused it.

He scanned the address—west side of Chicago—and checked the time. Chances were the insurance office where old Simeon worked would open around nine, and with the morning traffic, he could get there right about that time. How convenient. He'd take it as a sign that a small *chat* with Simeon was in order.

He scooped up the file and grabbed his favorite jacket, the Belstaff, which had taken the beating. Completely annoying. Add that to his list of complaints about this whole mess. Just another reason—albeit a minor one—to find out who was behind all this.

Or maybe, as his sister had said, he was good at talking himself into things. Either way, he'd pay Simeon Davis a call.

Chapter Twelve

Amanda walked into Lexi's garage-turned-office, a place she'd designed herself, and plopped onto the sofa in front of the desk. Who put a sofa in front of a desk? Lexi, that was who. Because it was her office and she could do with it as she pleased. She scanned the muted yellow walls and the shiny bookshelves loaded with design books and catalogs and samples and marveled at the change the place had undergone. A few months ago it had been filled with junk from the previous owner, and now it belonged in a home magazine.

"I can't believe this was once a garage. From inside you'd never know it."

Lexi sat back in her desk chair and took in the room. "Thank you. I'm so happy it's finally done. I knew when I bought this place I could make an office out of it. And the best is I can pull my car into the alley and open the bay door to load and unload it. No more schlepping those gigantic sample books if I can't find parking on my block. But you're not here to talk about my garage. You look a mess. What's going on?"

"And here I thought I cleaned myself up before coming in here."

Lexi shrugged. "You probably did, but I've never seen

you cry, so I know just by looking at your blotchy skin you had a good jag."

"It's been a rough week."

"Are you back in your place yet?"

"No. Hopefully today. The landlord got that worked out. The building department said it was a mix-up. I'd believe that if the skull hadn't gotten stolen, my bank accounts weren't frozen and my paintings weren't ruined." She let out a sarcastic grunt. "I'm my own reality television show."

Lexi leaned forward and held her hand out. "Honey, I'm so sorry this is happening to you."

Amanda took her hand, thankful for a friend to talk with. Something she hadn't done nearly enough. The fact that she had few true friends might be the reason, but that was her own fault. She had plenty of acquaintances, but people to share the details of her life with, secrets and fears, she didn't seek out. Doing that required emotional investments and, well…that was that.

Such a waste.

"And I haven't told you the best part," Amanda said.

"You can top all that's happened?"

"David Hennings."

Lexi drew her eyebrows in and Amanda rolled her hand. *Come on, Lex, you know.*

It took a few seconds, but Lexi's mouth dropped open. An all-around amusing look for the always cool and put-together interior designer.

"You and *David*?" She smacked her hand on the desk. "Good for you. The man is hotter than a two-dollar pistol."

Having always suspected Lexi might be insane, she thought this only proved it. How the hell was all this upheaval a good thing? "No. Not good for me. Not good at all. He's so, well, *hot*. In every way, if you know what I mean."

Lexi hooted. "I can't believe it. This is great."

She didn't understand. "It's not great. We're days into this and I'm already sad. Lexi, these people are crazy. I mean, they thrive on drama."

"Well, yeah, but it works for them." Lexi drew up, apparently thinking. "Ooohhhhh," she said. "Now I get it."

"Yes. I can't have that." She waved her hands in front of her chest. "It gets me too churned up. Like I don't know what to do with all these feelings. I've spent a long time building a life and I liked that life. Now the Hennings clan comes along and it all crumbles. And worse, I let myself have feelings for him and I'm already crying."

"Just hold on a second. You just said you'll be back in your place today. With that alone you're putting your life back together. I can promise you the fraud case will go away. It's a crock and you've got the best legal minds in the city on your side." Lexi leaned into her elbows on the desk, her gaze direct but filled with understanding. "I'm not minimizing what you've been through. It's a nightmare. Unfortunately, as you know, this is life. Bad stuff happens to good people. You rely on those who care about you to help you get out of that bad stuff. It's the way things work. You've just never let yourself have that. That's a shame if you ask me. Then again, what do I know?"

Apparently, she knew a lot. "Gee, Lex, don't hold back. Please. Be honest."

Lexi laughed. "I just think it would be nice to see you take a risk. And David is the perfect candidate. He's—"

"Not a conformist."

"Yes! He's a little unpredictable. Not what you'd think

of someone coming from his family. And, well, let's face it, he's nice to look at."

And he's great in bed. "I don't know, Lex. The intensity scares me."

"Of course it does. That's what's supposed to happen. But it should be a good scary. Don't you remember how I was when I met Brodey?"

"Total man hater."

"Ew. It sounds so harsh, but yes, true. He was different, though. I needed him in my life. He proved to me that he could be trusted. Neither of us is perfect and we've definitely been tested, but we got through it."

She glanced around the garage, the very place where a murderer had trapped her just a few months ago. But Brodey had shown up and the two of them, together, had overpowered the man. She brought her gaze back to Amanda. "What I went through in here was horrible. I still don't sleep well. But if there's one good thing that came out of it, it's that I know Brodey will always take care of me. Even when we're mad at each other. And I think you have to go through the tough stuff to really see a person's character."

"Even when he and his family are a little nuts?"

Lexi laughed. "Especially then. Did you forget my boyfriend's sister works for these people? Believe me, Jenna tells Brodey all the stories and we're not talking cray-cray here. They're *excitable*. But Jenna loves them. And yes, she talks about Penny and how loony she is, but she's a good person and incredibly loyal. They all are. Maybe…"

She hesitated and uh-oh. Amanda knew whatever would come next might hurt. "What?"

"I adore you. You know that. So anything I say is because I care. It's not meant—"

"Oh, just say it already."

Lexi laughed. "Fine. I think you're too stringent with the way you live your life. You're always afraid of the next bad thing. It has to be exhausting."

"You have no idea."

Again, Lexi smacked her hand on the desk. "My point exactly. A guy like David might be the perfect balance for you. He's a risk taker and you're not."

"You're saying I should lighten up a little?"

"Honey, you should lighten up *a lot*. Imagine the fun you'd have."

TRU INSURANCE. That was what the imprint on the door of the glass storefront said. Not what David had expected, but he could say that about the entire past four days. Standing on the sidewalk, the clouds overhead breaking up but not yet letting the sun through to warm the air, he glanced in both directions. At least two of the stores within his sight were empty, their windows showcasing a for-lease sign. The lack of foot traffic there weren't even a lot of cars driving by—didn't bode well, but it was still early on a Friday morning. Maybe things picked up later in the day.

Whoever did their prospecting might need a lesson or two on choosing a great office location. An insurance company didn't necessarily need foot traffic, but it never hurt. Or maybe rent was cheap because of the lack of pedestrian traffic and that was why TRU Insurance chose this location.

Did it matter? Hell if he knew. He might find out in the next ten minutes, though.

He pulled open the door and found a young redhead sitting at the first desk with a plaque that said RECEPTIONIST. There you go. Even if he found it bogus that the woman's name wasn't even on the plaque. Would it be so hard to put *Mary Jones, Receptionist* on there?

Not his problem. He glanced around at the four empty desks behind Mary Jones, the name she would forever be known as. They were standard-issue circa 1970s cheap metal, and combining them with the location, David got the feeling TRU Insurance wasn't exactly a huge money-maker. The hallway behind the desks led to a couple of doors and dead-ended at the rear entrance.

"Good morning," Mary Jones said.

"Hi."

"Can I help you?"

"I'm looking for Simeon Davis."

Mary popped out of her chair. "He's right in the back. Who should I say is calling?"

He could and probably should give a fake name, but—the *but* always got him in trouble—why bother? If Simeon didn't know Amanda, he wouldn't know David, either. If he did know Amanda, maybe he'd have gotten wind that David had been her sidekick all week.

Going with that theory and assuming Simeon was aware of David's connection to Amanda, he figured it wouldn't hurt for him to know they'd tracked him down.

Rather easily.

Plus, the Hennings name was legendary in this town. That alone might scare the pants off the guy.

Finally, he wasn't here to harass. Depending on your definition of harassment. All he wanted was to deliver a message—a very strong one—to Simeon Davis. Who-ever the hell he was.

Decision made.

"I'm David Hennings."

Mary Jones, a pretty young thing for sure, scampered

off and a minute later came back, followed by a man who looked like the photo Jenna had shared. He drew closer and David spotted the telltale mole above his eye.

"Hello." The man smiled—total greasy car sales-man—and extended his hand. "I'm Simeon. How can I help you?"

David shook his hand. "David Hennings. Is there somewhere we can talk?"

"Of course. My desk."

Okay. That worked. He trailed him to the last desk on the right. Apparently assuming this was a business meet-ing, Simeon took a legal pad from the drawer and grabbed a pen from a leather pencil cup on top of the desk.

Pen at the ready, he nodded. "What can I help you with?"

"Amanda LeBlanc."

He cocked his head and pursed his lips. "I don't fol-low."

Now, this was interesting. By the look on his face, ei-ther the guy was a great liar or he didn't know Amanda. At all. Not even by name. "You accused her of fraud and had her assets frozen."

Game over.

Simeon's shoulders shot back against his creaky chair. "I'm sorry. I can't help you."

He made a move to get up and David beat him to it by standing and blocking his path. He kept his hands loose at his sides. Nonthreatening, but readily available. "I didn't expect you to help me. I'm going to help you, though, and give you things to think about. Like how badly you want to be incarcerated. Because whatever this fraud nonsense is, you'll have to prove the allegations, which you can't do. Unless, of course, you manufacture evidence and lie.

And that, too, will put you in a cell. There's this thing called perjury. Judges don't like it. Don't like having their time wasted. Think about it, Simeon. Think about your wife and your kids." David waved his hand. "About your employment potential."

A woman entered the open area from the hallway, nodding at him as she passed. Simeon faked a decent smile for the woman's benefit, then slid a hard look to David. "We're done. Get out."

Gladly. "Sure. But be smart. Whoever you're working for, his name isn't on the complaint against Amanda. Yours is. And your life could go down the toilet because of it."

"Get. Out."

"Be smart, Simeon. Do the right thing."

On his way out the door, David's phone rang. Penny. Huh. Her two-point-five hours of cooldown must have ended early. That or their mother had gotten to her. He hit the button. "Hey. I was going to call you about before."

"Hi," she said, her voice breathy and rushed.

He pushed through the door and met glaring sunshine. He patted his jacket pocket but remembered he'd left his sunglasses in the car. Hadn't needed them earlier. "Are you okay?"

"Yes. Jenna just called me. She talked to the lab. We got a hit on the fingerprints from that key."

Whoa. Jack. Pot. Getting a hit off the prints meant the guy was in the system. And that meant he had a criminal record. "Rap sheet?"

"No. Did you know anyone who works with children needs to be fingerprinted?"

"Yeah."

"Well, big brother, you're not going to believe where this guy works."

"Tell me."

"The Dyce Youth Center."

HAVING RECLAIMED A portion of her sanity, thanks to Lexi, Amanda marched into the youth center with her head high, her makeup and hair repaired and her one remaining completed painting ready to be shown.

Life and business as usual.

Sort of.

Mrs. Dyce couldn't know it, but this little visit would restore Amanda's sense of routine. Bring her back to the existence she'd had before David Hennings had marched through her front door and upended her life with his presence and, after last night, a few bouts of borderline rough sex she'd never before even considered participating in.

What she needed was exactly what she was about to do. Show her work, explain the details, share her love of art. This was where Amanda belonged. Where she thrived. The safe zone.

Neutral.

Forget David Hennings. The man had already torn her up in a million different ways. Why give him more opportunities?

But maybe Lexi was right and she needed to lighten up. The time with him, for the most part, had been good, extraordinary even. No one could be perfect 100 percent of the time.

"Hello, Amanda," Mrs. Dyce said, striding toward her in gray slacks and heels and a black blazer. She wore a pearl necklace and earrings, and the minimal accessories screamed elegance and class and money.

Money that would help Amanda's bank account. And, considering that her assets were currently unavailable, a fresh infusion of funds would be nice.

"Hello, Mrs. Dyce. Thank you for letting me come by."

"I should be thanking you." She gestured to the large narrow box Amanda held. "Do you need help with that?"

She gripped the handle, lifting the painting a few inches. "No. Thank you. I'm used to it."

"All right, then. We'll look at it in the conference room. There's room to spread out in there."

Amanda followed Mrs. Dyce down the same hallway she and David had traveled earlier in the week. Mrs. Dyce stopped in front of a doorway—apparently their destination—just across from her office and waved Amanda in.

Once inside the conference room, a large space with a table for ten and leather cushioned chairs, Amanda set the painting down, resting the box against the wall while she rummaged through her tote for her portable easel. In seconds, she'd have it set up and be able to show the painting on it. As much as Lexi teased her about the pop-up easel, it came in handy for displaying her work in a pinch. Except...*whoopsie*...she'd forgotten it in the trunk.

"I'm sorry. I forgot my easel in the car. It'll only take me a second to grab it. Do you mind?"

"It's not a problem at all. Go ahead. While you're doing that, I'll see if my husband is still here. I'd like him to look at the painting with me. I always prefer to get his opinion on large purchases." The older woman smiled. "Keeps things running smoothly."

After that fight with David, Amanda was beginning to learn. "I know exactly what you mean." She held her finger up. "I'll be back in a flash."

She walked down the hallway to the door she'd entered from. The parking lot behind the building, a definite perk in Chicago, made for easy access. She popped her trunk, found the easel and headed back inside. As she climbed the brick steps, a man exiting the building pushed the door open and held it for her.

She glanced up to offer a smile and thanks and stared into the face of the man who'd stolen the skull.

Chapter Thirteen

Amanda stood on the step, unmoving, for a solid five seconds, maybe more, before her brain clicked. When it finally did, she whipped around, ready to run, but he clamped on to her arm.

"No," he said.

And the deep, shaky voice came back to her. *I don't want to hurt you.* She tugged, but his hand tightened and he stepped back, dragging her up the steps as she threw her weight into her heels, resisting momentum. *Useless.* The man outweighed her by at least one hundred pounds.

"Help!"

Someone had to be nearby. In the parking lot, walking the street, anywhere. She swung her head around. "Help!"

Nothing. Not a pedestrian in sight.

The man yanked and a blast of pain shot up her arm into her shoulder. He knew he had her. She kicked out, but he leaped just out of her reach. Missed.

"Oh, my God."

Amanda peered over his shoulder and spotted Mrs. Dyce holding the door partway open. Finally, someone to help.

"Call the police," Amanda said. "This man broke into David's apartment. He stole the skull I was working on."

Still holding her, the man angled back and his grip

slipped. Amanda yanked and—*yes*—freedom. She spun back to the door, sprinted toward it, made it four steps until he caught her and latched on to the back of her jacket.

"Stay still!" he hollered.

"Sssshhh!" Mrs. Dyce hissed. "Get her in here."

The words jabbed at Amanda, tiny swords stabbing at her ears, forcing their way in, but…what? She didn't understand. "I don't…"

What was happening?

But the man tugged her backward, dragging her down the hall, and Amanda started screaming. Two, maybe three seconds passed and the man's meaty hand clamped over her mouth. Still, Amanda screamed. The sound was muffled but at least it was there as the man hauled her across the tiled floor, her feet skidding, failing to gain traction.

He shoved her back into the conference room, where her painting still lay against the wall.

What's happening?

Without breaking stride, Mrs. Dyce closed the door, and the icy control in which she did it made Amanda shiver. Where was the caring, loving woman who'd helped the masses?

Slowly, she turned to the man, her cheeks sucked in, her eyes more than a little wild. But the control remained. Demented calm, that was what this was.

She moved closer to him, a few steps away. "How could you be so *stupid*?"

In minutes she'd transformed from pleasant and elegant to mean and scrappy. Unhinged.

"I don't understand," Amanda said.

"Shut up! You—" she poked at the man "—find my husband. Get him in here. *Now*."

The man scurried from the room, closing the door behind him.

Disbelief consumed Amanda. "What are you *doing*?"

Insanity. All of it.

"Stop talking, Amanda. Before you get hurt."

The entire episode was bizarre. *What's she doing?* And then the pieces, albeit odd pieces, started to merge. The visit to the center, chatting with Mrs. Dyce about the reconstruction and agreeing to work with the detective, all of it had been discussed. With a woman who had massive connections within the city.

But what did the reconstruction have to do with the Dyces? "You knew that man stole the skull? David almost got hurt!"

"Shut up. I tried to stop you. I tried. All I wanted was for you to go away. To give up on this *reconstruction*. And now look what you've done."

Amanda shook her head, disbelief stunting her thoughts. There'd be time for figuring it all out later. She eyed the door, but Mrs. Dyce stood in her path. *Get around her.* The woman had twenty-five years on her. If Amanda could get close enough, she'd shove her and maybe escape.

"You'll never get by me. Believe me. I'm not willing to let meaningless people destroy my life."

The door came open and a tall man with dark hair, graying at the temples, stepped in, his large frame filling the doorway. She'd seen Mr. Dyce on television plenty of times, but he appeared bigger now, more confident. Behind him was the other man. The messenger boy.

"That idiot!" Mrs. Dyce poked her finger. "He walked out when she was here. How *stupid*!"

"You witch!" the man said to her. "After what I've done for you?"

Mr. Dyce glanced at Amanda, his eyes darting. The

confidence from seconds ago slid away and his body became more erect, his movements jerky. He'd just been appointed to a presidential committee, an honor men in his position rarely saw, and his wife was detaining someone against her will.

"You have to let me go," Amanda said. "Whatever this is, holding me will only get worse for you."

"Stop talking," Mrs. Dyce said.

"No. You two are beloved in this city. After this, you're done. It's over. Tell her to let me go."

But Mr. Dyce's eyes were still bouncing around, that panic shredding him. "Scott, leave us," he said.

Scott, the lackey, slid his gaze to Amanda, then back to Mr. Dyce. "Whatever happens, I'm not going down for this."

"Oh, shut up!" Mrs. Dyce hissed.

"Shut up? I've been helping you this whole time."

"Just let me go," Amanda said, still not sure what exactly they were talking about. "I'll walk out and everyone is safe."

"Irene," Mr. Dyce said to his wife. "What are we doing? This is crazy."

The woman's eyes got huge. The kind of look fueled by rage and torment. "What are we doing? We're saving your career. *We* need to stay together on this."

"Yes. We do. But I just talked to Simeon. He's out. This plan of yours has gone too far. It needs to stop."

Simeon. What had she gotten into with these people?

"Wonderful," Mrs. Dyce said, sarcasm oozing. "What do you propose?" She pointed at Amanda. "She can send us all to prison. She has to go."

"No. She doesn't. Accidentally killing a homeless person is one thing. This? This is murder and I won't do it."

"Isn't this typical? Once again, on my own."

"Stop it."

"No. I was afraid that night and you were gone. You're always tending to someone *else's* problems. If you'd been available, this would have wound up differently." She held her hands out. "I had to protect myself and now we're almost there. Please. We'll just make her go away."

No. *No, no, no.* "David knows I'm here."

Mrs. Dyce marched to the credenza, where a brass sculpture of two children playing sat on the top. She picked it up, checked its weight and looked back at Amanda with that same menacing face from minutes ago. "Well, that's too bad for him, then, isn't it?"

The man—Scott—backed toward the door. "Lady, you are insane. I'm out. I was willing to help you six years ago, but now you two are on your own."

He slipped from the room.

"Irene," Mr. Dyce said, giving his back to Amanda.

Go! With the couple occupied, she ran. Bolted to the door, grabbed the handle and yanked. The door came halfway open. Freedom. *Run.*

Clunk.

A huge weight blasted the side of her head and she stared at the hallway, at her chance to escape, at freedom.

At least until it went black.

DAVID CHARGED THROUGH the back entrance of the youth center and scanned the doors on either side of the long hallway. A man strode toward him, a big guy in ratty khakis who looked…familiar.

Him. The guy he had chased out of the condo.

David kept moving, heading straight for the man, until something in his face changed. Recognition.

The man slowed, but David ignored him—*wait for it*—and moved just past him. The guy, thinking he'd dodged

one, kept his gaze glued to the door, but David whirled
and slammed him with a fist behind the ear.

Boom.

He hit the floor.

What most people didn't realize, and David learned
while working out with a buddy who was into Ultimate
Fighting, was that a well-aimed punch to the temple or
behind the ear would drop someone. Immediately.

Case in point: the unconscious man at his feet. Hearing
a commotion from behind one of the doors, he hustled
to it. Muffled, hissing voices came from the other side
and he halted, listened for a second. *Idiot...your career...
you did this*.

Gently, he turned the knob and suddenly the door flew
open, smacking against the interior wall. He flinched at
the bang, but his eyes fixed on something.

A body. On the floor.

Amanda.

She lay unconscious, arms and legs sprawled at her
sides while blood seeped from her head, and something
inside him went berserk. Just blew his mind.

Mrs. Dyce stood over Amanda, fiercely gripping a
sculpture. She directed her hard, almost desperate gaze
at David. "She attacked us!"

Liar. All David was sure of was one of them—most
likely Mrs. Dyce—had knocked Amanda out cold. And
that was a problem. For them.

"Irene, shut up." Mr. Dyce's voice climbed an octave
higher than his normal calm baritone.

David shifted his gaze between them. First he'd have
to take out Mr. Dyce. He was the bigger, more powerful opponent. By then, McCall would be showing up to
question Mrs. Dyce about the employee who'd broken
into David's condo. When he arrived, he'd find a whole

lot more than that. Between the two of them, they'd get this under control.

Lunging left, David drove his shoulder into his best friend's father's gut, propelling the man backward, off his feet, both of them crashing to the floor. They landed hard, David on top as air whooshed from Mr. Dyce. Behind him, Mrs. Dyce wailed at him to stop and Mr. Dyce started swinging, the punches missing their mark and sliding off David's arms and shoulders and the side of his head. David reared up, jabbed once, twice and the final time landed a cross on the jaw. Mr. Dyce groaned, a low guttural sound, and his eyes rolled back.

Mrs. Dyce. *Where is she?* David leaped to his feet and twisted in time to see her, on the move, a foot from him, sculpture in hand. He dodged left, ducking under her arms as she raised the sculpture. Before she could clock him, he shoved her, knocking her off balance, and she cried out, tipping forward until she dropped across her husband's legs, the sculpture still in her hand. She kicked out and swung the heavy piece, but the weight and her weird angle made her efforts useless. She swung wide. *Missed.* Breaths coming fast, he reached down, gripped her wrist and squeezed until she winced. She opened her hand and the sculpture fell. It thunked against the carpeted floor, and the thought of Amanda getting hit with that thing made his stomach flip.

He shoved Mrs. Dyce away, grabbed the sculpture with one hand and wrapped his fingers around the solid base. Not all that heavy—for him—but enough to split someone's head. At his feet, Mrs. Dyce began to sob. The wailing hit him wrong. Forget empathy or sadness for a woman he'd known most of his life. Those tears were tiny shards of glass scraping against him. Behind him, Amanda groaned and relief gripped him. At least she was still alive. Whatever Mrs. Dyce had to say, he wasn't interested. He shook the statue at her.

"Move and I'll crack *your* skull with it."

DAVID SWUNG AROUND the corner of the hospital hallway on his way to Amanda's room and received one hell of a shock.

He stopped short and cocked his head, wondering just what the next thirty seconds would bring.

Leaning against the wall outside Amanda's room— at least he assumed it was Amanda's room because why else would Penny be standing there?—his sister fiddled with her phone. Probably answering emails.

He started toward her and she glanced up. Spotting him, she tucked her phone away and stood tall.

If she was readying for a fight, he didn't have it in him. He'd been at the PD giving his statement, damned near frantic wondering how badly Amanda had been hurt. She'd regained consciousness, but they'd hauled her off to the hospital straightaway and no one had given him any updates on her condition.

"Hi," she said, nodding toward the door. "The doctor is in with her. She was kind of worked up, so they gave her something to settle her down. The doctor said she has a concussion but thankfully no fractures. There's a deep cut that they put staples in. Blech. Literally, she has staples in her head. They had to shave the area, and let me tell you, when she comes out of her fog, she is not going to be happy about her funky new hairdo."

"Oh, man. But no fractures. That's great."

"They want to keep her overnight, but the doctor thinks she can go home tomorrow."

David nodded, taking a second to absorb the relief bullying its way through the massive tension in his neck.

Crazy few days. And even with McCall sorting through the mess David had left at the police station, he still had work to do regarding his sister.

"Pen, what are you doing here?"

She shrugged. "After you called Dad, he told me you were giving a statement and I wasn't sure if Amanda was alone. I just didn't want her to be by herself while you were tied up."

On his way to the police station, he'd called his father and asked him to meet him there just in case that key he'd swiped came back on him. Which, so far, it hadn't, but man, oh, man, his sister had done this for a woman she barely knew. And he hadn't even asked.

"Thank you for doing that for her."

"You're welcome."

But after she said that she shook her head and pressed her lips together in a way that told him he'd once again screwed up. What now? He replayed the last ten seconds in his mind and it hit him. "I can see you're about to unleash on me. You don't have to. I know what I did."

"Well, *David*, you recognized the sign. That's progress at least."

He smiled. "Thank you for being here for her *and* for me. You knew I'd be worried about her being alone."

"We may not always get along, but you're my brother and I love you. You have this massive protective streak. I figured I'd sit with her until you got here."

He hugged her. Just reached across and wrapped his baby sister in a bone-crushing hug. And, lookie here, she hugged him back. Not one of those quick, barely touching hugs that had a mountain of tension. This was the real deal and something they hadn't done in years.

Still hanging on, he patted her back. "Thank you."

Penny released him.

"I'm sorry about before," he said. "And about Jenna."

"Forget it. Let's just please learn from it. I'm not always angling for a fight. Not anymore at least. A lot has changed since you've been gone. My life is different. I'm happy and intend to stay that way. I don't want to compete with you for Dad's attention."

What? He craned his neck, started to say something and stopped. "I'm confused."

"I know you think I'm a brat, but put yourself in my place for a minute. You were the one Dad wanted at the firm. You're the brilliant one. And Zac has always sort of breezed through, doing what he wanted and somehow managing not to infuriate the 'rents. After you chose not to be at the firm and he decided he wanted to be a prosecutor, the boys in the family became a nonissue. Me? I always wanted to be with Dad. Always. But, believe me, as much as Dad loves me and spoils me, he wanted one of his sons by his side. I was the runner-up. Sometimes that knowledge got the best of me. All I wanted was to prove myself and I took it out on you. I couldn't resist poking at you. I don't need to do that anymore and I'm sorry."

David ran his hand over his face. Was it tomorrow yet? Sure felt like it. The past few days had definitely taken a piece out of him and now his sister had damn near floored him with this revelation. All the fights and the vicious sarcasm and the general being a pain in the rear to each other and it came down to one issue. Pretty much the same issue for each of them. David had always resented being the outsider.

And so did Penny.

"Pen, I'm sorry. I never knew. Really, even if I had thought about it, I'm not sure I'd have figured out you were trying to break into the boys' club."

He'd been so wrapped up in his own life, he'd never

considered what went on in Penny's life. Or even Zac's. But Zac was…Zac. Nobody worried about him.

"You didn't know and I never told you."

"I don't want to fight anymore. I know I've said that before, but I can't do this anymore. And, listen, after the talk I had with Mom this morning, I think we've pretty much worn her out. She's about to dropkick us both."

Penny scrunched her nose. "Did she have the face? That one when she drills you with her eyes?"

"No. She had the face beyond the drilling."

"Ew."

"Yeah. Not good. She told me to take you to lunch once a week—just us—so we can get to know each other. After this conversation, that's a good idea. I'd like to get to know my sister again. And Russ. He seems like a good guy."

"He is. You two would probably get along. You're both bullheaded."

David laughed. "Harsh!"

"Oh, boohoo. As far as lunch goes, Fridays are usually good for me."

"Fridays?"

"Unless I'm in court. But I'd like to have lunch with you." She grinned, rubbing her hands together like the mischievous twelve-year-old girl she used to be. "Plus, it'll drive Zac crazy wondering what we're talking about."

Good old Penny. Always busting chops.

"Okay," he said. "Check your schedule for next Friday. Mom will go crazy. You'll get gummy bears out of it and I'll get brownies."

"Cha-ching!" they said at the same time.

"Ain't this great?"

The now-familiar voice coming from behind them

telegraphed things were anything but great. David turned to see McCall striding toward them.

"Not only do I get one Hennings," the detective said, "I get two. And both lawyers. Someone shoot me."

"Hello, Detective," Penny said. "You can't question her at the moment."

His sister. Right to lawyer mode. Gotta love her.

"Relax, Counselor. I'm here to update her."

The door to Amanda's room opened and the doctor stepped out. McCall flashed his badge.

"Hello, Detective. You can speak with her but not for too long."

"Thanks, Doc."

"We'll run a few more tests, but assuming nothing comes up, she can probably go home tomorrow. Let her rest, though. All of you."

"Sure thing, Doc." McCall said. "Thank you."

"I'll check back in a bit."

The doctor headed off and McCall jerked a thumb toward the door. "I'm guessing she won't mind you hearing, so come in and I won't have to do this twice. It's a helluva story."

AMANDA'S HEAD WAS coming apart. Well, coming apart might have been an exaggeration given the staples literally holding her skin together and the lack of a fracture—absolutely good news considering that she could be dead right now—but she definitely had pain.

The door to her room swished open and without lifting her head, she turned to see Penny enter the room followed by David and Detective McCall.

Immediately, her body craved David. Just being in the same room made her want to pull him close. Something she'd have to figure out how to deal with after the fight they'd had that morning. Who knew where they'd go from here?

She'd deal with that later. When her head wasn't coming apart.

For now, she hoped McCall had news for her. News that would inform her that she'd soon be back to some sort of routine. She didn't want to be greedy, but her routine would be the best thing for her.

She pushed herself up only to have the room spin. *That won't work.* Resting back, she felt around for the bed's remote.

"Hang on." David rushed to the side of the bed. "It's hanging off the bed. We'll wind it through the safety bars so it doesn't fall."

"Thank you."

He handed her the remote, their fingers brushing lightly. As usual, something inside her pinged. He did that to her, stirred her up, gave her a zap of something warm and hopeful, and suddenly she hated it. Twenty-four hours ago, it was a blessing she'd never experienced. Now, after her conversation with Lexi, it just confused her and she didn't know what she wanted.

Lie. She knew. She wanted him. Without the drama. The drama would decimate her. But she didn't want to be the person Lexi described her as, either. Didn't want to constantly be waiting for the next bad thing. Her mother would have expected more of her.

Slowly, she raised the bed enough that she could see but not bring a fresh bout of dizziness.

David ran his fingers over her cheek and she closed her eyes. She should pull away and not let him touch her. Touching made her feel the stupid zing and she couldn't think straight with that going on.

But just this once, after what they'd been through together, she'd let it happen. Comfort couldn't be bad.

"How's the head?" McCall asked.

"It feels like I got clubbed."

"Um," Penny said, moving to the other side of the bed. "Maybe because you did?"

McCall gestured to the gauze circling her head. "She must have whacked you good."

The staples holding her skin together proved it. Plus, she had to have part of her head shaved because the doctor, as he'd said, wanted better visualization. So, along with the injury, she'd look like a freak.

Bigger things to worry about.

For now, she'd stay grateful for the fact that she wasn't in the morgue. But that damned woman had inflicted a lot of damage to her life and when the medication wore off, Amanda suspected she'd be spitting nails.

Be grateful.

She sighed as McCall stepped up to the end of the bed. As much as she didn't want to discuss the incident, the detective was obviously here for a statement. And she'd give it to him. If for no other reason than to help him solve his case. All she'd been able to assume was that the Dyces somehow knew the woman whose skull Amanda was reconstructing. They also obviously had knowledge about her death.

She met the detective's gaze. "I'll tell you what I remember."

He held his hand up. "In a minute. Let me update you."

This sounded hopeful.

"We've arrested the Dyces and Scott Bench. He's the one who stole the skull cast."

"He was the man at the youth center, too," Amanda said. "I recognized him."

"Yeah. He's also your guy from the storage unit. He'd been following you and pulled the alarm."

"Bastard."

"You could say that. After the scene in the conference room, he got scared. Figured he'd wind up the fall guy for the Dyces, so he gave us the story. He's thirty-four and he's worked at the youth center for eight years. Known the Dyces since he was in high school. He grew up in a rough neighborhood and was heading down a wrong path. Couple burglary arrests and some petty-crime stuff. His mother took him to see Reggie Dyce speak at a rally, and the kid formed a relationship with him. They helped him get his act together. A few years went by and when he got married, they hired him to do maintenance at the center."

"He felt indebted to them?"

"Oh, yeah."

David cocked his head. "How indebted?"

McCall blew out a breath. "Enough to help them bury our victim's body."

"My God," Penny said.

Amanda sighed. The world simply terrified her. These people were beloved for their charitable endeavors and their dedication to helping others. Total frauds. "What happened?"

"There's a storage shed behind the center. One night Irene finds a hammer lying around the rec room, so she takes it back to the shed. It's winter and damned cold. While she's in the shed, she hears a noise and looks up to see some girl coming at her. Irene thinks she's about to get attacked. She must have been standing in front of the door. I'm thinkin' our vic was homeless and trying to get some shelter and when Irene came into the shed, the girl tried to run. Anyways, Irene claims she got scared and swung the hammer." McCall motioned like swinging. "Tagged her good. The girl dropped like a stone."

"She was dead?"

"At the time, Irene doesn't know. But Scott Bench is putting the trash out and hears the commotion. He checks it out and finds Irene in a state of total hysterics. He gets her calmed down, but she's going on about how they'd be ruined and all their hard work wouldn't mean anything and the center would have to close. Our boy Scott realizes he has a family to support and he's got a pretty good gig at the center."

"Where was Mr. Dyce during all this?"

"At some rally downstate."

"Which is why," Amanda said, "she accused him of not being around to support her."

David shook his head. "Tell me she convinced Scott Bench to bury the body."

"This guy takes hero worship to the next level. He's a street kid. He's seen it all and he wasn't gonna risk losing his job. Or going back to life on the street. Irene panicked and begged him for help and he told her he'd take care of it. They're a rotten combination, these two. He got his brother to help him and they dealt with the body. At least until I found it while walking my dog."

Stunned, Amanda simply stared. "She killed a young woman and threw her in the trash. The woman is evil."

"Hold up," David said. "When I took Amanda to the center and asked her to pass the sketch around, it kicked this whole thing off?"

Amanda grabbed David's hand. "No. That can't be. My building was condemned before that. She must have gotten her husband to reach out to someone at City Hall. But how did she know I'd agreed to help?"

"Wait," Penny said. "At dinner the other night Mom

said she talked to Irene. When she cornered you into telling Dad you'd help. This is *Mom's* fault!"

"No," Amanda said. "It's not. It's Irene Dyce's fault." She squeezed David's hand. "The conversation with your mom probably confirmed I was involved, but remember when we saw her at the center that first time and showed her the sketch?"

"What about it?"

"She commented on the detail. I bet she recognized her."

David dropped his chin to his chest and pounded on his head with his free hand. "You're right. Babe, I'm so sorry."

But Penny waved her hand. "Just knock that off. This was *not* your fault or Mom's. The woman is nuts. After Mom told her about the reconstruction, she was coming after Amanda anyway." She winced and turned to Amanda. "That sounded harsh. I'm sorry. I don't want him thinking this is his fault. My mother was already working the Dyces for their help on this."

"I know," Amanda said. "But what about Simeon Davis? Before Mrs. Dyce hit me, I heard Mr. Dyce tell her Simeon had backed out. What was that about?"

"Yeah. He got friendly with the Dyces after doing volunteer work for them, and when Simeon had trouble finding work, Reggie got the guy a job at the insurance agency. He was about to lose his house, so that job saved his butt."

"I don't understand how he knows me," Amanda said.

"He doesn't. The Dyces are in bed with the state's attorney. They helped get her elected. When you signed on to do the reconstruction, they made up some bull story about one of their volunteers being a victim of a check-cashing scheme and warned the SA she should look into it. They fed Simeon some line about wanting to make sure no other people got defrauded and asked Simeon to back them up. Make it look like more than one person got scammed. He did it."

"Because he owed them."

"Listen, this guy isn't the sharpest knife in the drawer. He took pride in the fact that Dyce came to him. He wanted to be the hero. Anyway, he went along with it."

David knocked his knuckles against the rail of the bed. "That's why the SA went into court saying if the assets weren't preserved, Amanda would deplete them before an investigation could be launched. Except, I went to Simeon and scared the hell out of him."

"Yes, Counselor, and thank you, but we're gonna talk about you butting into my investigation. Again."

"It's bizarre," Amanda said. "The lengths they were willing to go to."

"Yes, it is," Penny said. "But they've worked for years to reach a certain level. Mr. Dyce has just been appointed to a presidential committee. It's the pinnacle for him."

David huffed. "They wouldn't give up that status. People are so damned twisted."

"Yeah, well." McCall waggled his fingers. "I have the icing on this cake for you."

Exhausted, Amanda put her hands up. "Detective, I'm not sure I can take much more."

"You're gonna have to because we got a hit on your sketch. One of the syndicated crime shows ran it last night and someone thought she looked like the daughter of a neighbor. They called the neighbor and told them to check out the sketch online."

A hit. Just off the sketch. If it panned out, they'd have identified the victim before the reconstruction was even complete. *Don't.* Getting excited before they had a positive identification would be reckless. An emotional risk. So what? She could be hopeful. That was what she'd call it. Hope.

"Was it her?"

"It's close enough that we're getting DNA to be sure. She was a runaway. Been gone a couple of years and they'd lost touch with her. They didn't know where she was, never mind dead. That's all I got now."

McCall's cell phone beeped and he pulled it from his pocket. He read something on it and stowed the phone again. "Damn. I gotta go. I'll be back in a while to get a statement from you. All right?"

"That's fine. Thank you, Detective. This is great news. Sad, but great, too."

He set his hand on the blanket over her foot and squeezed. "It is good news. And thank you. If the DNA matches, you brought this girl home."

Chapter Fourteen

After McCall left, Penny made a performance out of checking her watch and announcing she had just a *ton* of work to do. The ton of work must have magically appeared after David, rather violently, jerked his head toward the door.

This family. Completely nuts.

But they were funny, too. And caring.

"So," Penny chirped. "I will see you both later. Call if you need something. Toodles."

Finger waving as she went, she fast-walked toward the door, something Amanda noticed earlier also. Penny fast-walked everywhere.

"She's a ball of energy, huh?"

"You could say that. It's her Napoleon complex. She's tiny, but she's deadly."

"You should make up with her."

David tugged gently on the hair poking from under Amanda's bandage. "I already have. Right outside this room. I showed up when the doctor was in here and I cornered her. Turns out, my sister and I have a few things in common. We're going to lunch together next week to discuss them."

"Really?"

"You don't believe me?"

"I absolutely believe you. I'm just surprised."

"I had a talk with my mother this morning after I infuriated everyone and generally made a jerk out of myself. Turns out, my mother is fed up with Penny and me fighting all the time. She came up with the lunch idea. It's a pretty good one. It'll give me a chance to get to know my sister again. Heck, maybe it'll be a weekly thing."

"I'm glad, David."

"Me, too." He glanced down at the safety rail. "Can I lower this?"

"Sure."

He lowered the rail and perched on the edge of the bed, his weight sinking the one side a bit. *Too close.* He should go. Let her be for a while. The doctor said she needed rest. And she should inform him that the closeness confused her, made her crave time alone to sort out her feelings. She should tell him.

Absolutely.

And yet she sat with her mouth closed and her thoughts flying.

"Is this okay?" he asked.

"Sure."

Again with the "sure"? That word needed to be banished. Forever. No. Not okay. That was what she *should* have said. Just thrown him out of here. Instead, he was sitting on her bed, way too close, and already she knew her life would never be what it had been. How could it be after all this? And maybe that was the point. That life meant bumps and bends and hills to be conquered.

None of which could be accomplished in neutral.

"Amanda, I'm sorry. For everything. For getting you into this mess, for tearing your life up and for blaming you this morning. No excuses. I'm an idiot sometimes."

Oh, she might love this man.

She bit her bottom lip but finally gave up and smiled. "You're funny, David."

"Sometimes I'm that, too." He shifted a little, facing her straight on, his soul-piercing gaze glued to hers. "Will you let me try to fix this? This week has been hell, straight up hell, but I knew we'd get through it. I knew. But when you walked out this morning, that did me in. I was mad and hurt and irritated at myself and everyone else. And then my mother got a hold of me."

Amanda laughed. "Poor baby."

He grinned at her. "Seriously, she's tough. And most of the time, she's right. Annoying, that. Since I'm coming clean, I might as well tell you that she has you lined up to be the next member of our family."

Gulp. "Wow."

David set his giant hand on hers, and his palm was warm as he curled his fingers around hers, cocooning her. She rested her head back and closed her eyes because this was the part of being with David she loved. That feeling of safety and warmth. With that, though, came the risk of heartbreak. *No neutral.*

Not with this man.

"Yeah. No pressure there. I think she has a point, though. When I'm not being a dope we're good together. I love talking to you and touching you. The minute you leave me, I want you back. And for a guy who spent years running, that's new. I like it. It makes me feel…lighter. Like dealing with my crazy family isn't so hard because I have you to make me laugh. To tell me when I'm wrong and not have it be a power struggle. To make me understand that it's okay to disagree and it doesn't mean you don't support me. I get that now. This morning, my emotions took over. I'm sorry. I can't promise my emotions won't get in the way again, but I won't blame you for it if they do. Never again."

"David—"

He raised his hand. "All I want is dinner. When all this gets hashed out, let me take you to dinner. We'll start again. Two people who've just met." He squeezed her hand. "Think about it. Please."

He stood, then raised the safety bar again. "Now I'm leaving because the doc said you need rest and they're gonna throw me out anyway." He kissed her lightly on the head, and his scent, the musky maleness she'd grown used to, surrounded her. He lingered for a few seconds before backing away. "I'll call you tomorrow."

Stop him. "Okay."

Then he turned and headed for the door. *Stop him.* But if she did, there'd be no neutral. If nothing else, he deserved better than that. Everyone did.

Even her.

"David?"

He stopped and tilted his head to the ceiling but didn't turn around.

"Yes. To dinner. And, if you're not in a rush, maybe you could sit with me for a while?"

He turned and strode toward her and instinctively she sat up. The room spun and she gripped the sheet, waiting for him to reach her again, and there he was, instantly by her side, leaning over the rail. But as fast as he was moving, he gently cupped her face in his giant hands and kissed her, a long, slow kiss that she wasn't sure she could ever live without again. Kisses from David were either fast and fierce or slow and gentle, each one different and surprising and perfect. This would be life with him. Different. Surprising. Perfect.

And definitely not in neutral.

Chapter Fifteen

One Month Later

David eased his car to a stop in front of a bungalow in Ina, Illinois, a small town almost five hours south of Chicago consisting of a whopping two and a half square miles. Amanda studied the gutter hanging from one side of the tiny house and the ripped screens on the two front windows. With a little work—maybe more than a little—the house could be adorable.

From what Amanda knew, nothing that had gone on in this house, not one single thing, could ever be considered adorable. This had been the home of Juliette Powers, the nineteen-year-old woman whose reconstruction sat in a box on the floor of David's backseat.

"This is it," David said.

"I see that."

Yearning for freedom and a better life, Juliette had run from this house at sixteen. Her mother's second husband had been abusive and getting nastier by the second, and Juliette had craved independence and a life free of yelling and fists. She'd been on her own, working odd jobs, living in shelters, for almost three years before her death.

Why she was in that storage shed the night she died, no one would ever truly know, but Amanda suspected Detective McCall's theory—that the young woman needed a place to hunker down on a cold night—was as close as any.

David shifted the car into Park and shut the engine. "You ready for this?"

She nodded. "I am. I didn't think I would be, but it feels…right. Juliette didn't get a happy ending, but we brought her home. That's what I'm hanging on to. She's safe now."

Three weeks earlier, David and Amanda, along with Detective McCall, had brought Juliette's remains—her skull and the hair found near it—home and attended her funeral. Now they were back. All because Amanda wanted Juliette to be remembered as a beautiful young woman, so she had finished her reconstruction on the second duplicate skull cast the lab had provided her. Scott Bench had disposed of the first one by tossing it off a bridge into the Chicago River. So many times, they'd tried to dump Juliette, to make it that she'd never be identified, but somehow, she refused to go unnoticed.

"I don't want this to sound condescending," David said, "but I'm proud of you. You've done an amazing thing here."

Amanda shrugged. "You helped. But thank you. I can't say I'm happy about it, but there's satisfaction in knowing who she was. Giving her a name again. We did that, David. Together."

"I know."

He leaned over the console and kissed her. Just a soft peck before backing away half an inch. She opened her eyes and met his alluring blue gaze that never failed to spark energy in her.

"I love you, David Hennings."

His eyes popped wide. He knew her well enough, more

than well enough, to know an admission like that, putting her heart out there, allowing herself to be vulnerable, didn't come easy. He had, in fact, cracked the code. By being honorable and trustworthy, he'd made it easy for her to love him. Case closed.

"Well," he said, "that's good news."

And then the idiot grinned. Just sat there with a smug smile and she wanted to throttle him. Let him have it because she'd just told him she loved him, and he wanted to tease her about it. Even so, she felt fairly confident his feelings ran as deep. The week prior he'd slipped and almost said it, but he'd stopped himself, probably afraid he'd spook her. Well, fine.

She reached to the floorboard and grabbed her purse. "I have something to show you."

"Finally a naked picture of you?"

"You wish."

She placed a folded sheet of paper into his palm and he pursed his lips.

"Go ahead," she urged. "Read it."

After opening it, he scanned it. The smile he'd just hit her with grew, and seeing it, seeing him happy and proud—of her—made something clog in her throat. She smacked her hands over her eyes before she started bawling. These past few weeks had been like this. One giant release of pent-up tears. Years' and years' worth. As healthy as it was to let all the fear and pain go, she'd prefer to ditch the waterworks. Just enjoy happiness for a change.

"The forensic workshop," he said. "You're going."

She dragged her hands down her face, then wiped them on her slacks. "I am. It starts next month. I'll be gone three weeks, but when I come back, I think I'll be ready to officially try forensic sculpting. I'm not afraid of it anymore. I'm out of neutral, David. With you, with my work, all of it. Thank you."

He leaned over the console again, wrapped his hand around the back of her head and hit her with one of his mind-melting kisses, more ardent this time, changing it up from a minute ago and reinforcing her belief that he would always offer surprises. After the years stuck in her safe zone, David had managed to pull her out of it and make her comfortable doing so.

He broke the kiss but held on. "I love you," he said. "You have to know that, right? I didn't want to rush you."

She nodded. "I do know. And thank you for not rushing me. For letting me get there on my own. I needed to say it first. With you, there's no neutral. There's just us—and your crazy family—and that's all I'll ever need."

* * * * *

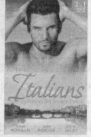

MILLS & BOON®

Why shop at millsandboon.co.uk?

Each year, thousands of romance readers find their perfect read at millsandboon.co.uk. That's because we're passionate about bringing you the very best romantic fiction. Here are some of the advantages of shopping at www.millsandboon.co.uk:

* **Get new books first**—you'll be able to buy your favourite books one month before they hit the shops

* **Get exclusive discounts**—you'll also be able to buy our specially created monthly collections, with up to 50% off the RRP

* **Find your favourite authors**—latest news, interviews and new releases for all your favourite authors and series on our website, plus ideas for what to try next

* **Join in**—once you've bought your favourite books, don't forget to register with us to rate, review and join in the discussions

Visit **www.millsandboon.co.uk**
for all this and more today!

MILLS_WEB